"*Calm Before the Storm* portrays believable characters emulating the Good Samaritan in arduous circumstances."
—*Church Libraries*

"Janice Dick is to be commended for her careful historical research in *Calm Before the Storm*. The action never stalls and she does a good job of trying to get into the mind and soul of German Mennonites who lived through unsettling times."
—Katie Funk Wiebe, *Mennonite Weekly Review*

"Janice Dick knows how to paint scenes that appeal to all the senses . . . pockets of language sparkle."
—Betti Erb, *Canadian Mennonite*

"Janice Dick combines a natural story telling flair with historical accuracy in *Eye of the Storm*. Dick writes clearly and concisely, holding the reader's interest. From her Christian position and her in-depth research, she produces conversations, historical data, and observations to explore pacifism versus fighting, Communism versus Christianity, the growth of Christ within the characters, and the ties between family, friends, and Christian denominations."
—Donna Eggett, *Christian Library Journal*

"Janice Dick has crafted a very interesting story of one of the most turbulent periods in Mennonite History, the Russian Revolution. Her two previous books are well written, and are obviously based on considerable research. The story is compelling enough to be of interest to any reader."
—Helmut T. Huebert, author of *Mennonite Historical Atlas*

"Janice has done a lot of research to make her stories authentic. These books will appeal to those who appreciate history with a touch of romance."
—Olivia Hardy, Kindred Productions

"Janice's books are carefully researched and reflect a conscientious attention to the details of history . . . but they are anything but dry history; her characters come alive in the reader's imagination. These absorbing stories have given us a new appreciation for a people that have refused to be molded to the world's standards."
—Martin and Janice Whitbread, Living Books Inc.

"I am deeply moved by your book. . . . This book is a tremendous gift to the Mennonite church as well as to the global community."
—Joanne Hess Siegrist, author, historian, and photographer

"*Calm Before the Storm* is well plotted, spiritually spot-on, and insightful. My favorite line: 'No man will ever be able to explain the workings of a woman's mind, and no woman will ever divulge the secret.'"
—Elma Schemenauer, author of seventy books

"Janice Dick weaves together historical research on the Russian Revolution with characters of her own creation, which remain true to the milieu of that era . . . I was caught up in the drama of family members with disparate personalities, each searching to fulfill a need. . . . *Calm Before the Storm* engaged my interest as a reader from the first paragraph to its dramatic conclusion."
—Shirley Bustos, educator, composer, and writer

"Janice Dick has captured the events described in her book accurately. She has brought to life effectively the personalities with all the resulting emotions."
—Henry Braun, educator and administrator

"Both a work of historic fact and romantic fiction, *Calm Before the Storm* weaves a colorful tapestry of suspense, sustained interest, and historical actualities. The story flows effortlessly and reveals the depth of Dick's research."
—Barbara Brennan, writer and editor

"Janice Dick, having become thoroughly familiar with the calamitous events featured in *Out of the Storm*, weaves a story of failure and faith in adversity."
—Hugo Jantz, missionary and preacher

"Janice Dick tells an intricate tale of persecution, courage, and passion in *Out of the Storm*. Lovers of historical fiction will delve deep into this story and not want to give it up until the final page is turned."
—Janelle Clare Schneider, author

OUT *of the*
STORM

Crossings of Promise

Historical fiction with a touch of romance

Dianne Christner
Keeper of Hearts

Janice L. Dick
Calm Before the Storm
Eye of the Storm
Out of the Storm

Hugh Alan Smith
When Lightning Strikes
When the River Calls

Heather Tekavec
The Cost of Passage

OUT *of the* STORM

JANICE L. DICK

Herald
Press

Waterloo, Ontario
Scottdale, Pennsylvania

National Library of Canada Cataloguing-in-Publication Data
Dick, Janice L., 1954-
Out of the storm / Janice L. Dick.

(Crossings of promise)
ISBN 0-8361-9271-0

1. Mennonites—Russia—History—20th century—Fiction.
I. Title. II. Series.

PS8557.I2543O98 2004 C813'.6 C2004-904841-4

Canadian Entry Number: C2004-904841-4
Library of Congress Control Number: 2004112141
International Standard Book Number: 0-8361-9271-0
Printed in the United States of America
Cover art by Barbara Kiwak
Cover design by Sans Serif Design Inc.

13 12 11 10 09 08 07 06 10 9 8 7 6 5 4 3 2

To order or request information, please call
1-800-759-4447 (individuals); 1-800-245-7894 (trade).
Web site: www.heraldpress.com

This book is dedicated to my parents,
John and Margaret Enns.
Dad was always my hero and Mom remains my greatest fan.
I love you both forever.

And to my husband's parents,
Walter and Edna Dick.
They have prayed for me and for these books,
and love me as their own.

I also dedicate this volume to the memory of
Benjamin B. Janz
(1877-1964)
Without his commitment and perseverance,
the events of this story would not have taken place.

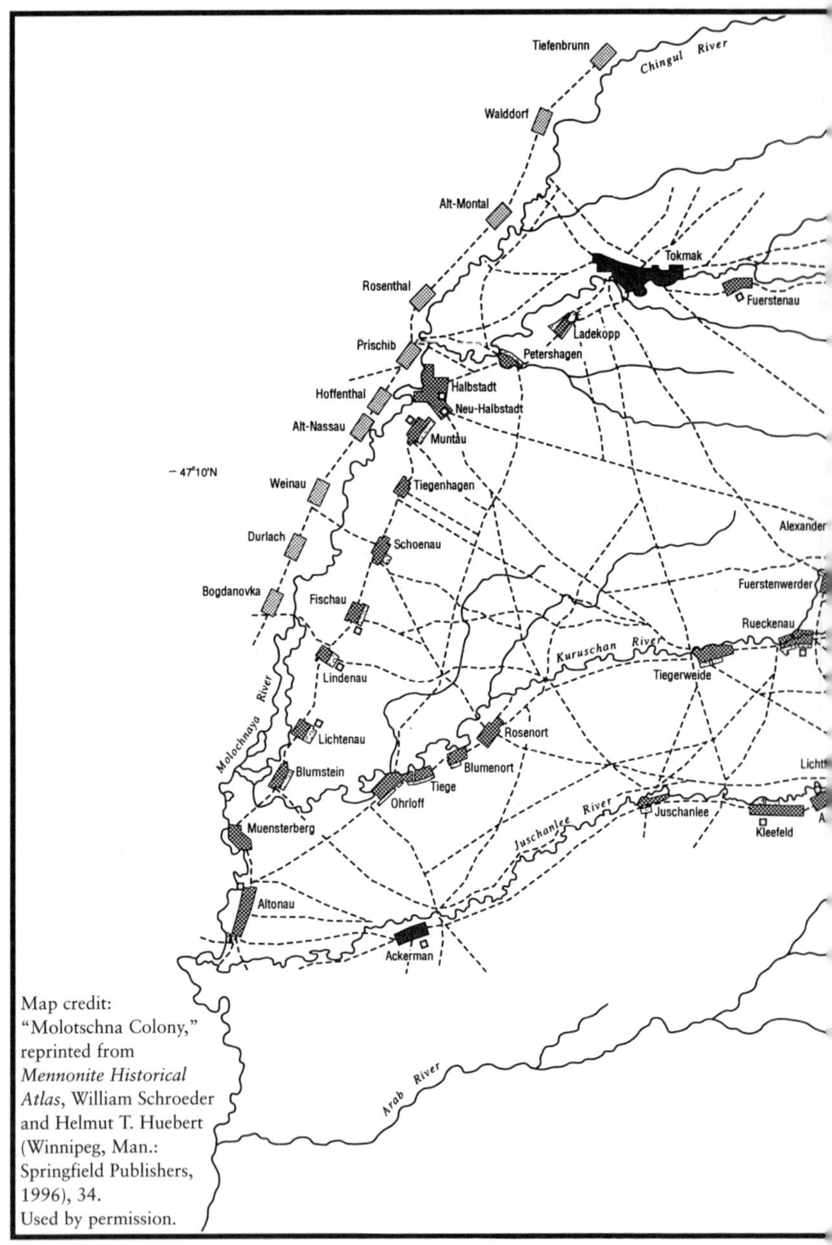

Map credit:
"Molotschna Colony,"
reprinted from
Mennonite Historical Atlas, William Schroeder and Helmut T. Huebert (Winnipeg, Man.: Springfield Publishers, 1996), 34.
Used by permission.

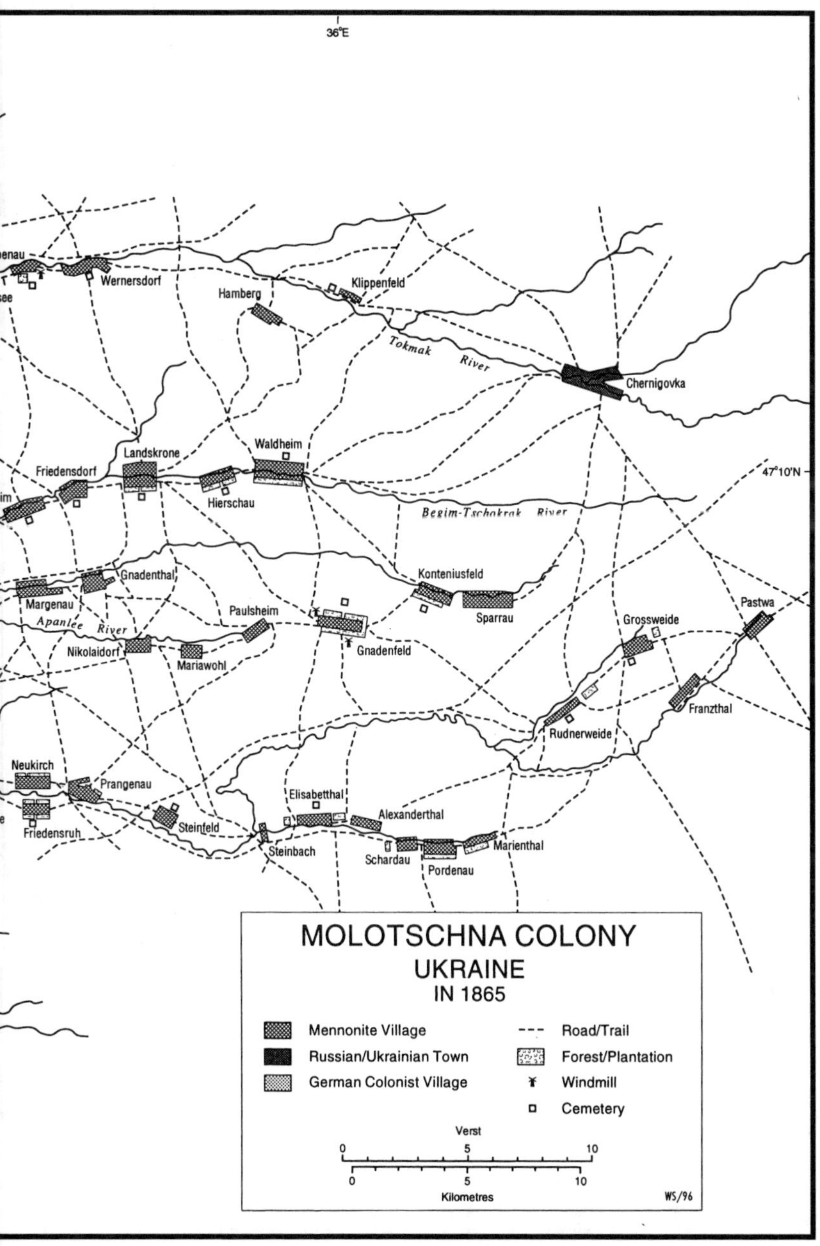
36°E
Wernersdorf
Hamberg
Klippenfeld
Tokmak River
Chernigovka
Landskrone
Waldheim
Friedensdorf
47°10'N
Hierschau
Begim-Tschokrak River
Gnadenthal
Konteniusfeld
Margenau
Paulsheim
Sparrau
Apanlee River
Pastwa
Grossweide
Nikolaidorf
Gnadenfeld
Mariawohl
Franzthal
Rudnerweide
Neukirch
Prangenau
Elisabetthal
Alexanderthal
Steinfeld
Friedensruh
Steinbach
Marienthal
Schardau
Pordenau
MOLOTSCHNA COLONY
UKRAINE
IN 1865
Mennonite Village
Russian/Ukrainian Town
German Colonist Village
Road/Trail
Forest/Plantation
Windmill
Cemetery
Verst
0
5
10
0
5
10
Kilometres
WS/96

And the Lord God spoke to Job
out of the storm.

Job 38:1

Prologue

I hold my breath steady
like everyone else
I want to stop rocking
back and forth.
We are all caught in this rhythm
boxed in like cattle.
I want to jump out and push.
The train is slow.

Slow.
As though there's time to stroll
once more along the rows of pear trees
heavy with fruit.
There's plenty of time
for one more game of lawn croquet
and afterwards a cup of tea
before bed.

Before the doors are forced
open, knives dance in the dark
riders fill the village street
with death, flames pounding
in my brain, my mother's screams
split the long summer evening
spun like a dream across gold decades
fragile as dust.

Who would have thought that we'd be rocking
scared, helpless as sheep
watching for the gate
for the star that must appear
and disappear
except for old photos
hauled half around the world.
I will lift them out
gently (if anyone should ask)
on long winter evenings
when the train is a black dot
in the distance. Frost
has shriveled our pear trees.

—"Train: 1929," by Sarah Klassen

PART ONE

September 1919–December 1920

We are most like beasts when we kill;
we are most like men when we judge;
we are most like God when we forgive.

Chapter 1

Katarina Sudermann shivered as the distancing autumn sun slanted through the trees of Alexanderkrone, Molotschna. The crackling tension in the colony bothered her as much as the weather. Even before she and Johann had fled here from the Crimea with her sister Anna, the state of affairs in the Mennonite colonies had deteriorated into chaos. They had come only because their home in the peninsula had been destroyed.

Katarina read the bad news in Johann's eyes. She kept up a pretense at supper for the sake of Anna, but as soon as dishes were done and her younger sister had slipped next door to visit the neighbor girl, Katarina confronted him.

"What is it? You have kept me in suspense since you arrived home from school."

Johann looked at his wife, took a deep breath, and walked to the window. He did not face her as he spoke. "It's Machno again. Only this time, he is in earnest."

Katarina's eyes widened at the mention of Nestor Machno, the self-proclaimed anarchist whose murderous band of miscreants left a wake of horror and tragedy wherever they went. "In earnest! What was he in when he attacked before? Was that just a taste of his savage intent?"

Johann turned to her then, anger in his own eyes. "You asked me, Katarina. Do you want to know or not? Please remember I am not the cause of this wickedness."

"I don't want to hear, but I must." She clasped her hands

in her lap to still their shaking. "Please tell me and I will not blame you."

"Very well. They are everywhere at once, it seems. They left more than eighty dead in Eichenfeld, in the Yazykovo Colony."

"That's just north of Chortitza, isn't it? Where else have they been?"

"They hit several other villages in the vicinity of Eichenfeld, killed another fifty."

"And besides the ones they killed," Katarina's voice trembled with foreboding, "there will be the unnumbered wounded in soul and body, those who wish they had died." She covered her face with her hands and her voice dropped to a whisper. "When will they come here to us? And where is my brother Nicholai? It's been nearly three months since he ran away. What if he met up with Machno's men? Kolya is only fifteen years old. What if . . ."

Johann gently pulled Katarina to her feet and wrapped his arms around her shuddering form. "Shh, Katya. We are in God's hands. Nothing comes to us . . ."

". . . but what he allows, I know, but I am so afraid. Is this the end of the world, the tribulation the Bible speaks of? How could it be worse?"

"I don't know. Perhaps it is our tribulation, but we must trust that God is in control." He held Katarina away from him and looked into her eyes. "You have always been strong, my love. Don't let that go. You have made your decision for God, and you cannot look back now, no matter what comes to us."

"Oh Johann, I know I must be strong, but I don't want to be. I want to fly away somewhere, far from this madness. Somewhere there must be peace."

He led her into the small parlor and they sat close on the settee. He stroked her hand and spoke softly, calmly. "I am going to visit Benjamin Janz again on Saturday. We are working on securing a place in some peaceful region of the world for our people. There are still quiet places, but it will take much work and considerable negotiation with the authorities. In spite of the turmoil around us, we must continue to make progress in the emigration issue. I think that is the salvation the Lord God holds out for us here.

"I will ride out early Saturday morning and be back by nightfall. You and Anna could spend some time with Susannah and Peter. That will make your day go faster."

Katarina leaned her head on Johann's shoulder. She sighed. "Mmm. I should spend more time with them. Susannah's little Marianna grows sweeter every day." She did not voice the longing in her soul as she spoke of the baby.

Katarina's eyes locked onto her husband's. "I'm so thankful you are still with me, Johann. I don't know how Susannah copes, not knowing where Gerhard is or what has become of him." She gripped the edge of his jacket as if she could keep him by holding on. Her heart murmured prayers heavenward, but it seemed they were lost on the way. Such faith—trust without proof—was difficult to maintain.

ꟹꟹꟹ

Paul Gregorovich Tekanin and Grisha shared a small meal with Father Serge in his private room in the Karassan Orthodox Church in Crimea. They had stayed with him since they had fled for their lives with Johann and Katarina. It was a long time to stay in one place.

A tension hung over the men as they ate their fish and black bread. Each waited for the other to speak, and finally Paul took the initiative.

"Father Serge, we will be leaving within the week."

Grisha winced, considering Paul's directness. He should have spoken; he would have used more tact.

The priest stared at him from beneath raised eyebrows. "Why, my friends? Are you not content here? Are you lacking anything?"

"My dear Father," said Grisha, "you have provided us with sustenance and security these last weeks. We will be forever grateful, but the times are getting worse instead of better, and our presence places you in danger."

Grisha would have continued but Father Serge interrupted him. "I am in the hands of God, and as such, I do whatever he asks of me."

"Yes, Father," agreed Grisha, "but your parishioners need you and I would not take you from them because we were too dense or too selfish to see the danger we are putting you in. I've seen the surreptitious looks we are given when we appear together."

Paul spoke again. "You are a friend we shall never forget, but the time has come for us to leave."

"Where will you go?"

"North to the Molotschna, I think. We will find Johann and Katarina, and see if we can be of service to them."

"So you have it planned. I did not suspect." Sadness etched the priest's kind face. "Well, I will not stand in your way. In fact, I would offer my blessing if this is something you have set your minds to."

"We would accept your blessing gladly. This is not a move we make lightly, but the times do not allow us to remain too long in one place."

Paul nodded. He glanced at Grisha, his faithful protector and friend, the only one who had walked every valley with him since they had come to know one another. Grisha was brother, father, mentor, conscience.

They parted from the priest the next morning. These days of political upheaval forced many partings, none easier than the others. Still robed as priests, Grisha and Paul Gregorovich walked north, following the Salgir River in the opposite direction they had followed it the previous summer. They spoke little and thought much as they walked into the setting sun of autumn.

ഇൾഇ

"Schwandorf!" Maria Hildebrandt tensed and clutched her satchel as the train conductor shouted her destination. The hour of truth approached. She had sent a telegram from Berlin announcing her coming. Would Dietrich be here to meet her? Would his family welcome her?

She had been traveling now for six months. It seemed like an eternity since she had bade farewell to Katarina and Johann in Halbstadt and left on this interminable trek with Benjamin Unruh through Russia and finally to Germany. But she would go to the ends of the earth to find Dietrich.

She repeated a prayer over and over as she stood and made her way to the exit. Stepping carefully down the temporary steps, with the help of the conductor, she shaded her eyes in the afternoon sun and searched the platform for the face she longed to see.

"Dear God, let him be here," she whispered. The station bustled with people of all description: soldiers returning to their homes, wives and mothers greeting them joyfully, children hiding from the men they no longer knew, seductively dressed women lurking in the shadows waiting for the unclaimed; each hoped the future would make up for the years the war had stolen from them.

As Maria's gaze scanned the crowd, she heard her name. She waved a hand in the air. Someone jostled her from behind and she tried again to find the location of the voice. A moment later she found herself looking up into deep blue eyes that twinkled as they regarded her, but the eyes, although very like

Dietrich's, belonged to a younger man of about her own age. He was somewhat slighter of build than Dietrich, and his hair a few shades lighter and windblown, not like Dietrich's carefully combed hair.

All Maria could say was, "Oh! You are not Dietrich."

Flashing her a wide smile, the young man offered her his arm and reached for her bag. "I regret that I am not. My name is Kristoph Kesselman, and I come in my brother's place. May I see you to our home?"

Maria could not move. "Then he is there? At his home? What has happened that he could not come to the station? Is he injured?"

Kristoph held up a hand, palm outward, to slow her questions. A shadow passed across his handsome face and his smile faltered. Shaking his head, he said, "No Ma'am, Dietrich is not at his home. He has not returned and we do not know where he is. I'm sorry to have to bring you these unhappy tidings."

Tears formed in Maria's eyes in spite of her resolution to remain calm and strong. She blinked them away and lifted her chin. "Very well," she said in a quavering voice. "That is no fault of yours. Please, let us leave this crowded place and go somewhere we can talk." She gave him a pleading glance and willed the tears to stop.

With a slight bow, Kristoph held her arm fast in his and forged a way out of the milling throng to a motorcar nearby. Wordlessly, he lifted her bag into the vehicle and opened the front passenger door for her. Once she was settled, he closed the door, and as he did, he caught and held her eyes for a long moment.

As Kristoph climbed into the driver's seat and started the car, Maria eyed him obliquely. What was the meaning of his long look? Surely he couldn't be thinking of her other than as Dietrich's chosen. She raised an eyebrow as she realized that he could indeed. She knew enough of men not to deceive herself there, but the realization brought a fresh stab of pain to her chest, and she hugged her satchel to her as a shield against it.

Chapter 2

As his feet carried him down the wide main street of Alexanderkrone, Johann's mind slipped back to Succoth Estate, Katarina's former home in Crimea, which had become his Eden on earth. It was there he had discovered true beauty: the estate with its mansion, parks, and orchards, the grace and love of Katarina, the integrity and strength of her father Heinrich.

Johann knew he would never fully adjust to the loss of Heinrich. The man who had been his father-in-law had also become his friend and mentor. He knew Katarina also suffered in her grief, and young Anna, sweet and pure as a dove, smiled through her tears and reminded them all, in spite of her youth, that they need not struggle against the will of God. He would bear them, He would heal them, He would eventually lead them all home at their appointed times, she said.

"Teacher, you look weary. Could I by chance lift your spirits with a listening ear?" Johann looked up, surprised, to find Abram Reimer at his side.

Johann smiled in spite of his grief. "Ah, my friend, you have found me out again. I'm afraid I do not hide my feelings well."

"Why should you? Should we not help each other by sharing our burdens? Is that not the meaning of Christian community? When one weeps, all weep with him; when one rejoices—which does not happen often these dim days—we all rejoice. Allow me to be your brother."

Johann blinked several times and pushed up his glasses with a forefinger. "Very well, and do not think me ungrateful for my hesitation." He walked slowly a few steps in silence, matching his stride to that of his middle-aged friend. "I miss Heinrich. I cannot accept the manner of his death. It plagues me day and night, and I'm sure Katya suffers as I do, surely more because he was her father." He turned to meet Abram's eyes. "How does one reconcile the reality with the promises of God that he will never forsake his children?"

"Has the Lord forsaken Heinrich?"

Johann lowered his head and stroked his moustache. In a small voice he said, "Perhaps not, but why must we go through this fire? Has God forgotten our plight? How am to care for my family?"

"One day at a time, Johann, one day at a time. Tomorrow has enough worries of its own. God will provide, and if he should call one of us home, that will be even better than remaining here. I don't understand either why the Lord allows such evil to be done."

He sighed and shook his head. "I'm afraid that faith is often nurtured in the school of adversity. It is the way of mankind. I wish it were not so, but . . . " his voice faded out and the two men walked together to Johann's house.

Katarina caught sight of them from the kitchen window and ran out to meet them. "Please tell me you do not bear bad news," she said, her green eyes wide.

Johann took her hand and held it tightly. "No, my dear. We were sharing the burdens we already bear, but now we will dismiss them for a time." Turning to Abram Reimer, he said, "Would you care to come inside?"

"Thank you, but I must hurry home to Cornelia. She has not been well. At first when Theodore and Katie Konrad came to live with us after their house was burned down, they proved to be wonderful company for Cornelia, but Katie's passing last month has saddened my wife, and Theodore's humorous tendencies have faltered in his grief."

"Give our love to her then," said Katarina. "I will visit her soon."

On the evening of November 11, Katarina met Johann at the door as he returned from a church meeting.

"What is that, Johann?" she asked, pointing to the west. The sky shone a hazy red on the winter horizon.

"I don't know," he said, mesmerized by the sight. "Must be a fire of some kind. I hope it doesn't spread; it's so dry here."

The next day Katarina stood frozen with fear on the path that led to their little house as her neighbor, Mrs. Franz, gave her the news. It was Machno again. Closer this time. As close as Blumenort, maybe fifteen versts as the crow flies. Mrs. Franz carried the news like a pelican carries rotting fish in her sagging bill. She had caught it and needed to get rid of it. The stench of it turned Katarina's stomach and filled her with the vilest dread. She began to believe their time had come, that she and her family would now be devoured by Machno's depraved appetite.

"Johann, they've come to Molotschna," she whispered fiercely when he returned home from the schoolhouse. "They have attacked Blumenort, Altonau, and Ohrloff. Where will they go next? It's only been a week since we buried the David Dicks from Apanlee."

"We don't know that the Dicks' murderers were Machnovitz," said Johann. "Could have been independent bandits."

Katarina stared at him incredulously. "Does it matter to you what brand of bandit shoots you?"

"Katya, we must keep our heads in this matter. It will do us no good at all to panic."

"I am quite ready to panic, Johann. Is there really nothing we can do?"

He rubbed a hand over his moustache and pushed up his eyeglasses. With a huge sigh he said, "Katya, I am not God. I am as helpless as you."

"You are not a woman either. They do horrible things to women."

"What would you have me do, Katie? Tell me and I will do it, if it is in my power. The local authorities are useless pawns in the hands of whoever is in power at this particular moment; we cannot depend on them for help. The *Selbstschutz* has tried to make a difference in defending our people, rightly or wrongly, but that has all backfired and we are now on the enemy lists.

"We are part of a huge sweeping cataclysm of history. Some of us will live, some will not. More than that I do not know, but if and until we are individually faced with the worst, we must pray and do what God requires of us. Please Katya, let us face this together. I feel like a target for your fear and anger, and I cannot withstand the arrows."

He stood waiting for her to respond. She stood trying to make sense of it. Neither found what they were looking for until Anna's slender arms encircled them both, pulling all three of them together. She looked up at them with calm determination.

"God will not forsake us," she said. Her voice sounded like an angel's, smooth, high and clear. And sure. "He has promised to help us in all our trials and so he will. Come."

She led them both by the hands into the little parlor and stopped before the settee. "I think we should pray." So Johann, Katarina and Anna knelt on the wooden floor, resting their elbows on the horsehair cushions, heads bowed in contrition before Almighty God. Through deep tears they asked forgiveness for their doubts and recommitted themselves to the One who had promised to keep them, while in nearby villages, mournful wails rose for the fallen.

Katarina watched the windows all that day, prepared to flee to the fields at the slightest sign of danger, but it did not come. Not that day. Instead, word of the growing typhus epidemic caused her to settle down and offer a helping hand at Dr. Bittner's office at the other end of the village. Not only was he battling an increasing number of typhus cases, he also had to deal with sporadic cases of smallpox, diphtheria, influenza, measles, and pneumonia. Katarina wondered at the doctor's perseverance and endurance.

Because of the number of patients and the instability of the times, most of the disease victims remained at home, with daily visits from the doctor. He did what he could, but even for those diseases for which cures had been discovered, he often could not find the necessary medicines, or afford them.

ຂ໑ຂ໑ຂ໑

Paul Gregorovich and Grisha traveled for two days in their priestly attire, then scrounged some peasant clothing and food at a bazaar in Dzhankoi, Crimea. By the end of the week they had reached Melitopol and jumped aboard a farmer's wagon for the last short jaunt to the Molotschna.

"You are almost home," said Grisha to Paul as they rattled into Altonau in the early evening.

"I have no home," answered Paul, his black eyes filled with pain. "I told you what I found last time I stopped there: no one lived in my village of Ackerman but a crazy old woman."

Grisha nodded his head and gazed into the sunset. "This world is not our home," he said. "In this world we will have trouble, so the Good Book says."

"A priest without a cassock," teased Paul. Then his face became serious as he continued. "One wonders how much trouble one life can hold."

They had stopped at the store on the main street, the

information hub of the village. A group of villagers gathered there, a world-weary bunch with lines on their faces and grief in their eyes.

"We seem to have come at an inopportune time," said Grisha softly, then changed his mind and asked them, "Has something happened here?"

The women in the group stifled sobs with their handkerchiefs and the men fought for composure. One of them, the eldest by Grisha's guess, heaved a tremendous sigh and told the tale.

"You must be strangers here. Machno has unleashed his fury on us in the Molotsch. He snuffed out eleven of our people here in Altonau and then went on to Ohrloff and Blumenort to kill more than twenty. We buried them yesterday. We are in sorrow and fear. If the madman does here what he did in Chortitza, many more of us are doomed. There is no place left to hide."

Grisha removed his cap in sympathy and respect, and Paul did the same. There were no words of comfort to salve the fresh wounds.

The man continued. "We are doomed, because we do not even dare to protect ourselves. We tried that once with the *Selbstschutz,* and it sealed our doom. Now we can only wait until that devil comes again." The cries of the women broke out in earnest at these words.

"Perhaps he has moved on," Paul suggested. "He attacks at random."

"Even lightning has been known to strike twice. No one is safe," the elder said.

"Who are you and what is your business here?" asked another of the men.

"This one is from Ackerman," said Grisha with a nod of his head toward Paul. "I myself am a wanderer. I have seen Petersburg through three name changes and then abandoned it for saner places. I see there are none."

Paul continued where Grisha left off. "We will most likely seek out someone in Alexanderkrone, a childhood friend of mine. Time will tell."

"You may stay with us then," said the elder. "It is not safe outside."

"Nor inside," retorted another. "Come with me. We will find a place for you tonight."

"We thank you," said Grisha sincerely. "We had not hoped for welcome, only rest."

"Rest welcome, then, and Godspeed to your destination tomorrow."

ᴥᴥᴥ

DEAR MIKA STOP
BANDITS TERRORIZE AGAIN STOP
MANY DEAD
& WE LIVE IN FEAR STOP
NO NICHOLAI YET STOP
J & K

The telegram from Johann and Katarina shook in Maria's hands. Kristoph looked on with concern in his eyes but did not interrupt her reading or her grief. He glanced over at his mother, sternness fighting with compassion on her face. She caught his eye and frowned.

Irmgard Kesselman had not welcomed the sudden arrival of this young woman claiming to be Dietrich's fiancée. Even though Maria Hildebrandt had been devastated by the news of her father and her home, Irmgard had viewed her with suspicion. She had taken care of the young woman during the months since she had come to Schwandorf, and she was slowly beginning to recover from the blow, but the care had been physical only, and Maria had deep emotional wounds. This telegram had brought more devastating news, and she wondered if Maria was strong enough to withstand it.

Now as Irmgard Kesselman watched Maria out of the corner of her eye, the ice of suspicion began slowly to melt.

"Well," she said, rising from her chair, "I believe a cup of tea would be in order."

Frau Kesselman made the tea and brought a cup first to Maria, who accepted it gratefully. Kristoph winked at his mother and turned to Maria.

"Would you care to tell us what the telegram says, or do you wish to keep it to yourself?"

Mika cleared her throat and nodded. "I would be glad to share it; the burden on my heart for my family is too heavy to carry alone." She told them of the dangers surrounding those she loved in a place she felt she had left many years ago, when it was only months.

When Jurgen Kesselman, Dietrich's father, arrived home from his work at the newspaper office, the atmosphere of the home changed considerably. Herr Kesselman had been quite taken with Maria from the start, inordinately proud that his son had chosen such a fine woman. He was a cheerful man, a gift he had bestowed on his sons also.

"Take comfort in the fact that they are alive and well," Jurgen suggested gently to Maria. "As long as there is life, there is hope, yes?"

"Yes, Herr Kesselman, but I can't help but worry for them, and we don't have any idea what has happened to my brother Nicholai. He left last summer and we haven't heard anything."

Kristoph spoke then. "I'd say not to worry. A young man like your brother would be very resourceful. I'm sure he wanted an adventure, and when the opportunity came, he took it."

"But why would he hurt his family so much, not leaving any word at all? That is unforgivable."

"You won't forgive him?" Frau Kesselman raised an eyebrow with her question.

Maria lowered her head. "Of course I will. I would forgive him anything if only he is alive and well."

"Yes," responded Frau Kesselman, a faraway look in her eyes. "Yes, so would I."

Her sadness brought Maria out of her grief and into this other woman's. She rose and knelt beside Frau Kesselman's chair. "I'm sorry," she said. "I forget that your grief is as great as mine. We must believe that both Dietrich and Kolya are alive and well, and that we will see them again."

The older woman regarded the younger. She placed an arm around Maria's shoulders.

Herr Kesselman clapped his hands joyfully and announced that tonight they would have a special supper. He would go straight to the bakery and buy some wiener schnitzel and they would celebrate life.

"And then, perhaps," said Mika, "we could talk about finding Dietrich."

"I agree," said Kristoph. "The time for waiting is over. We need to search for him ourselves."

"Any idea where to begin?" asked his father.

"We will discuss it after supper," said his mother.

ꕥꕥꕥ

Katarina took the tea Susannah Warkentin offered her and sipped it. Little Marianna slept peacefully in the bassinet in the corner of the room.

"She has grown so much in these last few months," she said.

"Yes," agreed Susannah, "I only wish Gerhard could see her." Her voice faded into tears.

Katarina could imagine her friend's pain, but she could not make it go away. She had no answers to Susannah's question: Why did God allow my husband to be taken by the White Army? Katarina also felt the unreasonable guilt that she still had her husband while Susannah waited and prayed for hers. And now she had a baby to care for, besides her mother and Katarina's brother, Peter.

Peter sat on a chair beside the bassinet like a guardian angel, a tall, thin angel whose dark hair tumbled onto his forehead in soft waves, shading his gray eyes. It was the eyes that gave him away. Sometimes Katarina saw confusion in them. She had also seen terror, but mostly Peter's eyes remained opaque, deflecting understanding. Besides Mama, Katarina knew him best, and she often felt she did not know him at all.

"He's always gentle," said Susannah to Katarina quietly. "I never worry about that."

Katarina was relieved, but she often felt she should be the one to look after Peter. After Gerhard had closed *Bethany Psychiatric Home*, Peter had clung to his nurse, Susannah. She did not complain, but Katarina still wished Peter would allow her to take him home.

One redeeming factor in the whole business was that Peter had bonded with Susannah's mother, Hannah. Since Susannah's father had been forced into the White Army along with her husband, Gerhard, Hannah had welcomed the presence of Peter even more. He did not require explanations. He simply lived each day as it unfolded, with rare words of observation to remind them all of his ability to sense the world through his own channels.

"Have you heard anything at all from Gerhard, Suse?"

"No, I haven't. I don't know if he is even alive." She raised her eyes to Katarina's. "That is what I live with." She took a deep breath and exhaled it. "Marianna is such a gift to us all. She is so good, just sleeping and eating, and when she is awake she is content. I am thankful for her, even though I am anxious for Gerhard. She is a part of him that I can hold close."

Katarina nodded. "I pray for you and for Gerhard every day. I'm sure the Lord hears."

"Oh yes, I'm sure he does," said Susannah with a touch of cynicism in her voice. "I just wish he would answer." Then, looking up at Katarina's pitying eyes, she said, "I'm sorry. You are a good friend to me, and I am becoming a bitter person. I know God knows best, but I don't necessarily like the way he is bringing it about."

"I wish I could do something to help you, something to make your life more bearable."

"Don't worry about me; I will survive. I think I will walk over to Neukirch to see how my sister Helena and her two little ones are doing."

As Katarina walked home along the dusty village street, she wondered how she would cope if Johann were suddenly called away. She had her own struggles with cynicism, wondering why she and Johann still had no children, but she could not unload her sorrow on an already burdened Susannah. Sometimes she wished for the dim holiness of Father Serge's church in Karassan. She would kneel there in the stillness and pour out her heart to her Lord. The churches in Alexanderkrone were far too conservative for that, so she shouldered her burden in silence, careful not to bother Johann with it. He had enough to worry about, not knowing how long he would be allowed to teach at the village school. These days everything could change in an instant, at the stroke of a pen . . . or the firing of a gun. She must reconsider her priorities.

ঌঌঌ

Johann and Katarina arrived at the Home for the Aged in Rueckenau in the early afternoon of a chilly November day.

Frau Anna Peters, Katarina's maternal grandmother, had awakened from her *mittag schlaff*, and welcomed her visitors with surprise.

"Well, well, what brings you two out on such a cool day?"

After hugs and shedding of coats, they sat together in Frau Peters's small sitting room. All around them hung pictures of her children and grandchildren, still and serious likenesses of those gone and those just gone away. The strong, hearty smell of cabbage borscht saturated the air of the rooms and caused Katarina's stomach to growl in anticipation.

"Oma," she began, not one to mince words, "we have been concerned about you here, with all the horrible things happening around us. We want you to come live with us. We have enough space, and I think the Home may not remain open very long if the political unrest continues to escalate. We want you to be safe."

"And I would be safe with you?" the old woman countered. "Abram and Cornelia tried to convince me to run off with them once before."

Katarina remembered the autumn of 1917, when Abram and Cornelia Reimer and their elderly neighbors, the Konrads, had come to Succoth for refuge from the chaos of the colonies. They had begged Frau Anna Peters to accompany them then, but she had refused.

"You would not be running off, Oma," said Johann. "I think you know the situation with many if not most of our Mennonite institutions these days. Everything is crumbling. We are offering you an alternative to the inevitable."

Frau Peters rocked in her chair, eyes straight ahead, hands folded in her aproned lap. Katarina conveyed to Johann with a slight shake of her head that patience and silence was their best ammunition in this encounter. Finally, Anna Peters looked at them and announced, "I will come. It is not my first choice, to be a burden to my grandchildren, but you are correct in saying I may have no option."

That said, she pushed herself to her feet and said, "*Nah yah*, we will have some borscht and brown bread, and then I must gather my things together. Come children."

"So here I am to crowd your little home, Anna," said Oma as Katarina ushered her into their house in Alexanderkrone. "Now you will have to put up with an old woman."

"I love you, Oma," said Anna as she wrapped her slender arms around Frau Peters's ample form. "A house with you in it would never be crowded."

"I believe the Annas will get along fine," declared Katarina with a smile. "I am looking forward to a Christmas filled with family and good memories."

Johann observed her happiness in silence, an unexplainable foreboding in his soul.

Chapter 3

Early in December Johann saddled up his horse and rode off to Tiege to see Benjamin B. Janz. He had first met Janz in the spring and had formed an immediate trust in the determined man who spent every spare moment working on government matters relating to Mennonite emigration. Johann had offered Janz his help and had, after some questioning, been accepted. Now that Johann and Katarina lived in the Molotschna Colony, it was much easier to keep in touch with Janz and his cause.

Johann knocked at the Janz door and was admitted by a dignified but clearly disturbed Maria Janz. At Johann's questioning look, she shook her head and murmured, "More bad news." Gesturing toward Benjamin's office, she returned to the kitchen.

Johann knocked softly at Benjamin's door and, at a murmured "yes," entered the room. Janz sat with his elbows on his desk, head in his hands. His worn German Bible lay open to the book of Job.

"Benjamin, what is it?" asked Johann, alarmed.

With a tremendous sigh, the older man looked up at Johann with red-rimmed eyes. "I do not understand God," he said. "I know how he answered Job sternly, and yet I ask him the same questions: Why do you allow evil, Lord? Why do the wicked prosper and the righteous suffer?"

Johann lowered himself into a chair beside the oak desk. "What has happened?"

Janz reached under his Bible for two sheets of rough paper, ink-smudged and water-stained, and handed them to Johann. "Read," he said, and sat back in his chair with closed eyes, his face gray.

It was a letter, dated December 6, 1919. Today was the 10th. "*This testament is written by Wilhelm J. Martens, formerly mayor of the village of Muensterberg, writing now from Steinfeld, Zagradovka Colony.*" Johann was immediately lost in the revelation that followed: "*I believe the end of the world is near. There can be no other explanation for the events of the past week. How else does one rationalize this unleashing of evil? My question, like Job's, is: what have we done to deserve this punishment?*

"*I write these things so they are not forgotten. I sit for long hours with head in hands, utterly bereft. But I must commit it to paper. On the afternoon of November 29, I, Wilhelm J. Martens, mayor of Muensterberg in the Zagradovka Colony of Ukraine, received a small delegation of riders to my village office. They arrived in a* droshky *with several more riders besides, all dressed as White soldiers. They were heavily armed and tried to make a scene. I prayed for grace and treated them with as much civility and necessary respect as possible. Finally they left. Thinking back, I now know they were looking for an excuse to cause trouble, but I gave them none. As it turns out, they did not need excuses, nor were they Whites. Only Machno's men could be that evil.*

"*After a matter of hours, the men—bandits all—returned with reinforcements and proceeded to the village center. There they set up a band and commenced playing loud dance music. What followed was macabre.*

"*The bandits, well stoked with Samogonka, fanned out and began killing everyone they came upon. I was at home by then, and my dear wife, knowing that they usually sought out the men of the villages as victims, insisted I hide. I made my secretive but swift way to the back garden and slipped behind a stone bench in a thicket of dense bushes. I could hear the music as plainly as if it came from my own house. And the screaming. It went on and on. Wagons of Russian peasants drove through the streets, freely helping themselves to whatever met their fancy. Fires were burning everywhere. And always the raucous banging of the drums. It was like a scene from hell.*

"After what seemed like a lifetime, the murdering thieves must have gone away and a deafening silence ensued. I cautiously picked my way back to the house. There was only sparse moonlight. The door was ajar and it wouldn't open all the way. I squeezed through and fell headlong over something in my path."

The writing grew erratic and difficult to read, but Johann was too engrossed to give up.

"It was my wife, or what was left of her. They use bayonets and axes and swords, these demons. I gently moved the body and opened the door to admit what little light I could. Scattered throughout the house, as if chased down in flight, were the bodies of our six children, ranging in age from toddler to eleven years. They had all been horribly disfigured.

"I backed out of the house as one in a trance and went to the neighbors' for help. What I found there made me retch uncontrollably. They were all dead, bodies strewn about, and their heads were placed on the windowsills. The husband, who had been hiding as I was, stood staring with the face of a stone statue.

"I could not rest. I crossed the street to another neighbors' house and found a similar scene, except here the heads of the mother and seven children were placed on chairs around the table.

"The teachers, Johann Martens and Heinrich Wolf, both lay dead. Wolf's throat had been cut. I could see where he had

tried to stop the blood with his shirt. The bandits had left bottles of Samogonka sitting on the table. Apparently they had taken a break to drink while their victims breathed their last.

"I went back for my neighbor and pulled him into the garden, away from the scene. Tomorrow we would face what had to be done. But the next day became a copy of the first. The bandits and peasants returned to continue their work. Some villagers were able to cross the Ingulets River to seek refuge in Shesternaya, but that was where the Machnovitz were headquartered, and most of these refugees were also killed.

"The women in our village were not all killed like my wife. Some were taken for the bandits' use, and in retrospect, I would rather my dear wife be dead than face a living hell with those devils. How can I say that? Surely this must be the end of days, to be so filled with horrors. Oh Lord, when will we be vindicated?

"I do not know how long this murderous rioting would have gone on, but on the evening of the third day, December 1, the bandits stopped their violence and left in a rush. Later, I saw the reason: a company of White soldiers approached.

"Final tally: At least 98 villagers dead—many entire families—but we are going by who is missing because most of the bodies are too badly mutilated or burned to be positively identified. One house remains standing, as well as a dozen or so smaller buildings, smoldering piles of ashes, carnage everywhere, bodies frozen in grotesque agony. Those of us who remain alive, although we are dead inside, are left to sort out the aftermath. And always the question looms: Why? How shall I endure this grief? How shall I ever in this life forgive myself for hiding and leaving my wife to face them alone? Has God turned his back on us?

"People are beginning to arrive from neighboring villages

to help us. We were not the only village targeted. They killed eleven in Schoenau, seventeen in Tiege, forty-five in Ohrloff, sixteen in Reinfeld and twelve in Gnadenfeld. But Muensterberg fared the worst. How low can men stoop? How dark can the world become?

"I fear I shall lose my sanity yet, with this burden on my soul. Therefore I write this testimony so the rest will not forget. We are not safe anywhere. We have no home. We can trust no one. Where shall we go now? We are birds without nests, sheep without shepherds. We are doomed."

The letter was signed by Wilhelm J. Martens in a shaky script. Johann handed the letter back to Janz, and his own hand shook. His stomach roiled and he left the house to stand on the porch and gulp in the cold, clear December air. Eventually he returned to the house. He sat again beside Janz's desk and they wept openly together.

"We must get out," said Benjamin. "We must set our people free."

ꟷꟷꟷ

Katarina looked forward to Christmas. Anna helped to create a festive atmosphere with her carols and hand-drawn cards, but something troubled Johann, and Katarina knew he was not telling her the whole truth.

"You are worried about your husband," said Oma.

"Yes, Oma. Your wisdom matches your years."

Oma smiled, then sobered. "There are some things that are possibly too difficult to speak of to the ones you love the most. You know the stories: bandits on the loose and the Reds are advancing south toward us. Johann can do nothing about either situation. He wants to spare you."

"Well, it doesn't spare me, not being informed. It just makes me worry more."

"Do you tell all the details you hear to Anna?"

Katarina was angry, and it took all her self-control to keep her voice calm. "Of course not, Oma, she is a child."

"The reason you don't tell her is not only that she is a child, but that you love her too much to force these thoughts upon her."

Katarina looked at her grandmother. "You are right, Oma. I need to put my trust in God and not in my husband. My faith is very small these days."

The old woman beckoned Katarina to her and took her hands. "Sit down beside me for a few moments, child," she said, "and we will pray for faith. It comes from God, you know."

That evening as the family sat at supper, an insistent knock interrupted them. Katarina's eyes grew wide with fear, but with a glance at Oma she willed herself to calm down.

Johann answered the knock and was greeted roughly by two Red soldiers.

"We are here for Johann Sudermann, schoolteacher."

"I am Johann Sudermann."

"You are to be ready by tomorrow morning to accompany us south to meet the enemy. Come to the Co-op Store at sunup. If you do not appear, you will be found and shot." They turned back up the snow dusted path and continued on to the next house.

Johann stood watching them walk away. Disbelief filled the ensuing silence as each member of the family fought their way through denial, anger, fear, and resignation. Perhaps peace would come eventually, but not tonight. Resignation would have to suffice.

Johann easily identified the fear in Katarina's sea green eyes and rested a hand on her shoulder. How many Christmases had they been separated? How could he leave her with the added responsibility of looking after Oma and Anna, especially with the bandit threat so real and so near?

"If the Reds are near, the Machnovitz will move on. That is a positive consideration," he said.

Katarina pressed her hands to her mouth to stop the sobs, but could not. Johann, with unashamed tears of his own, knelt beside her and held her, while Oma pulled little Anna near.

After a time Oma said, "We will be fine, Johann. Anna is not so little anymore and can help with many things, can't you, my dear? I will also do my share. We have many good friends and neighbors."

The people in Muensterberg had many good friends and neighbors too, thought Johann. "I have no choice but to place you all in the hands of God," he said.

Oma clucked her tongue. "I only hope God can live up to your high expectations of him."

Johann shook his head. "I'm sorry. Trusting myself to God is not nearly so difficult as trusting you all to his care. I know he is able, but I feel such a heavy responsibility, like I am deserting you in the worst of times."

Katarina turned toward him. "You are not deserting us, my dear husband," she said. "Perhaps it will be no harder facing the reality than the ever-present threat. It was bound to happen sooner or later. I only hope and pray you shall return to us unharmed and that . . . that we will be here to meet you."

Her tears came again, but Johann knew there were no options. Now was the time for courage.

Katarina walked with Johann to the center of town where a group of villagers assembled in front of the Co-op Store. They had slept poorly if at all, not wanting the night to end but thankful for the warning that gave them time to say good-bye. Susannah and Gerhard had not been so fortunate, Katarina knew. He had been taken away before her eyes, torn from her hands, her cries and questions ignored. At least she and Johann had been given some advance notice.

Katarina held close the hope that perhaps the civil war would end soon and Johann would be returned home, but she knew that was improbable, given the progress of the war. One never knew from one day to the next how the battles would come out.

As the sun pushed over the horizon, the commander began to call out names and unit leaders, and all the recruits lined up accordingly.

"Ask around for Kolya," Katarina reminded him for the tenth time, thoughts of her young brother Nicholai filling her mind. He nodded, squeezed her hand, and gave her a long look, then turned to his line. He carried a duffel bag filled with warm clothing, food, and limited writing supplies. He promised to try to keep in touch. Anna had given him a brightly painted Christmas card with her love, Oma had prayed a blessing upon him, and Katarina, well, Katarina loved him.

His figure blurred through Katarina's tears as he and the other men marched away. "Faith is believing in what we do not see," Oma had told them. Katarina clung to that faith as the distance between her and her husband grew. At last she turned, and Anna stood beside her to walk her home.

Johann had not been gone a week when Katarina's supper was again interrupted by knocking at the door. This time it was up to her to answer. Anna had flown to the window and peeked out the curtain. "It's two men," she whispered, terror in her voice.

Katarina took a deep breath, looked to Oma for support, and opened the door. It took a moment or two for her to recognize the two visitors, snow feathering their hair as they removed their hats, but then it flooded back to her: the forgiving, the disguises, the flight. She opened the door wide in welcome.

"Paul Gregorovich! Grisha! What brings you here and how did you find us?" She offered them chairs and pushed bread and cheese toward them. "Oma, this is Johann's dear friend, Paul Gregorovich Tekanin and his friend Grisha. This is my maternal grandmother, Anna Peters, and you remember my sister, Anna."

Both men smiled to a suddenly shy Anna and bowed respectfully to Oma. Paul turned back to Katarina. "Where is Johann?"

"Gone," said Katarina, trying to keep her emotions in check. "The Red Army forced him to join them. They left only days ago."

Paul fell into a chair. "We should have come sooner."

"How could we know?" countered Grisha.

They spoke of what had transpired in the last several months.

"Are you not afraid of being taken into the Red Army again?" asked Katarina. "Your leaving was not exactly acceptable."

Paul put a finger to his lips and smiled a slow smile. "I am a poor peasant who seeks work in the colonies. This colony is my home, and we might perhaps be of service to you."

Grisha added his own version, of which they were all aware: "Three women alone are not safe these days. We would be happy to stay in the garden shed and help where we can in exchange for a little food and anonymity."

"You have come at a most opportune time," Katarina said. "I will admit I would feel safer with trustworthy men nearby."

"We will try our best to meet your expectations," said Grisha, bowing slightly.

"We could share our Christmas with you," suggested Anna.

Katarina smiled. "Then it seems we have reached an agreement. I will find some extra blankets."

"We do not need much in the way of creature comforts, Ma'am," said Paul. "We are used to barns and straw, or grass and clear blue sky."

"It's almost Christmas and the air is cold." Katarina walked to the bedroom, then turned back and said, "I am greatly relieved to have you here. I thank you on behalf of Johann. This house could use some company, especially at this time of year."

The Sudermann house was indeed filled with people that Christmas, but the guests were not family and friends. As the Bolshevik Red Army rolled south to fight off General Denikin's Whites, troops pulled into the Molotschna, and they needed places to stay. Every available space was taken by the soldiers, and Katarina wondered why Johann, as one of their number, could not remain there as well. She was thankful, however, for the two ragged men, purposely scruffy, who had taken up residence in the garden shed. Their presence gave her a sense of security that she dearly needed at that time.

Susannah, although responsible for little Marianna, Hannah, and Peter, was also expected to billet army personnel. It was especially difficult for her because Gerhard was presently on the opposing side. He had been conscripted by the Whites in June and she had not heard from him since. She shuddered at the thought that one of these soldiers who now slept in Gerhard's home might eventually kill him. She tried to keep such thoughts away, but they hovered on the edge of her consciousness.

Generally, the Red soldiers were polite and respectful, especially to Oma, who had decided that people were people no matter where they were. Except Machno's men. Yet she knew of others who thought it expedient to be respectful of the bandits also, and it had saved their lives. Oma speculated that she would have probably lost her head rather than to bow and scrape before that lot.

Oma and Katarina protected young Anna as much as possible. She had grown tall and willowy in the last year, and her blonde hair curled in the same unruly manner as Katarina's. She was only eleven, but showed promise of becoming a beautiful young woman. Her sister kept her as busy as possible when soldiers were in the house, thankful that Oma was present to help watch over her.

Paul and Grisha also kept an eye out for Anna, who had become dear to them. She had a way of melting the coldest heart with her smile, with her eyes. Even though the Reds who were relegated to Alexanderkrone and area were for the most part decent men, Paul and Grisha kept close watch.

These Reds were not the violent ones with which Paul had thrown in his lot in Leningrad, but he knew the circumstances that could turn a man into an animal, and he would never trust anyone completely again. Except perhaps Grisha and Johann. To preserve his anonymity, Paul kept his head shaved. He could not remove the long dark eyelashes or disguise his coal black eyes, but he kept his hat low on his head when strangers were about.

Grisha didn't worry about his hair. Over the last couple of years his reddish mop and beard had grayed, and he was much thinner than during his days at PRAVDA. Grisha had also ceased to live in fear. He feared for those he cared about, but not for himself. Serving the Sudermanns gave his life purpose, and for that he was thankful. He would not worry about tomorrow.

In this blur of busyness, Christmas 1919 came and went, the most important consideration being how to provide food for the constant stream of Red soldiers coming to the door. That and the increasing occurrence of disease in its many forms.

ഇഇ

Maria Hildebrandt stared at the map of Europe spread open before her on the Kesselman's dining table. She and Kristoph had done the easy part: they had traced Dietrich's journey from Succoth Estate to Karassan, but then he and his companions had disappeared into oblivion.

"There were three of them traveling together," said Maria. "Father Serge told us so."

Jurgen Kesselman nodded from his easy chair. "We may be able to find out who the others were, but it would require an excursion to Berlin." His wife sat quietly crocheting, listening.

"I would be more than willing to make the journey," said Kristoph.

Maria sat straighter. "I will go with you." It was a statement, not an offer, and her posture intimated a will of steel. "We must gather whatever information is available."

"A word of caution," said Jurgen. "Since the Treaty of Versailles has been ratified, our country struggles to pay the huge war debt."

"A demanding agreement," said Kristoph.

"Yes. Millions of dollars are needed to repay losses in livestock, ships, railroad cars, and money, after pulling back our borders. And then there's the disarmament. Perhaps it would be advisable to wait a time before venturing off to Berlin. The army will be busy readjusting."

"How long, then?" Maria wanted to set out immediately. She had already waited many months since arriving in Schwandorf.

Jurgen frowned momentarily and then brightened. "It is almost February now. How about postponing your departure another month? Spring would make travel easier."

A troubled look crossed Maria's face. "Perhaps I shall go to Berlin now anyway. I've already lived off your generosity far too long."

"You will stay with us, as you have been. You are a part of

our family now and so you are welcome here for as long as you need our hospitality." Kristoph obviously spoke for his father as well, who nodded and beamed, but Frau Kesselman concentrated on her sewing.

"Mother?" prompted Kristoph.

Her hands stilled. "Of course you are welcome here. We will have to find you something to do, though, or time will be heavy on your hands. With the losses you have received, you need to keep busy."

Maria heaved a great sigh of resignation. She was not good at waiting.

ꙮꙮ

Katarina sat at the table in the little house in Alexanderkrone where she and Johann had taken up residence when they came to the Molotschna in September. Oma and Anna had already gone to bed, but Katarina could not sleep. For one thing, she was hungry. Food was scarce and the many billets only made the situation worse. For the first time since Christmas, the three of them were alone, except for Paul Gregorovich and Grisha in their garden shed. Those two did not demand, but scrounged and helped to feed the many expectant appetites.

Katarina wondered where Johann was now, how far away, and at what kind of place he received food and lodging. That thought alone gave her grace to continue to serve the Red soldiers as they passed through.

She thought of Mika, far away in Germany. Germany—the enemy—now cowed and disciplined. What a farce, she thought, consigning an entire country to the same opinion its leaders decided upon. They were all people just like her. She prayed for her sister and her determined search for her Dietrich.

Then there was Nicholai. For some reason, she believed he

was alive and well. She thought she would know if he wasn't. "He's so young, Lord," she whispered. "Please, please look after him and keep him from harm." In her soul she heard the answer: *Is my arm too short? What is impossible with people is possible with God.*

Even though the peace of the moment soothed her weary soul, Katarina soon felt the loneliness of missing Johann descend upon her. I must pull myself together and do something constructive, she thought. But what? She thought of Susannah, busy with her baby Marianna, and of the other young women with their growing families. What a comfort it would be to have children of her own, hers and Johann's. She sighed, then straightened. Why had she not thought of it before? Instead of wallowing in self-pity, she could make the most of her opportunities. She would begin to arrange it tomorrow. With a satisfied smile and a prayer of thanks, she rose and went off to bed and a more restful sleep than she had had in a long time.

Chapter 4

Word from the Chortitza Colony was bleak. It was bad enough in the Molotschna, thought Paul, but Chortitza suffered much greater losses than her sister colony. He had heard of unimaginable atrocities, of hideous murders and rape, of people—sick, elderly, young—driven from their homes in the middle of winter. Lack of food haunted everyone, and now the dreaded typhus raged through Chortitza in epidemic proportions, even reaching its withering hand into the Molotschna.

He could hardly fathom the plight of the people in Chortitza. He knew everyone's hearts either prayed for the comfort of their brothers and sisters or wondered when their turn would come. As miserable as it was to have the Red soldiers around, and as unnerving when one of them looked at him twice with narrowed eyes, their presence at least kept the Machno dogs at bay.

Katarina also heard of the horrors in Chortitza. Disease, hunger, cold, and hopelessness took its toll every day, and she wondered what she could do to help. Some of her neighbors and friends were organizing an aid shipment to the colony. She determined to find something to send along as well; she hoped they would do the same for her if and when she needed it.

What bothered her most were the stories of the women who suffered from the diseases carried and spread by the bandits and the soldiers. She had heard that more than one hundred women in Chortitza and some in the Molotsch were being treated for these diseases. At least their bodies were treated. There was no treatment for their permanently wounded souls. She shuddered, pleading with God to spare her that particular trauma. What is our life coming to when we bargain with God for a slit throat rather than being raped, Katarina asked herself. She must occupy her mind with other things.

"Anna, I have an idea," she announced the next morning at their meager breakfast. Both Annas focused on her face. "In the time we have before the next onslaught of soldiers arrives, we need to keep busy. It helps the time pass and settles our minds." She paused and looked to her grandmother for encouragement. The old woman nodded, curiosity lighting her bright eyes. "I would like to start a literary society. There used to be one here, but people have stopped coming. I would like to revive it. What do you think?"

Anna clapped her hands delightedly. "Yes, oh yes, Katya. We could meet at the schoolhouse because regular classes have been suspended for the present. Oma, what do you think?"

"I agree wholeheartedly. You start this group and help people take their minds off their troubles. How often would you meet?"

"I think once every week would be nice," said Katarina. The three of them put their heads together and discussed place, time, activities, and spreading of the word. The planning offered a short escape from the dismal realities around them. Katarina felt her heart warm at the thought of being surrounded by others who appreciated the written word.

Abram Reimer sanded the corners of the deacon's bench he had made for the entry of the church. The original one had been hauled out and burned by robbers recently. The bandits had not taken any lives this time, at least not directly.

His chin trembled as he remembered finding Theodore Konrad lying in pain in the backyard, where he had fallen while running from the bandits. The doctor couldn't say how many of Theodore's brittle bones were broken; that was not the greatest threat. It was pneumonia that took Abram's cheerful and witty companion from him.

Abram kept food on the table for himself and Cornelia by doing odd jobs for people in his carpentry shop. Most could not afford to pay him in actual cash, but they managed to find some form of exchange: vegetables, bread, fresh fruit from their orchards, the odd cut of meat from someone fortunate enough to have it.

Even in this time of leanness, Abram was amazed at the difference in financial status of his people. Most lived hand-to-mouth and shared with those who had less, but there were always a few who never seemed to lack. They pretended to be in want like everyone else, but their clothes did not show wear, their figures did not cease to grow, and their faces looked healthy in spite of supposed lack of food.

Abram's carpentry skills allowed him to put his time and talents to good use. He wished Cornelia could keep busier.

"Hello," called a voice he loved to hear, easing him from his own concerns for Cornelia.

"I am here, Katarina," he replied from the corner where he sat sanding the bench. "How good to see you. Have you stopped by to see Cornelia today?"

She smiled and nodded. "I have, Uncle. I gave her a pillow top design from Oma; she is working on it now."

"Thank you, Katarina. That will serve to distract her for the time being." He sighed. "She used to be busy all the time, baking, cleaning, gardening, all those things. Now I have to encourage her to get out of bed and suggest things for her to do."

"Her fears consume her. It has become a habit. There are

many people living in the prison of fear these days." Katarina walked about the workshop, admiring Abram's various projects. "I know, because I tend to fear myself, but now with Johann gone I am forced to be the leader in our home. I cannot afford to drown in my fears because the others depend on me, but it is only by God's grace that I can get up and face the day sometimes."

"You are a hero, my dear, and I admire you greatly."

"Oh no, Uncle. I am not brave at all; I am a coward."

He smiled his admiration at her. "Do you know what the difference is between a hero and a coward? I will tell you: both are afraid, but the coward runs away, while the hero faces her fears in the midst of her weakness. Yes, my dear, you are very brave."

Katarina smiled and reached up to pat her unruly hair. "As I said, God helps me, but sometimes we must help others who cannot help themselves. In fact, I have an idea for you and Tante Cornelia."

He sobered. "Tell me then; all ideas are welcome."

"Well, we are all aware of the terrible things happening in the Chortitza Colony, and some people here are talking of sending help to them. I propose that you both help in the organizing of this aid. We need to spread the word around, collect food and clothing, and arrange for it to be distributed over there. I think it would help her to be able to help others."

"Brilliant, Katya. You have my support, and I will talk to some of the men about delivering the shipment." His face grew solemn and sad. "Our brothers and sisters there in the Old Colony are experiencing evils that no one should ever have to face. We must do what we can.

"Now I have an idea to match yours, Katie. Ask Susannah's mother Hannah to help too. She and Cornelia are becoming good friends and the busyness would do them both good."

"I will, Uncle," she said, and threw her arms around his

neck. Without warning the sobs burst from her lips. He held her close, taking the place of the father she had lost, and soaking up the love of the daughter he had never had. "I'm sorry," she managed, between sobs. "Sometimes I miss Papa so much I think my heart will break."

Abram made comforting sounds and patted her back until she composed herself, then smiled his endearing smile as she kissed his cheek and went in search of Cornelia.

When she had joined the Sudermann household, Oma Peters had not expected pampering. Besides offering ideas to stretch the limited food supply, she also looked after their two pigs, seven chickens, four ducks, and the milk cow, but since the arrival of Grisha and Paul Gregorovich, she had much help. The difficulty of finding food for humans multiplied when applied to animals. It seemed almost heartless to feed animals when people were hungry, but Frau Anna Peters knew that eventually the family and others would be grateful for meat, and every day they thanked the Lord for fresh eggs and milk, for cream and butter.

She had not worked so hard in many years, but as she said to the family, "For such a time as this, all previous constraints are laid aside."

"I'm worried about Marianna," said Susannah to Katarina when the latter came to visit. "She is feverish and irritable. Would you look at her?"

"Have you sent for the doctor?" Katarina bent over the baby's crib and and touched her. Marianna's skin was hot and she fussed.

Susannah hesitated. "No," she said in a small voice.

Katarina began to ask her why, but realized she knew the answer. "Would he not accept some eggs or cream in payment?"

Susannah's face reddened and she moved to pick up her

whining baby. "We cannot spare them," she said quietly.

"Suse, she needs to see a doctor. With disease rampant all over the South, we cannot take chances."

Katarina took a cloth and dipped it in the bowl of water on the kitchen counter. She reached it to Susannah who removed some of Marianna's clothing and sponged her off. The whining turned to howls of discomfort and protest. "Her crying is only making her hotter," Susannah said.

"I will go for Dr. Bittner," said Katarina.

"Katya, I can't . . ."

"Don't worry; we'll think of something. We must look after Marianna."

Katarina found it difficult to concentrate at the Literary Society meeting that evening. Goethe and Schiller sounded stilted compared to the realities of disease and hunger, but as the evening wore on, she gradually relaxed into the beauty of the words of Fenelon read by one of the dozen or so attendees:

> *Cheered by the presence of God, I will do at each moment, without anxiety, according to the strength which he shall give me, the work that his Providence assigns me. I will leave the rest without concern; it is not my affair. I ought to consider the duty to which I am called each day, as the work that God has given me to do, and to apply myself to it in a manner worthy of his glory, that is to say, with exactness and in peace.*

Somehow the words found their way into her heart and granted peace to her spirit as she walked home through the deepening dusk.

"Measles," proclaimed Dr. Bittner. "Keep her quiet, draw the blinds against bright sunlight, give her lots to drink, and I will check on her tomorrow."

Susannah held little Marianna close to her heart as the doctor let himself out the door.

"Oh, my precious little one," she said. "We will take good care of you. We will make sure you get better." She continued to croon as she rocked the sick child in her arms.

Besides the literary group, Katarina joined the Concordia Choir. She loved music and the schedule of regular practices. It also availed her of the opportunity to mix with others on a social level. With Johann gone, the choir filled part of her loneliness. It blessed her heart to sing the deep alto notes in harmony with the melodies of hymns and folk songs. Concordia's able director, Mr. Isaac P. Regehr, expected strict attendance and discipline at practices, but afterwards, joined the others as they visited. The members often shared or recited poetry or essays during breaks in practice. The Concordia Choir proved to be a release of praise to God and a small haven of creativity and cultural challenge in the chaos of her corner of the world, and Katarina was thankful for it.

"Have you heard the news?" asked Mr. Regehr. "North American Mennonites have banded together to send a shipment of foodstuffs to help us in our time of need. It should arrive soon."

Katarina sat up straighter at the announcement. Perhaps help really was on the way.

"Benjamin Janz and Benjamin Unruh are both working toward emigration," added one of the young men.

"Unruh is heading off again to Europe and America with A. A. Friesen, J. J. Esau, and C. H. Warkentin on behalf of the the Union of South Russian Mennonites—VMSR—to find us a home," said another.

"I hope they find something soon. We heard thieves in the barn last week."

"I heard that . . ."

". . . bandits stole the Koehn's horses yesterday," Katarina told Oma as she returned from choir practice. "One of them was borrowed."

"*Ja, ja.*" Oma expertly treadled the spinning wheel while she spoke, letting the wool slide through her fingers. "Now they will have to ask for help again to do their farming. They can't sow their fields without a horse."

"I wish Johann were home. If they steal a horse or a set of harnesses, so be it, but what if they come into the house?"

"No use borrowing trouble, Katie. We're in God's hands."

Katarina sat down near her grandmother. "Aren't you ever afraid, Oma? Don't you ever doubt?"

"Of course I do, but it doesn't change the situation. Trust is better than worry."

Oma swayed gently with her work, soft wrinkles outlining her eyes, her mouth, her neck. Katarina leaned over and kissed her cheek.

When Katarina had heard of Unruh's planned expedition to Europe, she had asked him to forward a letter to Maria in Schwandorf. The letter was the encouragement Maria needed to convince the Kesselman family that it was time to begin the search for Dietrich in earnest.

"You cannot go alone," said Frau Kesselman. "It is neither safe nor proper."

Maria raised her chin. "I don't care if it's particularly proper, and it's safer than the situations my family members find themselves in daily. Don't you see? I must go."

"Then I will accompany you," said Kristoph.

"And that would lend propriety to the situation?" asked

his mother incredulously, a hint of her supposedly banished distrust of Maria Hildebrandt showing through her words.

"It's perfectly decent to ride the train," Kristoph answered.

Maria continued. "I am sure we could stay with the Schroeders in Berlin when we arrive."

Herr Kesselman added his confirmation. "It sounds like a good plan."

Maria guessed that in his heart Jurgen Kesselman wanted to believe Dietrich lived, that he would see him again. She knew he would love to begin the search, but he could not leave Irmgard alone, and he had a job at the newspaper office that he could not ignore. In the aftermath of war, one was exceedingly fortunate to hold a job, especially one that paid a decent wage. It was not something he could throw away, no matter how tempting the thought.

So Jurgen Kesselman did what he could by sending Kristoph with Maria. The two boarded the train for Berlin in March as the winter snow and rain receded into spring sunshine. The desecrated war zones were washed and cleansed, and new growth sprouted in promise of continued life and hope.

ഇഇഇ

Katarina grimaced as she cooked up a pot of *Prachasupp*. They had no meat at present—they were saving the chickens for eggs and the pigs for fattening—so she used what they had: potatoes, onions and flour, along with a bit of seasoning, to make the "beggar's soup." She cooked up the potatoes with the onion, salt and pepper, and bay leaf, meanwhile mixing the noodle dough from flour Paul Gregorovich had brought her. Then she snipped the dough off into the boiling water in little pieces and cooked it a bit longer. It would fill their stomachs if not their cravings, she decided.

No one complained about the plain fare. Paul and Grisha were thankful for food and Anna did not eat very much at the best of times. Katarina worried about her health.

Oma reminded them from time to time that they were fortunate to have potatoes and onions, and especially flour. You could make the most interesting things, she said, from these three ingredients. And salt. Always plenty of salt. If you were going to use salt or sugar, she said, then you shouldn't skimp on either. They still had salt, but Katarina knew the sugar was pretty well gone.

The way the crops looked this year, there would be few watermelons to make into syrup. They would all have to get used to a diet lacking in sweetness, that was a fact. As long as they could keep eating until the American aid arrived.

"We are standing guard at night again," said Paul Gregorovich. "People are so hungry they are stealing without a second thought. It will only get worse if things don't improve soon."

Katarina was surprised. "I didn't know you were staying awake at nights to protect us. I will take my turn tonight."

"I don't think so," said Grisha gently. "Tekanin and I are well able to trade off. We need to do something to earn our food, you know."

"But you do. You found us some flour. You find food for the pigs and the cow. You have patched up the back shed and fixed the holes in the roof of our house. I don't expect you to stay awake all night too."

"Katya," began Paul earnestly, "as long as Johann is gone, and perhaps even once he returns home, we will take care of you and yours to the best of our ability. Please do not deny me—us—of this privilege."

"Paul, I have forgiven you for what happened to Papa. You were not directly responsible. You do not need to keep paying for that."

Paul's face tightened and his lips formed a thin line. He continued in a quiet voice heavy with emotion. "I can never pay for that. At least accept what I give for Johann's sake."

"Yes. Yes, I accept on Johann's behalf and thank you with more than simple words can say. Your presence here is such a comfort and security for us all." She looked around the table at the nodding heads. Anna liked Paul, but was partial to Grisha, who brought her out of her shyness with his gentle ways. They communicated without many words, something Grisha had no doubt learned in the monastery. Theirs was a friendship of the spirit, the kind that lasted. It was good for Anna, thought Katarina, who had to grow up now without a father of her own.

Grisha walked with Katarina to the Literary Society meeting one night before Easter. He had insisted, said it would be dark when she returned home. Besides, he had said, he enjoyed literature, had written some of it himself, he joked, referring to PRAVDA'S pages. As they walked through the town toward the school building, Katarina was startled by noises in the trees at the side of the road. She gripped Grisha's sleeve instinctively, then let go, embarrassed.

"I'm sorry," she said quickly. "I thought I heard something."

"You did," he said. "It was the children."

"The children? What children?"

"The orphans; the homeless ones. There are many who have lost their entire families in this endless war and they band together to survive. Not just Russians but Mennonite children also."

"I heard the people of Halbstadt had taken in a large number of children from the Old Colony whose parents had either been murdered or died from disease, but I didn't expect them to be wandering around in the dark out here. How could we have missed their need?"

"They are probably not even from Alexanderkrone. Many Russian children have been left alone, and some of your own have also slipped between the cracks, so to speak, although the Mennonite church has done a good job of finding homes for the children they are aware of. One cannot hope to reach them all."

"I had no idea. Would they . . . are they dangerous?"

"I will walk with you after dark, Katarina. Do not worry about them."

"We should help them, feed them." She was quiet then, remembering that they had little to feed themselves, never mind handing it out to others. "At Succoth we always had enough to give away," she said. "Succoth is a dream from another life, another era. I don't think we will ever experience anything like it again."

Grisha started to refute her words, but stopped himself. "Yes, those days are gone, a brief glimpse of sunshine behind heavy clouds."

Katarina turned to look directly at Grisha as they climbed the steps of the schoolhouse. "Will these clouds last forever?" she asked.

He returned her sober gaze with one of his own. "For some of us they may," he said quietly, and then continued up the steps.

The latest group of soldiers who had demanded food and lodging at the Sudermann cottage belonged to the White Army. They had moved north again, pushing the Reds back before them. Katarina wondered when the craziness would end, this endless unrest and conflict, this Russian purgatory. She longed to know where Johann was, and the condition of his spirit. She knew the emptiness in the pit of her stomach was only partly due to hunger. If she had not had the responsibility of looking after Oma and Anna, she would have given up many times, but she would endure for their sakes and for Johann's. She would be here when—if—he returned.

Almost every day Katarina stopped at Susannah's to see how Marianna was progressing. The sweet child had suffered a considerable setback with the attack of the measles virus. It was uncommon, they both knew, for an eight-month-old child to suffer such a serious illness, but they also recognized that the life they found themselves in was anything but normal.

Katarina was grieved at the change in Susannah. When the White Army had taken Gerhard, they had also stolen Susannah's spirit. Even with Marianna, whom she loved with her whole heart, she was not the lively, cheerful person she had been. Not that Katarina expected her to be cheerful in their present circumstances, but she was only half the person she had been when Katarina had come to know her. All Katarina could do was to be there for her, to listen and support and love.

This day Marianna lay in a bassinet on the front porch of the house with Peter guarding her. He had become Marianna's protector, and Katarina was convinced he would put himself between Marianna and any danger that threatened her. It was good to see him with a sense of purpose, even if he did not discern it himself.

"She's much improved," announced Susannah as Katarina bent over the bassinet to stroke the baby's fair cheek. It was still marked from the measles, but seemed to be healing now.

"Thank God for that," said Katarina. "She is so thin; I think it took every bit of her strength to fight through this."

"The doctor refused payment. Said it was a sweet responsibility to look after such an angel."

Katarina smiled at Susannah's statement. She was not surprised. She entered the kitchen with Susannah and noticed Hannah, standing at the table, washing a stack of dishes in a bowl of soapy water.

"Company again too?" Katarina asked.

Hannah raised her eyebrows and paused to push her hair out of her eyes with the back of her hand. "It's a great time for hospitality in our village," she said. "Only two this time, though, and they moved on this morning. Apparently the Whites are still pushing north."

"Does it matter what color they are?" asked Susannah bitterly. "They steal our food in the name of Mother Russia and then march off to kill their fellow Russians."

"And steal husbands and sons in the bargain," added Hannah.

"We must stay above bitterness, Mrs. Loewen," said Katarina gently. "It only brings us down."

Hannah paused in her task again and then nodded her head. "Yes, Katarina, you are right. The good Lord has his reasons for allowing what he does—although it is far beyond me to know what they are—and I must depend on him day by day." She resumed her task with an attempt at lightness. "God only asks us to live this day, in his strength."

"You're right, Mama," said Susannah, and leaned over to give her mother a kiss on the cheek. "I'm thankful we can at least be together at this time."

"I must go, Suse," said Katarina. "I wanted to see how Marianna was doing. I am on my way to Widow Thiessen's to tidy up and do some laundry for her in exchange for more flour. She apparently had quite a store in her attic, but doesn't want to hoard it. What a blessed old woman she is."

"Drop by soon again," said Susannah with a smile. "You are a breath of fresh air to me." She gave Katarina an impulsive hug and said, "Give my love to Anna and Oma."

"Yes," said Katarina, pausing in the doorway. "Please pray for Anna. I don't know if it's just my imagination, but she doesn't look well lately. Knowing her, she is probably eating less so we all have enough."

"That sounds like her. Don't worry, Katya, everyone is weary with hunger these days. Pray the shipment from America arrives soon."

Anna sat quietly at the table peeling potatoes when Katarina returned home from Widow Thiessen's house. She worked slowly, as if in a daze. At Katarina's entrance, she perked up and concentrated on her job. "I'm sorry I'm so slow, Katya," she said. "I'm a little sleepy today." Her words slurred, and Katarina's heart beat faster.

"Anna, what's the matter? Don't you feel well? Come lie down and I will finish the potatoes."

"You can't do it all yourself."

Katarina put a hand to her sister's face and the heat of it alarmed her. Taking the paring knife from her hand, Katarina helped her from her chair and supported her to her room. "Lie down and I will get a wet cloth to cool your skin. You have a bit of a fever, I think."

"I'm sorry, Katie . . . didn't mean to make more work for you . . . just a bit of a nap and I'll be fine, I . . . " Her voice faded as she shivered beneath the quilt.

Her weakness frightened Katarina. She sponged Anna's face with a cool, damp cloth and, when the child had dozed off, went in search of her grandmother.

"Oma, Anna is sick. Would you sit with her while I go for Dr. Bittner?"

"Of course, my dear. She did look rather peaked this morning, but I didn't take it too seriously. Dear, dear. You go now, and I will sit with her."

Katarina returned shortly with the doctor in tow. "You were fortunate to catch me, Katarina," he said. "I was preparing for another check on my elderly patients in Lichtfelde. Now what seems to be the trouble, little Anna?"

They had reached her bedside, and although she tried to raise her head and acknowledge the doctor, who was one of her favorite people, she could not do so. Dr. Bittner kept his face expressionless as he examined the girl.

She's too thin, for one thing, thought Katarina, looking on, even considering how tall she's grown. Not enough reserve to fight sickness. It was the high fever that worried her, and the flush coming over her face.

The doctor completed his examination and gestured for Katarina to follow him into the kitchen.

"I don't want to alarm you, Katarina," he said.

"I'm already alarmed, Doctor," she said. "What is the matter with Anna and what can we do?"

"It appears to be influenza," he said. "You know as well as I do that we are limited in what we can do for her, but we will work together to do all we know." He enumerated Anna's care: sponge baths, sufficient water intake, rest, and concluded the list with a command: keep her away from anyone but those who live in this house. No billets. Katarina was only too willing to comply.

Katarina kept busy taking care of her sister. She missed the Literary Society gatherings, but it was difficult for anyone to attend regularly these days so the group gradually disintegrated. She was glad that at least the choir practices continued. She was ever thankful for her grandmother who took over most of the household chores, and grateful for the efforts of Paul and Grisha in securing food for the family. She really had no way of earning money at the present time.

One day in the first week of Anna's illness, Oma called from the sickroom: "Katarina, come."

Anna, who had been sleeping most of the time, suddenly sat up in bed, shaking and shivering. Her lips moved but no sound came forth. Her fingers grabbed at the covers as if to throw them off.

"Anna!" Katarina appeared through the doorway and rushed to the bedside. "Anna, what is it?" She tried to calm her sister, but the girl was hysterical. She mumbled something about fire and thunder and rain, and she raised her arms as if to shield herself from an unseen enemy. Katarina didn't know what to make of it or what to do, until Anna screamed, "Papa! Papa!" Then she knew the sickness had resurrected all the terrors of that awful night when she and her brothers and sisters had become orphans.

Wrapping her arms around her sister, Katarina crooned and stroked her hair. "Papa is with Jesus, Ännchen," she said over and over. "Papa is safe. We are safe. Shh, child."

Oma sat on the straight back chair beside Anna's bed and prayed, her wrinkled hand patting Anna's back. Together the two women calmed the sick girl, and eventually she lay back exhausted against the pillows. They stayed with her until she slept, fearful that she would repeat the episode, but she relaxed and slept soundly after that.

"She will start improving now, I think," predicted Oma, much to Katarina's relief. "She must have reached a low point, but she came through the battle. Thank the Lord."

"Yes, thank you, Jesus," Katarina whispered. She had lost enough in these last years: mother, father, both brothers—Peter was safe with Susannah, but only God knew where Nicholai was—and now Johann was gone too. She didn't think she could bear to lose sweet Anna.

"She is no longer a little girl," said Oma over a cup of tea. "She is stretching into a fine young woman, if we manage to find enough food to fill her frame." She shook her head and said, "*Ja, ja*, we have our share of troubles, but we still have our faith in God. He will never leave us, Katie, even in our darkest hours."

"Oma, how good it is to have you here. What would I ever do without you?"

Oma smiled and patted her hand as it lay on the table between them. "You would do what you needed to do, but I am glad I can be here to help." She raised herself from the chair and moved to check on Anna. Turning back, she nodded to Katarina: Anna would survive.

ഋഋഋ

As Anna entered her second week of recovery, Katarina came up with a plan to help her improve. "Anna," she said as she sat down on the chair beside her sister's bed. "I need you to help me with some planning."

Anna, sitting up against the pillows looking pale and thin, nodded and gave her sister a wan smile. "Of course, Katya, but what can I do?"

"Well, at choir practice last evening we were talking about having a *Jugendfest*. You know, a special Sunday when all the youth of the area can come together here in Alexanderkrone and sing together and have a social."

Anna leaned forward in her bed. "That sounds wonderful. Have the elders given their permission?"

"Yes, dear, everything has been cleared, but I need help with the details, and I know that you are always so good with details."

Anna smiled shyly and rested her head against the pillows. "I will gladly do what I can. Katya, you have so much to do and I have not been helping."

Katarina smoothed Anna's blonde curls away from her tired face and smiled. "Don't worry one minute. Oma and I have everything under control. Now you lie down," she eased Anna down and fluffed her pillow, "and Oma will come sit with you. I am going over to Susannah's to ask if she has some suggestions."

"That's a good idea, Katya. Susannah needs something to cheer her up too."

Katarina looked back at her sister and realized she had not fooled her at all. Anna knew exactly what she had been trying to do. Ah well, let her know. It would still give her something with which to occupy her mind.

ஐஐஐ

Katarina, her spirits cheered by her sister's improving health, hummed to herself as she walked the length of Main Street from hers and Johann's little cottage with the other *Anwohner* to the east end of town. She passed the school where Johann had taught those first short months, then turned north at the School of Commerce building and walked the short verst to Lichtfelde.

Arriving at the Loewen house, Katya knocked and pushed the door open.

"Hello!" she called. "Susannah? Hannah?"

She heard voices in the parlor and Susannah's call of "Come in, Katya."

As Katarina entered the parlor, Hannah greeted her. "So good to see you. You bring sunshine to our home."

Katarina felt shy with the praise, but in her heart she rejoiced that she could bring joy to others. After greeting Peter and giving Susannah and little Marianna hugs, she sat down on the settee beside Peter and began explaining her idea for the *Jugendfest*.

". . . so when the young people have finished their choir numbers, we could offer a light lunch—I know it would be hard to find the food, but I will set Paul and Grisha to it—and the young people could visit with each other." Katarina was so wrapped up in her idea that she didn't notice Susannah's attention waver.

Finally Susannah raised her hand and said, "One moment, Katya. I believe there is someone outside."

They peered out the window. A small wagon parked on the side of the street, hitched to a weary old horse. One man struggled to help another off the wagon.

"Soldiers again," said Katarina, bouncing a cooing Marianna on her hip.

Susannah grasped Katarina's arm in a viselike grip. Her face paled and she began to shake.

Chapter 5

"It's Gerhard," she cried, and ran to the door.

"It's Gerhard," repeated an awestruck Katarina to Hannah and Peter.

Susannah had run out to help the soldier bring Gerhard into the house. Her exclamations were interspersed with weeping and the raspy voice of Gerhard.

"I shouldn't come in . . . might infect you all . . . too tired to find another place . . ."

"Nonsense," insisted Susannah. "This is your house and you will recover here. Now let's get you up these steps. Ah, here is Katarina to help."

Katarina still held Marianna as she helped Susannah, while the other soldier, his cap pulled low over his youthful face, put his shoulder under Gerhard's other arm and lifted him one step at a time until he could be lowered onto a bed which Hannah had quickly prepared for him. Susannah knelt beside Gerhard and held his hand while Hannah rushed for a bowl of cool water and a cloth. The sick man gazed in wonder at Marianna but would not touch her.

"No, I must not come close. What a beautiful child." Then his hands fell slack and his eyes closed in exhausted sleep. Hannah bathed his forehead and Susannah began to remove the filthy, louse infested clothing. Leaving them to their tasks, Katarina and the young man who had delivered Gerhard moved back into the kitchen to give Susannah and Hannah room to work.

"Soldier," she said, "thank you for . . ." Words failed her as the soldier, in the tattered rags of the White Army, removed his cap and stood facing her. She stared at him in wonder. He was even taller than when she had last seen him, almost nine months ago. His hair had grown long and his top lip boasted a sparse moustache. The trials of the last months had added years to his face, and his green eyes revealed pain and apprehension.

"Kolya! Oh my Kolya!" Katarina sobbed as she gathered her brother in her arms. They stood thus for a long time until finally releasing each other.

"Nicholai." Her tears drowned out her voice and then Peter stood with them, sobbing mechanically and patting their backs. Katarina still carried a rather bewildered Marianna. She introduced the baby to Nicholai, who smiled and stroked her soft cheek with his finger.

"How did you come here?" asked Katarina once she had collected her breath. "Where have you been?"

"I was in the White Army, Katya. At first I wanted to be there, but later I was sorry I had joined up with them—I will admit that." He hesitated. "I, ah, I hated all the killing. I can't do that anymore." His eyes filled with pain and he covered his face in his hands. Quietly she held him, the dead brought back to life. He was a prodigal son returned with no father to welcome him and no fatted calf to serve him, but they would celebrate. Oh yes, they would rejoice together.

"I didn't know where you and Johann and Anna had gone, but I've found you."

"God brought you home, don't you see it?"

Susannah came into the kitchen then, her face a contradiction of joy and pain. "He's so ill, Katya," she whispered. "Would you find Dr. Bittner for us?"

"Susannah," she said, tears still coursing down her face, "it's Kolya."

Susannah started noticeably. “God be praised,” she whispered in awe. “You brought my Gerhard home.”

Hannah joined them in the kitchen, adding her surprise and joy to that of the others.

“He found me, you know,” stated Nicholai. “He risked discipline to speak to the commander of our unit, convinced him to let me go on account of my age. If he hadn’t spoken up for me, I’d still be there.

“Mrs. Loewen, I need to tell you: your husband . . . he was there too. He did not make it. He died at Christmastime. Gerhard was with him.”

Pain and grief filled the room where they gathered. Words could not stem the mournful wails of Hannah Loewen. Katarina helped her to a chair and sat beside her. Susannah nearly collapsed with the added sorrow of her father’s death.

“I think—I think Gerhard has typhus.” Susannah forced the words out of her mouth.

“Typhus?” Katarina did not want to face that fact. Johann had told her too many things about the dreaded disease, and she knew about his dear friend, Philipp Wieler, one of the many who had succumbed to typhus during the world war and the revolution.

Katarina knew typhus existed in the colonies, what with all the soldiers and bandits who had passed through and left their mark on the people and the villages and the landscape.

“Susannah, let me take Marianna home with me. She should not be here with Gerhard. She might come down with the disease. Peter must come too.”

“I know you’re right, Katya, but how will I let them go?” With a sigh and a lift of her chin, Susannah retrieved a few items of clothing and diapers for Marianna, and then took the fussing baby in her arms.

Katarina gave her a minute, then handed the baby clothes to Nicholai and took Marianna again. “We will fetch the doctor immediately, and I will come again tomorrow to see how you are doing."

"Kolya, you are just what the doctor ordered for Anna. She has been down with influenza, very ill, but I believe she is on the mend now. Your presence will give her another reason to want to get better."

"How long has she been sick?" he asked with concern, realizing how much had transpired in his absence. Johann had been drafted by the Red Army; Susannah had a child; Oma now lived with Katarina; they had taken up residence in a little house on the outskirts of Alexanderkrone; and the battles between Reds, Whites, bandits, and other factions continued in close proximity to the village.

"She has been in bed for three weeks," Katarina said. "The first week was frightening, and now she is weak and listless. I have been encouraging her with plans for a *Jugendfest,* which seemed to perk her up, but with you home she will surely get well."

They walked in a tight group: Katarina, Nicholai, and Peter, with Marianna in Katarina's arms. Not finding the doctor in his clinic, they left an urgent message with his wife and continued home.

"The air is warm, the birds sing as sweetly as ever, but we are consumed with sorrows," said Katarina as they made their way toward the small house that was now their home. "In spite of all the fighting and terrors, the Lord still takes time to coax the buds out on the trees and to paint the grass green." She remembered how bruised Johann's soul had been when he returned from *Forstei* service. He had needed to heal and to experience some peace while it was available. Now her brother needed that healing.

Nicholai raised his face to the sky and breathed deeply, then exhaled with a long shudder.

When they arrived at the Sudermann house, Katarina ran through the door, still holding Marianna in her arms, calling as she went. "Anna, Oma, we have visitors."

ೞೞೞ

As the cab slowed to a stop outside the Schroeder residence in Berlin, Maria felt nervous. This was where she had first come with Benjamin H. Unruh, expecting to find Dietrich, where she had received and read the telegram from her sister Katarina that their father had been murdered and their home burned to the ground.

Kristoph stepped out of the car and offered her a hand. Kristoph, ever the gentleman. He reminded her so much of Dietrich. She knew he had been interested in her at first, but she had communicated to him with certainty that she was only interested in Dietrich. Since then, Kristoph had taken on a brotherly role. He agreed with her determination in locating Dietrich, or at least tracking down what had happened to him.

I've become a dreamer, thought Maria to herself as she walked up to the house with Kristoph by her side. I often chided Katya for that and now I am doing the same thing. She shook herself and lifted her chin.

"Ready to take on the world?" Kristoph asked, a twinkle in his eye.

"I contacted your family before I left the colony," Benjamin Unruh said as they sat at tea in the Schroeder's parlor. "Nicholai had not yet returned; they had received no word about him. They live in a little *Anwohner* house on the edge of Alexanderkrone and have taken your grandmother Peters in with them."

Maria gasped. "I wonder how they ever talked Oma into it."

"There have been other changes as well: Johann has been drafted into the Red Army. He left mid-December and they haven't heard from him."

"Poor Katarina. Now she is in charge again. We must pray for her."

Kristoph lifted an eyebrow but said nothing.

Unruh continued. "The battles continue in the area. Last I heard, the Red Army of the Bolsheviks was requisitioning and demanding billeting in Alexanderkrone."

"Not again. How much blood can you get from a stone?" Maria's anger flared when she thought of Katarina trying to keep body and soul together for her family, and then having to billet soldiers too.

"Better than the Machnovitz," said Unruh.

Maria caught his eye and grimaced. "Yes. Anything is better than those bloodthirsty demons." She stopped to think on what he had told her of her family. What monumental changes had come to them all in the past twelve months. Ever since Dietrich left, the Hildebrandts and Sudermanns had experienced one tragedy after another. Well, she thought, her practical side coming forward, I cannot change the past, but I can do something about the present.

"Mr. Unruh, have you any idea how we might trace Dietrich's journey? We need to start somewhere, but I'm not sure where."

Unruh thumbed his moustache. "Germany is in upheaval since the Versailles Treaty was officially approved. I don't know what to tell you."

"You might approach the Commissioner of Defense," offered Herr Schroeder. "I could direct you there this afternoon if you wish—it's not far."

"We will expect you for dinner," said Frau Schroeder, the motherly woman who had been so concerned for Maria after she received the horrible news about her father on her initial arrival in Berlin. "As long as you are in the area, you are welcome to stay with us. We have plenty of room."

"Thank you, Frau Schroeder," said Kristoph. "We appreciate your gracious hospitality and will accept." He stood and leaned on the back of his chair. "Shall we, Maria?"

The Commissioner was in a foul mood. All his former planning and strategizing had fallen away in light of the treaty and its overwhelming demands.

"We lost many soldiers during this blasted war," he said, "and you expect me to know the whereabouts of every one?"

"No sir," said Kristoph calmly. "Just one—Dietrich Kesselman."

The man huffed into his thick moustache. "If he was enroute from Russia, how in blazes do you expect me to know where he ended up? If he didn't report to Berlin, he is dead. That is that."

Maria stiffened, but Kristoph shook his head very slightly at her and continued. "I realize you are a busy man. We will come back tomorrow morning. Maria?"

The man's brow furrowed and he smacked the desk with his fist. "Max!" he bellowed, his voice carrying through the open door to his secretary's desk beyond.

"Sir?" Maximillian Weissmueller appeared bewildered, shaken from his near comatose state in the next room.

"Search out any and all communications sent to or received from Commander Dietrich Kesselman since last year at this time. He apparently left southern Russia and headed back to Berlin at the very end of the evacuation. Traveled with two others, as far as we know. Find out who they were and what happened to them."

"Yes sir," answered Max, more confused than he had been previously. He withdrew to his office to make sense of his new assignment.

Kristoph swallowed a smile and bowed before the Commissioner. "My deepest thanks, Herr Commissioner."

"Yes, thank you," echoed Maria.

ജ

Gerhard responded well at first to Susannah's capable and loving ministrations. The wonder of a clean bed, uninterrupted sleep, cool water and adequate food, all given with love, stabilized him. Dr. Bittner administered sedatives periodically as well. The disease, however, had taken its toll.

For days Gerhard lay motionless beneath the thin blanket, his breathing shallow, his eyes hollow, his face drawn and old. Susannah sat by his side almost continuously, only agreeing to leave for short periods of time to rest or to catch a glimpse of Marianna as Katarina brought her to the yard. Suse did not dare hold her daughter, even though she washed carefully with the solution the doctor had given her.

Grisha ignored the warnings of the doctor and Susannah, and made almost daily visits to help take care of Gerhard. The household needed a man to bring calm and hope, and he believed he was that man for that hour.

"Mama, I don't know what to do," Susannah lamented. "The doctor has been here as often as he can, but there is no change. Gerhard lies here day after day with no apparent improvement. I've done all I know to do."

"Dear Susie, I'm sorry you have to endure this, after living without him so long. I pray daily for him." A faraway look descended on Hannah's tired face. "I don't know why God does the things he does. I don't understand him at all." Her eyes cleared as she looked directly at her daughter. "But I trust him. Now that I have begun to know God, I trust him with all I have."

Susannah smiled a sad smile and nodded her head wearily. "I know, Mama. There is a far broader picture being drawn here than what our limited eyes can see. Thank you for reminding me."

She rose to check on Gerhard, then called in a frightened voice from the next room. "Mama, come!"

Hannah ran into the sickroom to find Gerhard thrashing about wildly, his eyes wide.

"Mama, help me. We can't let him hurt himself. Help me hold him down until this episode passes."

Choking back her sobs, Susannah began talking to her husband, praying aloud, and holding his arms. He struck her in the face as he fought to escape the demons of disease that persecuted him. "Oh, Jesus, help us," cried Susannah as she wiped blood from her mouth with the back of her hand.

Hannah wet a cloth and washed Gerhard's face, while holding him on the other side. Eventually, he slumped back, went rigid, and lay still.

"Gerhard!" shouted Susannah. "Gerhard, don't you dare die. I'm doing all I can. Jesus, don't let him die." She washed him, massaged his stiff muscles, spooned warm, thin soup into his mouth, even though most of it dribbled down his face and onto his sweat-soaked nightshirt.

Hannah had gone for the doctor, and when she returned with him, the patient lay completely still, his eyes half open, unseeing, uncomprehending. Grisha had come and now stood aside for the doctor to do his work. Dr. Bittner examined the patient and showed them the rash on his body. "His temperature is very high again, even though he is quiet now. Be prepared for sudden episodes of delirium."

"It's terrible," whispered Suse, "but this stupor is almost worse to watch. It's as if he isn't there at all." She sucked in her breath to control her tears.

"He hasn't left us yet, Mrs. Warkentin. Keep caring for him

as you have been. I will give him another sedative. His fever may remain for several days like this, and then drop rapidly. Call me immediately if that happens."

Susannah turned panicked eyes on the doctor. He grimaced as he faced her. "A sudden drop in body temperature may send him into shock. If that happens, keep him very warm. Stay calm; panic does not help. We will do what we can but the Great Physician is in charge."

Susannah thanked him, dry-eyed.

"I will stay, Mrs. Warkentin," said Grisha. "I will help you watch."

ꕥꕥꕥ

Maximillian Weissmueller wore a small smile when Mika and Kristoph entered his office the following morning. "I may have something for you," he said, looking over his glasses at them.

Maria's heart beat double-time and Kristoph's head came up in surprise.

"*Ja*, I too am surprised there was anything to find out. Mmhmm. Sit down, sit down."

They sat on the edges of their chairs, waiting while the man shuffled papers. Finally, he straightened a small stack and adjusted his glasses. "It appears," he glanced at them, enjoying the suspense, "it appears that your Dietrich Kesselman of Schwandorf, Bavaria, received orders from Berlin in March of last year, 1919, to leave his post in southern Russia and return home immediately. Similar orders were given to others, among them Michael Schmitt of Magdeburg and Erich Jahn of Darmstadt." He looked over his glasses at them again and said, "None of them ever arrived here in Berlin. Mmhmm."

Maria's hand shook as she raised it to her face. Kristoph momentarily lost the sparkle in his eyes.

"However," Max continued, pleased with the effect of his words, "I have discovered that Jahn died of typhus. His family received a telegram informing them, and they contacted us. That's all I can tell you. Mmhmm."

Kristoph regained his composure. "That is something," he said. "Do you have the addresses of the other two men—Schmitt and Jahn? We will speak to their families and see if they have anything to add."

Max seemed at the end of his information, until Kristoph slid several marks across the desk. Max sat up. "Mmhmm," he said, sitting straight in his chair. "Perhaps I can find the addresses. One moment please."

Maria darted an angry look at Kristoph, who winked slyly at her. Armed with the addresses of the Schmitts and the Jahns, the two returned to Schroeder's for dinner and after that, to plan their next step.

ஐஐஐ

It had been a dreadful week after the last crisis for Gerhard. Many times Susannah had called on her mother to help hold Gerhard as he struggled violently with the horrible disease. Grisha had spent most of his days there as well.

Gerhard's temperature had dropped somewhat, but not as suddenly as expected. After another bout of frightening stupor Gerhard lay quiet beneath the blankets. Hannah had gone to see her friend Cornelia Reimer, and Grisha was off somewhere scrounging up food for them. Susannah sank to the floor beside Gerhard's bed and placed her weary head on the covers. "Oh Lord, how long?" she whispered.

"One moment at a time," a voice answered in her dreamless sleep, and then a hand gently covered her own. At first she assumed it was the hand of God comforting her. She wanted only to stay still and absorb the comfort as long as it lasted.

But as she sat there, she became aware that the hand was very warm, and that it shook.

Raising her head, she stared at her husband. He still lay unmoving on the bed, but it was indeed his hand that covered hers, and his eyes had closed in sleep. With a great soul-cleansing breath, she held both of his hands and sobbed out her relief.

"He's asleep and seems to be resting more comfortably," whispered Hannah to Grisha when he came by later. He held out a small round of cheese and a still warm loaf of black bread.

"The loaf is small and rather tough," he said, "but at least it helps fill the emptiness in here." He patted his stomach and smiled. "The cheese is something Paul managed to talk out of the cheese maker down the street. I don't know how the man does it, but he is becoming a master of persuasion."

"We greatly appreciate both you and Paul helping us out," said Hannah. She sighed as she looked over her shoulder. "Susannah is totally exhausted. I hope she does not come down with something yet."

"It must be difficult for her without Marianna. I hope Gerhard will recover soon and they can live as a family again. And you, Mrs. Loewen, how are you doing?"

"I am fine, thank you, and thank Katarina for the bread. Perhaps someday we can do something for you."

It doesn't matter, Grisha thought as he walked back to Alexanderkrone with a light step. As long as I do what God asks me to do, I am at peace.

Katarina looked around the little parlor with a joy she had not experienced in many months. Although Johann still served somewhere with the Red Army, she believed he was alive and as well as could be expected in this time of trouble.

She had more of her family around her now than she had had for a long time.

Anna, looking better than she had since she first became ill, sat darning socks, an art her grandmother had shown her. Oma sat nearby, rocking in the chair she had brought from the Home in Ruekenau, keeping an eagle eye on Anna's work even as she worked on her own.

Nicholai, tall and lean, still with a tiredness in his eyes, played a game of *Knippsbraat* with his brother Peter. With the snap of his finger, Nicholai sent the little black wooden disk sliding across the octagonal board to push Peter's white disks off the surface. Then Peter would try to do the same, but could never remember that his job was to aim at the blacks.

Katarina smiled as a prayer ascended from her heart, "Thank you, God, for your many blessings. Please allow Johann to feel your comforting, guiding presence this day too."

ജജജ

"We should begin with the Schmitts at Magdeburg," said Kristoph, pointing it out to Maria on the map. "It's only about 140 kilometers from Berlin."

"Yes," she replied, excitement tingeing her voice. "Perhaps we can find out something through them, and then," she traced the route west and south, "on to Darmstadt."

"That will be difficult, knowing that the Jahn's son is confirmed dead. I hate to open the wound again."

"Well, Kristoph, better that than not finding Dietrich. I'm sure they will be more than willing to help."

They all retired early that evening, intent on leaving first thing the next morning for Magdeburg. Kristoph slept soundly, while on the other side of the wall, Maria Hildebrandt lay staring at the ceiling with wide eyes until well after midnight.

She knew she should not set her heart on too much; it only would break again until one day it would be irreparable. But how could one not hope?

ഌഌഌ

Johann leaned wearily on his shovel and wiped his sweating forehead with the sleeve of his army shirt. He had been part of the Red Army for four months now. What irritated him most, besides being away from Katarina and her family, was never knowing what the next day would bring.

For the first while, he had marched south with his unit, pressing the Whites back. He had lived with his fellow soldiers in makeshift tents, reminding him of his *Forstei* days, and had been able to use his medical skills instead of killing the so-called enemy. He never knew when he might be facing Gerhard or others he knew who had been forced into the "volunteer army" of the Whites.

Then, without preamble, his unit officer had chosen half the men to go to an area south of Melitopol, near the mouth of the Molotschnaya River. So close and yet so far, thought Johann, frustrated that he had not yet been able to send word to Katarina of his location. She had no idea he was fifty versts from Alexanderkrone, cutting down trees to be transported to the cities for fuel, trees that had been planted by the *Forstei* before the turn of the century.

Even though Johann recognized the need for fuel, he would rather have been saving lives or helping Janz work on the emigration project.

"Sudermann, stop your daydreaming. Report immediately to the commanding officer."

Johann jerked at the sound of the supervisor's harsh voice. He had always tried to carry his share of the load, of the work, but this time he had been shirking and deserved punishment.

He shouldered his shovel and marched to a sturdy tent near the edge of the camp. He announced his presence and waited.

"Enter," came a voice from inside.

Chapter 6

Johann lifted the tent flap and blinked as his eyes adjusted to the dimness. "You wanted to see me, sir?"

"Who are you? Ah, yes, Sudermann. Teacher Sudermann. Come over here."

Johann approached the desk, his hat in hand. The commander motioned for him to bring the other chair to the desk and sit.

"I have need of your services, Sudermann. I cannot keep up with the copious amount of records required of me. I want you to do some copying for me. Here," he pushed a scrawled notebook at Johann and then some clean sheets of paper. "You copy this," he patted the notebook, "onto these," he pointed to the sheets. "I keep my notebook and the authorities get the papers."

"Where am I to work?" asked Johann, not wanting to sound too relieved.

"Right here for now," said the commander. "Here are pen and ink. Do a good job."

"Yes, sir."

"I have other things to do; I will return in an hour or two." The unit commander donned his cap and headed out of the tent, leaving Johann at the books, a contented smile on his tired face, his shovel abandoned outside the tent.

ꝏꝏꝏ

As more Bolshevik troops arrived in Molotschna from the North, people in the villages became wary. A couple of Red soldiers burst into the Sudermann house at noon one day.

"You!" One of them pointed at Nicholai and he rose immediately, fear blanching his face. "You will drive your wagon north for supplies. Alexis will go with you. Alexis! Take him!"

"I will be back as soon as possible," Nicholai murmured to Katarina as he left the house with the soldiers. He looked back, and the fear on his face reflected that on her own.

He did not return for almost a week. "I was forced to make daily runs back and forth for the Red Army," he said when he finally stumbled into the house late one night. "The horse is nearly dead."

"As long as you are safe, Kolya," said Katarina, concern etching her face.

"Of course I am." A slow smile transformed his face. "I may not have to transport Reds for a while."

Katarina's look questioned him.

"The Whites have taken Melitopol. They are on their way north again."

He continued to look at her with excitement in his eyes and she knew he had more to tell.

"When I was driving the supply wagon I once came very close to enemy lines."

Katarina gasped, but Nicholai held up his hand to stop her protests. "I didn't know where I was, but I made it through."

"Miraculous."

"Yes, well, a bomb fell beside my wagon. I crouched down and covered my head, waiting for the blast, and some White soldiers in the area ran for cover."

Paul Gregorovich had joined them, his face alive with interest, while Katarina felt only alarm.

"When nothing happened, we all stared at the bomb lying there. Someone threw a large rock at it, but again nothing happened. A couple of the soldiers approached the bomb. They kicked it and finally picked it up."

"Where were you when they were doing this?" Katarina's stomach was tied in knots as she thought about the scene her brother described.

"I pulled my wagon around and stopped to watch. From a safe distance." He smiled at Katarina. "Then the men opened the bomb and you can't guess what they found." He looked from Katarina to Paul. "Inside was a note written on a small scrap of paper. It said, 'We help in any way we can.' "

"Oh my," said Katarina.

"Traitors!" said Paul.

"Whose side are you on?" demanded Nicholai.

Paul shook his head. "My own," he answered, "but the factory workers who are doing this are traitors to the Communists."

"No matter who they are, they are certainly brave," said Katarina.

"It's not the first or only time something like this has happened," said Nicholai. "Sometimes the soldiers find sawdust or chaff in unexploded bombs."

"Makes one wonder if anyone is really on the side of the Communists, or if everyone is coerced by fear," said Katarina.

"The Bolsheviks have defeated the Poles," Paul informed them, "so now they will have more troops to send south. I think we will see more action here in the next while."

Katarina sighed. "We used to discuss weather and crops and family events, but now all we do is talk war and politics."

"These are the times in which we are fated to live," said Tekanin.

"Fated or chosen."

Paul made no reply.

ꟿ ꟿ ꟿ

Maria and Kristoph approached the Schmitt residence with eagerness. This was the first possibility of connecting with someone who might have a clue to the mystery of Dietrich's disappearance. Maria allowed Kristoph to knock and make the introductions, but she was ready to plunge in and find out everything she could.

Having settled into the comfortable front room, Mika and Kristoph told the Schmitts what they knew: Dietrich left Karassan in March of the previous year, in the company of two other German officers enroute to Berlin, and Erich Jahn had died of typhus somewhere along the way.

Frau Schmitt, a short, round woman with pink cheeks and faded yellow hair, dabbed her eyes with her handkerchief and rocked vigorously in her rocking chair as she listened to her husband tell their story.

"Michael was called back in the fall of 1918, but was allowed to stay on until he had completed his work. He waited too long, the authorities told us, and they would take no further responsibility for him because he had not followed orders." Herr Schmitt sat back and rubbed a hand over his bald head.

"Fritz, tell them about the telegram," prodded his wife, ceasing her rocking for a moment.

"Yes, my dear, I plan to. Now sometime in June we received a telegram from Lvov."

"We have it," interrupted his wife, sniffing into her hanky.

"Yes, my dear. Would you like to get it for us?"

Pushing herself out of her rocking chair, the woman hurried into the next room. They could hear paper being shuffled. She mumbled to herself as she searched, then called, "I found it," and hustled back into the room. She handed the envelope to her husband and he passed it to Maria and Kristoph.

> "LVOV COLD STOP LEAVING STOP
> MD"

Kristoph read the telegram under his breath.

Maria stared at the message.

"Tell him what we think, Fritz," said Frau Schmitt, her eyes darting from her husband to the strangers who sat on her sofa.

"Yes, Helga. At first we were perplexed by the message. The last letters would be initials, but they were not Michael's initials. We found out from the authorities in Berlin that he was accompanied by Dietrich Kesselman and Erich Jahn."

"The initials must have been those of Michael and Dietrich, so Erich would already have died in Lvov."

Herr Schmitt paused for his wife's explanation, then continued. "They said they were leaving and that Lvov was cold."

"It was summer," interjected Helga. "It would have been warm there."

"Yes, my dear. So *cold* did not refer to the weather."

"It must mean the surroundings, the general feel of the place," offered Maria, wracking her brain for explanation. "Perhaps *threatening* would be a better word, but they didn't want to let on that they knew they were in danger if someone should intercept their telegram."

"Exactly, *Fraulein,* but we have never been able to figure out what they meant or where they went from there." Fritz rubbed his head again, as if to bring out the genie who would unlock the mystery.

"It's not an army code," said Helga importantly. "We asked them, you know." She continued to rock, her chair creaking an accompaniment to their private thoughts.

Maria glanced at Frau Schmitt and wondered if she would rock herself right out of the door into the kitchen.

"Helga, my dear, why don't you bring us some coffee? It would do us all good."

"Shall I help you?" asked Maria.

Helga stared at her for a moment. "Oh no. I am perfectly

capable." She heaved herself out of the chair and bustled into the kitchen.

"She has been quite upset by everything, you see," said Fritz quietly after she left the room. "Michael is our only son. She has always been so proud of him and now, well, we don't know if he is even alive."

"Michael is alive," insisted Helga, from the other room. "I know he is."

"Apparently the telegram received by Erich Jahn's family originated from Lvov."

Kristoph leaned forward. "So Erich died in Lvov. If he was very ill, Michael and Dietrich may have stayed with him until he died. According to your telegram, the two of them moved on from there together."

"But where would they go?" asked Maria.

"What do you plan to do now?" asked Fritz as they sipped the strong, hot brew Helga had made.

"We will talk to the Jahn family," said Kristoph. "Perhaps they have some ideas as well."

"Hmph." This from Helga, rocking in spite of the hot coffee in her cup.

"We have spoken to the Jahns, but they did not welcome the intrusion into their lives," said Fritz. "Perhaps you will fare better than we. Their son is dead, you see, and they wish to forget and move on."

"Forget!" The word burst from Maria's lips before she could stop it. "When someone dies we do not forget. We owe it to them to remember. It is the least we can do in their memory."

Helga Schmitt looked at Maria as if seeing her for the first time. "I agree. We must never forget those we have lost."

Maria smiled as a lump formed in her throat. "If we find Dietrich, Frau Schmitt, we will most likely find Michael too. We must keep searching until we do."

Fritz sat forward in his comfortable chair. "What will you

do after you visit Darmstadt? Where will you go?"

"I suppose I will go all the way to Lvov if I have to," said Kristoph.

"We will go," added Maria. "I do not intend to sit in Schwandorf or Berlin while you go searching. I don't care what people think, either. I will accompany you wherever the road leads us."

Kristoph grinned at her. "Yes, we will most likely begin at the beginning. It may be a long and arduous search, but we will see it through."

Fritz sat in silence for several minutes, rubbing his head. The genie still did not appear. "Perhaps," he glanced sidewise at his wife, "perhaps I shall accompany you." Helga stopped rocking and stared at him as if he had lost his senses. He held up his hand to stop her exclamation.

"I have some connections here. I know people. The bank where I am manager is a large one with contacts in other countries. These connections are not always guaranteed helpful in time of war, but one never knows. My presence could also create a more acceptable appearance to your entourage."

Maria and Kristoph both showed surprise at Fritz's suggestion. Kristoph spoke for both of them. "We will think it over as we travel to Darmstadt. Then we will return here on our way back to Berlin and let you know what we decide. At first thought, it seems a good idea to me. Three heads are often better than two."

"Very well then," said Fritz, rising to shake hands with both of their guests. Helga followed suit but did not offer accommodation for the night. A stranger was a stranger, after all. One had to be careful. She wondered at her husband's wild idea. What was he thinking to link up with these people he didn't know from Adam and Eve? She was appalled. They would discuss it later.

ജ്ജ

Peter and Marianna had returned home to Hannah and Susannah's house, where Gerhard continued to make a slow but steady recovery, and Katarina's mind was mulling over a new idea.

"There are many orphaned children in our midst since the Machno terrors and all the disease," she said to Oma and Anna as they sat with their needlework in the lengthening days of May. "I think I may start up a kindergarten. It would not be only for orphans, of course, but would certainly include them."

"Why, Katarina? Do you lack for busyness?"

Oma, astute as always, cut to the heart of the matter. Katarina smiled and shook her head.

"Of course not, Oma, but I've thought it through. First, it would help the children, and the parents who struggle with daily life. The children would be occupied with something other than empty stomachs and playing hide from the bandits in the orchards. Second, we could work out a fee, say, a pound of butter or cheese, a basket of beans or a sack of apples, whatever they have to pay."

"And if they don't have anything? Will you turn them away?"

"Oma, you are teasing me. You know me almost better than I know myself."

"*Ja, ja*. Your idea is interesting. But think about it before you plunge ahead. Where will you have it? What will you feed the children? We have trouble enough coming up with enough food for ourselves."

"They would let you have it at the schoolhouse," offered Anna. "I'm sure they would. No one is going to school since the bad times anyway. Or the church. That's another idea."

Katarina nodded. "I think the school would be best, but we will inquire. Now Anna, do you think you are well enough to help me? I will need someone to keep the children busy and help them with their activities."

"Oh yes, Katie. I want to. I am feeling well now, especially since Kolya is safe home." Her sunlit countenance darkened momentarily. "He is sad, I think."

Katarina nodded. She had spent much time trying to think of a way to encourage Nicholai out of his sadness. His experiences of the last months were much too difficult for a young man of fifteen years. How could the army not have figured out his age? It was obvious. Perhaps they didn't care. Lives were expendable these days.

Word of the kindergarten spread through Alexanderkrone like a ray of sunlight in a consistently dismal sky. Something to look forward to. A slice of childhood for the little ones.

The authorities at the village office agreed, with some persuasion, to allow Katarina Sudermann to set up a kindergarten in the school. She thought of Johann's teaching days as she moved the big desks out of the way along the walls. Abram Reimer built a low table and benches for the students. Katarina was delighted with the results. She did not know he had cut down trees from his own orchard to make the furniture.

"I pray you have the strength to follow through," said Oma. "I know you have the heart, but it's difficult to complete our tasks without adequate food, Katie, and the problem grows." Her concern turned to a smile then. "Don't worry, girl. God will look after us. This old woman must have faith."

"The deacons are helping round up orphans," said Katarina. "They know who the children are and where they are staying. I hope the kindergarten is a distraction and a comfort to them."

One never knew, the doctor warned, when a relapse could occur or if the disease would pass to someone else, but life had to be lived. As Gerhard improved, Susannah regained a degree of the sunny disposition Katarina had seen in her at their first introduction. In spite of rumbling stomachs and accompanying weariness, life was improving.

Grisha continued to visit the Loewen/Warkentin household and soon he and Gerhard became fast friends. Susannah smiled at their deep philosophical discussions.

Katarina and Anna worked with the children, making crafts from used paper, playing quiet and not-so-quiet games inside and outside the schoolhouse, sipping weak lemonade from donated cups and nibbling on miniscule chunks of cheese and bread crusts. It was a party, a wonderful sabbatical from fear and drudgery.

Parents and children alike appreciated the kindergarten, and Katarina felt their gratitude in concrete ways. An assortment of edibles blessed the Sudermann table as payment for the kindergarten teacher, and Oma did her best to incorporate them into meals. She faced the challenge with the usual determination and humor.

"Two string beans for each of us," she would announce, "and a potato, and today a little bit of gravy."

"Gravy!" Nicholai appreciated food in quantity and quality.

"Gravy?" questioned Katarina. "How did you make gravy without meat?"

"I may be old, but I still have a few sparks left in this head of mine." Oma chuckled as she set the food on the table. "I'll show you after we eat."

With an attitude of contentment, they sat together, bowed their heads in thanks, and the simple meal became a banquet for their souls.

This evening Gerhard joined his family for supper. He sat at the head of the table where Susannah's father used to sit, with his wife on one side and her mother on the other. Marianna occupied a long-legged baby chair beside Susannah, and Peter sat stiff and quiet beside Hannah.

"We are a family again, praise the Lord!" said Gerhard in

a shaky voice. The typhus had weakened him considerably. The slightest activity put him into a cold sweat, and even his voice was a mere whisper of its former cheerful tenor, but his soul was on the road to recovery as his body healed, and all present were thankful.

Little Marianna could not take her adoring eyes off her father. She was unaccustomed to seeing him at the table, but seemed to like it well.

"Praise the Lord," Peter echoed as they bowed their heads to give thanks.

Gerhard continued to improve under the watchful eyes of his wife and mother-in-law. He played with Marianna and walked in the orchard in the mornings. By evening he was often tired and his chest hurt, but he slept well beside his wife.

It was time to make plans. How would they support themselves? Susannah had determined to find work laundering or sewing as she and her mother had done before Gerhard's return, and also to involve herself in some other paying job. Susannah had always worked by her husband's side, but it was difficult to convince Gerhard that she could be the provider for the family.

"War certainly changes one's perspective, doesn't it?" he said as they discussed his staying at home to take care of Marianna while the women went to work.

"War changes everything," said Susannah.

He caught her arm as she swept by him with some freshly washed towels and sheets. "Suse, what is it?"

She glared at him, but her face softened almost immediately as she looked into his beloved blue eyes.

"What is it? You have changed since I left last year. You've lost your bustling cheeriness."

"For your information," she said, planting a kiss on his

forehead, "I do not bustle. And if I'm not as cheery as I once was, blame it on the war, on the communists, on the bandits. It happens when you are robbed of what you love most."

He pulled her onto his lap. "*Liebchen*, it's a dangerous game you are playing, this blaming others. Our circumstances are beyond our control, yes, but our response to them is a decision we make."

Susannah blinked her eyes rapidly, fighting the tears. "I tried. I really tried to trust, but I couldn't. You were gone and I didn't want to trust."

"But I'm home now. Besides, your happiness should not rest in me alone. I cannot possibly meet all your needs."

"I'm sorry, Gerhard, but that's the way I felt. Now that you are back, I will eventually get back to being the person I was." She moved to her own chair then, conscious that her weight on his lap was too much.

"My dear, I am honored to know I mean that much to you, and blessed to be so loved, but I am concerned that you place all your store in me. I'm just a man."

"Gerhard, you are my man, and with you I will always be content."

"But what if . . ."

"No!" She shook her head emphatically and rose to take the towels and sheets to the bedroom cupboard. "We will not discuss it. You were gone and you have returned, and now we are a family again."

Gerhard's eyes widened with worry as he watched his wife exit the room. She did bustle, he thought, but immediately his mind returned to her words. He was not strong yet, although he could do most of the daily things he had always done and helped around the house as much as he could. But he was not God; he could not promise to be there for her always. He had seen enough of life to know that. And sometimes he had a feeling. . . .

ജ്ജ

Maria and Kristoph took the road from Magdeburg through Göttingen and Kassel and on to Frankfurt am Main. From there it was only a short jaunt to Darmstadt. Maria was nervous. Even with all the trials she had come through, all the losses in her life, she still felt uncomfortable confronting others with their sorrow.

Kristoph helped her out of the cab and held her eyes. "Don't worry, Mika. The worst they can do is throw us out. We can overcome that."

A small smile played at her lips. Like his brother, Kristoph was a master at seeing behind her mask to her fears. It was comforting in a way. She took his arm and they approached the house.

The reception at the Jahn household was somber. The house itself seemed to be in mourning. Everything was neat and clean, but there was a certain reserve, an absence of life that permeated even the furniture. Karl and Liesl Jahn and their young daughter Henny sat stiffly on hardback chairs, their faces frozen with repressed emotion. Erich was gone, they said. The telegram said that typhus had taken his life.

They did not say that Erich had always been the life and joy of their home, teasing and cheering both his mother and Henny, or that his father had great plans to train his son in the area of import and export. They did not share the fact that Liesl Goldman-Jahn descended from a long line of Jewish entrepreneurs, and that Erich had inherited his maternal grandfather's ability to turn any prospect into profit. Why would they say it? Erich was gone. The hope had been snuffed out in their home; their hearts were charred.

Karl retrieved the infamous telegram which lay on the desk in Erich's room, beside his favorite books and photographs. As Maria held the items and read the telegram, her eyes misted and her heart contracted with memories of Katarina's telegram. My papa's dead too, she wanted to say, and my heart aches for him.

They gained no further information from the Jahns.

"Thank you for your time," said Maria. "I'm sorry for your loss; war is not a kind master." She and Kristoph bade a somber farewell and took a train back to Berlin.

Maria and Kristoph stopped briefly in Magdeburg to welcome Fritz Schmitt to the search—he would meet them later in Schwandorf—then returned to Berlin for a last information check. It seemed Maximillian Weissmueller had indeed told them all he knew. They turned south then, to Schwandorf, to bid farewell to the Kesselmans before they set out on their journey.

Maria was anxious to commence with the search, but Kristoph persuaded her to take one step at a time. "If we miss a piece, the puzzle will not take on shape and we may take a wrong turn somewhere. As it is, we have little to go on."

"Yes, I know, and your mother will be glad to know we have a chaperone."

"Necessary, don't you think?" Kristoph winked at her.

She started to respond in kind, but choked on the words and turned away.

"Come, Mika," he said. "I only spoke in jest."

"There is no joking anymore. All that has changed," she whispered.

He took her shoulders and turned her around to face him. "Mika, don't give in. Life is worth living, even with our losses. Your papa is no longer in danger, as you yourself said, and we will find Dietrich."

She relaxed against him, unaware of the pain that tightened his face.

ƐƆƐƆƐƆ

Gerhard tightened his arm around Susannah's shoulders as they walked along the Juschanlee River. A host of sparrows twittered in the oak trees that stretched sheltering arms far above them.

"We are accompanied by angels," mused Susannah.

Gerhard turned to look into her eyes. "You are my angel."

"I'm not an angel, Gerhard."

"No more than I am God, but you seem so to me." He continued to walk with her at his side. "These last days have been wonderful. I know we are poor and hungry, but I rejoice in being near you and Marianna." If only it could last, he thought. He looked up at the birds so she would not read the fear in his eyes, the fear that dogged him much of the day and often in his dreams at night.

"You've improved so much lately," Susannah said. "I know you still tire easily, but I think you are over the worst. As your nurse, I give you a good report, but you must continue to rest much as you gain strength."

"Yes, Madam. Thank you for your prognosis." He smiled at her then and willed the doubts to flee, for the time being at least.

"You only have today," Grisha had told him when he confided his fears. "Don't allow tomorrow's sorrows to rob you of today's joys." Well, this was joy, and he would bask in it while it was today.

Several days later, Gerhard lay resting on his bed while Marianna chirped and gurgled beside him. A loud knock disturbed the peace of the moment. Susannah was still out working and Hannah had taken Peter to find food. Gerhard pulled himself into a sitting position and took a moment to allow his head to clear.

The knock sounded again, louder and more insistent this time. Placing Marianna on the floor where she would be safe for the moment, he answered the door.

"Gerhard Warkentin." Gogol Puchinsk stood facing him as he opened the door.

Gerhard nodded but did not smile. What did the mayor have to do with him? His stomach tightened.

"Warkentin, I have some business with you."

"Then speak it. I cannot leave; I am watching my daughter."

"Then I will come inside."

Hesitating, Gerhard moved back and opened the door a bit wider. The mayor pushed past him and seated himself at the kitchen table. He glanced around the room with raised eyebrows.

"I cannot offer you food," said Gerhard, reading his mind. "My mother-in-law has gone to see if she can find something for our supper. We are as hungry as everyone else." His eyes rested momentarily on the mayor's protruding stomach. He obviously had contacts. "Can we get to the reason for your visit?" He kept one eye on Marianna as she crawled toward him from the bedroom.

"Hmmph. Well. You need to know about the new tax. I have not received your contribution."

"What tax?"

"Each farm is required to provide the government with 280 eggs, ten pounds of butter and one thousand rubles."

"I do not have a farm. We have twenty chickens, a milk cow, and no money. How are we to—"

"—I don't care how you do it," roared the mayor, "but it must be in by next week."

The obnoxious man took his leave without another word.

Gerhard couldn't believe his ears. He checked with the village office the next day when the mayor was out and was only slightly relieved to have his tax lowered to half the amount, "because he does not have an actual farm." The whole instance bothered him thoroughly.

The following week, Mayor Puchinsk pounded at the

Warkentin's door again. This time Susannah was at home with Gerhard and Marianna.

"Warkentin, it has been brought to my attention that you did not volunteer for the army when they canvassed for recruits."

"What do you mean? I served with the Whites until April, when I became too ill to continue. They sent me home. The typhus nearly claimed me."

"In case you haven't noticed, Warkentin, it is the Reds who now dominate in this vicinity. They are moving down through the area and you are needed immediately to join up with them."

"Join the Reds? You can't mean that. I have only begun to regain my health. I'm still very weak."

Puchinsk exhaled and pulled back his shoulders, endeavoring to pull in his protruding stomach. "You will come with me now," he said.

"What are you saying?" cried Susannah, her alarm causing Marianna to whimper in her arms.

Without warning, Puchinsk pulled a gun from his waistband and pointed it at Gerhard. "Move," he roared.

"Gerhard!" Susannah grabbed his arm, horror etching her pale cheeks. "Please, you don't understand," she pleaded with the mayor, but he ignored her.

"Wait! Can't you see this is impossible? I would never survive another stint with the army. My family is hungry. I can't . . ."

"Warkentin!" he shouted, and Marianna began to cry. He lowered his voice. "I have tried to be lenient, but this decision is out of my hands. Do as you are ordered or you will be arrested."

Gerhard began to sputter, at a loss for understanding. He clamped his mouth shut and stared at the mayor who finally met his eyes. What he saw in those beady black eyes mirrored what he saw in his own whenever he looked in a mirror. Fear. Raw fear and helplessness in the shadow of the powers that be, whoever they were at that particular time. "Very well," he said in a voice both quiet and chill.

"No, Gerhard, please!" cried Susannah. Marianna wailed. Gerhard looked at her with stricken eyes. At his little Marianna. It was like a nightmare. Like his nightmares. Only now it had become reality.

Gerhard knew that in spite of the wanting personality of Mayor Puchinsk, he had been offered more leniency than he ever would have received from regular Red soldiers. He may well have been dead already for his stalling.

"My darling. God be with you. Marianna, my sweet little one."

Puchinsk grabbed him by the arm and hauled him from the house, Susannah and Marianna wailing in earnest from the doorway. Gerhard stumbled blindly beside Puchinsk, his hopes shattering into shards of grief, cutting his soul until it bled him dry.

Chapter 7

Johann signed the letter to Katarina, sealed it, and included it with the packet of envelopes to be sent to the Molotschna. He hoped the letter would find her. He had not written anything incriminating in case the mail was tampered with, just a short note letting her know where he was and what he was doing. He knew she would treasure the news.

Since that first day of copying, he had been called upon several days each week. Apparently, his work was satisfactory. He had several reasons to be thankful for his work: it offered him information about the state of the civil war; it afforded him opportunity to communicate with Katarina; and it gave hope that he would be able to avoid the inevitable combat which conflicted with his basic beliefs. He did not seek to avoid the battles for the sake of fear—he knew when the time came, he could endure the terror as well as any of them, and he had proved it many times—but for the sake of his conscience. He did not want to send a soul into eternity. Perhaps this copy job was God's reprieve for him for the present.

ꕤꕤꕤ

"Oma, I don't know what to do for Susannah," cried Katarina. "She has been completely distraught since Gerhard was taken again."

"Do you blame her, child?"

Katarina glanced at her grandmother. "Of course not. I just hate to see her so overwrought. I know I can't bring Gerhard back, but Marianna needs her mother. She had grown very attached to her father and now that he is gone, she clings to Susannah."

"And Susannah doesn't have the heart to meet her needs. *Ja, ja*, this life is a constant struggle." The old woman shook her head in pity. "I will think on it while you and Anna are at school. Do you have anything you need Paul and Grisha to do?"

Katarina paused to think. "Well, perhaps they could cut some wood for the stove."

The door burst open and Paul Gregorovich entered with an armload of wood. "Thought you might be wanting to bake something today, Grandmother," he said. Behind him, a grinning Grisha carried a sack of flour.

"Ha!" said Oma with a twinkle in her eyes. "How did you get flour without a pass to the mill? Some people will go a long way for fresh baking."

Grisha bowed low before her and swept his cap off his head.

"Put your hat on, old man," she chided, and then muttered, "Never a moment's rest. Bake some bread, patch some shirts, make a meal out of nothing."

Grisha smirked behind his beard while Paul and Katarina exchanged amused smiles.

Anna appeared from her bedroom. "Oma, I can stay at home today and help you. I don't mind."

At this, the old woman burst into laughter and the others joined in. "No, sweet Anna. You go help your sister. I will put these two to work and have all the help I need."

With a glance at Katarina, Anna nodded and fetched the box of wooden toys they took to the kindergarten each day. "Good-bye Oma." She smiled shyly at the two men.

"Katya," called Oma as the girls walked out the door, "don't worry about Susannah. Time will heal. I will go visit her today if my feet hold out. Now off to school with you both."

When Katarina and Anna returned home after lunch, Oma had fresh brown bread cooling on the table. It looked and tasted lovely compared to their usual fare of tough black bread or barley bread.

"What are you doing, Oma?" asked Anna, mumbling around a mouth full of bread.

The old woman sat at the table with a piece of old newspaper and the stub of a pencil. "Silkworms," she replied.

"Silkworms?" both girls asked at once.

"We used to raise them in the attic when I was young. All you need is a long table, mulberry leaves, and patience. And poor hearing. Once those little worms start munching, it sounds like rustling wind. We can spin the silk into thread for knitting or crocheting."

"Do we need more work?" Katarina asked wearily.

Oma looked up at her and smiled slyly. "Not you. Susannah. We will grow them in her attic and she will have the daily chore of feeding them and cleaning their trays."

"She's a busy woman, you know."

"*Ja*, and this will get her going each day. I spoke to her this morning and she is interested. First spark I've seen in her in a long while."

"Silkworms. Leave it to Oma to think of that." Anna giggled as she hugged her grandmother. "I'm so glad you're living with us now."

"*Ja, ja,* so am I, child."

ཙཙཙ

Nicholai walked the dusty street of Alexanderkrone beside

Grisha and Paul Gregorovich. There was no dew, even this early in the morning, and the dust choked them. Everywhere the ground was dry and cracked. Grass, fresh green in spring had turned a crisp faded brown. Fields sprouted weeds in patches, no germinating crops to challenge them. Here and there, volunteer wheat or barley grew, but there had been almost no seed to sow with; it had gone into bread to sustain life for the present.

"There are those who still have grain," said Paul Gregorovich. "I have seen them turn beggars away even though there are bags of wheat in their attics and hidden in their storage sheds."

"It's usually the wealthy ones who won't share," added Grisha.

"My father shared." Nicholai raised his chin. "He would not have turned people away."

"We did not know him," said Grisha, "but I believe he would have found a way to help as long as he had resources."

"That is true," agreed Paul, "but so is the fact that some of the rich Mennonites in their villages are hoarding food."

Nicholai was interested. "How do you know? Have you seen it?"

"I've seen their bulging bellies and their multiple chins, Kolya. They are not suffering hunger."

"The government officials are also finding enough food," said Nicholai. "Have you seen Mayor Puchinsk? He is a very fat man."

Grisha smirked. "He would be a comical figure if he did not wield so much power. Heaven help us in the face of such authority."

"The Russian peasants are starving, I know that," said Paul. "My own village of Ackerman was deserted but for one old woman when I stopped there last year, and she was completely crazy."

They walked in silence for a time, then Paul looked from Grisha to Nicholai. "I am going to Ackerman," he said. "Perhaps there is something there, something that would help us survive."

"What would you hope to find?"

"I don't know, but I am going."

Grisha nodded and turned back to Alexanderkrone with a salute. He did not question Paul's activities.

"I'm going with you," said Nicholai.

Paul hesitated, glanced at Grisha, and then shrugged. "As you wish."

"I will tell Katarina," said Grisha. "Don't walk at night."

"Or in the day, eh my friend?" Paul retorted. "I remember what a safe haven this colony used to be. Now there are no safe places."

"I will take the watch tonight," said Grisha as the other two started west down the dusty road.

ꚙꚙꚙ

Johann could imagine Katarina opening his last letter, telling her of his copy job near Melitopol. She would be relieved that he was near and out of the fray. Now he traveled west to Kherson, and it would be some time before he could contact Katarina again. He was still not that far from home, but certainly not where Katarina thought he was.

He entered the government building with outward confidence and approached the battered counter. Behind it, a man leaned back in his chair, his scuffed boots resting on a paper littered desk, his hat pulled forward over his eyes. His snores had apparently caused the plastered walls to crack and peel over time. Johann dropped a heavy book onto the floor. The sleeping man snorted and sat up, pulling papers to the floor with his boots and fumbling with his cap. Johann leaned over to pick up the book, giving the man time to regain some semblance of dignity, then greeted him.

"I am Johann Sudermann, sent from the Melitopol camp to work here in this office. I was told you were in need of a copy clerk."

The man continued to pull himself together, stretching his belted tunic over his ample stomach and pushing unkempt hair beneath his greasy army cap. "Hmmph. Copy clerk, you say?"

"I was sure you would know about this by the time I arrived."

"Oh, I knew, of course I knew. Just not sure when you would arrive, Sinderam."

"Sudermann."

"Suderam, yes. Just like the letter said."

"I have the letter here," said Johann. "My commanding officer gave it to me to pass on to you."

The burly man glared from under bushy brows, then snatched the letter Johann held out to him. He blinked and moved the paper around until he found focus. "Copy clerk," he muttered through his moustache as he read, "start immediately, make some sense out of your mess. . . ." He cleared his throat loudly and thrust the letter aside and glanced around him.

"If I may, Comrade ah . . ."

"Hmm? Oh, I am Shevchenko."

"Comrade Shevchenko. I could start with the papers on the floor, perhaps file them for you. I could organize them on the counter here."

"Yes, I was just going to do that, but now I tell you to do it. So do it now before you do anything else."

"Yes, Comrade Shevchenko, sir." Johann set to work at once, clearing up piles of papers and forms, sorting them on the counter, familiarizing himself with the office. Shevchenko wandered from one place to another, not finding anything to do. Finally, he hunkered down at his desk and stared through filmy eyes at a government form.

If the form was the usual, Johann knew it would take a good man a day to figure it out. As it was . . .

ೱೱೱ

"Silkworms!" said Susannah. "I can't believe I let Oma Peters talk me into this."

Katarina smiled. It was the first sign of life she had seen in Susannah since Gerhard was taken. "Kolya and Peter have been collecting mulberry leaves from the hedges in and around the village," she said. "The weather is nicely warm now, and the ounce of silkworm eggs that Maria sent from Berlin is ready to be exposed to the air. What a brilliant idea you had to send word to her there. I asked Abram Reimer to stop by and build some edges onto the low tables in the attic. He will add more table space as you need it."

Susannah wiped the kitchen table and swept the floor quickly. "Let's climb up and I'll show you how we have it arranged." She pulled a cord to release the ladder from the ceiling of her bedroom and the two women hitched up their skirts so they could climb.

The attic had been swept and cleaned. Two long, low tables ran its length. "It will be good for Peter to have something worthwhile to do."

As it will be for you, thought Katarina. "Oma was telling me that an ounce of eggs—three *zolotniks*—will produce 40,000 worms, which will nibble away almost thirty *pud* of leaves."

"I won't turn away any offers of help," said Susannah. "I must keep up with my laundry and cleaning work around the village. It will earn us enough to eat until I can spin the silk."

"Oma will help. She says she misses spinning, and I think she may convince Cornelia Reimer to help as well."

"I must get back downstairs. I hear Marianna crying for her supper."

"Remember, Suse, we will help you in every way we can," said Katarina once they had climbed down the ladder again.

"I know you will. You already have. Katya, I appreciate your friendship so much. I could not manage without you." Susannah closed her eyes and struggled for composure. "I have to cling to every bit of hope there is," she whispered. "Hope is what keeps me going. Hope and faith."

ƐƆƐƆƐƆ

Anna loved the children. As she knelt beside little Sarah and helped her with her scrawled drawing, she pretended she was grown up with a class of students to teach. "Jakie," she said firmly, rising quickly to catch the boy as he romped around the room, "we sit still in kindergarten. No running in the classroom."

All the children seemed excitable today. She was in charge while Katarina stepped out to talk to the mayor at the village office. Katarina would only be gone a few minutes. Anna could keep peace until she returned.

Jakie stood at the window again, unable to keep his seat. He wheeled an invisible horse around and galloped to another window, shooting an imaginary gun.

"Jakie! Sit down immediately." She moved to the window to take his arm and her heart leaped to her throat. Scruffy soldiers, possibly bandits, rode down the street in the direction of the school.

"Quickly, children," she said, as rehearsed. "Let's play a game of hide-and-seek. We will hide in the orchard and Teacher will come find us when she gets back."

She herded them toward the back door and sent up a prayer of thanks for Jakie. The children galloped excitedly on unseen horses, racing out to the orchard behind the school. Once there, Anna bribed them. "If we are very quiet, Teacher will bring us a treat when she finds us, but we must be very quiet or the game will be over and there will be no treat at all. Shh. Quiet now."

When the waiting became long, Anna calmed the children with stories. They were all very glad to see Katarina when she "discovered" them later. It had been a long game and they were tired of it. Katarina praised them for playing so well and led them back to the schoolhouse where roasted zweiback awaited them. She had hoarded the ingredients until there were enough for the buns, then roasted them and saved them in the back of one of the storage cupboards for just such a time.

The children, happy for something tasty to chew on, skipped home with their parents or older siblings that afternoon.

"What happened, Katya?" asked Anna with fear in her eyes. "Was it soldiers or bandits?"

Katarina sighed and shook her head. "It was soldiers this time, Änya. I was just returning to the school from the village office when I heard them. I managed to hide behind the woodpile, but I had to wait there until they were gone. They stopped at the village office and wouldn't leave. A couple of guards stood out front, and I could not risk leading them to the school. All the while I worried about you and the children."

"You shouldn't worry, Katie. We were fine." A shadow crossed her angelic face. "I was frightened, but we were safe. I am afraid of the soldiers, they aren't usually as bad as the bandits." She shuddered. "I am terrified of the bandits."

"Anna, you were very brave. Thank you for taking care of the children until I could get here. I know I can count on you." Katarina picked up her supplies to go home. "I won't leave you here alone with them again. That was not a good idea."

ꕥꕥ

It took the rest of the morning for Paul Gregorovich and Nicholai to walk to Ackerman. They spoke of the revolution and the civil war, although Paul was reluctant to tell many of his experiences.

"I caught a ride north from Crimea on a wagon transporting White soldiers," said Nicholai. "I said I intended to join them as soon as we reached their next outpost." He rubbed the back of his neck with his hand and shook his head. "They didn't know why I would do that if I didn't have to. They didn't understand about my wanting to do something to stop the evil.

"I tried to keep my enthusiasm up, but even to me it started to become plain that the White Army had no idea how to fix the injustice in our world. They had no plan at all but to destroy the Bolsheviks. And they wanted a Constitutional Assembly—I think that's what they called it—which would then know what to do and how to do it."

They continued to walk in silence and then Paul said, "You don't have faith in the strength of the Whites then?"

Nicholai shrugged. "They may win some of the battles, but if they don't know what they want, then power is no use to them."

"Yes, power. Power and greed. That's what they're all after, you know. They spout great ideals and plans, but it all boils down to climbing to the top of the mountain and pushing everyone else back. They care nothing for the people, for you and me."

"What do you think will happen, Paul?" asked Nicholai,

wide-eyed at the affirmation of his worst fears.

Paul Gregorovich shrugged. "Who knows? If the Whites win, they won't know what to do with the power. If the Reds win, well, there will be a bloodbath, that's a sure thing."

"But why? Why always violence?"

"Ha! You sound like Grisha. Because it's the quickest way to achieve a desired end, that's why. And once one faction is in power, the others must be destroyed in order to maintain that power." Paul glanced at Nicholai and then put a hand on his shoulder. "Ah, Kolya, do not take the full weight of the world on your young shoulders. You cannot carry it."

Nicholai blew out his breath in a frustrated sigh. "I know, Paul Gregorovich, but I had such plans to make a difference and now I see I can do nothing. Nothing at all. Life becomes more and more difficult for my family, for all the people in our area and all of Russia. There's never enough food to go around, there's no seed to plant crops, everyone lives in fear. And I can do nothing."

Again silence descended on the two travelers. Finally Paul spoke. "Your brother-in-law, Johann, would say that God is in control. He would say that this world is a proving ground for the next and we are to be faithful to what God calls us to do, no matter what the circumstances."

"Do you believe that?"

"I don't know what I believe anymore, but I know what I don't believe. I don't believe we will ever have freedom, at least not during my lifetime. I don't believe that good wins over evil—look around you."

"Do you believe in God?"

"Do I believe in God? I honestly don't know. My heart says yes, but my head tells me this is absurd. So far nothing has proved to me that there is a God. Maybe one day I will know."

Nicholai's concentration was almost audible. "I think I

do—believe in God, that is. I know Katarina and Johann do. They seem to know him. And my . . . my father did, even at the end, I know he believed."

"My father died too," said Paul, "fighting for the right. Nothing changed. Last time I was in Ackerman, a crazy old woman said my mother had died and my sister had run off with a soldier. I have no one left anymore. Maybe believing in God would be a good thing, eh? Someone who won't go away and leave us."

"God promises to be with us always," said Nicholai thoughtfully, "even to the end of the age. Maybe knowing that makes it possible to live through times like these." He looked up at Paul for his response.

"It's better than nothing, I suppose. Certainly can't hurt. There's Ackerman, past those trees there. At least that's where it was. Who knows if it still stands today."

"He what?" Katarina stood with hands on her hips.

"He walked with Paul Gregorovich to Ackerman," said Grisha. "Paul will look after him."

Katarina shook her head. "That boy will never learn. Always flirting with danger."

"Mrs. Sudermann—"

"Katarina."

"Katarina. Give him some credit. He found his own way to the mainland. He survived months in the White Army. He will return safely from Ackerman. I think he is at a loss as to his purpose."

"And Tekanin will help him find it? That is difficult to believe."

"I thought you had forgiven Paul."

"I have. Most of the time, I have. But that doesn't mean I trust him with my brother."

"Then trust your brother to the Lord and ease your load.

God will look after him as he sees fit. I know it is not easy to let him go. Unfortunately, he will go whether you want him to or not."

Katarina sighed. "Yes, I know. I just don't know how much more I can let go of. How much does God require of me?"

"Only as much as is best for you, Katarina."

Nicholai matched Paul's determined steps through the dusty streets of the town, now deeply rutted from army and bandit wagons. He stumbled once, but Paul did not see. Tekanin's pace quickened as they approached a decrepit *izba* on the southwest side of the village. Nicholai's pulse increased as he noted signs of life in and around the tumble-down building. Was the crazy old woman wrong? Did Paul's mother and sister still live? Were they waiting until he would return for them?

Without waiting to knock at the door or call, Paul Gregorovich opened the door and walked in. Nicholai bumped into him from behind when Paul stopped still in the doorway. Nicholai peered around his friend and they both stared wide-eyed at an old man sitting on a rotting mattress in the corner of the one-room house.

The man made no move, nor did he show any sign of alarm. He merely blinked at them. "What do you want now? Take it and leave us. We will die soon anyway."

"Who are you?" demanded Paul.

"That is my question," said an angry voice behind them. "By what right do you barge into our home?"

Chapter 8

Paul and Nicholai both wheeled around to face a gaunt young woman standing at the entrance to the *izba,* a sturdy stick in her hand.

"Do you want us to go in or come out?" asked Paul, a smile tugging at the corner of his mouth as he watched the slight woman glare at him. The smile only added fuel to her fire.

"In!" she commanded. They complied. There was no place to sit, so they stood in the middle of the room.

"What do you want with us? We have already given more than we have."

"Now how is that possible?" began Paul, but seeing the pain in her eyes, he did not demand an answer. The answer was common and sad, especially common with one as pretty as this girl must have once been.

"This used to be my home. I lived here with my mother and sister until six or seven years ago. Last time I came to find them, they were gone, Mother dead, so said the crazy woman, and Sonya run off with a soldier. I had to come back once more." Paul spoke and waited for a response.

The woman stared at him, obviously analyzing his words.

The old man spoke then. "They are not here. Only a few squatters seeking shelter from the weather and the bandits. Sometimes we are successful; sometimes not." He glanced at the girl. She lowered her weapon and sat on the mattress next to the old man.

Paul sat on his haunches near the fire pot while Nicholai leaned against the wall. "Who are you and where did you come from?" Paul asked.

The girl sighed. "I am Pava and this is my father, Igor. We came across the Molotschnaya before winter set in. The soldiers had driven us from our village; we had nowhere to go. We came across this village one day and claimed shelter. It looks as if either plague or sword drove these people away."

She shrugged. "What does it matter? We live until we die and then it's over. The dead are blest." She crossed herself and looked toward the dark corner by the mattress. A stone was table to several small icons, a primitive altar of shallow hope.

"Pava. You and your father are welcome to stay here. Do you have food?"

Pava frowned. "We are starving. We can offer you nothing."

"No," said Paul. "Do you need food? I could perhaps find you something."

"Why?" Again the frown and uncertain fear in her dark eyes.

"Because I am also a hungry Russian trying to survive. Here," he pulled a fist-sized sack of roasted grain from his pocket. "I traded a rabbit for this yesterday. You are welcome to it. We will not eat here, this is for you and your father."

Pava stared at the proffered food, then at Paul. The shadows lifted from her eyes for a few moments, hinting at something she had considered dead: a faint glimmering hope. With something akin to reverence, she reached out and took the sack of grain. Her eyes locked with Paul's, then she clutched the grain to her chest.

"There is no charge for it," said Paul, holding her eyes. "We will go now."

"Come again," said Igor. "If you have extra, we will not turn it away. Not for myself, but for my daughter, you understand. I wish her to live."

"I will do my best, Father," said Paul. He motioned Nicholai toward the door. They ducked out, then Paul turned once more and lifted a hand in farewell.

Nicholai stole a glance at Paul, but said nothing. He did not belong to this group. He still had family, home, enough food to ward off starvation. He still had some hope.

It was very late when Paul and Nicholai returned to Alexanderkrone. Grisha stood guard in the shadows near the gate. Paul followed the garden path to the little shed where he and Grisha stayed. Nicholai entered the main house quietly, but even so, Katarina met him in the kitchen before he had a chance to find his bed.

"Thank the Lord you are home," she whispered, pulling a shawl around her. "I've been so afraid."

"I am fine, Katya. I am a man now; you don't need to worry about me."

"Oh Kolya, I always worry. It doesn't matter how old you are." They sat opposite each other at the scarred kitchen table. "I stopped at the village office today," she said, playing with the fringes of her shawl, "to renew our permission to continue with the kindergarten." She paused, tension apparent in every move. "Some Red soldiers stopped there also. They said the Whites, now fighting under General Peter Wrangel, have reached the Crimea. Some are even as far as Melitopol."

"Melitopol. Isn't that where Johann is?"

She nodded, unsure of her voice.

"He'll be fine, Katya. He knows how to stay out of trouble."

She shook her head. "There is no place without trouble these days, Kolya. I am so afraid for him. My hope each day comes from believing that he is coming back, that I only have to hold things together until he returns. I long to hand the reins over to him again."

"I'll help you, Katie, if you let me. I know I'm young and

you see me as little Kolya, although I'm not little at all anymore." His sister smiled wearily. "I will find work in the village and help bring home food. I can't take Father's place," his voice quavered, "but I can help to keep our family together."

Katarina looked at him, sitting across from her, and saw him with new eyes. He was a young man now, handsome, muscular, and tall. His experiences over the last number of months had forced him to grow up, to mature. She still saw the child in him, her cheerful, carefree little brother, but that persona had somehow taken second place to the man who sat across from her now. She smiled and reached for his hand.

"I love you, Nicholai. I love the little Kolya of the past, and I love the man you are becoming. I welcome another set of shoulders to share the load. Thank you. Forgive me when I forget who you are."

He smiled too, a crooked, almost shy smile. "I love you too, Katya, and don't worry too much about Johann. I believe he will come back."

"We have to believe that, Nicholai."

Over the following days, military carriages rattled through the villages with more frequency. At first, the residents sought shelter in great fear, but gradually, they adjusted to the disturbances. Sometimes the soldiers stopped for food for themselves or their horses, but, for the most part, they were decent and even courteous. Katarina imagined Johann would be as kind as he could be to anyone who helped him.

These were White soldiers, definitely more decent than the Reds, but Katarina did not look forward to battles on her doorstep. If only they could settle their differences in someone else's front yard. She only worried they would force Nicholai to join them again. He had grown in physical appearance, but he was still far too young to fight in the army. Surely they didn't conscript fifteen-year-olds.

She thought of Johann that day as she played with and taught the kindergartners. How sweet and innocent they were, in spite of the many struggles they had already experienced. She wondered how many of them would have permanent scars on their hearts and souls from these devastating times.

All that day they heard the faint roar of cannons in the distance. Katarina explained it away and distracted the children from their preoccupation with war. Who could blame them? They had already seen too much.

Katarina heard the pounding of hooves at the same time as she became aware of the wild whoops of the riders. *Machnovitz!* Her heart squeezed in her chest as she looked around her at the wide-eyed innocence of the children. "Come quickly," she cried, and herded them like a mother hen into the basement. Then she remembered Anna, who had run home to gather some materials for today's lessons.

"Oh, Lord, protect her," she cried silently in the darkness, all the while trying to shush the whimpering voices. She couldn't leave them alone here, that was certain. There was no one else nearby to help. Nicholai had gone to Kleefeld with Grisha, but perhaps that was a good thing; he could have done nothing but get himself shot or bayonetted.

Katarina tried to keep the threatening shudders from becoming full-blown hysteria. She had to remain outwardly calm for the children and trust Anna to God. "Please God, please God, please God . . ." she murmured, holding little Manya to her chest.

She could hear wildness outside, but had no way of knowing what was happening. It seemed like days, but in truth was perhaps an hour until someone called softly down the stairs. "Mrs. Sudermann, are you there? They are gone now."

She tried to answer, but it took several tries to make her voice work. "We are here." She ushered the children up the steps into the protective arms of several parents who had been sick with worry about them.

"I must go check on Anna," she explained, arranging for each child to be taken home. "She was at home, was going to follow me in a few minutes."

Understanding, they sent her off, exchanging worried glances. Things happened these days, and no one was immune. Especially young girls and women. They prayed as they watched Katarina run down the steps of the hall and into the dusty street toward her house.

As long as she lived, Katarina would never forget what she saw upon entering her yard. She ducked through the rose trellis, which sagged to one side where the supports had splintered. Bruised, broken flowers stained the ground along the walk. The door of the house stood wide open but no sound broke the shattered stillness.

Katarina's vision wavered, but she forced herself to move forward. Grasping the door frame, she leaned in and listened again. Perhaps Anna had hidden in the garden or the garden shed and wasn't here at all. Then she heard a sound, like the faint bleating of a lamb. In a fog of fear, Katarina moved toward the sound. Through the kitchen, down the hall to Anna's bedroom.

Anna sat in a crumpled heap on the floor. Her dress was torn and bloody. She had pulled the blanket from the bed, and now held it around her like a shield from the world. She whimpered, not the cry of a child in fear, as the kindergartners had cried, but that of a wounded animal. Falling to her knees beside Anna, Katarina reached for her, but Anna scooted away in horror, looking at her but not seeing.

"Oh, Lord God, help us!" The muted cry leaped from Katarina's heart as she looked at her sister. She was one of the flowers, crushed, broken, robbed of beauty and innocence. Katarina began to speak softly to Anna, all the while edging closer to her, her heart like a stone in her chest.

“Ännchen, it’s Katya. I’m here now. I know I’m too late, but I’ve come. They are gone. The bad men are gone. They won’t hurt you anymore.” *Oh, Lord Jesus, why? Did you not hear my fervent prayers? Have I sinned that you did not hear me?* “Anna dear, let me hold you. I will wash you and put clean clothes on you. I will help you and not leave you alone ever again. I promise, Änya. I promise.” *Oh, dear Jesus, help us.*

Gradually, with much patience, Katarina succeeded in calming Anna to the point where she allowed herself to be held, but she could not reach her soul, as if it too had been molested, too raw for consolation. There were no tears from Anna, although Katarina made up for that with her own; hot, angry tears at the horror that had broken the stem of Anna’s purity.

A sound at the door caused Anna to shuttle into a corner again, and Katarina to stiffen with apprehension.

“Katarina! Anna! Where are you?”

Nicholai. Oh, Lord, what now? If he was angry before, he will certainly go off to kill someone in revenge when he sees his sister. Worried prayers continued to pour from Katarina’s heart as she answered him. “We are here, Kolya. Please come quietly.”

ঌঌঌ

The town of Kherson sat comfortably at the mouth of the Dneiper River, separated from the Black Sea by a westward jutting peninsula. The government office in which Johann worked was situated in the center of the city, a low stone building on another dusty street. He spent most of his time editing government documents and organizing files. His predecessor, if there had been one, obviously knew nothing of organization.

An eye for detail is the key to a successful project, thought Johann as he riffled through another ream of paper from the cabinet in the corner of the room. As he worked through the papers, his eye caught one entitled *Comrades' Benefits*. He couldn't believe anything of the kind existed. The contents of the memo also surprised him: all office workers in the Red Army system were to be allowed to take leaves of absence from time to time, with the supervisor's consent, of course.

So, another thing Comrade Shevchenko had kept from him. Johann was beginning to understand how the man worked, and also how to work with him. One had to watch one's step, but neither did the Communists appreciate weak people.

"Comrade Shevchenko," said Johann that afternoon before locking up the office for the day. "I am going home to see my family tomorrow. I will return by the end of the week."

Shevchenko glared at him from beneath bushy brows. "This is the army, Suderam. You don't come and go as you please."

"We have accomplished much in the last while," countered Johann, knowing that his supervisor had done very little of it, "and I know you wouldn't want the inspector to see that I have not been allowed my leave, when he comes by the following week."

If Shevchenko glared before, he virtually sparked now. Gauging Johann with narrowed eyes, he turned away and pretended to work. "I will mark you down for four days," he said with a growl, "and then you will be back at the desk. The new regime has no time for vacations."

"I appreciate that, sir, but in these volatile times, I must check on my family. I will be back after four days."

When Shevchenko left, Johann locked up the office, stopped by the little room in the inn that had become his by virtue of his employment, gathered a few things, and began the journey to Alexanderkrone with a heart lighter than it had been in months. He was going home, even if only for a short visit. Katarina would be thoroughly surprised.

ꕥꕥꕥ

The smoke-filled air of Berlin made Maria cough. It was so dirty. She missed the clean air of Succoth.

"It's progress you smell, Mika," said Kristoph. "This city is working hard to come out of the aftermath of war, and they shall succeed. You wait and see."

"They may succeed, but I may succumb," said Maria, coughing again.

They spent an evening with the Schroeders and Benjamin Unruh before boarding the train again for Schwandorf.

Unruh was also packed to leave. "I have a few stops to make in Europe," he said, "and then I am off to America with Friesen, Esau, and Warkentin of the *Studienkommission*. There are certain men I wish to meet with to find an opening for our people there."

"Have you heard from your wife?" Maria couldn't imagine her alone with the children at such a tumultuous time, while her husband lived in peace and freedom, traveling thousands of miles from her.

Unruh pulled a letter from his vest pocket and waved it in her direction. "God be praised, I received a long letter from her. She and the children are well and cared for."

"You are fortunate to have the opportunity to travel."

"Someone must do this work, my dear. One cannot accomplish it from one's parlor."

"I understand," said Maria, "but I'm glad I am not the one left waiting." Even as the words left her tongue, she knew they were meant for herself as well. She had been left. But she would not sit and wait. No, she would seek and find.

Somewhere, Dietrich waited for her.

"The news from the Molotschna is not good, though," continued Benjamin Unruh. "The Reds have temporarily taken over the colony, but the Whites still linger, pressing the boundaries. The people never know from day to day who will be in charge of the villages."

"Do you not fear for your family?"

"Of course I do, but I can only be in one place at a time. This is what is required of me at present."

Maria set her mouth in a firm line. She worried about her family. How were they faring in the colony? What else had happened in her absence that she would not find out for weeks or months? She shook her head to clear it.

"I will bid you farewell then and Godspeed in your travels. Tomorrow Kristoph and I will return to Schwandorf and prepare for our journey east. I thank you for all you have done for me. I know I would not be here if not for your generosity."

She shook his hand and retired for the night, her mind on Dietrich. Where could he be? Would she ever find him, or was he dead somewhere, buried in an unmarked grave? She tossed and turned that whole night and welcomed the morning with its easier farewells. The clacking of the train wheels lulled her into sleep shortly after she and Kristoph set out next morning. And then we head east to Dietrich, she thought as she drifted into sleep.

ꕥꕥꕥ

Johann's few days in Alexanderkrone proved to be both a blessing and a curse. His longing to see Katarina was fulfilled, but their parting brought fresh pain. His relief to know she was safe nearly drowned in the river of sorrow over Anna's condition and the near explosive political and military situation.

"Yesterday the Reds were in charge," said Johann. "Today the streets are filled with Volunteers."

"I've heard," said Katarina, "that some of our people are considering leaving with the Whites when they move on."

"I wouldn't recommend that," said Johann, "but I don't want you facing anything more like Anna did." He shook his head and rubbed his faced, removing his eyeglasses and setting them on the table.

"She doesn't speak at all. Oma managed to get her to sip some soup, but she won't eat. We will surely be forced to billet more soldiers in the near future. The Reds are pulling in by the wagonload. Anna will be terrified of them."

"Would she go to Susannah's?"

Katarina shook her head. "She doesn't trust anyone besides me and Oma, not even Kolya. Besides, Suse will have her own billets."

They were silent awhile, then Johann asked, "How is Susannah doing? This must be a terrible time for her."

Katarina reached over to take Johann's hand and held it between hers. "It is terrible. She cries a lot, can't seem to stop. Then she is stronger for a time, but often, she just dissolves in tears."

"At least she has her mother with her."

"Yes, that's a blessing, but it doesn't take the place of a husband and father, and Hannah has her own sorrow to deal with." She leaned closer to him and he touched her face and smoothed her unruly hair back from her forehead. "Please be safe, Johann. Stay whole for me. I can only do what I do because I know you are coming back. I'm not strong enough to be on my own."

"You would do whatever you had to do, Katie, I know you would. If I dealt the cards, you know I would promise to be with you forever. I'm not in immediate danger where I am now. Rather a soft job, actually." He smiled and then sobered again. “But you know I have no more control over the situation than you do. Promise me you will commit yourself to God. God will never leave you. Promise me, Katie?”

She nodded as the tears dripped from her chin. “I promise to try. I . . . I know all these things in my head, but the fear sometimes makes me forget and panic.” She searched his face. “How long must we go on like this?”

Johann shook his head as he put his glasses back on. “I don’t know, my love, but there will be an end. There has to be. I haven’t been able to contact B. B. Janz for quite some time, but I know he will be working feverishly on emigration business.”

“You think we will be forced to leave, then?”

“Katarina, it’s the only way. Look around you; there’s nothing left of this country.”

Chapter 9

As Johann prepared to go back to Kherson the next morning, Paul Gregorovich appeared. They strolled out to the back garden together. They had been able to talk a good deal this visit, and Paul's presence gave Johann a measure of calm about leaving his family again.

"What do you think, Tekanin?" asked Johann. "How is the situation shaping up?"

"Not good." His shaved head gave him a strange appearance to Johann, but it helped hide his identity. "The Reds were firm here, so we thought, but now Wrangel's Whites have pulled in. It's only a matter of time until the conflict begins, and it won't be pretty. I can hear cannon fire again today."

Johann sighed. "I don't know why I expected good news. How long, do you think, until the fireworks?"

Paul shrugged. "Who knows. Not long though. I'll do my best to keep them safe. You know that. Grisha and I are committed to that."

"I know and I thank you from the bottom of my heart, but you are a man and the enemy is an army—two armies and assorted bands of embodied demons. Even your best cannot stand against that."

"Where is your faith, brother? You always spoke of trusting God. Is that only for the good times?"

The two men locked eyes and Paul continued. "I know this is a case of the blind leading the blind, but listen to yourself, man. If your faith is no good in trials, then it is no good at all.

Prove to me that it is as worthy as you have always told me."

Johann looked away first. They stood leaning against the back fence, faces to the morning sun. "It's not my God I'm doubting, Paul Gregorovich. It's me. Am I strong enough, dependent enough on him to trust him with my family? That's the question that haunts me." He shifted his position to face Paul. "If they did to my family what they did to the people in Muensterberg and Zagradovka, I don't know if I would remain sane. Look what they did to Anna. I cannot be here to protect them."

Johann's reasoning did not satisfy Paul. "My friend, if you really believe your God controls this world, and that he has our best interests at heart, then you must trust him. With your family and yourself. Even with your cynical friends." He smirked, but Johann had no smile to match Paul's.

He stared at the ground, dug at it with the toe of his boot. Finally, he heaved a huge sigh and grasped Paul by both shoulders. "I have a long journey yet today, and much time to think. I will pray and listen for the Lord's encouragement. I need to hear it from him, but you, my dear friend, have pointed me to him. You're an amazing man, you know?"

Paul laughed, a smile lighting his handsome face. "No, no, I am just a *muzhik*, just a crazy peasant who wanders through life without understanding."

"You know the facts."

"Ah, but knowledge and belief are two distinct entities, am I not correct?"

"You are so close."

"Pray for me then, Sudermann. Who knows, perhaps this great God will speak to me too."

"I think he already does."

Paul laughed again and slapped Johann on the back. "Come back soon, friend. I will try to keep hell at bay until you return. Make sure you bring your God with you."

"You needn't be afraid of our guests, Anna." Katarina tried to coax her sister from the bedroom to the table. It was suppertime and the Cossacks billeted with them needed to be fed. Oma busied herself over the stove, but she could not do it alone. Katarina had been glad to share the burden of her fears with Johann on his leave, but now he had returned to Kherson.

Anna shook her head fervently and pulled away. Katarina did not know what to do. She couldn't leave the girl alone in her room forever, but the child was obviously and understandably terrified of strangers. Eventually she gave in. "I'll bring you something to eat here then, but tomorrow we will eat together."

Anna remained mute, sitting on her bed, hugging her knees. It broke Katarina's heart to see her so, but at present she had to see to her billets. "I will be back as soon as I can, Anna." She smoothed her sister's golden hair and bent to kiss her. There were no words of comfort to take away the terror.

Back in the kitchen, the soldiers spoke of leaving. "I saw at least a dozen of our aircraft fly over today," said one. "From Melitopol to Gross Tokmak, I'd say."

"Yes," said the other. "I predict we will be gone before sunup tomorrow. We will stop those dirty Reds from coming back."

"How many troops do they have at their disposal?" asked Nicholai, wide eyed.

The first man huffed into his moustache and scratched his sideburns. "Cavalry, about twelve thousand, I've heard, and then twenty-five thousand infantry." He smirked. "Nothing to fool with, eh? But we will outmaneuver them."

Nicholai determined to talk to Paul and Grisha about that. He had run off to join the war effort, and now it had come to him, now that he didn't want it.

Later they visited, the White soldiers and Katarina and

Oma. These were Cossacks from the Don region, and they were a decent and polite lot.

Oma sat spinning silk into fine thread, thread that had become far too expensive to buy at a store. Who could afford a thousand rubles for one spool? So Oma kept the wheel spinning until it became too dark to see.

ജജജ

Fritz Schmitt, the father of Dietrich's companion Michael, arrived in Schwandorf on June 10, prepared for the journey. Maria's bag was packed; she knew she needed to travel light this time. Kristoph spoke assurances to his mother, trying in vain to convince her she was not losing another son.

"We will return, Mother, and we will bring Dietrich with us, but it will take time. Don't worry every day. Light a candle in the church on Sundays and say a prayer for us and for Dietrich. We need you to be strong for us."

His father, at his desk, slipped a number of bills into an envelope and brought them to Kristoph. "Come back when this is gone. It should last a long time if you are careful with it. You might want to give some to the lady," he motioned with his head to Maria, "in case you are separated. I'm sure Schmitt has his own supply."

"Thank you, Father," murmured Kristoph, suddenly struck by the seriousness of this adventure. He tended to take life lightly, with a smile and a joke, but he knew they faced danger on this journey, and he felt full responsibility for Mika. He would never forgive himself—Dietrich would never forgive him—if anything happened to her.

A passenger train took the three travelers on the first leg of their journey. They intended to get as close to the border of Ukraine as possible and try to pick up the scent. The more Kristoph thought about it, the more ludicrous it seemed.

How would they locate two men who had been missing for more than a year? What had he been thinking?

He looked over at Maria, beautiful in sleep, her head resting against the back of the seat, and he knew why he sat on this train enroute to nowhere. Until they found Dietrich, a feat beyond his comprehension in spite of what he had told his mother, he would be here for her. He didn't let himself think about what would happen after that.

He glanced over his shoulder at Fritz Schmitt and knew he no longer carried his secret alone. Schmitt raised an eyebrow and turned back to his newspaper.

ഇഇഇ

All through the month of June, trouble surrounded the colony. The Reds had seemed entrenched in south-central Molotschna, but the Whites again pushed them back.

On the sixteenth, White aircraft flew overhead and the world of south Molotschna became a living hell. Although the village of Alexanderkrone was occupied by Whites, their own planes began dropping bombs.

Soldiers ran for cover, innocent citizens stood in shock in the street, not sure which way to run. Screams and cries filled the air.

Two soldiers burst through the door to find Katarina urging Oma and Anna to climb quickly down to the cellar.

"Hurry!" they shouted, motioning Nicholai and Paul Gregorovich down as well. The soldiers followed the family into the cellar, pulling the trap door shut after them. There they sat together until the worst of the bombing ceased.

"How could this happen?" asked Nicholai later as they stood surveying the devastation outside. "Why are your planes bombing your territory?"

"Miscommunication," answered one of the Volunteers.

"That's crazy!"

The soldier stared at him with narrowed eyes. "This is war, son. Things aren't always as clear as we would like them to be. It happens."

"The Whites have put themselves to flight," muttered Paul Gregorovich, shaking his head.

As Katarina busied herself with household duties one day in late June, Paul Gregorovich slipped in through the door and motioned her to come. They stood together watching the parade of Bolshevik soldiers marching hurriedly past the house and on up the street.

"What's happening?" Katarina asked.

"I'm not sure," said Paul. "This morning I could hear gunfire between the Reds and the Whites somewhere between here and Lichtfelde. I thought perhaps the Whites were driving the enemy out, but the Reds are coming back. It could mean more fighting in our backyards."

Where are you, Johann? Katarina's mind cried out for him, but outwardly she nodded and ran to find Nicholai. Oma had heard and now prepared poor Anna to flee. Katarina heard her whimpers.

"Quickly, everyone," she urged. "To the woods by the river. Quickly."

Oma held Anna firmly by the hand and all but dragged her out of the house. Paul and Grisha stood at the door, ushering them out. Nicholai helped Katarina carry a few blankets and a little food tied up in a towel. They hurried through the garden and out the back gate, which Grisha stopped to latch again. Then they moved quickly on through the fields and down to the Juschanlee.

Katarina's mind whirled as they ran. They did not flee alone. Many families, it seemed, had a similar idea. Katarina wondered where Susannah was hiding. It was either the cellar or the trees. She wondered how they would all "hide" in the small woods.

Nicholai had given his blankets to Grisha and now held Anna's other hand, helping Oma to carry her along. The girl's legs pumped, hardly touching the ground. Her eyes were wide, terrified.

They reached the place Paul had scouted out for them, and dug in behind a large rock, into a small hollow overhung with poplar and willow branches. It was cool there, the ripple of the river playing a soothing melody nearby as if to negate the chaos a short distance away.

Time slowed then, as they sat with nothing to occupy them except wondering how long they would be there. Katarina felt sorry for complaining about their former situation. At least they had been within four walls. Now only a thin roof of leaves veiled them from the late June sun.

Grisha watched them: the old woman—the wise woman he called her—humming a tune and stroking Anna's hair; the girl beginning to calm to her touch but still so scarred by the viciousness of her attackers; the boy, trying to be brave, trying to hide his confusion and fear; the woman, her faith evident in everything she did, even now as she whispered encouragement all around; and his tall, dark friend, who had experienced much sorrow, yet still grasped for hope.

Grisha observed and then began, in a quiet voice, to tell a story. His practice with the brothers at the monastery did well for him. He soon captured the interest of all, and for a short period of time, in the midst of approaching mayhem, he allowed them to escape their fears. It was the least he could do.

Eventually, Nicholai snuck away from the hiding place in the woods, much to Katarina's dismay, to find out what was going on in the village. He did not return by nightfall and Paul set out to find him while Grisha stayed with the others.

All seemed quiet in the village the next morning as Grisha, Katarina, Anna and Oma cautiously pushed open the back garden gate. Others had been returning all morning, and the guns had gone silent. In fact, everything appeared to be as they had left it.

Paul cracked open the door of the gardener's hut where he and Grisha stayed and then joined them. Katarina froze and stared at him with eyes full of fear. "Kolya?"

Paul raised a hand to calm her. "He is safe; I saw him. He returned too soon and has been volunteered to collect bodies and cart them to a large grave being dug near the old cemetery."

"He's alive. He's well. He is well, isn't he, Paul Gregorovich?"

"Well, but considerably shaken and exhausted, I would say."

"And could you do nothing to help him?"

Paul tensed at the tone of her voice. Her former deep-seated anger at him sometimes bobbed up like a dead thing floating to the surface, and overcame her determination to forgive. "I myself was enlisted to dig the grave, Katarina. I was thankful the Whites took charge and not the Reds, or I would most likely be swinging by now."

Katarina grimaced and turned away. "That was unfair of me. I'm sorry. Everyone seems to forget how young Nicholai still is. He should not be coerced into such a situation."

"Katarina," Grisha broke in, "war is no respecter of age. Remember the little children, the orphans who roam the streets. They are also too young to deal with their situation, but there it is. I think Nicholai will survive. The Reds are gone and I for one am thankful."

Paul agreed. "The battle was not heavy here; Nicholai will be home soon. Some of our villagers who refused to leave their homes were shot, either accidentally or purposely, and there are dead soldiers."

Mercifully, Oma had taken Anna to her room and set about

to occupy and distract her. Katarina tried to stop thinking of Nicholai dragging dead bodies onto a small wooden cart and pushing them through the familiar street, past the school to the old cemetery. She couldn't block it out, so she talked to the Lord about it as she worked.

That evening after the sun slipped exhausted below the sighing horizon, Nicholai quietly opened the door and stepped into the kitchen. He walked to the table and sat, eyes empty. Katarina sat next to him and rubbed a hand over his shoulders. Grisha joined them. No one spoke; there were no words to say.

Have you forgotten us, Lord? Katarina kept her inner turmoil hidden as she ministered to her brother, but Grisha recognized it, and prayed her soul would not become hard because of the suffering all around her.

The village had filled up with Red soldiers, at least one thousand of them, moving south again. An apparent victory for them.

"Some of the Germans have been handing over White soldiers to the Reds," said Nicholai as the family sat around the table for the evening meal.

Katarina looked up in shock. "Are Paul Gregorovich and Grisha all right?"

Nicholai nodded. "They're smart. They don't trust anyone. You won't see them anywhere until the Reds leave."

"If they leave."

Nicholai replied with silence. Katarina felt a shiver run down her spine.

The apparent Bolshevik victory, however, did not last. Whether the Whites had regrouped or set a trap, the Reds soon changed direction and ran back from where they had come.

That night Katarina billeted several Whites again. One of

the Cossacks who had previously stayed with them stopped by for a short visit before his contingent left.

"The world has gone crazy and I am here to see it," said Katarina as they sipped tea out on the verandah under a pale three-quarter moon.

"I have been conscripted into the Volunteer Army," said the Cossack, drawing on his cigarette, "and my brother is forced to fight with the Reds." He looked over at Katarina and blew a puff of smoke upward. "Yes, it is crazy. All I want is to go home to the Don and live peacefully. But I am here." He rose and stamped out his cigarette in the dust. "Thank you for your kindness. I wish you safety."

He untied his horse, pulled himself into the saddle and saluted with two fingers to his hat.

ঌঌঌ

Information on the civil war passed through the office in Kherson, providing Johann with details about the situation in and around the Molotschna Colony. The news bothered him. Johann knew the White Army presented a serious problem to the Reds. He had managed to avoid five or more White divisions on his return from Alexanderkrone to Kherson. They camped strategically in a large semicircle starting west of Halbstadt and continuing south along the left bank of the Dneiper. The Markov Division sat across the river from Berislav, with the Kornilov Division a short distance south. Shevchenko informed Johann on his return that the White front also faced the Reds from north of Halbstadt down through Waldheim and Gnadenfeld, extending to the Sea of Azov.

Johann had returned to Kherson on June 10. After that, the Whites pulled back for a few days, supposedly under pressure from the Reds, but they continued to impose substantial damage on the Red Army by way of their aircraft. So the Reds moved mostly at night. They occupied the colony all the way down to Alexanderkrone, and Johann prayed fervently that further conflict would not take place in the village.

At five o'clock on the morning of June 20, in spite of the fact that the Reds outnumbered them by ten thousand infantry and double their cavalry, the White divisions closed in. General Peter Wrangel depended on superior strategy.

According to the facts that came in via telegraph, Johann learned that several Red divisions panicked and fled westward toward Halbstadt, while others broke through to the south, all to be turned back to the area around Ruekenau, where they were centered. Continued White onslaughts from land and air eventually forced the Reds to call a retreat. The Whites pursued and caught up with them near Hierschau, inflicting more losses. The Reds continued their hasty retreat, leaving behind two hundred guns, forty cannons, three thousand horses and two thousand men.

ഋഋഋ

Some of the wounded brought into town were Bolsheviks, some were Volunteers. It didn't matter to Katarina. They were people caught in the same net of turmoil she was. She was thankful for the training Johann had given her back at Succoth. She knew basic medical skills. Very basic. Mostly she witnessed fear and discouragement in the men and boys who were brought to the house.

Anna spent much time at Susannah's with little Marianna when there were soldiers in the Sudermann house. Oma or Nicholai walked there and back with her. There she felt needed and more secure. Susannah did not take in many billets.

On Sunday afternoon, Katarina attended a practice of the Concordia Choir. Director Regehr also had a heart for the many wounded and lost soldiers in the area, and he led his choir mostly in Russian songs that afternoon. They practiced in the schoolhouse, and before long, had acquired an audience of Cossacks. The White soldiers watched and listened quietly, some with tears in their eyes at the songs of their homeland, of the steppes with wild rye waving in the keening wind, of the song of the nightingale in spring.

During a break in practice, one of the Cossacks approached Director Regehr and asked if he and some of the other Cossacks might sing for the choir. The request was eagerly granted and the Russians took their places in the middle of the schoolroom floor now cleared of desks.

Rich voices joined in melancholy harmonies as the men clapped in time and stamped their boots on the wooden floor. Katarina and the others found the rhythm intoxicating and could not keep their hands or feet still.

The tempo of the song increased and a shiver of excitement ran down Katarina's spine. The men divided into two groups, all the while singing, clapping, and stamping. One group squatted on their haunches and kicked their legs out—left, right, left, right. The other group danced upright, kicking their booted feet high in the air, twirling and leaping. One of them grabbed a meter stick from the teacher's desk and held it out in front of him, one hand on each end of the stick. With a deftness which defied the eye, he jumped over the stick, one foot first, then the other, then back. Again and again with slight variations.

The choir rose to its feet, cheering and clapping and the Cossacks danced on. Katarina's heart thrilled, remembering the fierce, free-spirited gypsies she had befriended as a child in the Crimea, and their colorful, controversial dance at hers and Johann's wedding. That life seemed like a faded dream, but for now, this exhilarating experience had helped both the Mennonites and the Cossacks to forget, even for a short space of time, the tragedy and travesty in south Russia. It had been a celebration of life and joy in the midst of fear and death.

ഇഇഇ

The German train clattered through Plzen and on to Prague, where Maria, Kristoph, and Fritz Schmitt climbed aboard another train and continued on to Ostrava and finally to Krakow. The three, dressed inconspicuously in plain traveling clothes, switched to a rickety coach for the remainder of the ride to Lvov.

"I think this is as far east as we should go." Schmitt had obviously researched the route before joining them in Schwandorf. "It's too dangerous, and we know they sent word from Lvov." The three disembarked the coach and found a dim corner in a dirty pub.

"But the telegram," said Maria. "They were fearful here. They would not have stayed long, I think."

Kristoph calmed her with a smile. She noticed the challenging twinkle in his blue eyes. "Now we must deduce which direction they would have gone," he said. "Obviously not east, but otherwise we cannot be sure. It depends on what they encountered here."

"Death," said Schmitt, sobering them all. "They encountered death. Erich Jahn died here. People might remember."

"Doctors, hospitals, any medical clinics or even the inns are worth investigating." Kristoph turned to Maria again. "Do you have the picture of Erich?"

"Of course." Did he think she was witless?

"Just checking, Mika. Thinking aloud."

She sighed. He could read her mind.

"Don't think too loud," added Fritz. "We are not among friends."

They set out, systematically checking street by street, Fritz on one side of the street and Kristoph and Maria on the other. Day followed weary day, and each nightfall, their hopes were dashed once again. No one had seen or heard of the three young men. Or at least they were not willing to talk about it.

Kristoph watched people's eyes and hands as he asked his questions, and he didn't think they were any closer to finding the trail. They had been gone from home an entire month, and so far nothing useful had turned up.

Maria sat lost in thought, staring at the eastern horizon from the window of their tiny flat. Some distance east of here, her father lay buried and her remaining family struggled to survive. Had Nicholai returned? Was Katarina managing without Johann? She hadn't heard from them in months. Anything could have happened.

She shook her head, willing herself to put aside what she could not know or control. Oh Lord, she prayed silently, closing her eyes, please keep them safe. And Dietrich. Please Lord. Not for my sake alone, but for his family.

She opened her eyes to find Kristoph staring at her, his mouth slightly open. He took a deep breath, as though he had forgotten to breathe, and forced a smile to his lips. "Did you say one for me as well?"

ଌଓଌଓ

Shevchenko was a fool in many respects, but Johann gave him credit for knowing when to fold his hand. Now that the Reds had been overcome and the Whites remained behind to make sure of it, his commander had gone into hiding. Apparently, he did not care what Johann did.

Johann pulled himself into the saddle of a flea-bitten nag once requisitioned from some poor Ukrainian farmer and clucked his tongue. "Come on, old girl," he urged, "let's go home. We'll see if either of us survives this trek." The horse stretched her neck high and bared worn yellow teeth before snorting and setting one split hoof in front of the other. Johann laughed in spite of himself. "I agree," he said. "I completely agree."

They followed the Dneiper to Kakhova the first day, then veered east and north toward the Molotschna. Most of the White encampments had dispersed toward the front earlier, but a few outposts remained to secure the region. Johann avoided them by riding mostly at night; the area did not offer many trees for shelter.

At the end of the third night—a long night for both horse and man—he drew near the colony. Then, without warning, gunfire erupted to his right. He coaxed his steed into a draw and slipped from the saddle. The mare would be in no worse danger if he used her as a shield than if he didn't. He stayed there for the rest of the day until the evening star blinked into view and the moon positioned itself beneath it. He cautiously led the horse back to even ground, mounted and set out. He hoped to gain the safety of the colony in no more than an hour. The mare, exhausted from steady walking, plodded pitifully along and Johann promised rest and food once they reached their destination.

Johann had seen no trace of military movement, but something bothered him. He would not feel safe until he reached home. Several times he stopped to listen, but he heard nothing. Shaking his head, he urged the horse on.

He never quite remembered where the shot came from, but as the moon smiled placidly from a sky now embroidered by a million stars, a bullet caught him in the upper arm. Pain spiked down through his arm to his fingers and he dropped the reins with a surprised cry. His mount stopped, as if resigned to the fact that death awaited her, and she'd rather have it now than move another step.

Johann dropped to the ground, crawled to the shelter of a stand of water poplars and rolled out of view. Bandits, he thought. Must be bandits. Whoever it is has no way of knowing whether I am Red or White, so it probably isn't either of them. It must be someone who thinks I have something he needs . . . ah, the horse.

Best to move as far from the horse as possible, he decided. "Thanks, old girl," he murmured as he slunk away, bent double from pain. When he had left a good distance between the mare and himself, he dropped to the ground and looked after his arm. Only one wound, as far as he could tell in the moonlight, which meant the bullet remained in his arm. He removed his shirt, tore off the sleeves with his teeth, and put it back on. Then he tied one sleeve tightly around the arm to stop the bleeding and bandaged the wound with the other. Working with one hand offered definite challenges.

Faint from shock and loss of blood, Johann stayed where he was for several minutes, trying to catch his breath. Then, knowing he would need help soon, he pushed himself to his feet and moved through the trees to a field on the other side. He stumbled along a path worn by cattle, and finally, all energy drained away, he reached Ackerman. He remembered Paul telling him the village was deserted, but surely a few people must have returned by now. He sincerely hoped so, because he knew he would not walk another twenty versts to Kleefeld.

The quietness of the hamlet disturbed him, and he began to think Paul may have been right in saying it was deserted. Well, he would find shelter nevertheless. By instinct, he staggered down the street to the blacksmith shop and made for the hovel that had been Tekanin's home. Quietness prevailed as he eased the door open. Holding tightly to the handle for support, he moved inside.

The dingy interior of the hut shimmered in the light of a single candle. He saw a mattress on the floor, on which lay a scrawny old man. The man stared at him without blinking, without speaking.

Johann stared back, too exhausted to respond. Then, without a word, he fell headlong to the dirt floor.

Chapter 10

"Have you seen Susannah lately?" Oma asked as she brushed and braided a silent Anna's golden hair.

Katarina looked up from her mending. "No. I haven't had a chance to go see her. Terrible of me, but I am kept so busy with the household and the kindergarten." She resumed her stitching. "I should go this afternoon. I'm sure she would appreciate a visit."

"Would you like to go too, Anna?" Oma asked. "We could visit with Mrs. Loewen and Peter and play with Marianna. Wouldn't that be nice?"

Anna frowned and turned her head away. Her face reddened and she picked at the fabric of her dress.

"You don't have to go anywhere if you don't want to," Katarina assured her.

A tear rolled down the girl's hot cheek and fell to her lap. Oma held her, rocked her, and spoke soothing words. "Don't worry, my child. Your heart will heal. We love you."

Katarina set off to Susannah's alone. Suse met her at the door, a thin, pale replica of the Susannah she had met at *Bethania* several years ago.

Susannah forced a smile. "Come in, dear Katya. It's been so long."

"I know and I'm sorry. We live only a short walk away, and yet we haven't seen each other."

"Well, you're here now, and it's a timely visit, I think."

Katarina wondered what she meant by that. Peter sat on the floor of the parlor with Marianna, humming almost imperceptibly. He did not greet his sister, but allowed her hug.

"Mother's gathering laundry from the neighbors. She won't be back for a little while, so we will have tea in the kitchen."

Susannah put the kettle on the stove, then took it off to fill it from the pail on the counter, then placed it back on the stove. She reached into the cupboard for cups, set them on the table, then carried them back to the counter. She stopped herself and said, "Tea, Susie, tea," and found the tin in the back of the cupboard.

Katarina watched in fascination as her usually calm friend tried to remember how to make tea, and wondered what bothered her so much as to make her forget such a normal routine. She found out soon enough.

When Susannah finally mastered two cups of tea and sugar and teaspoons, she sat at the table near Katarina and held her eyes. "Katarina, we're . . . I'm going to . . . um, I'm going to have another baby." Her eyes swam with tears she refused to shed. She waited for her friend's response.

Katarina's shock stole her breath for several moments. "How could you . . . Gerhard was . . ." She counted back and realized that, yes, Susannah could be pregnant. "Oh, Suse. I don't know what to say. I'm surely happy for the child you carry, but it will be so difficult . . ." Her words trailed off.

Susannah turned her cup in her hands and stared into the dark liquid. "It's . . . I'm still in shock myself, and I know I will love this little one as much as I love Marianna, but . . ." She began to sob quietly, her face in her chapped hands. "Oh Katarina, my life has become such a tale of woe. How will I ever endure it?"

Katarina pulled her chair over next to Susannah's and held her friend while she wept.

There were indeed no words to help. Except one. Neither

of them had noticed little Marianna's entrance. She toddled unsteadily to her mother's chair, grasped onto her skirt, and looked up with wide blue eyes. "Ma-mama?" she queried.

Susannah dried her tears with her apron and reached down for her little girl. Marianna sat very still in her mother's embrace for several moments, then wriggled away.

"Ma-mama!" she exclaimed with satisfaction.

Both women smiled through their tears. "She needs you," said Katarina, "and so does your unborn child. Somehow the Lord will see you through."

"I dreamed of Gerhard last night," said Susannah. "He called to me and I saw his face clearly. He looked like he did when Nicholai brought him home—tired and sick." She looked up at her friend through eyes that threatened to overflow again. "I'm so afraid for him. I'm sure he is suffering."

"Susannah, we can't know that."

"Oh, but Katarina, how could he not be? He had not yet recovered from the aftereffects of typhus. He was weak yet; I think his heart suffered damage. The army gives them no rest, the food is terrible, the water no doubt dirty. I'm sure he is ill again."

Katarina sighed and shook her head. "There is nothing you or anyone else can do, Suse. We must trust him to God, who is merciful."

"God, who is merciful. Where is this God when the way becomes so dark there is no pinpoint of light ahead?"

"Dark?" Marianna mimicked.

Susannah smoothed the blond head. "You are my faint light," she said. "For you I must continue." Her other hand rested on her stomach.

Katarina too had asked the question many times, and like Susannah—like Job of old— silence met her queries.

ꕥꕥꕥ

Paul managed to steal away by himself the next time he visited Pava's *izba*. The plight of the young woman and her elderly father had not left his mind since he had found them there in his old home. Neither had Pava's face left his memory. He set off in the early morning, his night watch complete, without telling even Grisha. His life was his business, after all.

The heat of late July branded his back before he had traveled far on the road, but he pulled his worn cap over his growing curls and trudged on. He arrived with the sun high overhead and lifted his hand to knock at the broken door. His hand stilled at the voices within.

"Who is he? What are we to do with him?"

"Can't just throw him outside, daughter."

"He could be dangerous. Why would he come here?"

Then the sound of something heavy being dragged. "Don't do it, girl."

Paul knocked and called out, and every noise stopped. Pava's face appeared in the crack of the door and after hesitating a few moments, she let him in. A look of guilt crept across her fine features as her eyes moved to her now obvious secret: a body in the middle of the floor. Paul gasped and moved back, then rolled the body over. His heart constricted as he recognized a pale and unconscious Johann.

"How did he get here?" he demanded, stooping to examine him. "How long has he been like this?"

Pava watched, wide-eyed. "Just another beggar who showed up early this morning. Don't know who he is." Defensiveness surfaced in her voice.

Paul stared up at her. "This man is my friend. We've known each other since childhood and he is like a brother to me. He has saved my life more than once."

He turned back to Johann and untied the makeshift bandage. "He's been shot," he said. "We have to get the bullet out, but I don't know how. Do you have any water at all?"

Pava scooped a bit of tepid water from a rusty old kettle on the fire and held it out to Paul. He raised Johann's head and slowly poured a trickle into his mouth. Some of it ran down the man's chin and beneath his collar. Suddenly, Johann's face twitched and he swallowed and coughed. Blinking his eyes in the dimness, he tried to focus.

"Paul?" his voice rasped, and he grimaced in pain.

"I'm here, Johann, but I don't know what to do. You've been shot, and we need to get the bullet out."

Johann tried desperately to shake the stupor from his mind. "Boil . . . water." His head rolled back.

"Pava!" shouted Paul. "Get water. Boil it. Quickly." She grabbed a tin pail and ran from the hut.

"Johann, I know it's easier to faint, but I need you to tell me what to do. I won't let you die for lack of trying."

Old Igor sat shaking his head on his corner mattress. "Give him more drink, son," he said. "If I had stronger, I'd offer it." The old man dragged himself off his mat and stirred the fire to life, adding a few twigs.

Johann came to again and forced himself to concentrate. "Clean the wound. Sterilize a knife." He clenched his teeth until the spasm of pain passed. "Tighten the tourniquet." He raised his head and tried to see his wound.

Sweat poured from Paul's face and ran in rivulets down his chest and back. The temperature inside the hovel soared with the newly kindled fire. Pava returned, panting, with a bucket of water. She hurried to heat it over the coals and came to crouch near Paul. She found an old rag and soaked it in a dipper of water to bathe Johann's face. The coolness revived him further.

"All right," Johann's voice was thin, weak. "Boil the rag, pull it out with a stick and wash the wound. Throw a knife into the boiling water." He winced and shook his head again.

Pava retrieved the steaming rag from the water and held it

out to Paul Gregorovich on the end of the stick. They glanced at each other, then he took it gingerly and washed the wound.

"Again," said Johann, gritting his teeth. He moaned as Paul worked, knowing the pain would only worsen.

Paul lost his nerve for a moment as he held the knife ready.

"Straight on," rasped Johann. "Don't cut an artery."

Paul dragged in a deep breath and sliced into the flesh. Johann arched his back and emitted a long groan. Pava turned away with her hand over her mouth.

Paul turned his head toward Pava and she wiped the sweat from his forehead. Gradually, she took her place at his side again and helped hold the patient. She couldn't believe now that she had intended to dump this man in the bush for the wild animals to find. When had she so lost her humanity and compassion? Several scenarios crossed her mind, too painful to dwell on. What mattered was that Paul had arrived in time to stop her.

Paul located the bullet and pulled it out. He cleaned the wound thoroughly once more and bandaged it. His patient shuddered and slipped into unconsciousness.

"You must look after him for me, Pava," said Paul. "I will get a wagon and a horse and come back for him."

Her face blanched. He trusted her to do this, when she had almost left this man to die? But what other choice did he have? He couldn't carry the man on his back all the way to Alexanderkrone. She nodded. "I will do my best."

"I'm going back now. I brought you a little bread and a few crumbles of cheese." Her eyes widened as she reached for the food. She smiled at her father and he winked at her as if to say I told you so. "If his fever soars, bathe his face with cool water, and keep giving him water to drink. Clean water."

He held her eyes for a moment to make sure she had heard him. She nodded again, but her mind was on the food. She was excessively thin, Paul noticed. Gaunt. Like her father.

Well, he would do what he could. He would do it for the mother and sister he had lost.

Katarina's heart burst with joy at Paul's news, not that Johann was wounded, but that he was near, and coming home today. "We will find a cart," she said, and thought immediately of the rickety old glorified wheelbarrow Nicholai had used to collect bodies after the battle of the Molotschna. She shuddered.

"Jakob Dyck has a small buggy," said Grisha. "I will fetch it." He left in a hurry while Paul went to borrow a horse or an ox.

"We will have him home soon, Katarina," he said with a smile as he stood in the doorway.

"Your heart is right, Paul Gregorovich. Thank you for saving my husband." She turned away. "I will get my things ready."

Katarina sighed and sat at the table, her hands clasping and unclasping. Her Johann was alive and coming home. Her excitement wouldn't allow her to concentrate on anything else. She stood and paced the floor until she heard buggy wheels, then ran outside, Johann's medical bag in her hand.

The condition of Pava's hut horrified Katarina. She had seen the inside of the servants' houses at Succoth, but never such a dark, filthy place. The mattress on which the old man sat was covered with bugs and stains. She shuddered, then remembered the men she had nursed at Succoth. If she still had those resources at her disposal she would bring these two unfortunate souls home and look after them.

But times had changed. She barely had enough food for her own family. No servants stood by to make meals and clean the house. No extra rooms waited, prepared and vacant for guests. There was no end to the number of poor who needed help. She could not save the world. The realization always disappointed her.

Pava stared at her from a corner of the hut. She would not speak, other than a few lonely syllables to answer Paul's questions. They came from different worlds, the two women, and yet both had suffered. At that moment Katarina felt truly blessed. Her losses had been great, but obviously, Pava had fared much worse.

Johann had passed a restless night, and Pava looked tired from sitting at his side. Katarina thanked her in Russian and knelt at Johann's side. "My darling, I am here. I've come to take you home."

Johann peered at her from glassy eyes. His face tilted in a weak smile of recognition. Carefully, Katarina, Paul, and Pava lifted Johann to his feet and helped him into the buggy. He gritted his teeth to the pain.

"Thank you," said Katarina, taking Pava's hand and reaching for Paul. "You saved his life."

"No," Pava whispered, shaking her head. "I didn't . . ."

"Please accept my thanks."

Pava stared after the buggy as it rolled back east to Alexanderkrone. So much had happened, so much had changed since Paul Gregorovich had appeared at her door. Sometimes she felt the unfamiliar tingling of hope inside her, an emotion she had all but forgotten these last desperate years. Perhaps if she prayed more, God would remember her. Perhaps he already did.

"There's good news!" Nicholai bounded into the house and stood before Johann, who sat resting in Oma's rocker. The fact that Oma had suggested he sit there proved her joy at his homecoming. Out of respect, no one sat in Oma's rocker except Oma.

Nicholai lowered himself onto another chair and sat on the edge of it. "I've heard the Germans are coming. Soon. They're marching to join the White Army and destroy the

Communists. We shall be free, and we won't have to leave our country."

Johann listened, eyes narrowed. "Where did you hear this?"

"At the mill. I found some work there while you were gone, and people come and go, you know, and they say it's true."

Johann pursed his lips and pushed his eyeglasses up with his finger. "It sounds like a good thing, Kolya, but don't get too excited yet. I'm not sure how the Germans could return. They've lost the war and are deep in debt with the conditions of the Treaty of Versailles. I can't see it."

"Well, it's true, whether you believe it or not." Nicholai stood and left the house while Johann shook his head.

Paul entered the house as Nicholai left. "What's the matter with him?"

"Oh, another rumor. He is naive and then angry when anyone contradicts what he says. People say the Germans are returning to free us from the Reds. It's not possible."

Paul smirked. "Why would they do that? Good will? That's not how politics work."

"Yes, well, he believes it."

Grisha opened the door and poked his head in. "Paul Gregorovich, there you are. I'm going to the villages around to see if I can trade some eggs for milk. Since the cow is dry, we need some milk for Anna."

"I'm talking to Johann. Go ahead without me."

Grisha nodded and backed out of the door. He stood there wondering if they even needed him anymore. Paul had found Johann again—he heard them laughing on the other side of the door now—and Gerhard was gone. He missed Gerhard; he was a good man. With a sigh he turned from the house and set off for Kleefeld. He knew where he could be of use, but no one must suspect or he would endanger them all.

ഋഋഋ

His fever soared and his hands shook. He knew what came next. The uncontrollable shudders and rigidity. The lapses into unconsciousness. This time, there were no loving hands to bathe his fevered head, no clean bed to sleep in once the drenching sweat had been washed away, no warm soup to feed his disease-ridden body, no words of comfort. No, this time he would not recover, not without a miracle.

Miracles happened; he had seen them, experienced them. But he doubted it. He'd had a feeling about this, but hadn't been able to bring himself to talk about it. Well, didn't make much difference now. He would never see any of them again. He tried to still his shaking but it only worsened. He sat down beside the road and leaned his head against a tree.

"Hey you, get moving," roared a voice. He slumped sideways and lay still, face to the ground.

Someone kicked him in the side, but he could not move. "Aagh! Leave him. He won't make it anyway."

His mind shattered into blackness.

ജ്ജ

Throughout the long, hot summer, Katarina worried about Anna. She spoke a few words now and then, but only in answer to her family's questions. She did not leave the house except to use the outhouse, and then only in the company of Katarina or Oma.

Life, although lean, had taken on a routine of sorts. The Whites patrolled now and then, but the Reds were not much in evidence in the summer. Ordinary commerce had turned into a farce. "A wheelbarrow full of paper money won't buy you a loaf of bread," said the townspeople. Many kinds of paper currency had completely devalued. Katarina had managed to save as many *Grivni* as possible, but those ten-kopek notes were only accepted in Ukraine, and no one knew for how long. The entire country suffered in economic despair.

The Reds returned and drove out the Whites again, this time sending them fleeing to Crimea where heavy fighting followed.

Katarina closed the kindergarten for the safety of the children, Anna and herself.

In early November, Johann and Katarina received a letter—a miracle in itself—from Wilhelm and Agnetha Enns. They had not seen the Ennses since leaving Crimea the year before. The letter comforted and troubled at the same time, reinforcing the belief that there were no safe places left in Russia. Katarina read the letter aloud that evening after supper.

> *Dear Johann, Katarina, and Anna,*
>
> *It is 20 October as I write these words. We don't know, of course, if this letter will arrive at your door, but we thought it would do no harm to send it. We pray you are in good health.*
>
> *Has Nicholai returned? We sincerely pray he has. If not, he is in God's hands. Trust in the Lord and he will give you the desires of your hearts.*
>
> *We also send greetings to the two who traveled with you. We heard they moved north to find you. May God bless their loyalty.*

Grisha and Paul Gregorovich glanced at each other. Katarina smiled at them both and Johann acknowledged them with a nod of his head.

> *We are well, although considerably troubled in spirit. Until recently we had decided to remain here at Tomak in the Crimea, in spite of emigration talk. We have our house and most of our workers are loyal, but lately, things have happened here to cause us to reconsider our former decision.*

As you know, the Reds have moved south again, this time all the way to Crimea, sending the Volunteer Army fleeing before them. Heavy fighting resulted in places, also other incidents, one of which I will describe for you.

It happened at the Bible School at Tschongrau. The school opened for classes after harvest as usual. Teachers and students were settling in when a Red Army unit showed up and arrested them all—yes, teachers, students, staff, everyone. The Reds commanded the prisoners to stand against the brick wall of the school in a row to face a firing squad. Meanwhile, some of the soldiers rounded up the entire village, both Mennonites and Russians, and forced them to attend the execution.

The man in charge then demanded the townspeople to reveal publicly how these prisoners had taken advantage of the people. No one said a word, because the accusation was so preposterous. Finally, one of the villagers gathered his courage and shouted that these men should be released as they had only been friendly with everyone.

With no one to accuse them and no false witnesses, the Reds let the men go free. The teachers—A. H. Unruh, J. W. Wiens, and Gerhard Reimer—told their story in the Mennonite Brethren Church in Karassan on Sunday last. What a rejoicing that no one had been hurt or killed (Agnetha asks me to include that they were all considerably shaken). And what a revelation to us that we must consider the safety and freedom of our children.

And so, Johann, when you are next in contact with Mr. Janz, please include our names on the emigration list. We will be glad to come to whatever gathering

point he should prescribe when the time comes. Until then, we wish you God's mercy and grace in this tumultuous time. In spite of the circumstances, we are a happy family here, and for this we praise God.
In Christian love,
Wilhelm and Agnetha, David, Sarah, Tina, Philipp

Johann rode to Tiege to see Benjamin Janz the next day.

ꕤꕤꕤ

"Ah, it's been a while, my friend." Janz seemed sincerely glad to see him, thought Johann.

"Yes, I've had a few setbacks."

Janz knew about his conscription, but Johann explained about his transfer to Kherson and his mishap on the way home.

"It's good you came today," said Janz. "There is much to do. Our brothers are being inducted into the Red Army at an alarming rate. An All-Mennonite conference has been scheduled for 19 February, but that is still some time away."

"Where will it be held?"

"Alexanderwohl. We need to find a way for our men to be allowed alternate service. They are being trained to kill."

"The Communist government is a formidable foe."

"Someone must do it, Sudermann. We cannot allow these things to happen unchallenged."

Janz stared at Johann. "We cannot lose faith. This is only the beginning."

"I realize that, sir, but what about the *Selbstschutz*? How does one negotiate a nonresistant stance for men who have taken the law into their own hands and fought aggressively against the anarchists?"

"Ah, there's the rub. We have shot ourselves in the foot, so to speak. We must now retrace these unprecedented actions and try to find a way to explain them to ourselves and to the authorities."

"I will meet you in Alexanderwohl for the conference in February then," said Johann, preparing to leave.

"Johann. Help is on the way for us. I've just heard that the American Mennonite Relief (AMR) organization has formed a board, the Mennonite Central Committee, which is sending a shipment of aid to us here."

"Food aid?"

"*Ja*. They are concerned with our plight and wish to help. If we can hold on for a while yet, we will at least not have to starve."

ꕥꕥꕥ

The changes bothered Grisha. He thought about them as he stood guard in the quiet of the waking day. He had noticed the steady influx of Red soldiers in the area of late. They demanded billets again. If he faced the news honestly, he realized the Communists controlled most of Russia. The South proved the only real White stronghold, and it seemed to be slipping. Their short reprieve, however welcome, was about to end.

He knew, however, that there were ways to make it more difficult for the Reds to take over. Nothing loud and bold, just obstacles to slow them down. Since his arrival in the Molotschna he had maintained a free spirit, coming and going as he pleased with few questions to answer. He did his duty by the Sudermann household, and that with heartfelt commitment, but it was not all he did.

Paul continued to spend significant time in Ackerman, often not returning for days at a time. I've lost him, thought Grisha, his heart heavy, but he has found a companion. He will survive without me.

Katarina daily served her family, her friends, strangers. She visited Susannah frequently, helping her with her silkworms, and Anna finally agreed to go with her, only to find her heart renewed by little Marianna. Grisha saw the change in Anna and sent thankful prayers above.

Grisha worried for Nicholai; a boy forced to grow up too soon, he carried too much pain in his heart. Unless he changed his thinking, he would become a cynical man, sour to life, missing its few but undeniable joys. Grisha had tried to speak with him about it, but Nicholai always replied with an "I'm fine" and walked away. He could not force the boy to listen to him, an old man with nothing to show for his life.

"My Russian friend," Oma poked her head out the door, interrupting Grisha's thoughts. "I could use a little help here if you can take time from your musings." Oma. The strongest soul in the lot. Grisha loved her like his own grandmother.

"I suppose I could afford a few minutes of my precious time," he countered.

"Well then, I could use some water from the village well. Ours seems to be dry. I realize it's a woman's job, but perhaps you can be back before you are recognized."

"I will go out of respect for you, Oma, and if I suffer, I suffer."

Oma's mouth twitched but she maintained a straight face. "Be brave."

Grisha chuckled as he carried the pails toward the well at the center of main street. Even in want, life could be tolerable, as long as the warmongers stayed away. As he passed the village office, he noticed a small gathering of Communist soldiers, and he knew it was not to be. How long did they have until the whole scenario played itself out again? Why did the Molotschna have to be the battlefield? How paradoxical, that it should be so: battles fought on the land of peacemakers. Perhaps it was as some of the elders now said, that the Mennonites had sealed their fate with their participation in the *Selbstschutz*, that this present persecution belonged to God's discipline for straying from his precepts.

He shook his head. He didn't know what he thought about it. What was it the monks had often quoted? "In this world you will have trouble." The words of the Christ.

Grisha took a deep breath as he set the pail on the wooden planking and pumped the handle. He hoped his present covert involvements would not heap new troubles on those he had come to love. His actions were in their best interests.

Well, that may not be completely true, he admitted to himself. He wanted to thwart the arrogant powers that had forced him to fear, to leave his home, to lose Paul twice, to hide his actions. If he had his way, the Communists would not have an easy transition.

ℬℬℬ

"Katarina, I am thankful the kindergarten is shut down for now. There are so many soldiers about; it's not safe for you to go out." Oma helped Katarina wash the dishes after supper.

A loud pounding on the door interrupted them. Katarina looked to Oma with fear in her eyes. With quiet urgency, she ordered Nicholai from his place at the table to hide in the bedroom. She opened the door, her heart pounding. Three Red soldiers pushed their way in and demanded food.

"We had no harvest this year," said Katarina, "but we will share what we have."

The men laughed. "What choice do you have, eh?"

She thought again of the difference between these men and the Cossack who had sat on their verandah with them only a couple of months ago. Her musings were interrupted by a roar.

"Hurry up, woman. We are hungry!"

She and Oma rustled together what food they could find

and served the men, all the while fearful that Nicholai might come out to defend them. They prepared themselves to have to put up with them for the night as well, but the soldiers left as soon as they had eaten.

"*Das vedanya*," said the youngest, leaving the door open to an early winter wind full of ice. Katarina hurried to close it and leaned against it, a great heaving sigh escaping her.

"They've gone, Katya. Collect yourself now. We have done our duty again and God saw fit to give us a restful night."

"Yes, and Kolya is safe." She turned to find him standing at the door of his room, leaning against the door frame, a brooding look on his young face. They stared at each other, a thousand thoughts flying back and forth but none spoken.

"Good night, Kolya," she said, touching his sleeve as she passed him.

ঌঌঌ

After weeks of searching, Maria, Kristoph and Fritz moved from Lvov back to Krakow. Perhaps the men had made it this far—except for Erich. They would try here.

Krakow was as different from Lvov as day from night. Maria could understand enough of the Polish language to get by, because it fell somewhere between German and Russian. Kristoph, on the other hand, spoke Polish fluently, as did Fritz.

During the second week in Krakow, when Mika felt decidedly discouraged with the entire effort and wondered if she had fabricated the whole image and person of Dietrich from the beginning, they found a clue.

Chapter 11

Fritz had been inquiring at hospitals while Kristoph and Maria targeted inns and public places.

"Have you seen these men in the past year?" asked Kristoph, showing the pictures of Michael and Dietrich to an innkeeper in one of the poorer districts.

The man glanced at the photos and shook his head. "No, no."

As Kristoph turned to leave, the man said, "At least, I don't think so." Kristoph turned back and stared. The man shrugged.

Reaching into his pocket, Kristoph pulled out a few bills. "Will these improve your memory, Mr. . . .?"

The man's eyes lit up. "Wisniowecki. Show pictures again." He held them nearer the light. "I maybe see them. Bad light in here."

Kristoph grimaced and slid him two more bills. The man squinted at the photos once more. "Ah, it comes back. Last year. Two young soldiers. German I think, but they spoke the Polish good. Stayed a while. Used to come in often. One not looked too good."

Maria tensed. "Which one?"

The innkeeper pursed his lips.

Kristoph thought he might have to hand over more money, but he would have done anything at this point to draw out this man's cooperation. Finally, after months of searching, they had found their first real clue.

Wisniowecki chose Michael's picture and pushed it across the counter toward Maria. "That one, he not look good." He took a drink from a glass behind the bar. "Then the other one here," he tapped his finger on Dietrich's photo, "he come alone."

"What had happened to his friend?" Maria demanded.

"How does Wisniowecki know that, eh?"

Maria rolled her eyes. "Do you know where they were staying?"

"No, no. I mind my own business, eh?"

"Let's go, Maria," said Kristoph. To the innkeeper he said, "We may be back. Keep that memory sharp."

Wisniowecki nodded and smiled. It had been a profitable night.

ꕥꕥꕥ

The Reds returned to the Molotschna in December, having dispatched the Whites. They brought with them fear, smallpox, and typhus. They left, most of them, taking everything of value and leaving behind a devastation not yet known to the Mennonites.

Johann and Katarina faced Christmas of 1920 with empty hands and scarred souls.

"We must summon our courage for the sake of the rest," said Katarina. "We have to be their example."

"My dove," said Johann. "Always looking beyond yourself to others."

His unexpected tenderness brought tears to her eyes. She reached across the table to hold his hands. "I can't stand to see my family floundering in fear. I don't want them to carry this time as an excuse to stop hoping, to stop striving. We have to help them."

"And we will." He smiled at her in the lamplight. Even in

the dead of winter, a sprinkling of freckles danced across her nose and cheeks. Her hair, ever curling out of its pins, shone bronze in the low light. But it was her eyes that inspired him most, green as summer grass, deep as the ocean, filled with faith even in a winter of worry.

"The choir is caroling tonight," said Katarina at breakfast several days before Christmas.

"Even this year? What is there to celebrate this year?" Nicholai's hardness struck a note of alarm in Katarina's soul.

"Even this year, Kolya," she said. "Do you think times were easy the year the Savior was born? They were probably as poor as we, if not poorer."

Her brother didn't reply.

"Where will you sing?" This from Anna. She and Oma had secretly been crafting small gifts for members of the family, and the work had pulled her out of her self-imposed silence.

"There are many people in need of encouragement this season, and a reminder that the Christ who came at Christmas lives for them even in sickness and need. The widow Thiessen will be expecting us, and Susannah—she's due any day, you know; and the Voth girl—the youngest—is still recovering from typhus."

"Her brother died." Anna's eyes were large in her thin face.

Oma put her arm around the girl's shoulders. "He is with Jesus."

Anna reached for her spoon and mechanically ate her thin porridge.

"Maybe they'll give you *Prips* and cake like last year," said Johann, lightening the moment.

Katarina laughed. "Maybe. I miss real coffee, but one can get used to it."

"If one must." Oma twinkled, then turned to Anna. "If you help me with the dishes, we can get to work." She winked and Anna responded with a smile that did not quite reach her eyes.

Johann accompanied Katarina to the church where the choir congregated. Oma had insisted she bundle up from her head to her feet, but the night was mild and calm. Friendly chatter skipped through the group as they set out on their trek of goodwill.

Widow Thiessen had indeed been expecting them. "*Kommt herein, kommt herein*," she called from her chair by the window. She sat where her daughter Lena had placed her earlier. Lena had stopped by Katarina's on her way home to her family and asked if Katarina would help her mother to bed when they stopped there. First they sang, drank *Prips* and ate the little cakes Lena had left for them. Widow Thiessen sang all the words with them, her wrinkled cheeks wreathed in smiles. Katarina and two other girls helped the old woman into bed and settled her before running through the snow to catch up with the others.

Katarina hadn't felt so free in what seemed like years. She felt like the girl from another life who had run out on a Christmas morning to find the gifts left by the *Weinachtsmann*. Papa had been there then, and Mika and Peter.

"Katya, hurry up or we'll lose them."

She quickened her steps and caught up, out of breath, at Susannah's. Then to Voth's and on again. By the time they dropped her off at home well after midnight, Katarina's feet ached, but her heart soared. Fresh air, friends, music, all these together cheered her and gave her faith and strength to continue.

Katarina and Johann shared a cup of hot tea before retiring to bed the day after a lean but joyous Christmas.

"The people of Friedensfeld were not as fortunate as we were this Christmas," Johann told her. "They had a surprise visit from the Machnovitz as they gathered for worship on

Christmas Day. The beasts stormed the church, threatening with guns and swords."

"On Christmas Day?"

"The bandits no doubt planned it that way. The congregation expected sudden and violent death, but God spared them. The bandits stole from them and left. The minister, Aron P. Toews, had his hands full trying to calm his flock after that."

Katarina looked away. For a short time she had been able to convince herself that life was good, that nothing had disrupted the beauty of this place, of these people, but she knew she deceived herself.

She wished Johann hadn't told her the news. She wished he could make her world safe again.

"I talked to B. B. Janz again last week," he said. "He already has many names on the emigration list. He doesn't know how long it will take to arrange it all, but if anyone can do it, he can."

As much as Katarina wanted to be thankful for this information, her mind could not fathom leaving everything she held dear to travel to a far country she knew almost nothing about. She wanted safety, but she wanted it here. She stood by the window watching fat, fluffy flakes of snow coast down to a thickening white carpet outside. Johann came up behind her and put his arms about her waist.

"We will get through it. God promises to rescue us when we trust in him."

"I want more from life than to get through. How much will we lose before we are rescued?"

"God knows our limits, Katya. He will not fail us."

She sighed and turned in his arms. "Promise me?"

He smiled into her eyes. "His promises are always trustworthy."

PART TWO

1921

Send some rain, would you send some rain?
'Cause the earth is dry and needs to drink again,
And the sun is high and we are sinking in the shade.
Would you send a cloud, thunder long and loud?
Let the sky grow black and send some mercy down.
Surely you can see that we are thirsty and afraid.

But maybe not, not today,
Maybe you'll provide in other ways,
And if that's the case . . .

We'll give thanks to you with gratitude
For lessons learned in how to thirst for you,
How to bless the very sun that warms our face,
If you never send us rain.

Nichole Nordeman

Chapter 12

"I've heard *Bethania* has reopened," said Katarina. She needed to distract Susannah from the pain and from her low mood. Between labor pains, they spoke of trivial things.

Susannah rested, drenched with sweat even though the January cold stretched icy fingers through the walls into the little house. Hannah sat ready with towels and water. The bassinet stood ready to receive a new occupant.

"How many residents do they have now?"

"Over sixty, I think. I don't know where they come from or where they will go if the political situation deteriorates again."

After the next contraction, Susannah said, "It's ridiculous. How do they intend to find food for so many in these times?"

"I don't know. It probably won't last. The School for the Deaf in Tiege opened again as well, but there are only two of the previous thirty-some."

"Why don't they just give up?"

Susannah groaned and the time for distractions ended. Katarina and Hannah readied themselves for a long night, but they knew Susannah would work the hardest. If only they could keep her spirits up. She needed all the strength she could get, emotionally as well as physically.

ഌഌഌ

Leaving Maria with Fritz in the flat, Kristoph went out into the evening under the pretense of getting some fresh air. He made his way swiftly to the inn and began questioning patrons about Michael and Dietrich. He didn't like bringing Mika into places like this any more than necessary, but he knew she would insist if she knew where he was heading.

"Excuse me, this man visited this establishment fairly often in the past months. Do you know his name and where he lives?" Kristoph pushed Dietrich's picture in front of a couple. His intrusion obviously annoyed them. They waved him away.

He moved to the next table and the next until Wisniowecki beckoned him to the counter. "You disturb my customers," he said.

"It's important," returned Kristoph.

"So is my living."

Kristoph sighed. "I'm sorry. This man is a friend who disappeared last year. We need to find him."

"Yes, but you not bother my customers. Listen," Wisniowecki leaned toward Kristoph in a conspiratorial manner, "I not see that man for many months. He go away, I think."

Kristoph tried to read his eyes. Was he lying to get rid of him or was he telling the truth?

"If he comes again, I let you know, but I don't think so."

Kristoph closed his eyes as another door slammed shut in his mind. "Thank you," he whispered. He walked a long time. What now? He wished he had Maria's faith. On the other hand, she too appeared discouraged of late.

"God, if you can hear me, if you would deign to bend your ear to a sinner such as I, show us what to do. If Dietrich is here, don't let us overlook him. Whatever the case, help us to know if he is dead or alive." His experimental prayer dissipated into the cold air like the puffs of breath he exhaled.

ഌഌഌ

Nicholai sat in church wishing he were anywhere else, but he had run out of other places to go. He no longer accompanied Paul Gregorovich to Ackerman. Paul and Pava did not need him, in fact, they usually forgot he was there. Grisha occupied himself with certain clandestine activities that Nicholai knew to be decidedly unhealthy if discovered. Johann spent his time with Katarina and Anna, or riding back and forth to Tiege to work with Benjamin Janz.

So here he was, sitting at the *Jugendverein*, supposedly enjoying himself in the presence of a couple of dozen others his age. The youth meetings helped distract the young people from the growing severity of their situation, and encouraged healthy interaction between them.

In spite of the famine, mothers always provided some kind of snack, which Nicholai appreciated. The games were entertaining once he allowed himself to become involved in them, but he found the other young men immature. The girls were just silly, giggling and batting their eyelashes, all trying to gain the attention of the boys.

Except one. Nicholai had noticed her at the last meeting. She smiled generously and took part in the games, but not in the giggles. He watched her as she sat around a table of young people playing *Mensch, Ärger Dich Nicht*. Her mind seemed far from the game, from the people, from the room in which she sat. It was as if she were struggling beneath a heavy burden. She glanced up, aware of his gaze. He looked away, but not before she sent him a hint of a smile.

Justina Epp. That was her name. She lived in Kleefeld with her mother and a couple of siblings. He glanced her way again and discovered her eyes on him.

Nicholai found it all confusing, this tingling he felt when Justina looked at him. He avoided her for the rest of the evening, but her face filled his mind, a clean open face, her hair partially pulled back, the rest of it hanging down her back. He desperately wanted to talk to her, even as he left the meeting without so much as a backward glance.

"His name is Gerhard," said a weary Susannah. Her mother, Hannah, wrapped the tiny squalling boy in warm blankets and held him while Katarina tended to Susannah. Then the new mother reached for her son and, for a short moment, her many trials faded at the sight of his face, puckered and blotchy.

Katarina left with the linens and towels, Hannah left to spread the word, and mother and baby were alone.

"Such a fine little man you are," she said, pulling the blanket away from his face and stroking the wisps of fair hair on his head. He stared in the direction of her voice.

"It's a challenging time you've chosen to come into this world, my little one, but we will do our best for you." Susannah smiled and the baby stared. "This is not an easy life, my sweet one, but for some reason the Lord sent you to us. I suppose we needed you, although how we shall manage another mouth to feed, I don't know."

The baby's face puckered again and he began to wail. "Shh, shh, not to worry. God will provide. Come, my love." She held him close and sang softly a Russian lullaby her mother had sung over her. Baby Gerhard calmed again and nestled into her neck.

"Dear God," whispered Susannah, "I give you this babe. I do not know why you entrusted such a treasure to me in this time of need, but I ask that you give me faith. Faith to believe you will provide for us, faith that tomorrow will be better than today, faith that my Gerhard is in your hands, wherever he is. And faith to raise this child as you want me to.

"I am so very weary, Lord, with daily struggles and gnawing fears. I give you myself. Do with me as you will. Only give me strength to trust you and to obey. I have gained nothing by trying to get through on my own. I need you desperately. Take over in my life and in the lives of my family." She drifted off to sleep before reaching the "amen," a young woman no longer alone. Her most important battle had been fought—at least for today—and she slept more peacefully than she had in many months.

ꙮꙮꙮ

The atmosphere in the church in Alexanderwohl crackled with tension. It had been a long conference, culminating in the formation of the organization of the Union of South Russian Mennonites, the VMSR. Benjamin Janz, newly elected chairman, stood. "Gentlemen, before we close this meeting, we will take a vote. You are asked to reaffirm your stand on the issue of nonresistance."

Beside him, Johann wondered what his friend and mentor would say.

"This assembly gives us the task to go and intercede before the Communist government and insist that all Mennonite young men are nonresistant, but all of us and the government know what has happened through the *Selbstschutz*. It will be extremely difficult to assert that we are non-resistant."

A murmur shuddered through the assembly. Janz continued:

"Furthermore, we ourselves do not know if we really endorse this view. Perhaps we want to assume such an attitude now, but if another situation develops we will shoot again."

Johann waited for the tension to erupt at Janz's painfully honest words. It did not.

"If we really want to adhere to nonviolence in the future, then now is the occasion to confess. What has happened has unfortunately happened, but we are sorry that it did. This must be settled here today.

"I have no intention of forcing anyone to conform to my standards, but if we do not agree, I must resign from the leadership of this organization and request that you elect a new chairman. I call for the vote. Do we affirm nonresistance or not?"

Benjamin sat down. The church was quiet until the count came in.

"Affirmative," called Heinrich Friesen. "It is unanimous."

ꕥꕥꕥ

They decided they would leave Krakow the next day. Maria wore her discouragement like a heavy coat, and neither Kristoph nor Fritz could think of any more options in Krakow. They had canvassed the city from corner to corner, and each day returned to their dingy flat without a single lead. Perhaps it was time to turn back. Perhaps neither Michael nor Dietrich would ever be found.

Fritz Schmitt had long ago given up hope of finding his son, Michael. When the innkeeper told them that the one in the picture named Michael had appeared very ill, and then ceased to come to the inn with the one named Dietrich, he knew his son had died. He mourned quietly, but in truth, was not surprised. How often did one find a loved one who had disappeared in war, especially a soldier traveling through enemy territory?

The ominous task of communicating the probability to his wife now consumed the elder Schmitt. He often walked the streets as well, whether by sunlight or moon glow, or sat at the inn nursing a mug of beer.

This night Maria sat alone while Fritz and Kristoph walked, independently, in the winter night. Overcome with desperation, she tied a scarf over her head, lifted her long woolen coat from the peg by the door, pulled the collar up around her ears, and set off. She could not sit alone in the dreary rooms another minute.

Her footsteps led her subconsciously to Wisniowecki's inn. She knew her lone walk was dangerous in the war-torn city, but she no longer cared what happened to her. Without Dietrich, what purpose did life offer?

She entered the dim, smoky room and settled at a small table in the darkest corner, facing away from the other tables. Warming her hands on a cup of steaming tea, she thought of her ridiculous hopes of finding Dietrich. Gradually, her frozen fingers and toes warmed, but she kept her coat around her shoulders and her scarf in place. Wisniowecki had not seen her come in. A woman at the counter had made her tea.

Maria sat for an hour, lost in memories, hopes, and dreams, trying but unable to rid herself of them all. *I wait all my life for a man like Dietrich and he is taken from me.* She discussed her situation silently with God. *I know I don't deserve better, but why bait me? Why give and take away again? Have I not suffered enough for my sins?* The questions tormented her soul.

"Is safe now." Wisniowecki's voice drifted into her roving mind. "Sit by the fire and drink some."

Maria turned slightly at the scrape and thump behind her. Through the hazy dimness of the pub she watched a tall, thin man hobble to a table by the fire, leaning on a crutch. When he sat, she realized one of his legs was missing below the knee. Her heart felt pity, but she reminded herself not to stare.

As she was about to turn away, the man glanced in her direction. Electricity shot through her as if she'd been struck by lightning. Her eyes opened wide and a groan escaped her lips. She tried to speak his name, but her voice betrayed her. She stood on shaky legs and her scarf slipped down around her collar.

The man stared, first in confusion, then in anger. Reaching for his crutch, he stood abruptly, his chair crashing to the floor. "What are you doing here?" he shouted in German. Then, turning to the bar, he bellowed in Polish, "Wisniowecki, you snake! You filthy liar! What would you not do for your stinking money?"

Maria stood in total shock.

"Dietrich?" Her voice rasped in the sudden stillness. She came to herself and rushed toward him.

"Don't come any nearer," he warned in a voice of iron, his hand held up to stop her. "I do not . . ." The words seemed to stick in his throat. "I do not want to see you . . ." again the pain-filled hesitation, "ever again."

He turned and thumped his way back to the door behind the counter. Smashing it open with his crutch, he stumbled through and let it slam behind him. The room resounded in silence. Mika stood like a stone statue in the middle of it. Then, the self-possessed Maria Hildebrandt who had never swooned in her life crumpled to the dirty floor with an audible sigh.

Chapter 13

"Why you let him in when she is here?"

"I did not know it was her, Leszek. She had that scarf on her head."

"Well, you make trouble now."

"What do we do about her?"

"I do not know to fix this."

"But Leszek, we have to do something. We cannot let her lie there on our floor in the middle."

With an angry epithet, Wisniowecki turned away and the woman approached Maria, by now coming out of her faint. She sat up groggily and then leaned back into the woman's arms as she tried to absorb the nightmare that had unveiled itself before her eyes.

"Why?" she asked, tears marring her view of the woman.

Silence.

"Please," she pleaded. "Why is he so angry?"

"You not see his leg?"

"Yes, of course. But I've been searching for him for more than a year. Why would he not be overjoyed to see me? We were to get married the day he left. We loved each other."

The woman shrugged and helped her to a chair by the table she had previously vacated. She fetched her a fresh pot of tea and sat down with her.

"He does not want people see his leg," she said simply. "Says he cannot go home no more. No hope he has."

"That makes no sense," countered Maria. "I don't care if

he has one leg or none—he is my Dietrich."

"Yes, that is how woman thinks, but man, well, to him is different."

"But how can he be convinced that I love him still?"

"I cannot tell you." The woman rose and placed a hand reassuringly on Maria's shoulder. "You try. Maybe you find way."

Before the pot of tea had grown cold, Maria pulled her wraps closely about her and headed for the door. As she passed the counter, she said to Wisniowecki, "I'm coming back. You can tell that angry man in there that he can't get rid of me that easily. He once made a promise to me, and I hold him to it." She turned and walked quickly out into the darkness toward the flat.

ഇഇഇ

"I've been called back into the Army." Johann told Katarina the news as she sat knitting stockings from the silk Oma spun. Katarina's needles stopped mid-stitch.

"Oh no, Johann. Not again." Her face paled and her eyes filled.

He sat down next to her on the sofa. "I am still in the Red Army," he said. "It won't be so bad, Katya. I will be doing office work again."

"Where?"

"I am to go back to Kherson, but who knows where from there. Now that the Whites have been effectively crushed, the Reds are consolidating their strength. I could be posted nearer to the Molotschna."

"Or farther away. Oh Johann, how am I to do it without you again? I'm not strong enough."

"Katie, we've been through this. At present I have no choice. This is exactly what B. B. Janz is working on: a way to obtain the release of Mennonite men from the Red Army."

"How will we keep in touch?"

"I will find a way, my dear."

"When do you leave?" She set aside her knitting and took his hands.

"Tomorrow. I just talked to Mayor Puchinsk, or I should say he talked to me, and I must present myself in Kherson in two days. I will take the train, which shouldn't take two days, but one never knows what delays we may be faced with on the way."

Katarina sighed. "I wonder what it would be like to go to sleep at night without worries about your family, about getting enough food to eat, about horrible diseases caused by filth and evil. I can hardly remember Succoth, you know. It seems all a dream to me."

"Yes, our Eden. Like a glimpse of heaven."

"No, heaven will exceed Succoth by far, and we will all be there together."

They sat in silence, absorbing each other's presence. Then Johann packed his few things, bade the household farewell, and left before daybreak.

ꕥꕥꕥ

When Maria pushed open the door of their flat and stormed in, both Fritz and Kristoph jerked in surprise, at the suddenness of her entry and at the fire in her eyes. Kristoph rose to meet her, afraid that she had come to some harm.

"Where have you been? Why did you go out alone?"

"He is here," she said without preamble, her voice shaking, her finger pointing to the floor. "Was here all along. Thinks he's going to send us packing. Well, I did not come all this way to run back in defeat." She shrugged out of her coat and threw it unceremoniously onto a chair. Standing in the middle of the floor, hands on hips, she said, "Tomorrow I am going back to talk some sense into him."

Throughout her tirade, the two gentlemen stared at her in shock.

"Dietrich?" Kristoph took her by the shoulders and made her look at him. "You found Dietrich?"

She looked into his eyes and the enormity of the situation struck her. Tears boiled up, running in angry rivers down her porcelain face. Her shoulders began to shake with sobs and she fell against Kristoph. He led her to the sofa and sat beside her, holding her against him, a look of astonishment on his young face. Fritz sat rubbing his bald head, new hope springing up in his breast.

When Maria had spent herself crying, she told them of the surreal meeting. They all decided a good sleep was the thing before launching out to rescue the man who did not want to be rescued. Maria's sleep was fitful, and she awoke while the winter world still slept. And she prayed. Prayed that she could talk sense into her beloved, convince him of her love, of their need for one another, of his promise. Her anger and hurt gradually gave way to thankfulness that he had been found, and found alive, and to determination that they would figure out what to do.

As soon as Fritz and Kristoph awoke, the three headed down to the inn, where a weary Wisniowecki brooded at the counter.

"We've come to talk to Dietrich," announced Maria.

"He don't want to talk to you."

"I will talk to him, if I have to break the door down myself."

"He give me orders that nobody he will speak to. Especially you."

That comment cut to Maria's heart and she stepped back as if struck. Her determination began to seep away, and she sat wearily in a chair. Fritz laid a hand on her arm, but Kristoph pounded his fist on the counter, rattling the glasses that stood there.

"Where is the brute?"

Wisniowecki shook his head, but couldn't help a glance toward the door behind the bar. Kristoph marched around the counter and through the door.

The room he entered was small and scantily furnished. His brother sat at a table in the corner, head in his hands. At Kristoph's sudden entry, Dietrich's head jerked up and he tried to stand, but fell back onto the chair.

Kristoph reached down, picked up the crutch, thrust it at Dietrich and said, "Stand, coward. I want to talk to you eye to eye and I am much too angry to sit."

Dietrich's left eye twitched, and he pulled himself upright, leaning on the crutch. He set his mouth in a thin line, raised his chin and waited.

Kristoph leaned into him. "What have you been doing, hiding here like a coward while we search every dark corner of this rat infested city?"

"I am not a coward. It is for the best."

"Ha! Best for whom? For no one."

"In case you haven't noticed," Dietrich controlled his voice, but he could not block the pain from his eyes, "I am no longer a whole man. I cannot walk without this stick."

"Rubbish! Maria loves you, not your leg. Good heavens, man, can't you see that? Don't you know it?"

Dietrich turned his face away. "It's too late, Kristoph. My heart has become like a stone within me. I cannot love anymore."

Kristoph grabbed his brother by the collar and they stood nose to nose. "Do you have any idea what you are doing to that woman out there?" His outstretched arm pointed to the door through which he had come. "All she has done is love you, so much that she has searched everywhere, taken dangerous risks in order to find you. And when she does, you turn on her like a madman. Well, in my opinion, you are completely mad to turn away from such a love. Completely and absolutely mad."

Dietrich flinched as if he had been struck. "You're in love with her."

Kristoph's eyes widened. He let go of Dietrich's collar and the elder brother fell back onto his chair, his crutch crashing to the floor. Kristoph took a deep breath.

"No," he said. Then in an agonized whisper, "Yes. Yes I am. I didn't intend for it to happen, and then there was the possibility we would never find you or you would be dead." He sat down at the table and stared into space.

The silence grew. Finally, Kristoph raised his head and spoke, his voice heavy with emotion. "What I feel doesn't matter. She loves you. I'm your brother and will never be any more than that to her. But believe me, if you persist in your ridiculous denial, I will spend the rest of my days trying to change her feelings for me. I've always looked up to you, my brother. Now, when it matters most, don't disappoint me. Don't be a complete fool."

Kristoph wiped his eyes with the back of his hand and stood. With one last look, he walked out, leaving the door open.

Maria stood at Kristoph's approach. He looked at her with such pain in his eyes she was afraid something had happened to Dietrich. Then she understood. "I'm sorry," she whispered. "My dear brother." She stood on tiptoes, kissed him on the cheek, smiled, and bravely walked behind the counter into the little room where Dietrich sat.

She seated herself in the chair recently vacated by Kristoph and stared across the table into Dietrich's wide blue eyes. In an even, low voice, she said, "You once made a promise to me. You said you did not want to leave me ever. Do you remember?"

"That was before I lost my leg. I am not the man I was. You need to realize that."

"So 'ever' only means as long as everything stays as it is?"

"Maria, it's not just the leg. I've lost my hope, my will to live." He looked past her and lifted his chin. "Go back to Germany with Kristoph. He loves you, you know. He would give you a life that would satisfy you. You would soon grow tired of this shell of a man I've become."

Maria stood to her feet, and for all his soldierly experience, Dietrich winced at the anger in her eyes. "What do you take me for? I am no longer the selfish coquette I once was. That woman is gone. That entire life is in the past. Everything has changed, except my love for you. Your brother is a dear, wonderful man, but he will never, could never, bring to me what you already have in our short time together.

"Now, we are going back to the flat to pack up our few belongings, and then we will come for you. Be ready."

She stood and marched toward the door.

"Mika."

She stopped. She turned.

He grabbed his crutch and pulled himself up.

"Mika, could . . . could 'ever' begin again?"

She was in his arms in an instant, holding him up as he wept, their tears mingling as words of love tumbled over each other to fill the gaps left by war and time and fear.

They met the next day in a huge old cathedral on the route between the inn and the flat, and exchanged vows that would bind them together in love for as long as they both would live. Kristoph and Fritz Schmitt bravely stood witness, each grieving his own inevitable but heartbreaking loss. Dietrich and Maria spent their wedding night at the inn, and the next day the foursome boarded a train for Germany.

ജ്ജ

Katarina knocked at Susannah's door, a gift in her hand. She had worked long hours on the fancy baby dress and looked forward to giving it to Susannah for little Gerhard.

Susannah's mother opened the door. Her eyes were red from crying and her face puffy.

"Hannah, what is it? Is Baby Gerhard sick?"

Hannah shook her head, unable to speak. She opened the door further and motioned her visitor inside. Katarina dropped her gift on the kitchen table and waited for Hannah to compose herself.

"It's . . . it's Helena. My daughter Helena from Neukirch. Her . . . husband, Jakob . . ."

Katarina placed a hand on the woman's arm to calm her. "What happened to Jakob?"

Hannah burst into fresh sobs. "Dead. Killed. He . . ." She stopped to wipe her eyes and blow her nose. "He went to the Old Colony with a wagon load of goods for the people there. They have suffered so terribly from the Machnovitz and the famine and disease. Anyway, a group of bandits caught him, stole the wagon, horse and all, and shot him." Again, she was overcome with weeping. "Now . . . now my Helena is a widow, with three little children. Why do my daughters suffer so much?"

Susannah had joined them, and wept along with her mother. "She was so happy with Jakob and the children. Perhaps we will go spend some time with her."

"We will take turns," said Hannah. "I will go for a while, then you go. We need to help her."

Katarina wondered when her turn would come. Yes, she

had lost her father, but she still had a husband. Perhaps childlessness was her cross to bear. Or perhaps it was a blessing. It seemed this life was fraught with grief.

ꕤꕤ

Upon his return to the army office in Kherson, Johann set about to catch up the work that had collected in his absence. Shevchenko had been replaced by another man, a Communist to the core by the name of Malenkov. The man was Shevchenko's opposite in almost every way: tall, slim, neatly dressed, hard-working and articulate. Unfortunately, the one thing he had in common with his predecessor was the most dangerous: Bolshevik fervor.

After a month or so, Malenkov introduced a new assistant, Svetlana Kamarovskaya. Within the space of two more weeks, her efficiency had put Johann out of work.

"You are being transferred to Tokmak," said Malenkov. "Comrade Kamarovskaya and I can handle the work here. You begin next week."

Johann boarded the train immediately and chugged home to Alexanderkrone.

"Katarina," he called as he entered the house. She stood stock-still in wonder.

"Johann?"

"I have been transferred to Tokmak, beginning on Monday. It's only Thursday yet."

"Tokmak! That is less than twenty-five versts from Alexanderkrone!"

They beamed at each other as it it were Christmas all over again.

"I shall likely be home most weekends," he said.

Johann's position at Tokmak proved another time of

learning. Things had changed since the end of the civil war. The Reds did not need to occupy themselves with the Whites, and concentrated on taking charge of Ukraine.

Johann found out, in dealing with the various office memoranda, that trouble still brewed in the north. Although the most serious setback to the Communists had come from the South, the factory workers still called numerous paralyzing strikes in Leningrad.

In March, a third and unsuccessful revolution was staged near Leningrad, by sailors at the Kronstadt Naval Base. The rebellion was quelled by the army, but not without bloody fighting and the execution of all who took part.

The tenacity of the people amazed Johann. Those northern city dwellers faced the same encroaching hunger as their southern neighbors, yet they did not give up easily.

The most difficult part of the job for Johann was the grain seizures by the Communists. He knew the state of the farms—no seed, no rain, no feed for their few remaining animals. He knew the people themselves starved, and yet Lenin persisted in bleeding them when they were already wounded.

Ah, thought Johann, that is what he is trying to do. He must break the back of any remaining resistance. He must keep the people in a perpetual state of need and reliance, keep them totally off balance. Only then can he gain and maintain power. Starve and subdue.

And so the dinosaur struggled on, wounded and starving, even as the rest of the world rebuilt their walls and healed their wounded and planted new crops. The winds of drought and famine and fear blew over the land, threatening to bury the dinosaur deeper than it had so far been buried.

Johann fought the tightness in his spirit as he reached across the desk for another file, a list of names of more men who had become fodder for the Communist beast. He opened the file and began to transcribe the names onto a government form. They loved forms and lists, this new regime. The depth of information the *Cheka* possessed on so many citizens caused him to shudder. It was as if a huge evil eye watched continually as the ants scrambled for food and shelter. An iron fist kept them subdued, squeezing the life from them.

He needed to talk to Benjamin Janz.

ꕥꕥ

"Anna? What's the matter?" Katarina entered her sister's room, followed by Oma, who had summoned her. The girl lay pale and still beneath the blankets. Her eyes were closed, but Katarina knew she was not asleep.

"Anna," she whispered as she settled herself on a chair beside the girl's bed. "Oma says you are not feeling well. What's the matter?"

Anna's eyes finally flickered open, and as her gaze shifted to meet her sister's. Katarina's heart clenched. Where she expected to see pain or fear, she saw nothing.

"Anna!" She turned to her grandmother beside her with wide eyes. "Oma, it's not typhus, is it?"

Oma tried to calm her with a quiet voice, but it did not work.

"Oma, typhus is rampant everywhere. Do you think Anna has caught it?" She turned back to Anna and began to check her for symptoms. "We've kept ourselves and our house clean, Oma. We shouldn't get typhus."

"Many soldiers of both Red and White armies have been housed beneath our roof. One cannot always stop the spread of disease with soap and water."

"Anna, do you have a headache?" She checked the girl for rash and fever.

"Is she feverish?" asked Oma anxiously.

"Yes, very hot, but she is shivering."

"Keep her covered then," said the old woman, reaching into a bureau drawer for another blanket. "Best to get her to sweat out the sickness."

"No rash," said Katarina, with a small measure of comfort. "Not yet, anyway. Oma?"

Her grandmother laid a hand on her shoulder. "Lord, please keep our Änya. Help us to know what to do for her. We ask you, the Great Physician, to heal her."

Anna's eyes had closed and she lay quiet, her breathing shallow, her pale cheeks hollow. Katarina clung to Oma's hand on her shoulder, her own prayers racing heavenward for this innocent victim. Was this the onset of typhus, or some vile disease left by her attackers? Or was she just too fragile a soul to exist in the mad world that had overtaken them?

ꙮꙮꙮ

Grisha turned the corner from Lichtfelde to Alexanderkrone, and nearly collided with an apparition in the semi-darkness, a small, bent form cloaked in an enormous dark shawl. He began to apologize, but stopped cold at a shriek emitted by the phantom.

"You evil creature," screamed the little old woman. "You cannot come here."

Grisha instinctively grasped her scrawny arms and was surprised at her strength. "Don't be afraid, woman. I am not an enemy."

"The enemy! The enemy has come!" She flew at him again, swinging something at his head. He ducked and wrapped his arms around her to stop her attack.

"Quiet, woman. I will not hurt you, but you must stop struggling." His words had no effect whatever on the distraught woman. She continued to scream and struggle.

A couple of villagers walked by, leaving a safe distance

between themselves and the struggling Grisha. "She's crazy," they called as they hurried by, "wanders around attacking the unsuspecting. I'd let her go, if I were you."

Grisha had decided to do just that when rough hands grabbed him from behind. "What are you doing to this woman? Let her go at once." The voice of one of the constables sent chills up Grisha's spine. The last thing he wanted was to face the police. If they should ever find out about his covert occupations, he would be a dead man.

"You're coming with me," the constable said, dragging Grisha away.

"The woman is crazy! She attacked me. You can't arrest me for that."

"I can arrest you for anything I want," the constable replied, tying Grisha's hands behind his back. "Unruliness and insolence are not allowed. You will think about that while you sit in jail, and if fate is cruel, you will have more to fear than an Alexanderkrone cell."

Grisha's heart pounded within him. Who would even miss him? What would he eat? How long would he last if they discovered his secret work? He tried to keep himself from falling on his face as the constable pushed him along the street.

On the other hand, did it matter what happened to him? Perhaps his time was finished. Perhaps he had done all he could. Paul didn't need him. Not now that he had met Pava. Katarina had Johann close almost every weekend. They would miss him, yes, but they did not depend on him. He was expendable. His work against the Bolsheviks was important, but there were always others to take it up. Yes, perhaps he had reached the end of his path.

Chapter 14

"Don't be ridiculous!" hissed Johann from the free side of the bars. "We need you and I will negotiate your release."

Grisha shook his head. "I've thought a lot about it these last couple of days, sitting here with nothing else to do. I've wasted much of my life on empty dreams, chasing after the wind, regrets that will remain. I cannot change those things now, but I have tried to atone for at least some of my past mistakes."

"You can't do that, Grisha."

"Can't do what?"

"Atone for your mistakes. Only Christ can do that."

Grisha smiled. "Yes, I know that. My time at the monastery profited my soul, but I have tried since then to do some good, to help some people in whatever way presents itself. I will continue as I am able, if I am released."

Now Johann sighed. "You will get out. I have connections, but you need to be very careful, for all our sakes."

Grisha took the warning to heart. "I work alone, mostly." His voice was barely audible and Johann had to lean into the bars to catch the words. "I will keep doing what I started, and will most likely end up here again, or in some other place of incarceration. You must release me from your hearts. Get me out of here and send me off, and then never think of me again."

"How can we do that?" Johann's voice rasped in frustration, his hands gripping the bars. "You saved Paul's life, I don't know how many times. You took care of Katarina and our household when I was absent. I will not turn my back on you."

Grisha's hand came up to stop further words, and a sad smile crept onto his weathered face. "Don't take it so hard, man. Life is brief, always has been. We are born, we live a little—for good or for evil—and then we die and go to our reward. Do not fret for me."

Johann hung his head as his hands slipped off the bars of Grisha's cage. He stood. "I will talk to the mayor. You are not the only one to come into contact with the crazy woman. They cannot keep you here on that charge. Now eat what Katarina sent so you have the energy to leave."

Grisha smiled and nodded. His heart felt at peace, now that he had talked it through. He would live each day as if it were his last, and pray that God would bless his efforts.

ꝏꝏꝏ

Maria sat next to Dietrich on the westbound train, watching the scenery flash swiftly past on the other side of the windows and listening to Dietrich's tale.

"I am not a nurse; I am a soldier. Erich's suffering almost undid me. Michael stayed with Erich through the last excruciating days and nights while I made it my responsibility to find food and drink and blankets.

"Most likely, it was Michael's compassion and commitment that cost him his own life. Such close proximity to Erich no doubt exposed him to more germs than his weary body could fight." He remembered the lice that crawled over them all.

"We buried Erich in a small cemetery on the outskirts of Lvov, and then carried on to Krakow. We stayed for a time so Michael could regain the strength he needed to continue on to Germany, but instead of improving, he grew weaker.

"Then came the accident: I was in the pub, getting something for Michael to drink, to help him through. A fight broke out and I found myself in the middle of it. Someone fired a gun and shot me in the leg. The innkeeper and his wife did their best to treat the leg and I went back to Michael.

"He was so bad I couldn't leave him. My leg infected, and one day while Michael lay in a coma, I ventured out to the pub again for help. They tell me I collapsed from fever and didn't wake up for several days. When I did, I was frantic for Michael. They came with me and found him—dead."

Dietrich's composure broke. He tried to hide his brokenness from Maria.

"No more struggling with this alone," she whispered as she stroked his hand. "We are together now. Rest and you can finish the story later."

He let his head fall back on the seat cushion, but his eyes fluttered open again. He could not forget, but as he looked at Maria, a faint glimmer of hope began to birth in his chest in spite of his utter despair. Perhaps with time . . .

ꙮꙮꙮ

"We're losing her." Oma's whisper sent chills up and down Katarina's spine.

"No! We can't just let her go."

"Child, Anna has no will to improve, and we cannot force her to do so."

"Oma, do you suggest we give up?"

The old woman shook her head. Her hands were tightly folded on her lap. "Katarina, the change must come from inside her, from her own faith in God."

"But when we are too weary to exercise our own faith, then the faith of others keeps us afloat."

Oma sat silent, then looked directly into her granddaughter's desperate green eyes. "Anna is a fragile soul tossed about on rough waves. She has been broken, and has not the strength to heal or to withstand more pain. She seems to have chosen instead to float away from us."

"You sound as if we should let her go, let her drift away."

Oma sighed. "I don't know what to do for her. I have prayed and talked and encouraged and prayed some more. I have no more ideas. Who knows what she has yet to suffer? I cannot blame her for longing for heaven."

Hot tears sprang from Katarina's eyes. "I too have longed for heaven, but I do not believe this is Anna's time. I will not let her go. I have lost enough." She rose and slipped into Anna's room, wiping her tears fiercely with her sleeve. She watched the slight rise and fall of the quilt, noted the dark blue circles under her sister's eyes, saw the scrawny arm as it lay on the covers, and her heart quaked.

Anna's eyes fluttered open. She focused on Katarina and then smiled. "Do not cry for me, sister. I'm not afraid, and it will be easier for you if you don't have to worry about me."

"Anna! I . . ."

"I wasn't made for such a time."

Katarina pulled the wooden chair closer to the bed and sat, taking Anna's hand in hers and rubbing it. She forced herself to smile.

"Anna, now it is my turn to speak. You have been more like a daughter than a sister to me since Mama died. Her death left me lonely. I have lost Peter to Susannah, Papa was murdered for his faith, I may never see our sister Mika again, and who knows what will happen to Nicholai. Johann is closer now, but we never know how long that will last with this senseless new regime. Please, Anna, don't you leave me too. I could not bear it. I need you."

Anna listened silently, her emotions flitting through her eyes like pictures in a book.

"If you decide to leave me, Anna, I cannot stop you, but I beg you to stay. Please." Katarina's tears began to fall on the quilt, quiet sobs shaking her body.

Anna reached out her other hand to her sister. Her own tears began to squeeze out onto the pillow. "I'm sorry, Katya. I didn't know you would miss me that much. I thought it would be easier for you without me."

Katarina stared at her incredulously.

Anna grimaced. With a huge sigh she said, "I see I've been selfish."

Katarina tilted her head and cried again. "Oh sweet child." She held her in her arms and they cried together until Anna fell back on the pillow in exhaustion.

"Dear Jesus, please let me keep her," Katarina begged. "Please make our Anna well."

Meanwhile, Oma sat in the kitchen with her head bowed, praying for the Lord's will to be done in Anna's precious life.

ꕤꕤꕤ

Johann had government business in Kharkov, the capital of Ukraine. He took the train east from Tokmak to Chernigovka. The line branched off north again through Wasskressenka.

Johann had not spoken with Benjamin Janz for a long while, and had recently received word that his friend and mentor was presently in Kharkov. As chairman of the VMSR—the Union of South Russian Mennonites—Janz's mandate was to negotiate for the release of the many Mennonite young men who had been forcibly inducted into the Red Army. 1921 had already been a year of mass induction. Johann felt for these men, even though he himself served in the Red Army against his will. By the hand of God, he knew, he had been granted a reprieve with this office position. He did not take it for granted.

With his position came a certain degree of knowledge and power, those two enigmas that stood sometimes together and sometimes at odds. If one knew too much, he could be doomed; if one knew too little, the same fate applied. Ignorance was definitely not bliss. Not in this world.

Johann had been able to secure a temporary freedom for Grisha, on the condition that the man not show his face in Alexanderkrone again. Katarina had cried when she heard, and Oma, rocking in her chair, had bowed her head in intercessory prayer. Paul had been there as well. His face pale, he had clasped his friend in a strong embrace, looked long into his eyes, and slipped away in the direction of Ackerman.

The train jostled Johann from his remembering, and he gathered his papers, slid them neatly into his briefcase, and exited the car. He found Benjamin Janz in a small room on Butovsky, deep in concentration, several documents lying on the table before him.

"Good of you to stop by," said Benjamin, offering him a chair.

"I'm here on government business, which gives me the opportunity to see you as well. How are you doing?"

Benjamin frowned, then sighed. "My reason for being here is to negotiate the release of the young men, as you know." He lifted his chin and stared past Johann. "My priority seems to be shifting, however, to one much more basic and imminent: the survival of my people."

He focused on Johann. "The famine is severe. The situation escalates every day."

"What about the aid shipment promised from America, from the Mennonite Central Committee?"

"Blocked outside our borders, and the general Communist inefficiency and bureaucracy keep it that way. The children are dying. In some villages, especially in the Old Colony, they sit with distended bellies and stick legs and arms, faces drawn and old. We must have help soon or it will be too late. It's already too late for some."

Johann's heart constricted at the thought of Susannah's little Marianna starving like that. "What more can we do? Katarina says she still manages to find food, although it is never enough. How does one deal with a corrupt system?"

Benjamin sat up straight in his chair and reached for one of the documents before him. "I've been granted an interview with an influential official here in the city, but I must wait until two days hence to see him. He may be able to help."

"Is there no one else you could speak with sooner?"

"No. This is the man. To speak with anyone else would be a waste of time, possibly even counterproductive."

"I wish you well with the interview. Is there anything I can do? I have some influence in Tokmak now."

Benjamin thought about the offer. "Find out how many Mennonites from that area have been inducted this year. Send me the information if you can. I believe there is still some mail service inside the country."

"I would be glad to do so. If only we could still communicate beyond our borders."

"I have found a way."

Johann stared at Benjamin incredulously. "How?"

"German diplomatic courier." Janz smiled victoriously, then his smile died. "I have sent many letters, but they seem to do no good. No one cares about our life-and-death dilemma here in Russia." He looked at Johann. "What more can a man do? My knees are worn and stiff from praying, but our situation only worsens."

Johann sat silent, then placed his hand on Benjamin's shoulder. "I will pray for you, brother, for your faith and your health and your spirit."

"And my family?"

"Of course. How long since you've been home?"

"Two months. When one begins negotiations, one must be always available for contact. I have much to do here. In summer," he looked out the window at the new leaves on the poplars, "I will travel to Moscow to speak to the Central Executive Committee of the Communist Party about the ongoing appropriation and division of our land in Ukraine."

"That's a heavy responsibility."

"Responsibility is always heavy, Sudermann, but it seems I am suited to it. Or so the VMSR thinks."

They visited a while longer, spoke of their families, of circumstances in the Molotschna, of Anna's illness, of Susannah's Gerhard, of Janz's wife on her own in Tiege with their children. Then they prayed together and Johann left to see to his own responsibilities. He was considerably sobered by the creeping, sinister darkness descending on his people—on all the Russian people—and he felt almost completely helpless to stop it.

ꕥꕥꕥ

Katarina had emptied out the last sack of grain, including the dust, and Oma had mixed it with a little oil and yeast. It baked into a hard, black bread that brought tears to poor Anna's eyes as she tried to swallow it. Oma soaked it in warm water for her, and she managed to gulp some down. Now even that bread was gone and Nicholai was determined to do something about it. He set out for the mill to see if the miller would give him credit on a little flour. Sometimes Johann came home on his weekends with a bit of money, so they would eventually pay it back.

Miller Baerg was a good man. He did what he could for those in need.

"Nicholai!"

The sound of someone calling his name stopped him in his

tracks. He turned to see Justina Epp hurrying his way. Out of breath, she stopped for a moment when she reached him. "Nicholai. Are you going to the mill?"

His face flamed right to the tips of his ears. He hated when that happened. Either Justina didn't notice or chose not to point it out.

He nodded in answer to her question.

"May I come with you? I haven't gone before." She looked so uncertain that Nicholai relaxed.

"Come on," he said, turning back to the road. "It's nothing."

She frowned and walked beside him. "I don't have any money to pay him."

Nicholai looked over at her but kept walking. "Neither do I."

"What if he doesn't agree to credit?"

"Then we negotiate."

She thought about that. "You mean we offer to pay another time, or work to pay for it?"

"Something like that."

"Well, I don't know how to do that, but I'll watch you."

Nicholai's heart beat a little faster. He didn't know how to do it either, to beg without seeming to. He hoped Miller Baerg would be as reasonable as he was purported to be.

Nicholai glanced at her again. "Why did they send you to the mill? Can't your brother go?"

Justina's voice was so soft he could hardly hear it. "He left on the last emigrant train. He's going to Winnipeg, Canada, ahead of us to avoid the army. I hope he gets there."

"So do I."

"We're glad he could get away, but it feels lonely without him. Mama hasn't stopped crying."

Nicholai cleared his throat. "I was in the army. The White Army." He straightened his shoulders as she stared across at him.

"Why would they take you? You're too young."

"They didn't. I went of my own accord."

Justina was confused. "Why ever would you do that?"

"Sometimes a man comes to the point where he has to try to make things better. I thought I could do that. I wanted to join the *Forstei*, but it closed down before I was old enough. So I took off to join the Volunteer Army."

"How old were you?"

"Fifteen. It was just last year."

"Why did they let you in? Even the Russians don't induct boys under age."

He didn't know if he would tell her. Would she think him brave or stupid? For some reason he wanted her to think him brave. "I took my brother's certificate of birth. He is a few years older than I. They didn't question it, because I was already tall."

Justina raised her eyebrows. "I suppose you were very brave to do that," she said, and his chest puffed out, "but wasn't it rather risky? I mean, you could have been killed without anyone ever knowing where you were and all your bravery would have profited you nothing."

Nicholai's chest sank again. "Sometimes you have to do what you have to do." He felt her eyes on him, but she said no more about it. Gave him the benefit of the doubt. He appreciated that.

"I'll go first," said Nicholai as they approached the mill, "and then I'll wait until you are done."

When they left the mill later, Nicholai and Justina each carried a small sack of flour, and she congratulated him on his newly acquired job at the mill.

ꕥꕥꕥ

"I have been transferred to the mayor's office in Alexanderkrone," Johann told Benjamin Janz, who had allowed himself a rare visit to his family in Tiege.

"Thank the Lord."

"Yes, and I am free to come and go as long as my work is done. I came to discuss emigration plans."

"I leave for Moscow tomorrow to discuss that exact topic with the Communist Party Central Committee," said Janz.

"Weren't you just there?"

"Johann, these things are not accomplished at once. They take much time and patience." He paused and tapped his pencil on the desk. He regarded Johann for a long moment. "Would you be interested in coming with me?"

Johann raised his eyebrows as he considered what Katarina would say. "I might. How long do you plan to be gone?"

"That all depends. A week, two weeks? One never knows."

"If I decide to come, I will be at your door at daybreak tomorrow," said Johann finally. "Katarina is used to managing without me. I'm sure she will not disagree."

Janz closed his lips in a thin line. "The women carry much of the burden in these times. We go, and do, and they stay and wait. Through all my travels and absences, my Maria has never complained. She knows she also serves who stands and waits. Sudermann, without Maria, I could not accomplish what needs to be done."

Johann felt gently chastised. After entering the names of Wilhelm Enns and his family in the registry of emigration, Johann took his leave with the words, "I will go home and talk to Katarina, and if she is willing, I will see you on the morrow."

They left together the next morning from Tiege. Janz had business first in Kharkov.

"I need to find out," he told Johann, "if the Commissariat of Foreign Affairs is interested in distributing the American Mennonite Relief shipment in the South. We need them as an ally if we will ever get that aid into the country."

After a few hours' stop in Kharkov at the Communist

headquarters there, Johann and Benjamin again boarded the train.

"Our situation approaches desperation, Johann." Benjamin Janz's eyes bored into Johann's as the train carried them northeast to Moscow. "Communist soldiers are moving back from Crimea through the villages. They are demanding food our people do not have and stealing anything they deem useful or set their fancy to. Food is becoming scarce, and since most of the seed was stolen or destroyed or used for food, next year will only be worse."

"I thought the Commissariat of Foreign Affairs in Kharkov agreed to help."

Janz frowned. "My discussion with Commissar Manzev proved successful, yes, but even with him on our side, the acceptance and distribution will take time. Local authorities do not always cooperate, laws or no laws. I have, however, been given permission to invite Alvin J. Miller, the American Mennonite Relief representative, to Ukraine for further aid negotiations. That is a significant development.

"By the way," he said, locking onto Johann's eyes, "when we meet with the Russian officials, I will do the talking. Do you understand this?"

Janz's demeanor brooked no disagreement. "Of course," answered Johann. "I come to learn and to support."

"And to pray," added Janz. "Prayer is the most important thing. I have written another letter to America. We must have food immediately or we will perish."

Johann stared straight ahead as the train whistled through a village. His heart squeezed in his chest. His pulse pounded in his ears. So far they'd always made it, always survived. Would they really die here in this despairing land, forsaken by all? Beside him Janz murmured something and rubbed his hands over his face.

Chapter 15

In Moscow, Johann watched in amazement as Janz worked. The man instinctively knew the best path to efficient and effective negotiations. They entered an imposing stone edifice near the Kremlin. Even though they could have spoken with any number of workers, Janz held out for an interview with the top official. They would have to wait four days to see him.

"We do not waste our time with those with little knowledge and no influence," Janz said quietly to Johann as they left the building and approached another government office, "but we contact as many of these officials as possible."

"Why?" asked Johann. "Is it not confusing to deal with so many at once? Would it not be better to pick the best and follow them through?"

"It depends on the situation. Sudermann, you and I may not be able to convince them of our earnest request, but they may be able to convince each other, *ja*?"

Johann admired the self-control of his mentor. He never appeared rattled by responses to his inquiries, never gave up where there was any hope of progress, never divulged more than the person needed to know.

"You play your cards close to your chest," observed Johann later that evening as they ate in a small establishment near the government offices.

"Ah, but this is not a game. This is a matter of life and death. Tomorrow we go another round."

The next day, Benjamin and Johann continued their meetings.

"Why do you wish to leave this wonderful country, Comrade?" asked the official sitting across a battered desk from them. "Have you a bone to pick with the government?"

Janz remained calm, long legs crossed, hat in his hand.

Don't you know he's baiting you, Johann wanted to ask, but then he realized they all knew it. Janz, however, had a greater purpose than his own pride. He represented an entire ethnic group and he would not be put off by sarcasm or intimidation.

"What we have here," he said, ignoring the official's question, "is a large, formerly productive segment of Russia almost totally devastated by war. To leave such normally fertile land unused would be unthinkable for the Communist government. But as a result of the world war and the civil war, many of the Mennonite people are too poor to regain their former status. My proposal is twofold: first, rebuild the land and business destroyed by war; and second, remove those unable to contribute to this reconstruction. Allow them to emigrate."

The official studied Janz for some time, then leaned forward to write something on the paper in front of him. He looked up at him. "And why should we allow traitors to escape, those who have fought against our government?"

Janz maintained amazing control. "That is a problem we are discussing with your comrades in the department." He uncrossed his legs. "We will leave you now. You are a busy man with many important things to do. Thank you for your time. I hope to be able to speak with you again next week before we return to Kharkov."

They rose, shook hands, and left, Johann wondering why Benjamin had not explained his stand on the self-defense fiasco. "Not a wise move at this time, Sudermann. We will leave the two men to discuss this . . ."

". . . and convince each other," finished Johann, a smile tugging at his mouth.

"You learn quickly, my friend. Come. We need to talk with Alvin Miller today yet about coming to Ukraine. He has been allowed into Moscow where he is trying to gain cooperation from the Communist government." Johann hurried to keep up with Janz's long strides.

The two men were able to return to Molotschna after only one week, having spoken to several influential Communist officials about the necessity of emigration as well as some suggestions for its implementation.

ഋഋഋ

"She was doing so much better," said Katarina to Johann on his return. "She decided to try, to eat, to gain back her health."

"What happened to set her back again?"

"Fear." Katarina whispered the word, which came up from her own soul as well.

"Fear of what?"

Katarina turned to face Johann. "The Halbstadt arrests. We heard about them. In the secondary school. Young men and women too, stripped, thrown on the ground and beaten almost to death."

"They are looking for weapons left behind by *Selbstschuetzler*. We have no weapons."

"It doesn't matter to them. They gather hostages and shoot them until someone comes up with the required quota.

"And there is the fear that we will all starve eventually, even if the aid shipment arrives. There's no more food, Johann. Miller Baerg has been gracious, but we cannot expect him to feed us all from his own dwindling supply."

"I will speak to the mayor," Johann answered.

"You've done that before. Either he doesn't care or he can't do anything for us. Everything is falling apart. There is no more good news anywhere."

Johann sat silent for a long minute, then gently contradicted her. "There is some good news, Katya. Machno is gone."

She stared at him, the very mention of the man's name causing her to shudder. "For how long this time?"

"For good, I think. I suppose Lenin and Trotsky didn't need him anymore, and he became like a fly buzzing around their heads, so they made sure he left."

"Where did he go?"

"I don't know. Poland? Romania? Far from us anyway. And I am home."

Katarina looked at him, read his eyes and leaned against him. "Yes, you are home. Thank the Lord."

He wrapped his arms around her and buried his face in her curls. "You are my home, Katarina."

They released each other then to talk of the pertinent problems that did not go away, even through love.

ﻌﻌﻌ

"Katarina!" Johann's call was quiet but urgent. She appeared from Anna's room and he met her in the middle of the kitchen.

"How is Anna?"

"Better today. Why? What is happening?" She knew from his face that something was wrong.

"We have to get you all away quickly. The Reds are coming to do more weapons searches here in Alexanderkrone. This afternoon. Mayor Puchinsk just found out. We can't subject Anna to that, or you either."

"But where will we go this time?"

They both sensed a presence and turned as one to see Paul framed in the doorway. They sighed with relief.

"I heard what you said, Johann," said Paul. "Bring them to Ackerman. I know it's a long walk, but it would be safe. No one bothers us there."

Katarina contemplated the situation, then nodded. "Yes. I don't know if Anna can walk that far, but we will help her. Oh Johann, what about Susannah and Marianna, and Peter, and...?"

"No time. Get Anna ready. I will find Kolya."

Paul had disappeared again, and the fact irritated Johann. Tekanin came and went as if he had not a responsibility in the world.

"I will go warn Susannah," said Johann.

His irritation dissipated swiftly when he and Paul returned at the same time, Paul with a small wagon, the kind children played with. Where he found it no one knew, no one asked.

"This is for Anna," he said. "I'll go to the mill and warn Nicholai."

Katarina sent him a look of sheer adoration. "Thank you."

"But why are we going out today?" asked a pale Anna.

Katarina smiled at her. "It's a beautiful autumn day, the leaves are falling, and the sun is still warm enough to give you the kiss of health. We will have an adventure."

Anna eyed her sister doubtfully, but could not refuse one who had so tenderly cared for her all these endless months. "Is Oma coming?"

"No, Oma is not coming," said the old woman herself. "I am going to Cornelia Reimer's house. She and Abram need help cleaning out their cellar. I think Susannah and her family will come help as well." Frau Peters glanced meaningfully at Johann and he understood. Katarina heaved a sigh and breathed a prayer that these dear ones would be safe in their hiding place. Thank God for Johann's warning.

Paul Gregorovich pulled Anna's wagon, allowing Johann to return to work without suspicion of duplicity. The sun smiled down on them as if their world were still the Eden it had been a few short years ago.

Katarina forced herself into a pleasant mood, even though the edges of her mind played pictures of beatings and shootings, and she worried about Oma and the Reimers and Nicholai. She looked down at Anna, a blue woolen shawl thrown over her shoulders, her blonde curls spilling over it like spun gold.

"Princess Anna," she said. "You are the Cinder Girl on her way to the ball."

"*Ashenputtel.* That's one of the Grimm's stories," Anna said, her eyes twinkling as she lifted her face to the sun and reached out to catch the leaves floating lazily to the dusty ground. The adults quickened their steps, down the length of Alexanderkrone's main street, across to Kleefeld and beyond.

"I don't know that one," said Paul. "How does it go?"

"You tell it, Katya."

"Well—Anna, you must help me remember—there was a little girl whose mother died, and her father eventually married another woman with two beautiful daughters."

"Very beautiful, but exceedingly cruel," added Anna.

"Yes. They forced the girl to work hard with the servants and sleep on the hearth among the ashes."

"That's why she was called *Ashenputtel.*"

Paul nodded and smiled at the girl.

"Let's see," said Katarina, losing herself in the story, identifying with the poor girl's loss. "*Ashenputtel* visited her mother's grave every day and planted a twig there. She watered it with her tears and it grew into a fine tree."

"And the birds lived there in that tree and sang to the girl, and when she needed them, they helped her with her work."

Katarina encouraged Anna with a smile and a nod and the girl continued the story.

"The king of the land held a three-day ball for all the beautiful young women of the kingdom so his son could find a wife. *Ashenputtel* wanted so badly to attend the ball, but her stepmother only made her work harder, even when the birds helped her finish her chores on time.

"So she ran to her mother's grave and cried . . ."

Katarina remembered another girl weeping at her mother's grave. No birds had come to her rescue then, but her God had.

". . . and the birds flew down with a beautiful gown and slippers for her. She went to the ball and the prince danced only with her. It was all right for her to dance because she was almost a princess, right, Katya?"

Katarina grinned in response.

Anna continued with the fairy tale, more animated than either Katarina or Paul had seen her in many months. "The next day the birds brought her a more beautiful gown, and the third day her slippers were made of pure gold. Every night at midnight she disappeared before the prince could follow her. She was so beautiful her stepmother and stepsisters did not recognize her, and when they came home from the ball, she had left her fancy clothes at the tree and lay in her dirty work clothes in the ashes.

"But the third day, the prince devised a plan to stop her disappearance. He had his servants spread cobbler's wax on the steps, and as *Ashenputtel* ran away, one of her gold slippers stuck in the wax and stayed behind.

"The prince took the shoe and went to the house where *Ashenputtel* lived. The stepsisters tried to put on the shoe, but it wouldn't fit. Finally, *Ashenputtel* tried it, and of course it fit perfectly, so the prince took her home to be his bride."

"That's the story," said Katarina to Paul.

"No, Katya, that's not the end," said Anna. "The stepsisters followed them to the wedding and tried to be nice to her so they could have an important place in the palace, but the birds pecked out their eyes and they lived the rest of their lives in blindness because of their wickedness. That's the end of the story."

Paul raised his eyebrows. "That's as good as any Russian

tale," he said. "Justice prevails."

Anna remained silent for a moment, thinking about Paul's comment. "It's too bad justice doesn't prevail in our world."

ꕥꕥꕥ

"The news is not good, my friends," said Benjamin Unruh as he sat across the table from Dietrich and Maria Kesselman. "I have recently received a letter via diplomatic courier from Benjamin Janz in Kharkov. He writes that the famine is growing more severe. Apparently there was no seed grain left to sow, and as a result, no crops are maturing. There will be no harvest, no food for the people of the South."

Maria frowned. "I thought Holland and America sent aid. What happened to it?"

Unruh raised his bushy eyebrows. "What happened to it? It sits in Constantinople, blocked from entering the country. The AMR has sent Alvin Miller to Moscow to negotiate with the Central Executive Committee to allow entry of the aid shipment into the country, but so far he has not been able to enter the country himself."

Maria looked at Dietrich, concern and fear filling her expression. "What can we do?" she asked in a small voice. Dietrich covered her dainty hand with his strong one.

"Sometimes care parcels make it through," suggested Unruh. "I sent one to Janz for his family; he said he had difficulty finding enough food for them."

"We will assemble a parcel immediately," said Maria, rising to follow through on her statement. Then, remembering, she smiled at her husband and bent to retrieve his hand-carved Bavarian walking stick. He pushed himself to his feet, positioned the cane in his left hand, and offered Maria his arm. She looked up at him, love glowing in her face, and his smile answered hers.

"Thank you for contacting us," said Dietrich to Benjamin Unruh. "We will bring our package here tomorrow morning."

"Good. It will leave by courier in the afternoon."

ꝏꝏꝏ

Katarina remembered the ramshackle *izba* as it had been when Paul had discovered Johann there with a wounded arm. The single room dwelling stank horribly and even the gloomy darkness of the windowless hut did not hide the filth. She wondered what Anna would think.

The hut looked the same on the outside, but as Paul opened the door, a surprising sight met Katya's eyes. A window had been uncovered, letting in the bronze sun of the fine fall day, and Pava stirred the embers of a fire to life in preparation for a noon meal. The former smell did not assail her, nor the filth so immediately apparent on her previous visit. Pava, a Pava with hope, had changed things.

Pava smiled warmly at Paul as he entered, and came to meet him. When she saw he was not alone, she stopped and looked to him for explanation.

"Pava," he said quietly, reaching for her hand. "Johann found out there were to be weapons searches in Alexanderkrone today. I have brought Katya and Anna here for safety. The girl has been very ill."

Pava recognized Katarina, and nodded for them to enter. Anna's shy smile brought an answering one, and she invited them to sit on the stumps brought inside for that purpose.

"We've been telling the story of *Ashenputtel*—the Cinder Girl," said Anna. "It's very sad but it ends happily."

"Not for the stepsisters," commented Paul.

Thin old Igor lay stiff and still on the mattress in the corner of the dim hut. Anna saw him at once and looked up at Katarina, her eyes spilling over. She moved over to Igor's side and sat quietly beside him. Igor reached swollen fingers to gently pat Anna's hand.

"Sweet child," he said. "Why you should be born into a time like this."

Katarina darted a look at Anna. These were almost the same words the girl had expressed just weeks ago. That she did not belong to this world. The thought chilled them both.

"You've made a home of this room," said Katarina, trying to shake the fear inside her.

Pava gauged her eyes, then nodded to accept the compliment. "Paul helps me. He brings us food." She glanced at Paul.

"I work a bit here and there, at the cheese factory, at the mill where Kolya works, on the *kolchos*, anywhere I can procure food."

Katarina turned new eyes on Paul Gregorovich Tekanin. He had indeed been helping, but not her. She did not need him like Pava did. She understood why he stayed away for long periods of time. Pava and Igor were alone. They needed him.

ꕤꕤꕤ

"You are tired, my dear," said Oma to Susannah as they sat side by side in the cellar of Abram and Cornelia Reimers' house. "These times are very hard for you, *ja*?"

Susannah's head drooped in the flickering candlelight. Marianna leaned against her, playing with a wooden doll carved by Abram. Susannah propped Baby Gerhard against her to nurse him. His stubby legs kicked impatiently, and then he settled down to drink.

"*Ja*." Her whisper carried a world of weariness.

"Come Marianna," said Hannah. "Come sit with your *Grossmama*." Marianna went willingly, and Hannah carried on a whispered conversation with Cornelia Reimer. Abram sat silently beside a fidgeting Peter. The skinny young man pulled at his hair, at his clothes, all the while murmuring the phrases he heard around him.

"As much as I miss Theodore and Katie Konrad," said Abram, "I'm thankful they don't have to face any more of this terror. They are forever safe now."

"Forever safe now," said Peter.

"I need Gerhard," Susannah whispered to Oma as she nursed her son. "They had no right to take him away again. He was still sick. How could he leave me with two children, my mother, and a boy with problems in his mind?"

Oma listened to the list of woes and, although her heart broke for this young woman, only twenty-three years of age, she sensed a bitterness in her soul.

"Who are you blaming?" the wise woman asked bluntly.

Susannah turned her face toward Oma and frowned. "What do you mean?"

"You say *they* had no right, and how could *he* leave me. You blame the Communists and Gerhard himself. I don't imagine Gerhard would have gone if they hadn't forced him, do you?"

"Of course not, but it's not right that I am left alone to deal with these losses. What happened to the verse about God taking care of widows and orphans, of what is right and just and good?"

Oma sighed and thought through her response. "I have found in my life that living happily ever after is for fairy tales, rarely for real life. As for being alone, you are not."

"I am alone!" Susannah argued, causing the rest to stare in her direction. She grimaced and lowered her voice. "I am alone without Gerhard. We had only a few short years together, and almost all were fraught with fear and insecurity. I loved him . . . I love him. I need my husband, and the children need their father."

"As I said," continued Oma without mincing her words, "life is not a fairy tale. Sometimes the only one we have is God. I think he is the one you are bitter toward. Why did God allow Gerhard to be taken, why did he allow you to bear another child to take care of?"

Susannah pulled Baby Gerhard close and leaned to kiss his blond curls.

"Why is it so hard to find enough food; how long must we live in fear and uncertainty? Am I correct, Susie?"

Susannah stroked her baby's head.

"I have seen the work of bitterness, my dear. It is never good. It wounds, and then pours salt on the wound. It hurts most the one who clings to it for meaning."

"How . . ." Susannah's voice blurred through her tears. "How can I stop it? I have no strength. My anger and bitterness is all that keeps me going. And my prayer that somewhere Gerhard is safe."

Oma wondered how to phrase her next words. "Sometimes, Susie, acceptance is our first step. We do not know whether or not Gerhard is alive. Chances are not so good, *ja*? Only God knows, so we must trust him with our loved ones.

"I know this is hard to understand and even harder to do, but I've found it best to concentrate not on what we do not have—or what has been taken from us—but on what we do have. Many, many of our people have lost loved ones. It is a rare thing that a family has not been touched by death or disease or both. Johann told me, according to the records he has seen, over 4000 people in the colonies have perished through disease."

"And the murders."

"*Ja*. Another 250 were murdered. That is the raw truth, but we must look at today. We sit here protected from possible death because Johann was able to warn us of the weapons searches. So far our children survive. We have homes to live in. We have our faith in God."

"Do we?"

"I cannot answer that question for you, but I encourage you to examine the depths of your heart. I think you will find there what you need."

"I can depend only on myself?"

"No, no, child. In the depths of your heart, I believe you will find the One you have lost sight of. God waits for recognition. God alone can give you the peace you long for, the peace the world cannot give. Trust him, my child."

Little Gerhard finished his meal and pushed away from Susannah. Gaining his hands and knees, he scuttled away into the unlit corners of the cellar.

"I'll get him," said Abram.

"I'll get him," echoed Peter.

They both scrambled after the baby, bringing him back with a mouth full of dirt.

Susannah grabbed him. "Phooey. Spit, Gerhard, spit. Dirt is not to eat. Stay where it is light."

"Stay where it is light," repeated Peter.

Chapter 16

Why did I survive? Dietrich asked himself the question again. More and more often of late, he wondered if somewhere there was a plan for his life. Perhaps fate—or God, as Mika named it—was a force to consider. Perhaps . . .

"Schwandorf!" The shout of the conductor jolted Dietrich from his musings. He turned to offer Maria his hand. Their eyes met and he marveled again that this beautiful woman loved him, had waited, sought him out, and not given up hope, even when he had lost all hope. If there really was a God, he must find him and thank him.

His eyes scanned the crowd for his mother and father.

ꝏꝏ

"I'm glad you were at the mill when Paul Gregorovich came to warn us, Nicholai." Justina smiled at him.

"I'm glad I was there too," said Nicholai sincerely.

They sat together near the river, under the trees planted generations ago by their forebears. They shivered, partly from the chill November air, partly from the excitement of being here together on the edge of danger.

"You're very brave," she said.

"Huh. I'm hiding, am I not?"

"That makes you not only brave but smart. And gallant."

He grinned. "Why gallant, pray tell?"

She laughed lightly. "Gallant because you speak like a knight, and because you rescued me."

"It's all Katarina's fairy stories. She was always full of them. I shouldn't have listened."

She smiled again and leaned her head against the tree. "Sometimes I wish we lived in a fairy story, or at least in the world we used to know. That was almost a fairy story, wasn't it?"

Nicholai remembered. "We lived in a three-story house with vines growing all over it, and orchards, and a river, and our own little chapel. We had cattle and horses and crops in the fields. I played with the servant's children all the time."

"Servants? You must have been very rich."

"My father was. They killed him, you know. Hung him in his own barn."

Justina remained silent.

"Burned the house and the orchard and everything. Except the church. That's when I ran off to join the army. I had to do something to stop all the violence."

"By killing someone else's father?"

Nicholai jumped to his feet. "You have no idea what you are talking about!" His words came out too loudly, and he looked around in fear that he had given away their hiding place. He glared at her, but his fierceness had no effect. In fact, the look in her eyes silenced him. He sat down again beside her.

She faced straight ahead as she spoke. "We were in Blumenort when the bandits came. They rode into the village shouting and cursing, singing dirty songs. We had nowhere to go. They slashed my father with a saber and he fell bleeding. Mother ran screaming for the back door, but they chased her down and . . . and . . . misused her. She screamed and screamed." Justina's entire body quaked as she told her story. "Meanwhile, my father lay bleeding to death. My brother was not at home or they would have killed him too.

"Another bandit dragged my sister into the garden and had his way with her."

Nicholai's face had gone white, his eyes huge, and he shook like the dry leaves still clinging to the poplars around him. He had to ask. "Where were you?"

She didn't look at him. "I ran into the garden; there was no place else to go. It was a game of cat and mouse, and I was the mouse."

He stared at her profile and grated out his anguish. "Did they catch you?"

She let her head fall onto her knees and became as still as a stone. Nicholai knew the answer. Her shoulders shook, but he couldn't touch her.

Finally she lifted her head and her eyes were dry. "You won't want to befriend me now, and I understand that, but I have enjoyed our friendship to this point. You are a fine young man." She pushed herself to her feet and started to walk away.

Nicholai jumped up and called after her. "Where are you going? It may not be safe yet."

She stopped and turned to him. "Does it really matter? When once your soul is devastated, what more can they do to you?"

Nicholai cleared his throat. "Please don't go back yet."

"Why not?" Her eyes begged him.

"My sister . . . she . . . they caught her too."

She came back and laid a hand on his arm. "I'm sorry. How is she doing?"

"Not well. She got sick after that and almost died. She doesn't seem to want to live anymore."

They sat again.

"I didn't either," Justina said. "I thought my heart was dead. But then I noticed you at *Jugendverein*, and I decided maybe there might be something left of life yet."

They looked at each other for a long time, two young people old beyond their years.

"You may be right," he said.

They waited until dark, talking of many things, and then ventured back, hand in hand, to the villages.

ꕤꕤꕤ

"Dietrich!" Her voice rose above the crowd as she pushed her way toward them. Maria stepped back and allowed Dietrich's mother to enfold him in her arms.

The scene brought tears to her eyes, especially as she thought of the reunions she would never, could never have with her parents. They were gone forever from her. Well, maybe not forever, but she would never see them again on this earth. And when would she see Katarina and Johann, Anna and Nicholai and Peter?

Dietrich reached back for her and drew her to him. "Mama, I know you have met Maria, but I would like to introduce you to my wife: Frau Maria Kesselman."

Dietrich's mother regarded Maria for a moment, then opened her arms. "Welcome home, daughter. Thank you for your determination in bringing my son home again. I owe you so much."

Maria basked in the welcome. Perhaps she would yet have a mother to share with. "You owe me nothing, Mother Kesselman."

Jurgen also shed tears at the miraculous reunion with his eldest son. Kristoph stood back until everyone had been sufficiently greeted and wept over, then stepped forward.

"I believe we have some celebrating to do. Shall we?" He led them to the car and drove them toward home, where food and stories kept them going for the rest of the evening, and many evenings thereafter.

ꩡꩡꩡ

The morning after Paul Gregorovich and Katarina had fled with Anna, a knock sounded at Pava's house in Ackerman. Paul cracked the door to see who was there and then opened it wide.

"Sudermann, what happened in your village?"

Johann nodded to Pava and sat on the stump next to Katarina. Anna was apparently in conversation with Igor, but he kept his voice low. "They've gone. They got their quota of weapons."

"Can we go home now?" asked Katarina.

"Yes," he said, "I think it is safe now." He looked again toward Anna.

Pava spoke up. "I need to get water from the river. Would you like to come with me, Anna? It's pretty down there."

Anna turned questioning eyes on Katarina, who nodded her assent, and they left.

Katarina looked to Johann for explanation.

"It was gruesome," he said. "They beat people, terrorized homes, and shot at random until enough weapons were given over."

"How many died this time?" asked Paul quietly.

"Eight, I think. Unless more die from their beatings. Several of the youth were kicked around. I had no power to stop it." Johann hung his head.

Katarina said, "You were not expected to stop it. God placed you in the mayor's office so you could at least warn some."

"Mayor Puchinsk is in trouble with the authorities. They are removing him from his job."

"What did he do now?" asked Katarina.

"The usual: drunk all the time, extorting money from Communist coffers, not filling out required forms. It doesn't take much and Puchinsk is as lazy as an old bull."

"Are they sending someone else to take his place?" Paul asked.

Johann didn't answer, just shook his head.

"You?" This from Katarina.

"For now. It's an opportunity to help our village, but it can also be my undoing. It's a risk either way. I will, however, be able to travel to Kharkov on business, allowing me to connect with B. B. Janz. "

Katarina stared at him. "For such a time as this."

"Let's go home," he said.

ꙮꙮꙮ

"Who can that be?" Katarina stared out the window as a cart filled with furniture and household goods, pulled by a half-dead cow, stopped in front of their house. A man and woman approached the door.

"Watch the cow," the man ordered gruffly.

A skinny youth appeared from behind the wagon. "She won't move without a whip, Father."

The man growled in return and the woman's eyes flitted from one of her men to the other.

"Johann, it's your family." Johann, ready to leave for the mayor's office, opened the door.

"Father! Mother! Where are you going?" he asked, his eyes on the heaped-up cart.

"We are going to Batum to find Ernst," said the senior Sudermann, defiance in his eyes.

"We came to say good-bye," said his mother, tears spilling down her cheeks.

Johann pulled the door wide and Katarina came to greet them. She gave her mother-in-law a warm hug and her father-in-law a brief handshake. It was all he would allow.

"We have no time for dallying," he stated. "Mother insisted we stop here."

"I should think so," retorted Johann. "We may never see each other again."

His mother brought her apron up to catch the flood of tears, and Johann frowned.

"I'm sorry, Mother, but I think this is a mistake. B. B. Janz is working diligently to acquire permission for our emigration. You need passports and emigration papers. Without them you cannot leave the country, and you certainly cannot return."

"We do not wish to return. This country has betrayed us." The older man glared at his wife who continued to weep.

"Come, sit for a little while," encouraged Katarina. She helped Johann's mother to a chair and sat beside her. "Where are the children?"

"Guarding the cart and cow."

Johann stepped from the house and greeted his brother and sisters. His young brother, Willy, a boy of about twelve years of age, stood with his hand on the cow's neck. Willy was the only son left at home now that Ernst had fled to Turkey. Johann's sisters gathered around him. Although they saw each other from time to time, living only in the next village of Kleefeld, they never seemed to tire of his visits. And they loved Katarina.

"Quite a journey you are taking," Johann remarked.

"If we make it," said Willy.

"We all wanted to wait," said Mariechen, lowering her voice and glancing around, "but Father would not hear of it. I think he misses Ernst."

"I will try to dissuade him yet," said Johann.

"Don't bother. It only makes him more angry." Willy's eyes showed the fear he felt and Johann's heart grew sad for him, for all of them, but mostly for his father, who would bear the responsibility if—when—things went wrong.

Johann sighed. “Well, come in then for a cup of tea before you leave.”

“Can’t,” said Willy. “Have to watch that our frisky young cow doesn’t run wildly off with all our earthly possessions.”

Johann chuckled in spite of the situation. “Come inside. I will watch from the window.”

They stayed perhaps an hour before Mr. Sudermann ordered them on their way. Even though Johann had never been close to his father, had in fact been at odds most of the time, he felt orphaned as he watched the rickety cart sway down the lane, then turn onto the road that passed Ackerman.

His father intended to travel to Melitopol, then across the isthmus to Crimea and down the coach road to Sevastopol. After that, they would need to book passage on a boat to the Black Sea port of Batum. How would they ever find Ernst? He may have gone to Batum, or to Constantinople. He may have died or gone on to North or South America. Johann sent a prayer heavenward for them. They would need it.

ꙮꙮꙮ

“I have a petition for the Central Executive Committee of the Ukrainian Communist Party,” said Benjamin Janz to Johann, who had come to Kharkov.

“What kind of petition?”

“For emigration.” Janz eyed him, then slid the petition across the desk for him to see. Johann scanned the document, then looked at Benjamin for clarification.

“We need Mennonite landowners in order for reconstruction to happen,” he began, “but the civil war created many refugees. These refugees are unable to add anything to the economic restructuring, so my proposal is to remove them, thus killing two birds with one stone, as it were: relieving the famine with fewer mouths to feed, and ensuring a better chance of a future for those who remain."

"So you see an economic future for those who remain?"

"No," stated Janz. "No I do not."

"But then why . . . I don't understand."

Janz's urgency surprised him. "No, Sudermann, we do not have any kind of future here, but this is where we begin. We cannot simply approach the highest powers of the land and tell them we want them to set our people free. We must negotiate. Always consider their perspective, their response. It's in the timing."

Johann still felt confused, but he had seen Janz's tactical skills succeed before. "How do you think the authorities will respond to this petition?"

Janz pulled the document back toward him. "I have no allusions that it will go smoothly. There still and always will remain the glaring fact that the colonies were the counter-revolutionary strongholds of the South during the civil war. The *Selbstschutz* has greatly reduced our credibility with the Communist government. Let us pray together before you leave, Sudermann."

Johann bent his head and folded his hands as Janz prayed. "Loving Father," he cried, his voice a call for mercy, "here we are, thy servants in a time of great distress. We have no wisdom, no power of our own to draw upon. But Lord God, we beseech thee to grant us a measure of thy grace sufficient for the task thou hast laid on us. Grant openness from the men who will consider this petition.

"Thou canst turn the hearts of kings, O mighty God. We call on thee to do so now, and to make a way for thy people here in this Egypt to again cross the sea to freedom.

"In the name of thy dear Son and our Savior, Jesus Christ, amen."

ឌឌឌ

Nicholai saw Justina more often than he could have hoped for. She had begun calling on Anna, and their friendship proved a great step to Anna's healing. Nicholai did not know what they talked about, but they understood each other even without words. Justina spent hours playing games with Anna, and Nicholai joined in when he finished his day's work at the mill.

They carefully rationed out the small bag of sunflower seeds Katarina had saved from the wild sunflowers in the fields behind their house. What they had taken for granted before now became a treat fit for royalty.

The village of Alexanderkrone struggled to overcome the fear and loss caused by the arms search, and they were not alone. Many villages experienced similar trauma. Johann brought Benjamin Janz news of the horrendous beatings and shootings of hostages for weapons, but Janz already knew. He had, in fact, prayerfully composed an extensive memorandum regarding the situation. His purpose was to present it to the Commissariat of Justice, but he struggled with whether or not he should go ahead with the plan.

As December winds blew, Benjamin Janz sat on a cold bench in a park in Kharkov with a trusted friend, Heinrich Kornelsen. Together they discussed the plan and prayed for wisdom. Was it the right thing to do? Would it halt the senseless beatings and killings, or would it only exacerbate matters?

All day the two men agonized over their decision, and in the end, they determined to go ahead. The results were astounding, even to Janz and Kornelsen.

ꟸꟸꟸ

Johann saw Janz again in Alexanderkrone.

"The Department of Justice has called for a prompt inquiry

into the situation of violence in weapons searches." Janz looked pained and Johann could not understand why.

"Is this not what you petitioned them for?"

"*Ja*, I wanted to put a stop to the violence, but they have exceeded my expectations in a way that may harm us. The Commissariat has demanded hearings in various villages. At each hearing, a Communist official and I are to be present."

"How could this bring harm?"

"They may say too much," said Janz, exasperated at Johann's slowness of mind. "If I am there, the villagers will feel free to speak their minds, and some of them will reveal things that should not be revealed here and now.

"I am responsible for the outcome. It was my decision and I shall bear the consequences, along with the innocent. It is a dark time, Johann, a very dark time for our people in Russia."

Johann felt a heaviness descend upon him. He knew things were bleak; he was the interim mayor in Alexanderkrone, but Janz's words reminded him, convinced him that their lives were on shaky ground.

"Chairman Makar of the Ukrainian Committee for National Minorities will begin a tour of the colonies by January. We must pray God that he sees and hears only what is beneficial for our people."

Johann cast about for some kind of encouragement, some bright spot on a bleak landscape. "Do we really stand alone? Are there not other men involved in the emigration process?"

"Yes there are. Gerhard Ens has sent messages from Rosthern in the west of Canada, and David Toews is also in Rosthern. I sense in Toews a great commitment and courage for this task. And A. A. Friesen from the Russian *Studienkommission* works with us also."

"And Benjamin Unruh," added Johann.

"Unruh is a key contact. But nothing is happening, Sudermann." He slapped his hand on his thigh. "My family is hungry in Tiege; my wife is tired and lonely, although she would never reveal it; and we still have no food.

"I have written again to America. I told them to forget about the condensed milk and the chocolate. Just send us bread, bread, bread! And flour as quickly as possible. I do not know what more I can do. And now, by my decision, I may have made matters even worse. The celebration of the of arrival of the Christchild is near, and there is no joy for us."

"You have done much good already, Benjamin," said Johann, "and I have no doubt you will succeed in convincing the government about the emigration as well. Do not despair."

Janz sighed. "There is much to do, but now," he rose and shrugged into his coat, "I will spend a few quiet days with my wife and children for *Weinachten*."

ꕥꕥꕥ

"How is my favorite mayor?" asked Katarina when Johann arrived home for supper from his job as mayor of Alexanderkrone.

He tried to smile in return, but could not. The distinct sadness in his eyes chilled Katarina.

"What has happened now?" she asked in a small voice.

He sat wearily at the table and leaned his head in his hands, thankful that Nicholai was not yet home and Anna remained in her room with Oma.

"I have found something out," he said.

PART THREE

1922

Daily bread, give us daily bread,
Bless our bodies, keep our children fed.
Fill our cups, then fill them up again tonight,
Wrap us up and warm us through,
Tucked away beneath our sturdy roofs.
Let us slumber safe from danger's view this time.

Or maybe not, not today,
Maybe you'll provide in other ways,
And if that's the case . . .

We'll give thanks to you with gratitude,
A lesson learned to hunger after you,
That a starry sky offers a better view
if no roof is overhead
And if we never taste that bread.

Nichole Nordeman

Chapter 17

Katarina sat down beside Johann and pulled his hands away from his face. "Tell me."

"I found out about Gerhard," he said.

She wanted to ask all the questions screaming in her mind, but she waited.

With a sigh that sounded like it came all the way from his feet, Johann said, "I found record today of Gerhard being taken into the Red Army back in May of 1920."

Katarina frowned. "We knew that before."

"I know, but I also found a memo that he was no longer part of the unit he had been assigned to. 'Too ill, left behind,' it said. He's dead, Katya. Gerhard is dead. I need to tell Susannah."

"But could he not have survived somewhere? Perhaps a villager found him and took him in? It happened to you in Ackerman."

"No, Katya. There is no chance. In fact, they probably shot him just to make sure. I see the records. I work for the enemy. Gerhard is dead."

Silently she nodded. "I will come with you." She took her shawl and followed him out the door.

Hannah met them at the door. "Come in, come in," she said. "You are in time for supper."

"We have not come for supper," assured Katarina, trying to smile. "I would not impose on you like that unless I brought food."

"We need to talk to Susannah," stated Johann, his face sober.

Hannah studied his eyes for a moment, glanced at Katarina and showed them in. Susannah held Baby Gerhard on one hip as she stirred the thin soup on the stove. Her face sobered too as she greeted her friends. She pulled the soup pot off the hottest part of the blacked surface and turned again to face them.

"Shall we sit in the parlor?" she asked.

"That would be fine," said Johann, searching his mind for words both clear and kind.

Hannah reached out for little Gerhard, setting him in the tall chair. She began feeding him and Marianna, and ladled a bowl of soup for Peter. Johann and Katarina followed Susannah into the quiet parlor. They sat and Susannah looked at them expectantly.

"Susannah," began Johann, "as you know, I have been working in the mayor's office."

She nodded.

"Well, I happen to have access to the village records. Comings and goings, births and deaths, are all documented."

Her eyes widened but she waited in silence.

"I discovered documentation of Gerhard's induction into the Communist army, and . . " he hesitated and then forced himself to continue ". . . and also a memo noting when they . . . when they left him behind."

"Left him behind?" Susannah gripped the arms of her chair. "He was discharged?"

"Not exactly," said Johann.

"Oh, for heaven's sake, Hans, just tell me, please."

"Gerhard isn't coming back, Suse. The only way they would leave him behind is if he was next to death."

Susannah rubbed the wooden arm of the chair, sliding her fingers along the fine carvings. "Is there any chance...?" Her voice thinned to a desperate whisper.

"No, Suse. There is no chance. We must bid him farewell now. We must carry on."

Silent tears dripped from her blue eyes onto her dress. She sat immobile until Katarina cast a concerned glance at Johann.

"I'm so sorry, Suse." Katarina came and knelt beside Susannah's chair and put a hand on her knee. "But perhaps it is better to know than to wonder every day . . ."

"No!" Susannah pushed out of her chair and backed away from them. "It is not better. You cannot know for sure. He could be alive somewhere—he could be. Someone may have found him and helped him."

"That's what I thought at first too," said Katarina, "but I don't think it's probable."

"That's fine for you to say," replied Susannah, "with your husband sitting next to you. Well, I don't believe it—I won't believe it. I will continue to trust that my Gerhard will return. He must . . ." She covered her face with her hands and wept.

Katarina was unable to comfort her friend, and finally Hannah shook her head and said they should go. She would look after Susannah. It would take time. She also had her other daughter to look after. Helena was due to give birth to a fourth child in the spring. Why did both her daughters have to lose their husbands while they were with child? Sometimes Hannah wondered if God really knew what he was doing in Russia.

ꙮꙮꙮ

The First General Congress of the VMSR, the Union of South Russian Mennonites, convened in Margenau, Molotschna, January 3, 1922. Johann walked the nine versts from Alexanderkrone to be part of the meetings. He arrived late; Katarina rationed what little food they had and they were all beginning to feel the effects, the general lack of energy. Johann was exhausted when he finally reached Margenau and Benjamin Janz was already speaking.

"Brethren, I have thoughtfully and prayerfully considered my position as chairman of this union, and I have decided to resign."

Before he could go on, several of the attendees stood to their feet. "We cannot accept your resignation, Benjamin. We need you at this time. You have begun negotiations for our young men in the army. You have prepared and presented petitions for emigration. How can you step back now?"

Janz rubbed his chin with his hand and spoke from his heart. "I am weary, brothers. I miss my family and they need me. It tears my heart to leave them every time I travel to Kharkov and Moscow. I see them so rarely that my children barely know me. I'm tired of being gone."

"Perhaps you have been chosen for this sacrifice, Benjamin," said Bernhard Neufeldt. "The goals of this union will require much sacrifice before they are met."

Johann stood to add his voice. "I have seen your sacrifice, Benjamin," he said, "but I have also seen your wisdom, your communication skills, your perseverance. I believe we need you in order to succeed in our efforts. I'm sorry, friend, but I beg you not to resign."

Others raised their voices in agreement and finally Benjamin raised his hand to stop them. He sighed. "Very well. I will do it. Perhaps I can help our youth as well as society. But don't leave my family in the lurch if things become difficult."

The delegates promised and the meeting proceeded.

"Makar has completed his tour of the colony, but the government officials at Kharkov proved unsympathetic to the complaints of the Mennonite people. So, I will make another journey to Moscow after this conference is over."

ᐅᐅᐅ

Benjamin Janz sat in his home in Tiege, a rare occurrence these days, surrounded by his wife, Maria, and his children: Peter, Helena, Gertruda, Maria, Jakob, and baby Martha. It was good to be home, to see how his children had grown—Peter was already fifteen and the baby toddled around on chubby legs—and to share the days with his wife. Their Christmas celebration had been meager. Where Maria had found wool to knit mittens he did not know. She amazed him.

Later, Benjamin moved to the desk in his bedroom to again look over the government documents stacked there. Darkness stared back at him as he gazed out the small window. His mood matched the darkness. His hope for his people diminished with each sunset, and his weariness deepened with each daybreak.

A sharp knock on the door jolted him to alertness. Night visitors. What could this mean? So many men had been taken away in the night and never heard of again. Torn away from their families without a word of explanation. Was it now his time? Were these dark feelings premonitions of his fate?

Resolutely, he rose from his chair and started through the kitchen to the door. His eldest daughter, Helena, had already answered the summons. She met him in the kitchen, her eyes wide with questions.

"A man outside wants to talk to you, Papa," she said, alarm pulling her features taut.

"Who is it?"

"I don't know. I couldn't see him." She turned frightened eyes to the door. Maria sat stiff in her chair, her knitting still, her eyes on her husband.

Benjamin straightened his shoulders and approached the doorway. He was, after all, in the hands of the God whom he served. Nothing happened without his divine assent. He stood in the doorway, framed now by the light from the oil lamps, then stepped out into the night.

"Are you Benjamin Janz?" a voice from the dark asked him.

His heart pounding, he replied, "Yes, I am he."

The man did not come into the light and Benjamin could not see anything of him. The voice said, "I have come from Mr. Benjamin Unruh to convey greetings and best wishes to you. He wants you to know that abroad everything humanly possible is being done to help you and the colonies here in every respect. Do not lose courage, and do what is possible. You are not alone; the Christian community abroad stands for you wherever possible.

"And now farewell; I must go."

Benjamin stood staring into the darkness of the night, but with the words of the man—or was it a divine messenger—the darkness in his soul began to lift and the light filtered in. Wordlessly, he closed the door.

He knew now that he could continue his work, that it was important, and that he did not work alone. He felt a part of a larger community, one that spanned continents and crossed oceans.

"Thank you, Lord," he murmured.

ജജജ

When Johann came home from the mayor's office one day in mid-January, he brought a visitor with him. Katarina turned from her supper preparations in surprise.

"This is Kornelius Penner," he said in explanation. "He has come here from Chortitza to find work."

Katarina dried her hands on her apron and shook the man's hand. "Welcome here," she said. "Supper is about ready."

"It doesn't take as long to prepare as it used to, Katarina tells me," said Johann by way of conversation. "There is little choice these days. It's black bread and thin soup or flat barley bread and thin soup."

"Any food is welcome to me," said Kornelius.

"Well then," said Katarina, compassion rising in her at the hungry look in her guest's eyes, "have a seat at the table. Oma! Anna! *Kommt essen, ja?*"

Oma greeted Kornelius with a warm smile, Anna with a shy one. The girl continued to improve, but progress was slow. They prayed that nothing would interfere with her restoration. Typhoid fever ran rampant through the Ukraine; many families had already counted losses due to that plague. The other plague was starvation. The specter of hunger stalked the previously fertile land, as fields lay fallow and weed-choked. Any remaining seed had already been swept from the corners of bins and storage cupboards to be baked into tough bread.

Nicholai returned from his work at the mill just as Johann prepared to ask the blessing. He shook Kornelius's hand and took his place at the table.

"We still have not found a way to bring in the food shipment from MCC," said Johann as they settled down to eat.

The smell of meat wafting up from the soup quelled Johann's appetite. He had finally felt compelled to reveal to Katarina the source of the bits of meat he brought home. At first she had gagged at the thought, but hunger had a way of broadening one's tastes. Besides, there was not enough food to share with dogs and cats these days. All in all, it was not so bad if one didn't think about it too much. It was better than crow. That tasted like rubber however Katarina or Oma fixed it.

"I don't mean to make light of your situation here," said Kornelius, "because I know you are rationing your food carefully, but in the Old Colony there is no food left. If aid does not arrive shortly, the children and old ones will certainly die.

Many have already. Everyone is so tired. They are ready to give up."

"Is that why you came? You did not want to give up yet?" Johann finished his bowl of soup.

"*Ja*. I will not die without a struggle. I want to go to America."

"They say life is not easy there and the climate can be harsh."

"Work gives purpose to life; I am not afraid of hard work, and a man can withstand cold if he has a full belly."

"Well said," agreed Johann. "Is your name on the emigration list?"

"I put it on months ago already. Now I wait."

"Is your family still in Chortitza?" asked Katarina.

Kornelius shook his head. "I have no family left."

"What happened to them?" asked Nicholai.

Kornelius's spoon stilled in the bowl and he took a ragged breath. "They are all dead from one plague or another."

Nicholai grimaced. "I'm sorry. I should not have asked."

"*Ja*, I am sorry too, but the Lord gives and he takes away again." He did not add the words, *Blessed be the name of the Lord*, and Katarina remembered how she had felt after her father had been killed.

Johann said, "You are welcome to stay with us for as long as you need to. We will share what the Lord has given us."

"I thank you. I shall try my best to contribute."

Johann considered. "Perhaps you will accompany me after supper to take some flour to a neighbor. She has no man in the house and we try to help her."

"Of course." They set out for Susannah's in Lichtenau soon after supper.

ᘓᘓᘓ

"There must be something we can do, Dietrich," exclaimed Maria as she paced their parlor in Berlin. The couple had taken up a small residence there to be closer to information about Maria's family. They visited the Kesselman family in Schwandorf often, but felt this situation suited them better. Besides, Dietrich was in a position to receive some monetary compensation from the German army for his physical injury, and the contacts for such things headquartered in Berlin.

Dietrich looked up from the forms he was filling out. "We have sent care parcels, my dear. We continue on the alert should the situation allow us to step in. For now, I see no other help we can give."

She settled on a chair opposite him and leaned her elbows on the table. "I know, but it seems so indifferent to do nothing." Her fingers drummed a staccato rhythm on the tabletop. Dietrich lifted his eyebrows imploringly.

"I'm sorry," Maria said, smiling a little. "I'm driving you to distraction."

"Yes, you are. You have done so ever since I first set eyes on you."

She met his gaze and lost herself in his eyes. "I love you, Dietrich."

"And I you, my little Russian princess. But I think you need something to fill your time. Have you thought of visiting at the hospitals or teaching in a school?"

Maria wrinkled her pretty nose. "I despise hospitals. I only helped in Succoth because it was there and I needed something to do."

"So now you need something to do again."

She stood and resumed her pacing. "I don't know, Dietrich. I can fold sheets and make beds, but I'm not much good with sick people."

"Yes, well—wait a minute! I have a splendid idea. You could help people in Russia to contact their relatives in

America and vice versa. Many are desperate to know how their families are, and regular mail has been stymied at the borders."

Maria stopped her pacing and stared at him, her mind whirling. "Do you think I could help? How would I get involved in something like that?"

"I don't know. Talk to Unruh when next he is here. Or some of his cronies. You could relay information by diplomatic courier."

She sat down at the table, pulled out a piece of paper, and began a note to Benjamin H. Unruh. If there was a way to help, she would find it.

ଧଧଧ

"Some flour for you, Susannah, and soup bones for tomorrow's supper." Johann handed her the packages and introduced his companion.

"This is Kornelius Penner from Chortitza. He is here to secure passage to America."

"Really. I hope you find your way there." To Johann she said, "Thank you for the food. One gets used to the soup."

Johann agreed. "Better than the alternative," he said.

"*Ja*, that is true," said Kornelius. "Such soup is lifesaving."

"Johann," said Susannah, "I don't like to ask when you are busy with your own family, but is there a chance that Nicholai could come chop some wood for us? Mother is not strong enough these days—I fear she will come down with something if she gets too rundown—and I can't seem to gather enough energy to do it."

"Of course. I will ask him."

"Let me do it." They both looked at Kornelius in surprise. "I need to earn my keep and this is something I can do." To their hesitation he said, "I may look like a specter, but I assure you, I can chop wood. Especially after a bowl of soup and bread. Where is your ax?"

Susannah smiled, one of the first smiles Johann had seen her muster in a long time. "Johann will show you; I must go to my children now. And, thank you, . . . Mr. Penner."

ꕥꕥꕥ

Janz sat solemnly at his desk in the small room in Kharkov, writing a letter to Benjamin H. Unruh in Germany. He missed his wife. He wondered how the children fared. Loneliness ate at him like the ever-present gnawing of his stomach.

"*February 18, 1922. Until today no bread has arrived,*" he wrote. "*The colonies are suffering severely. Harder from Fuerstenau is dead. At the orphanage in Grossweide nine children are sick and swollen, as are sixteen people in Waldheim. In the Old Colony a number, especially children, are dead.*"

He rubbed his large hands over his face. When would it end? When would relief come? After the First General Congress of the Union in January, and what he had come to call his "visitation," he had taken up his burden and carried it with energy. Now, looking at the end of February, the energy had been replaced by sheer determination.

He had continued to follow his well thought out plan of approach to the Communist authorities, his obviously contradictory policies: rebuilding the economy of the Ukraine, and emigration. Not only the authorities, but also his fellow Mennonites often questioned him as to the incongruity of this approach. Should we not concentrate on reconstruction, they asked, and then perhaps emigration would be unnecessary?

"They have no idea," he muttered to himself, signing the desperate letter and sealing the twice turned envelope. "If we stay, we will be swallowed up by the system. Already we are losing our traditional biblical values."

He pounded the desk with his fist. "I will not allow my children to be devoured by the Communist beast. I will persevere. I will guard them against the looming monster, God help me."

ഋഋഋ

"I will stand guard tonight," said Nicholai after breakfast one morning in early March. "The thieves are becoming bolder each day."

"Bolder and hungrier," sighed Katarina. "I wish I could help them. They come begging at the door and windows every evening. I have to make sure everything is locked or they come right in."

"I've never seen it so bad," said Oma, shaking her head. "Everyone is desperate. I should go check on Hannah Loewen; Susannah said she wasn't feeling well."

"Most likely lack of food," said Katarina. "Like the rest of us." She refused to let the thought of typhus or typhoid fever dwell in her thoughts, especially when connected with those she knew and loved. Perhaps by denying its presence she could deny its power.

Oma did not comment.

"I will grind up some of the corncobs we kept for the animals. It would be a shame to starve if help is around the corner. Then again, we have waited two years. It is hard to believe anyone even remembers our situation. I wonder how Mika and Dietrich are."

She thought of the parcel of brown bread, cheese, and chocolate they had sent a week ago. What a miracle that it had come just then. She turned to her work and Oma pulled a shawl around her stooped but sturdy shoulders for the short walk to Lichtfelde.

"Where is Kornelius?" Katarina asked Nicholai as he prepared to leave for his work at the mill. "I haven't seen him after supper in several days."

"He stands guard at Susannah's house or helps dig graves. That's what he told me."

"Dig graves?"

"Some of the men have been digging fresh graves in the cemetery so they are ready when needed. They are so exhausted from hunger they aren't sure they will be able to dig them later, and we are always needing more graves."

Katarina fought the tears as she listened to her young brother's words. How their world had changed. Death, once a known but rare specter, had become a constant companion. It hovered over every household, waiting to catch another weary soul.

Johann returned in time for supper, bringing several parcels for people in the village, and one for themselves.

"It's from Saskatchewan, Canada!" exclaimed Katarina. "Anna, it's from Canada."

Anna joined them at the table, supper preparations momentarily forgotten in favor of the brown paper package tied with tough twine.

"Here, let me," said Nicholai. "I have a knife." He pulled the blade from his side pocket and cut the string. Katarina's hands shook as she unwrapped the layers of brown paper. Several components fell out onto the table, one a small sack marked with the words *milk powder*. Another label read *rice*, and another *beans*. And a small sack of fine, plump wheat.

"Uncle George has sent another package of cheese," crowed Anna, holding the paper-wrapped block to her chest. "I love cheese."

"It doesn't matter how old cheese gets," commented Oma, "it's still good to eat. Shall we slice some to go with our soup?"

"Yes, yes. Oh, Katya, we have fresh black bread, soup and cheese. We are rich."

Katarina smiled at Anna's reference to fresh black bread. It was in actuality almost indigestible, but one had to admit it was better than eating field mice and crows. Tomorrow she would bake real bread again, and there would be enough to send along a loaf with Kornelius for Susannah.

Kornelius knew he would stand guard for Susannah as long as he could stand at all. The hard black bread from Katarina Sudermann felt like an anchor in his stomach, but it gave that underused organ a sense of purpose, something to gnaw on in anticipation of eventual digestion.

He didn't know why he felt so strongly about helping Susannah. As he patrolled the perimeters of her tiny yard each night, he analyzed his thoughts. Was he using Susannah's presence to ease the memories of his Sarah? Was he over-indulging his already strong sense of compassion? Did Susannah's need stir his chivalrous nature?

She had certainly given him no encouragement. He knew she appreciated his help, but she could not discern his commitment to her cause. He could tell by the way she stared at him when she thought he didn't see. She did not share of herself; he knew her story only from Johann and Katarina.

Neither did he uncover his hidden grief. Memories of his Sarah remained locked away in his heart, to be examined and cherished and wept over in the privacy of the darkness.

Kornelius remembered when he had first met Sarah. She was seven and new at school; he was ten and not interested in girls. Sarah spent her time playing with Kornelius's younger brother and sister. He knew her well, at least he thought he did.

Somewhere along the way—he could never figure out when—she became a young woman. For a while he had avoided her, not knowing how to work it all out in his mind. Why would he be drawn to his sister's friend? But it wasn't long before her laughing eyes put a claim on his heart. As the years passed, neither of them ever wondered about their future. They would be together as soon as they were of age to marry.

The war and the revolution had changed many things, but not his love for Sarah. Her inner strength buoyed him up when his spirits flagged. Her encouragement kept him going even in the worst times.

He stood by her too, when the Reds took her father away, and when her mother died of the pox. He cried with her when her younger brother lost his life in the last *Selbstschutz* standoff. They had clung to each other as their world fell apart around them.

Then Sarah herself had become ill with typhus. In spite of the warnings of friends, he had sat with her through the ragings and the deadly quiet. A few times she had recognized him, and he knew she would not stay in this world for him. "You must find your life without me," she had said, and then slipped into a coma from which she never recovered. He remembered his anguished pleading with Sarah and God. Neither had given him the answer he begged for.

He had not taken much thought for God since. Why would he rely on Someone who remained distant and unreachable?

Probably what drew him to Susannah, he thought as he checked the mulberry hedge for beggars, was that he saw the same frustration and hurt in her that he felt. He could read that much in her eyes, in her stiff demeanor. She too had experienced loss and pain. She knew what it was to lose one's hope. So he, Kornelius, decided to be her hope, let it lead where it may.

Chapter 18

Reluctantly, Benjamin Unruh shared his latest letter from Benjamin Janz with Maria Kesselman. He saw anxiety spread across her fine features as she read:

"The gulf between need and possession, production and consumption, availability and demand, daily grows wider and deeper in all areas, and with incredible rapidity leads into the dark future, the night, ruination, toward catastrophe."

Maria looked up at Benjamin Unruh. He said nothing.

She continued reading. *"That I today must live to see this calamity of my people makes me wretched, old and ill."* He went on to plead for help for his own family, who suffered alone in Tiege while he traveled yet again to Moscow to petition the government for permission to emigrate. *"Herein lies our only hope,"* he wrote.

"Janz is in despair," remarked Unruh.

"Of course he is. So am I, and I have no lack of food."

"I believe change is coming soon." Unruh meant his words as encouragement. "The American and Canadian proponents of Mennonite Central Committee have been working constantly to win their way into the country with aid. The food and goods are at the border. They only need to unlock the doors."

"What is the delay?" asked Maria. "Why is the food being withheld?"

Unruh shook his head in frustration. "A variety of reasons. As long as the Whites lurked about, the Reds had no time to worry about feeding the people. You know about the difficulties of coming to terms with the new regime. They are not about to be pushed into anything. There is the ever-present corruption of the local officials. They will take a share of anything that does come through."

"I pray help would come soon enough for my family. For all of them." Maria shuddered at the thought of the many starving people in her homeland. If she had not followed her heart to Dietrich, she too would be there, skinny and swollen, tired and listless, ready to give up hope. She handed the letter back to Unruh and put on her coat. "I will go pack another parcel. Perhaps it will keep them alive another few days and help will come."

ᏇᏇᏇ

Kornelius knocked at Susannah's door. He knew she would not mind this intrusion. She opened the door and looked inquiringly at him. He stood beaming at her for a moment, then whisked the loaf of fresh, fluffy brown bread from behind his back with a flourish.

"For you, my lady," he said, bowing and holding it out to her.

Susannah looked at him with a mixture of irritation and interest. He was such a skinny man, so gaunt and yet so gallant. She smiled in spite of herself. "Where did you steal this?" she asked in jest.

Kornelius's smile disappeared, replaced by a slight frown. "You belittle me, Madam. I am an emissary from the Sudermanns. They received a parcel from Amer—from Canada—and wish to share it with you. I am not a thief, Mrs. Warkentin."

"I'm sorry. I did not mean it so. Please forgive me. Sometimes I think our trials have robbed me of all kind and gentle ways."

Kornelius relaxed. “You are forgiven. Please take the bread; it is manna from heaven.”

This time Susannah accepted the gift from his hand. “Thank you.” She turned to take it into the house for her family, but something stopped her. Turning back, she said, “Mr. Penner, would you share this bread with us?”

Surprised, he stuttered for words. “I . . . if you . . . yes, I would. Thank you.”

“The mayor is going to Halbstadt to bring home our food,” Johann exclaimed as he entered the house mid-morning near the end of May.

“Is there a parcel again? How did you know? Why would they send it to Halbstadt?”

“There is a very big parcel. Janz and Miller and the others have at last been successful. The food shipment from the United States has arrived.”

“The Mennonite Central Committee shipment? It’s here?”

Johann grabbed her and danced her around the kitchen until they were both breathless. Oma came out of Anna’s room and watched them in amusement. “I may report you both to the deacons. It must be very good news or you would not make such fools of yourselves. You have no idea how to dance, either of you.”

Her comments set them all to laughing, which brought Anna into the kitchen as well. “We will have food soon!” Katarina could not contain her relief. Perhaps the outside world had not forgotten them. Perhaps they would not have to die here after all.

Just then Kornelius knocked softly and entered the house. He looked from one to the other, wondering if he were interrupting a family secret. But Johann immediately got up to greet him and put him at ease.

“We are celebrating, my friend. The food shipment has

finally arrived in Halbstadt. I am going immediately to collect it for our village."

Kornelius wore an expression of wonder and incredulity. "The shipment has come?" He stood in the doorway in amazed wonder. "I must tell Susannah," he said over his shoulder as he left the house.

ꙮꙮꙮ

Johann brought back a parcel from Mika and Dietrich and some for other villagers, but the main shipment was being sent out by wagon the next day. Many villages had already set up kitchens in churches and schools for allocation of the anticipated foodstuffs.

In Alexanderkrone, the distribution center had been set up in the school, ready since the beginning of March. When the food arrived, Johann immediately set about organizing supplies and reckoning ration amounts.

"The note suggests a ration of gruel and a piece of bread for each person signed up on the first list—those in urgent need. That comes to about two and a half cents per person per day. Not a lot of food."

Kornelius, helping to unpack the food, said, "Not a lot, but more than we had. It will keep us alive." More to himself he said, "I'm sure Susannah would be willing to help here. Her mother can look after the children, and then they would have enough to eat. I will tell her as soon as I finish here."

"Why don't you tell her now." Johann saw the light in Kornelius's eyes and felt hope. "Ask her if she would come tomorrow; we will need much help."

Kornelius eyed Johann hesitantly.

"Go on. Tell her all volunteers receive double rations."

Kornelius smiled, nodded and slipped out the door.

Johann and Katarina busied themselves unpacking and sorting through the foodstuffs, while others cooked and prepared the food for the villagers who stood in long lines in the street. The queues had begun forming last evening when news of the food swept through Alexanderkrone. Johann had remained at the school all night to prevent theft. He too knew hunger.

"The Communist government has claimed twenty-five percent of the shipment," he said to Katarina.

"What? How can they do that?"

"They just do. They say it's their share. Maybe that was the condition on which they allowed it into the country, who knows."

"It's despicable."

"Yes, well, we will use what they have left us."

"This much gruel and bread for each person," instructed Katarina as men and women who were able came to help with the distribution.

"There are Russians in the crowd," one woman reported. "What do we do with them?"

"They are hungry," answered Johann, wondering why he should have to explain, "so we feed them. Women and children first."

A warm spring sun beamed an additional blessing on the heads of the hungry that day as they accepted their food. The blessing passed from person to person, down the line.

Kornelius showed up mid-morning, a dark look on his usually pleasant face.

"Where is Susannah?" asked Katarina, who had been looking forward to working together with her friend.

Kornelius frowned. "Her mother is ill; she cannot leave her. I have come in her place."

"What's wrong with Hannah? Surely food will help."

Katarina could see it pained Kornelius to be the purveyor

of bad news. "Susannah insists its just weakness and that she will soon get stronger, but I think it's consumption. I've seen it before."

"Tuberculosis? Johann, Kornelius says he thinks Hannah Loewen has TB."

Johann stood with a large bag of grain in his arms. "Hannah?" He closed his eyes for a moment. "What else must Susannah bear?"

"I should go to her, Johann. Can you do without me here for a bit?"

"Of course, Katya. Kornelius, you do what you need to. If Susannah needs you, feel free to go. I have many volunteers here."

Kornelius already held the door for Katarina, who stopped to gather a few rations for the individuals in Susannah's household. She also needed to see that her brother Peter remained well. Perhaps she should take him home with her, give Susannah one less responsibility. Oma and Anna could watch him. Yes, she decided. She would bring Peter home.

Katarina dreaded seeing Hannah ill, watching another person waste away without being able to help. She steeled herself, determined to help Susannah all she could. Beside her, Kornelius walked in silence, his anger apparent in his stride and in his manner. She wondered how he would endure this, another reminder of his own losses. Katarina could see he had come to care for Susannah, but it was not a mutual feeling.

"I am a married woman," she had told Katarina when she had commented on Kornelius's commitment.

"Susannah, Gerhard is not coming back. You know that."

"How do you know? By some memo written by the Russians? I do not believe it. He will come."

Katarina felt at a loss with Susannah's denials. They had talked of it before, with similar results.

"I appreciate Mr. Penner's kindness, but neither he nor I

have any feelings toward one another besides an understanding of grief. Please do not mention this again."

Katarina had not mentioned it, but Johann told her that Kornelius had spoken with him. He wanted to know the truth about Susannah's husband. Was there absolute proof that he was dead? Johann gave him the facts and expressed his own certainty, but absolute proof was difficult to confirm.

Now as she approached Susannah's home, Katarina felt a strong tension. She must help where she was needed and leave the rest alone.

"Susannah?" she called from the doorway.

Susannah appeared from one of the bedrooms, her face thin and pale, her golden braid, once neatly coiled around her head, now unpinned. She carried little Gerhard on her hip. He was no longer a baby, and Katarina could see how his weight wearied Susannah. Katarina's brother Peter trailed behind them.

"Katarina! How good of you to come. I was about ready to put my head out the door and call for help." She set Gerhard on the floor and after staring at Katarina with his fingers in his mouth, he ran to Kornelius.

"Hello, little man," he said, scooping the boy up easily and tossing him in the air. The child whooped with pleasure and Susannah almost smiled. Kornelius addressed Susannah. "May I take him outside with me while I collect wood and feed the cow?"

"Feed the cow?" said Peter with the exact inflection of voice Kornelius had used.

"Yes. Put his jacket on him. The autumn breezes are cool."

"The autumn breezes are cool," said Peter, following the two outside.

"Where is Marianna?" asked Katarina.

"Mr. Penner took her over to Abram and Cornelia's earlier. One of their neighbors has a little girl she likes to play with.

Marianna needs more than sickness and sorrow in her life."

"Looks like little Gerhard is comfortable with Kornelius," said Katarina after they had gone.

"Yes, Mr. Penner is good to him, and to Peter," said Susannah curtly.

Katarina changed the subject. "How is your mother? Has the doctor diagnosed her yet?"

She nodded. "It's consumption. That confirms my resolve not to emigrate. Mother would never be allowed to go."

Katarina's brow furrowed. "May I see her?"

Susannah nodded.

Hannah greeted Katarina weakly when she entered the woman's room. She lay still and pale beneath the worn comforter. Her hair had thinned and her eyes wore a sad expression.

"Ah, Katarina. Haven't seen you in a long time, but I'm sure you've been occupied."

"I'm sorry, Hannah," said Katarina, settling herself on the chair beside the bed. "How are you feeling?"

"Tired," said the woman, "always tired. I want to help Suse, but now I am another burden for her."

"You're not a burden, Hannah. She would gladly take care of you."

"I am a burden, Katarina. She has two little ones to look after and Peter, and I need to get out of bed and help her. Besides, Helena had her baby last week. He's a little one, with the famine and all. Lena needs me too." Hannah threw the covers off and tried to sit up, but fell back, gasping for breath.

"Please, Hannah, stay in bed. You must rest so you can recover."

"Recover? You make it sound like I have a disease. I'm just tired. I'll sleep today and by tomorrow I shall be up again. Then I will go to Neukirch and help Helena."

Katarina turned to look at Susannah, who stood in the doorway of the bedroom. "I've told you, Mother, you have tuberculosis—consumption. You will need months of rest to get over it."

"I have no such thing," declared Hannah, raising her head off the pillow. "I'm just tired." Her head fell back and her eyes closed.

Katarina stood and took Susannah by the arm. "She doesn't believe she is ill. Has the doctor spoken to her?"

"Of course," said Susannah, blinking back unbidden tears. "She doesn't believe him either."

"I will take Peter home with me," said Katarina. "You do not need him to look after as well."

"No, don't worry about Peter, Katya. He is no trouble. Sometimes he watches the children for short periods of time, and he has latched onto Kor . . . Mr. Penner almost as quickly as he attached himself to Mother."

"Are you sure? He is my brother, and I will take him home if you wish me to."

"Katarina, Peter and I developed an understanding and a trust at *Bethania*. I vowed then that I would always take care of him, unless you request otherwise. The only way I would change my mind is if our situation endangered him. He has become part of my family."

Katarina took Susannah's rough hand. "Thank you, Suse. Times have been so hard for you," she rubbed a thumb over the calluses marring a hand too young for such marks, "but I still see my first real friend when I hear you talk like that. You have a generous, loving heart."

Susannah's head drooped. "Years ago I gave myself to the Lord to use as he wished, and at first I believed I had found my calling in nursing. Then Gerhard won my heart and I was the happiest woman in the world. And then, my life began to crumble."

She wiped tears with the back of her hand. "*Bethania* closed because of the incessant and cruel raids of the Machnovitz, we had to leave, my father died, Gerhard had to join the army, and then . . ." her voice thinned as she cried ". . . and then when I thought I had him back, they took him away again. Everything is gone and God seems vindictive. I don't know what I've done to deserve this." She sobbed brokenly and Katarina moved close to comfort her.

When her sobbing had ceased, Katarina said, "You have suffered many losses, Suse, but don't forget the good things. God gave you Gerhard, even if for only a short time. He gave you two children to remember him by. He allowed you to be with your mother in her need, and even to show her the way of salvation. You said yourself that Peter has been a joy to you. And now, in your desperate need, God has sent Kornelius to help you."

Susannah took a deep breath. "Well," she said, "it does no good to cry, does it? Only robs our strength. I'm sure you have work to do at the American kitchen. Thank you for bringing the food. Tomorrow I will ask Mr. Penner to stand in line for us. You do not need to bother yourself to bring the rations to us."

Katarina sighed. "I will come again soon. If you need something—anything—send Kornelius to us and we will come." She hugged her friend again and hurried home to make their meager supper. She would not stand in line. Not yet. Not as long as she could stir up a thin soup and bake dusty bread. Others were in more serious need.

Nicholai did not return home for supper that evening and Katarina worried. When he entered the house late in the evening, she questioned him immediately.

"Did something happen to make you so late?"

He no longer brushed off her concerns, recognizing them

for what they were. His time away in the army had made him aware of the blessing of a caring family. Katarina felt like a mother to him and he cherished her concern and love.

"There was trouble at the mill last night—vandals. When I got there this morning, Mr. Baerg was already busy fixing and cleaning up the damage. We wanted to get it operational again for tomorrow. People need flour."

"Do you know the identity of the vandals?" asked Johann.

Nicholai shrugged. "We have a pretty good idea, but what can we do? They were probably hungry."

Katarina frowned. "Morality is lax these days in all areas. Those who still have food hoard it for themselves while their neighbors starve. People kill for bread. How can a simple thing like food turn people into animals?"

"We have not suffered as much as some," commented Johann gently. "We are all capable of anything, you know. Even gentle spirits can become twisted in the darkest days."

Katarina sighed, knowing it to be true. She prayed for strength to maintain her integrity and her focus. Help me focus on you, Lord, she prayed in her heart.

ഌഌഌ

"Any changes in the status of emigration since the food shipment arrived?" Johann sat across from Benjamin Janz in Kharkov.

"If you are asking whether emigration is still a priority, my answer is yes."

"But why? The war is over, the rains are coming again, we are receiving food and promises of seed. Even tractors. If we work hard at reconstruction, can we not rebuild our country? Emigration is extreme. And now we have Lenin's New Economic Policy."

"*Ja*, that will change things."

"You mock," said Johann. "What is it about the NEP you don't approve of?"

Benjamin leafed through a file and retrieved a folder. "Here we are. It talks about private trade, private property, individual rights, a generous touch of entrepreneurial possibilities."

"It also promises the cessation of grain requisitions for farmers, and free market sales opportunities for them," added Johann defensively. "Sounds good to me."

Janz's eyebrows lowered and his eyes sparked anger. "Lenin has come under considerable fire for this policy, Sudermann. It is merely a temporary solution. It is in direct contradiction to the socialist policies of the Communist regime; it cannot last. You work in a government office, can you not see that?

"Lenin is a Marxist, as are Trotsky and Stalin and Kamenev and all the rest. Speaking of Lenin, you may not have heard, but he is seriously ill, and I have enough contacts in Moscow to be aware of the changes creeping in. There are sinister forces afoot, Sudermann, and we do not want to stay to find out their power."

Johann frowned. "Are the new faces and names really so sinister? Tekanin worked with Stalin during the revolution."

"Josef Stalin has been working his way into the Central Committee of the Communist Party. Mark my words, Johann, we will hear much from him yet. You think the tsars were iron fisted, watch the man of steel, watch what these Communists will do. No, Sudermann, we must leave this place while we can. These present days are only a lull in the Russian storm."

"But if we work our way back to our former financial stability with the help of this new economic policy, if we become self-supporting and economically beneficial to the country, why would the government renege on such policies as the NEP?"

"Johann, we are the least of their concerns. We are a few poor citizens tucked away in a corner of a vast country in the midst of enormous change. We are nothing but a puff of smoke on a distant horizon."

Johann felt the intensity of Benjamin's words. They caused him to reexamine his relief at some of the recent political changes. Perhaps he wanted to deny the urgency of the situation because it meant emigration, and emigration was a traumatic and irreversible decision. As much as he wanted to distance himself from that decision, he knew he must face reality.

"How are negotiations for emigration progressing, Benjamin?"

Janz's eyes lit up. "The VMSR has received approval by the government here in Kharkov. We have thought it best to change the name of our union to remove reference to Mennonites as such. It will henceforth be known as the VBHH—*the Union of Citizens of Dutch Lineage*—a change suggested by Commissar Manzev in Kharkov. Anything associated with the Germans is not to our benefit at this time. We continue to work toward our goal of mass emigration; I cannot tell you more at this time."

Johann sighed. "I would like to add more names to the emigration list: Susannah Warkentin, her two children and her mother, Hannah Loewen. So far she adamantly refuses to leave and now her mother has TB. Her husband was taken by the Reds a year ago this spring and died of typhus while in their army. Susannah denies that he is dead, but his fate is obvious."

"*Ja*. You would have heard by now if he had survived. I will add the names. If she refuses to go in the end, there is no harm done."

As Johann drove the buggy home, scattered raindrops spit on fields overgrown with wild grasses and waving weeds. He wondered if the promised tractors and seed grain could restore the ravaged landscape to its former fertility.

One Alexanderkrone farmer reported to the village office that he had managed to grow out only one *dessiatine* of wheat this past year. All the rest had blown away. He had salvaged only eight pud of wheat and a little corn and rye to feed his family of eight. He had probably been forced to sign up on the first list when the kitchens were set up.

Johann, as interim mayor, had access to the town records. He knew the "haves" and the "have nots," and the "haves" were as rare as guns in the colonies these days.

Chapter 19

The news that awaited Johann at his arrival back at the village office in Alexanderkrone nearly sent him into shock.

"You have been demobilized." Comrade Vasylenyk handed him the memo from Moscow.

"Demobilized," Johann repeated. "Have I done something wrong? Have I forgotten to fill out some of the required forms? I don't understand."

Vasylenyk stared at him incredulously. "You're done, man. You are a free citizen, you and others of your age. Don't quibble with good fortune."

Johann stared back at him in shock. "Demobil . . . oh yes, yes. I misunderstood. Do you have a mayor for the village?"

"That is not your concern, but according to our reports, you have done a good job of filling in. We could use you as a secretary here if you are willing."

Johann nodded. "I know the work and would be willing to continue for the time being. Thank you for the offer."

Vasylenyk smirked at Johann's misunderstanding and shook his head as he marched out of the office.

Johann stood and stared after him. He was a free man. After several years of serving the Red Army of the Communist regime, he was now an ordinary citizen. Relief flooded him. He didn't mind the work, in fact, it interested him and allowed him to have a certain amount of influence and knowledge of political happenings. As village secretary, he could maintain that knowledge if not the influence, and be free to resign when the time came for emigration.

This would be good news to offer Katarina, something to offset the less than good news of the tax forms Vasylenyk had given him. He wondered which he should present first.

"You have been released from the army?" Katarina stood staring at him, then threw her arms about his neck with a hug that nearly knocked him off his feet. "Then we are free to emigrate without that extra red tape to worry about."

Johann managed to catch his breath again. "I may be able to stay on as village secretary for a time. That would entitle us to a bit of extra food and information. I've been able to help Benjamin Janz with some information here and there because of my work."

"That would be wonderful," she said. The summer sun had brought a healthy glow back to her face, now generously freckled. He savored the vision before letting the other shoe fall.

"I also have a matter of concern to share with you."

She sighed. "Isn't that always the way? Never rain without clouds. What is it now?"

He pulled an envelope from his shirt pocket. "A tax form."

"Tax form? We already paid our taxes for this year."

"Yes, but they have been raised. Substantially."

"How much?"

"Very much. Communist wisdom has increased taxes on the land, whether fallow or seeded, and on cattle."

"Well, what is the problem? We have neither land nor cattle at the moment, except our scrawny cow."

"We have a house that sits on land. If we don't pay these higher rates, we may lose possession of our house."

"So what happens if we don't pay? Would they force us to live on the street while our house sits empty? Or while beggars and thieves seek shelter under its roof? What are they thinking?"

Johann sat down in his chair. "Whatever their motive, we must try to pay."

"But how?"

"I may be able to negotiate a slight decrease because of my recent mayoral position, and if Miller Baerg pays Nicholai for his work at the mill, we might be able to come up with the amount. I will see what I can do."

"Then I will try not to worry." She focused on him. "I'm sorry I get so worked up about these things. I'm afraid, you know, of what will come next. That they won't let us go. I want to go, Johann. I've thought about it every day and have come to realize there is nothing left here for us. By the way the new regime is treating us, there is not much hope for the future either."

ജജജ

Janz presented his emigration list to the authorities in Kharkov in August. It consisted of 17,121 names.

"Seventeen thousand names!" shouted Specter, Chief of Mobilization. "What are you doing—systematically emptying the country?"

Janz remained calm. "You requested a list. These are the applicants who have already signed up. There may be more."

Specter glared at him. "You will have to condense this," he said, waving the document in the air as if it were contagious. "We were expecting approximately three thousand, not seventeen. Have you lost your mind?"

Janz responded as if they were having a pleasant chat over a cup of tea. "At last report, there were steamers coming from America to collect the first three thousand—the most desperate. More are expected in the future. There are fifteen thousand prepared to leave immediately."

"I must speak with Krassikov of the Commissariat of Justice. I cannot give you an answer on this . . . this false assumption."

"That is an excellent idea, sir." Janz stood and extended his hand. "Thank you for your time. I await your answer."

Specter reluctantly shook the proffered hand and glowered at Janz's retreating figure. "That man . . ." he muttered. "For three years I have not crossed myself, but if I could ever free myself of Janz, I would cross myself three times."

"How was your meeting with the Kharkov government?" asked Johann of Benjamin Janz when next he saw him.

Janz shook his head. "Not good. Not good at all."

Johann was shocked. "But I thought you had gotten somewhere with the Kharkov authorities. You told me the VBHH had been officially recognized by the Communist government."

"*Ja*, that is all true, but the ships they are sending, Johann, those ships are to dock at Odessa, and that city has now been quarantined due to a cholera outbreak. We cannot move anyone in or out of there."

"Why Odessa?" moaned Johann.

"Besides that, the contract with the CPR, the Canadian Pacific Railway, is apparently for 2,500 to 3,000 people. That is only the tip of the iceberg. And now the Canadian government is demanding medical inspections by their own and Russian doctors both here and in Latvia. There is no end to the obstacles we face."

"I've heard that the German and Dutch governments have both offered to help rehabilitate Russians of German ancestry. They are willing to supply money and goods to enable our people and others to get back on our feet here. Is this possibly the easier answer to our dilemma?"

Janz sat with his head in his hands. "Of course it is an easier answer, but is it the best way? Do you think I work day and night at this emigration for enjoyment? I did not ask for this task."

He rubbed his large hands over his face and stared out the window. "I don't know, Sudermann. Sometimes I wonder if . . . no! There are thousands waiting to leave this country. They have suffered intensely. I cannot disappoint them now."

Janz looked at Johann and said, "The Russian government has refused to allow Canadian doctors to make inspections here as per CPR demands. So we go another round."

ꕥꕥꕥ

"A letter came today from Batum," said Katarina. "Your sister Mariechen writes."

Johann took the letter and read with great concern:

August 1922 *Batum*

Dear Johann and Katarina,

We are finally leaving this place. I thought we would all die before the time came to go. I will tell you some of what we experienced here.

When we left the Molotsch, we traveled down to Crimea and arrived safely in Sevastopol. The journey was hard on Father. As stubborn as he is (he will not read this letter), I think sometimes he doubts his decision, but he would sooner die than admit he was wrong. And so we almost did.

There was no place for us to live when we arrived in Batum. It was winter, and here that means cold wind and rain every day. We sheltered under our wagon for a week until we finally secured a corner of a basement room in the city. We were not lonely there, as rats and other squatters kept us company. But we were cold, and Father's rheumatism bothered him much. We tried to find enough to eat, but never did. Only enough to stay alive.

The sun came out in spring, but there is much sickness here in these dirty and crowded conditions, and many were not well enough to take advantage of the fresh air and sunshine.

Neither did we find Ernst. He may have gone to Constantinople, who knows? Perhaps we will see him in the new world.

We are leaving here next week, bound, we think, for North America. I don't care if we end up in Mexico or Paraguay or South Africa, as long as we get away from here. This has been a dark pit of existence. It's been almost impossible to get passports and visas. We almost gave up hope, but we weren't allowed back into Russia, so we had to keep trying. There are a few here who have been negotiating for us, and it seems they have finally succeeded.

Many of the Batum refugees have died, but so far, our family is alive. We almost lost Willy, but spring and Mama's prayers brought him back.

So I write farewell. We will try to send a letter when we arrive at our destination. If you have already gone, we will write to Katarina's Uncle George in Canada. We have his address.

Mama sends her love. This experience has aged her greatly. Pray for us as we do for you.

Mariechen Sudermann

"Johann, I've heard that the emigration is finally underway."

"Don't get your hopes up too high," he cautioned. "Odessa, where the ships were to dock, has been quarantined.

Even if the ships arrive, no one will be allowed in or out of the city."

He hated to see the disappointment flood her face. He hated to be the purveyor of bad news again. He was about to leave the house when a knock sounded at the door.

"Paul Gregorovich!" Johann was pleasantly surprised by Tekanin's arrival. "Come, have some supper with us. We have a little more, don't we, Katya?"

"Of course," she said and went to fetch another bowl. She spooned some of their small portion of fried potato skins and eggs onto a plate and added a slice of brown bread, made the day before from wheat Nicholai had brought home from the mill.

"Thank you, Katarina," said Paul. "And Nicholai. How are you, my friend?"

Nicholai nodded with pleasure. Paul usually brightened up even a dismal day. His dark hair, allowed to grow out into curls, and his black eyes gave him a debonair look which made them all feel more alive.

"Where are little Anna and Oma?"

Katarina looked at Johann. He said, "They walked over to Lichtfelde to see how Susannah's mother is doing. She has tuberculosis."

"Why is it that the women and children always suffer the most, when it is the men who start the wars?" The silence was filled by spoons scraping bowls.

"How is Pava?" asked Katarina.

"She is well. She sends her greetings, as does Igor."

"Thank you. Do you have enough to eat?"

"We manage. Our diet has changed like everyone else's but so far we have not starved. They gave us food at the American kitchen yesterday. They are generous to include us."

"Why wouldn't they?" asked Johann.

Tekanin smirked. "Well, the food comes from Mennonites in America for Russian Mennonites. I do not qualify."

"If you are hungry and in need, you qualify. That is the way we have tried to follow for generations: to feed the hungry, visit the prisoners, clothe the naked."

"This truth brings me closer to believing in God than any preacher," said Paul, holding Johann's gaze. Johann looked back at him, depths of understanding passing between the lifetime friends.

Finally, Johann asked, "Have you heard from Grisha? Anything?"

Tekanin pursed his lips and nodded. "That's why I've come." He glanced at Katarina and Nicholai.

"Come out on the porch with me," said Johann, "and we can visit over a cup of *Prips*."

When they had gone outside, Johann asked his question again. "What of Grisha? Where is he?"

"He is in trouble," said Paul. "He has kept up his underground resistance to the Reds and has accomplished a few things, I think." He chuckled without humor. "Interesting how the cause he once gave his life to is now the one he is resisting. He is in prison is Kharkov."

"On what charge?"

"Exactly that: resisting the government."

Johann frowned. He had seen the inside of a couple of village jails in his mayoral work. He had tried to free some of the young Mennonite men who had ended up there for various reasons or no reason at all, and he'd even been successful in a few cases, but Kharkov was the capital city of Ukraine. That made intervention much more difficult. And a charge of resisting the government was extremely serious.

"I am no longer the mayor of Alexanderkrone, Paul. I don't know what, if anything, I can do."

Disappointment pinched Paul's handsome face. "I didn't

know where else to turn. Grisha has always supported me, even when I didn't deserve or appreciate it. I suppose that was most of the time. I can't let him down now."

"What do you propose to do?"

Paul shrugged. "I don't know, but I will find a way to help him if there is one."

Johann worried about his words. "Before you do anything drastic, let me inquire about it. I still fill the secretarial position for the village. Perhaps there are some strings I can pull. Vasylenyk has been fair to me over the last months. He may be the person to start with. Let me see what I can do."

Paul nodded. "You are a good man, Sudermann, a true Christian if ever I saw one."

Johann smiled. "Coming from you, those words mean much to me. Will you stay with us tonight?"

"No, but thank you. Pava will be waiting and I have a long walk ahead of me."

"If I had a horse, I would offer it, but I'm afraid my cow would not take you farther than the edge of town."

They laughed lightly together and clapped each other on the back, and Paul disappeared into the darkness of the December night.

Johann read the news in the Communist newspaper just before Christmas: Russia had become the *Union of Soviet Socialist Republics—the U.S.S.R.* Trotsky remained in charge of the Red Army which finally and completely defeated what was left of the White faction at Vladivostock on the east coast of Russia, off the Sea of Japan.

In spite of Lenin's New Economic Policy and the somewhat dubious feeling of *svoboda*, Johann felt a disquiet in his soul. What did the announcement of this newly christened republic portend for the Russian Mennonites?

He knew his people. As Janz had said, the Russian

Mennonites held their historic faith very dear. They valued spiritual, economic, and political independence; they clung to their German ethnic roots and they rejected socialism for capitalism. All in all, not a good fit. No, Johann was having serious doubts about the future of his people in this country.

ꕥꕥꕥ

"Grisha has been transferred to Lubyanka." Johann's whispered words caused Paul's hair to stand on end.

PART FOUR

1923–1924

Grant us peace, Jesus, grant us peace,
Move our hearts to hear a single beat
Between alibis and enemies tonight.

Or maybe not, not today,
Peace might be another world away,
And if that's the case . . .

We'll give thanks to you with gratitude,
For lessons learned in how to trust in you,
That we are blessed beyond what we could ever dream
In abundance or in need,
And if you never grant us peace—

But Jesus, would you please . . .

Nichole Nordeman

Chapter 20

"Lubyanka?!" Paul shuddered as thoughts of the notorious prison in Moscow filled his mind. Beautiful architecture could not hide the aura of evil that clung to the infamous institution. "Still on the charge of resisting the government?"

Johann nodded. The two men met in an old barn on the western outskirts of Kleefeld.

"You know you are being watched also?"

"Yes." Paul pulled his cap lower on his forehead in a subconscious gesture. He had shaved his head again. "I am careful."

"Make sure of it. I don't want to lose you after we've found one another again."

Paul snorted. "What about when you leave for America?" He hadn't meant to sound like a sniveling child, but he hated the thought of Johann's leaving.

Johann rubbed his whiskered cheek and kicked at the floor with his boot. "We are from two different worlds, Tekanin. For a short time those worlds merged, but that time is swiftly drawing to a close, and we will have only memories. Neither of us can read the future. I only know my future is not here, and there is no way for you to leave."

"I do not wish to leave. I am Russian. This is my land, my soil, my home. Pava is here. But I will miss you."

"I'm glad you found her."

Paul narrowed his eyes and peered at Johann by the light

of the hand torch set on the floor. "No, I do not approve of the arrangement, but I am glad you are not alone. You are my brother and I wish the best for you."

"You never change, you . . ." Tekanin's voice failed him and he turned away. He cleared his throat and tried again. "You have been a living sermon to me. Do not write me off. Not yet." He regained his composure. "Pava has helped me to survive. She fills the emptiness in me. She is also good at hiding me—a deceptive little woman. I will take care of her. But what do we do about Grisha?"

"What can I do? The name Lubyanka causes me to sweat. I have no power in that direction."

"But you can pray."

Johann was silent. Paul's plea touched his heart. "Yes, I can pray, and I will. Grisha is in the hands of God. Only a miracle can break Grisha out of that fortification of demons."

The miracle knocked at the door of the Tekanin *izba* in Ackerman at dusk not two weeks later. Pava peeked out the window and summoned Paul with fierce whispering. A moment later, Grisha was grabbed by the arm and pulled swiftly into the little house.

Paul Gregorovich stood and stared at him. "Grisha, where in blazes did you come from? How did you get here? Are you alone? Where are you going to go?"

"One question at a time, my impulsive friend," answered a grinning Grisha, grabbing Paul in a hug. "I come from Lubyanka." He spit on the dirt floor in contempt. "I do not understand why they let me go, but I could not have escaped on my own. There is no way out of there except death." He shuddered.

Pava busied herself making strong tea, all the while keeping an eye fixed on the miracle before her. "You must be frozen," she said, and handed him a cup of the brew.

The men sat on the large stumps hauled there for that purpose. Grisha blinked away the mental apparitions that assailed him and sipped the scalding liquid. "Ah. Thank you, Pava. I don't mind the cold. It is refreshing. You take a deep breath and feel it down to your toes. The air is clean and free. I don't mind the cold when I am outside."

Paul became impatient. "Where are you going? You can stay here too, but I don't know how long it will be safe."

"I know. I probably shouldn't have come, but I needed to see you once more. We have been like family for many years."

Pava sat with her father on the mattress in the corner.

Paul frowned again. "What do you mean, once more? Where are you going?"

"Paul, I do not know what my future will be, or how long I have. Life is fragile, one day at a time. This chance came to follow my heart here, and I took advantage of it. Either I continue my subversive activities or I become a hard core Communist. You know the first will eventually seal my fate, and second is not an option for me. So I come to bid you farewell."

Paul Gregorovich stared at Grisha, the man who had saved him from death and destruction more often than even he knew. He saw the abundance of gray in his mentor's hair and beard. It almost totally hid the red. His stocky build had thinned considerably in the years of homelessness and famine, but the eyes were the same—deep blue, true.

"Why is everyone leaving?"

Paul's plaintive words caught Grisha's heart. "I do not wish it, but we both know I cannot stay."

Pava rose from the mattress and came to stand beside Paul. Her eyes glistened.

"When do you go?"

"Tomorrow before daybreak. The nights are still long. I can be far away by sunrise."

Tekanin bent his head in resignation. He felt the finality of Grisha's words. With a shuddering sigh, he said, "Give us a bite to eat, Pava, and then we must let the man rest for his journey."

ଌଌଌ

"It is dark," said Benjamin Janz to Philipp Cornies, a colleague from the Union of Citizens of Dutch Lineage, the VBHH. "Nothing to see; nothing to feel; nothing to appraise; no support, no foundation, no future. Everything is all factual material for negative conclusions, for negation. For a long time I have worked, hoped, striven—with one word—*believed.*"

The cold winds of January beat against Janz's quarters at No. 4 Butovsky in Kharkov, and Cornies suspected at least a part of Janz's discouragement connected itself to the freezing weather and his lonely Christmas. Janz had remained in Kharkov through the changing of the year, in the midst of a campaign to convince the authorities there to come to an agreement with the Canadian Mennonite Board of Colonization and the Canadian Pacific Railway. He could not give up, now that he'd come this far.

"The little chest with our entire hope and faith floats as a last wreck upon the billows of the Russian flood, and seems destined and compelled to sink in it."

"Do not lose faith, brother," said Cornies. "We will yet see the rewards of your labors and ours. The people rely on you to lead them."

"How can the blind lead the blind, my friend? If circumstances don't soon change, I must capitulate, step aside."

"You are not a man to capitulate in the darkest hour, Benjamin. Rely on your faith."

Janz looked at his friend wearily. "And if that commodity is scarce?"

"We will pray for you, for your increased faith. Do not despair."

ꕥꕥꕥ

"I thought our situation was improving," said Johann to Kornelius. "The war is over, rain has begun to fall again, and the crops are growing, but the government's hand of control is tightening. The Cheka now takes an active part in all negotiations with our people, so B. B. Janz told me. They are leading weapons searches again. If they don't find the number of guns they have decided upon, they select people by lottery and shoot them."

"It gets worse instead of better," said Kornelius.

"I try to keep things in perspective, but now, as village secretary, I have to find some landowners from the village to form a committee to monitor theft. The Communists want petty crime under control, and have made it our responsibility. They don't give us credit to govern ourselves as we have for generations, but we are supposed to take care of the details they don't want to bother with."

Kornelius nodded. "Johann, you have been an important ally for the people of Alexanderkrone, in whatever capacity you have served the village. No one expects you to do more than you are able."

"The Communists do."

"Even they cannot get blood from a stone. Do your best, talk to the authorities about the rest."

Johann sighed. "You are right, of course. Thank you for listening. I needed to talk to someone, and I hate to unload everything on Katarina. She has her hands full looking after the household and helping Susannah when she can."

"Don't worry about Susannah. I will make sure she and her household are taken care of."

The young people met in the large parlor of the Kroeker home in Alexanderkrone, since religious gatherings were no longer allowed in public places such as the school and the church.

"Strange that a youth group cannot meet in the church," said Justina as they enjoyed a plate of rolls and tea after the Bible study. The other girls stared at her.

"Why would you concern yourself with that, Justa?" asked Greta Kroeker. "Let the men worry about that."

Justina set her teacup on the table and leaned forward to face Greta. "I consider it because it affects all of us. If these hard times have taught me anything, it is that we must be aware of what is happening around us. That kind of knowledge can sometimes protect us."

"Sometimes," answered Greta, and Justina saw the glint in her eyes. "God allows some to suffer anyway, but perhaps that's a punishment."

Nicholai, who had been listening intently from the other end of the table, spoke up. "And some, when they fail to understand God, create a smaller god they can explain."

Greta stared at him, eyes blinking, trying but failing to come up with a witty reply.

"Don't pick on Greta," said Heinz Letkemann. "She doesn't know what she's talking about."

Flustered and embarrassed, Greta pushed back her chair and stood. "I'll get more tea," she murmured.

Muffled giggles broke out in the parlor as the door closed behind Greta. Justina's chair scraped back and she stood as well. "We gathered this evening for a Bible study," she said. "We study in order to pattern our lives after the Savior. Obviously we have learned nothing tonight about following him." She picked up her teacup and followed Greta into the kitchen, leaving behind a surprised and hushed group of young people.

After a bit more stilted conversation, they began to take

their leave. Nicholai slipped out into the clear night and pulled a deep breath of crisp air into his lungs. He saw Justina then, on her solitary trek back to Kleefeld.

"Justina," he called softly. "Wait."

She stopped and glanced behind her, then continued to walk. Nicholai grimaced and broke into a trot, catching up with her.

"Why don't you wait? I want to talk to you."

Justina tossed him an aloof glance and kept walking. "Then talk."

Nicholai laughed and shook his head. "I don't understand. I stood up for you tonight. I didn't want Greta to say something that would hurt or embarrass you in front of everyone. Why are you angry with me?"

"You didn't want her to tell the whole group that I've been raped? Is that what you're trying to say? Why? Because it would have embarrassed you?"

"Justina, please! All right, I would have been embarrassed too, but my first thought was for you. Greta was trying to grab attention, and she does whatever she can to get it. I don't trust her."

"So you responded by striking out against her."

"I didn't, Justina! Please stop for a moment." They were by now on the outskirts of Alexanderkrone, walking along the dirt road to Kleefeld, in the shelter of hoarfrosted poplars and willows. The snow sparkled like a field of diamonds in the moonlight.

Justina stopped and turned to face him.

He took her elbow and led her back into the trees, away from the eyes of others heading home from the meeting. "Justina, some of those present tonight will already know about what happened to you, in fact, I'm sure there are others who have suffered as you have, but I didn't want your suffering thrown out for all to see. It would not have helped anyone. I . . . I couldn't stand to see you face that."

Justina blinked rapidly, her chest heaving with the effort of maintaining her composure. "Why not?"

"Because I care about you. You're . . . special to me."

A tear squeezed out from each eye and slid down her face, glistening in the cold light. She said nothing.

"Justina, you are different from the others. You have character, substance. I can relate to you on a deeper, more meaningful level that I ever could with any of the others. Please, don't shut me out."

She trembled and he drew her into a gentle embrace. "I've lost a lot in my life already too. I think I can understand."

She cried then, her face in his shoulder.

"I was wrong in the way I defended you," he whispered. "I will have to apologize."

Justina pulled away and held his eyes. "I respect that. Nicholai—"

"—I'd like it if you called me Kolya, at least when it's just the two of us."

She smiled as she brushed away her tears. "Kolya."

Her eyes flitted from his face to the trees, to the moon, to the snow-covered ground at her feet. "Kolya, does it not bother you that I . . ."

"That you were molested? We have all become victims. Your heart is pure." He turned her face toward him again. "I hope that you can find a tiny place in that heart for me." His statement was a question which begged an answer.

Justina's shy smile gave him what he was hoping for. He tucked her arm into his, checked the road for other travelers, and led her out of the trees. "May I see you home, my lady?" he asked with a slight bow.

She inclined her head to him and answered, "Yes, you may, kind sir."

ȣȣȣ

"Good morning, Susannah. Where is your family today?" Katarina asked as she poked her head in the door.

Absentmindedly, Susannah answered. "Mr. Penner and Peter took both Marianna and little Gerhard for a walk to the mill for flour. Mama is asleep in the back bedroom, and I just returned from visiting my sister. Helena is determined to leave Russia with her children. She does not want them to remain here under any circumstances." She hugged her arms around herself. "I can't imagine her not being there in the next village."

She focused on her friend. "Katya, now the government wants 42 million rubles per person in taxes!" Susannah's hair had come out of its braid and hung in tired wisps around her shoulders.

"We will most certainly pay for Peter, and quite possibly we can help you with some money."

"That's very kind, and I accept the help for Peter, but you already have enough to pay for: you, Johann, Anna, Oma. And what about Mr. Penner? Does he fall under your household as well? No, Katarina, I appreciate your generosity, but you don't need to be responsible for my household too."

"Well, we will see how it works out. Have you anything to sell?"

Susannah shook her head, pushing the stray hair behind her ears. "The cow is dry. No milk or cream or butter. We need the few chickens we have left for eggs. I thought perhaps our cow would calve this spring, but now I don't know. We didn't have much to feed her."

"Have you been sending her out to the pasture with the herder?"

"Of course, Katya, I'm not stupid."

"Suse, please, I'm asking for information, not chastisement."

Susannah looked away. "I'm sorry. In spite of your offer to help, I feel I am on my own. No one can help me."

Katarina, praying for patience, led Susannah to a chair and

told her to sit. She pulled out a chair beside her, placed her elbows on the table and laced her fingers under her chin. "Susannah," she began. "I will not lecture you on your attitude, because I have not suffered the experiences you have. I don't know what it's like to be a widow in such a time as this—" She held up a hand to stop Susannah's expected denial of her widowhood. "Yes, you are a widow and you would benefit from accepting the situation. What I want to say is that I miss my old friend, the Susannah I met eight years ago at *Bethania*.

"This young woman met me with a round, healthy face wreathed in smiles that emanated from a joyful heart. I'll never forget your hair, thick and honey gold, braided and wrapped around your head like a crown. Sometimes it resembled a halo. You were energetic and positive, full of hope. And that was before you and Gerhard became an item, so you can't give him the credit. I think you glowed because of your relationship with God."

"Much has happened since that time, Katarina. That Susannah is gone, that heart is empty and broken."

"I disagree. I think you are hiding her inside. You keep her locked away to prevent more pain. I understand the response, but it's not good for you. Let her out. Bring our old Susannah back. Let us help you deal with the pain."

Susannah sat silent for so long that Katarina wondered if she had drifted into a daydream.

"Susannah?"

Her friend focused on her again. "Did I really look like that? Was my joy so evident? I look in the mirror sometimes—by accident, not on purpose—and I wonder who the stranger is who stares back at me. She is thin, pale, unkempt, unhappy, and often unkind."

"Do you like her?"

"I despise her, but she is who I have become. If you hadn't

known me before, you would not now waste your time trying to change me."

Katarina smiled. "That's where you're wrong. Kornelius . . ."

"What has he to do with anything?"

"Allow me to speak, Susannah. Kornelius did not know you in better days. All he knows is the woman you see in the mirror, and yet, he cares for you anyway. He sees the treasure you have locked away in your heart."

"I'm not interested in him. I will always love Gerhard."

"Suse, do you think Wilhelm Enns did not love his first wife, or Agnetha her husband? I'm sure they struggled to work through that problem, but they have found great joy in living their lives together."

"They know their first spouse is dead. They saw them die or at least someone did." Her anguished eyes pled for under standing. "I don't know that. How can I betray my vows of faithfulness?"

Katarina took Susannah's hands and massaged them with her thumbs. "Suse, I'm not asking you to marry Kornelius. All I'm asking is that you allow us and him to glimpse the real you. Go back to your first love, to Jesus who saved you from sin, and let him heal you. He will lead if you will let him. You don't have to keep fighting alone."

Susannah's voice choked with unshed tears. "I've tried before, but I can't seem to do it. It seems the anger holds me together."

"You can't hold yourself together. Only the Lord can do that. Won't you give him the opportunity? He waits with arms full of blessing."

Susannah began to weep, sobbing out her anger and her pain. Her mother appeared in the doorway, pale and drawn from her fight with TB. Katarina led the woman back to her room, made her comfortable and explained what they had been discussing.

"*Ja, ja*," whispered Hannah. "She has changed something awful. I am sorry she has to bear the brunt of the load for the rest of us. When I am better, I will help." Looking up at Katarina, she said, "You do what you can for her. I would appreciate it. She once shared her faith with me, and now her own is challenged. It's sad."

"Pray, Hannah, and I will do what I can." She smoothed Hannah's hair and headed back to find Susannah at the sink, washing her face with cool water. She still shuddered, but the tears had dried, at least for the present.

"Come sit down now," ordered Katarina. "I am going to fix your hair." They visited while Katarina brushed and braided, and the conversation that began with difficulty soon developed into the familiar banter of two friends.

When the time came for Katarina to leave, Susannah threw her arms around her and hugged her fiercely. "Thank you, dear friend," she cried. "Thank you for braving the anger and forcing me to see the truth. I will try again, God helping me."

Katarina laughed. "Go look in the mirror, Suse. You're thinner than you were, as we all are, but you look amazingly like someone I used to know. You're even beginning to sound like her."

Susannah smiled and kissed Katarina on the cheek. "I may need regular reminding, but I don't want to go back to the person I've been these last few years. Keep at me, won't you?"

Katarina nodded and hurried home with a light step that matched the feeling in her heart.

Chapter 21

A light rain had begun to fall, soaking into the parched ground. It filled the fissures in the soil and flowed in little rivulets in the fields, the yards, the orchards, the roads. As darkness fell, Johann sat by the fire reading a memorandum from the state to the village office. It spoke of reconstruction, of bringing back the fertility of the land, of increasing the numbers of cattle and horses, the latter being almost nonexistent since the civil war.

Katarina played a game of *Knippsbraat* with Anna, Nicholai and Kornelius, and Oma rocked in her chair, her knitting needles clicking briskly.

Johann looked up from his reading and surveyed his family. His opinion about the emigration was changing once again. What could they complain of anymore? They had food, relative peace, health, and work. The demands of the Communist government appeared harsh, but that would settle down. As he had argued with Benjamin Janz, Lenin had relaxed the socialist concept for now, and Johann had faith it could continue that way. If the concessions benefited reconstruction, why would the government change them? It would be all right here yet. Perhaps they would not have to leave the country.

Katarina glanced up from her game, the concentration of competition still on her face. He smiled and she answered with one of her own. She didn't agree with him, he knew. They had discussed it before. But they may not have a choice.

The cholera epidemic had blocked the planned evacuation last summer, and the Russian government had refused to allow foreign doctors on their soil to make the required inspections.

The Canadian Mennonite Board of Colonization was still having difficulties getting a contract with the Canadian Pacific Railway, and was running short of the required funds. All in all, it seemed hopeless. Even Janz, as much as he believed emigration to be the only viable answer, experienced doubts now and then about the possibility of such a venture.

In bed later that night, Katarina launched into the topic Johann had dwelt on during the evening, the one he didn't want to discuss with her again.

"It's only a lull in the storm," she whispered, her head propped on her arm on the pillow.

Johann rolled his eyes and looked in the direction of the ceiling. "Katya, the Mennonite Central Committee continues to send us food and the rains are coming. Farmers will soon be planting the seeds sent us by the MCC. Tractors have arrived to help with the plowing and they're sending horses too."

"And all religion is being banned from the schools. No one who has ever preached behind a pulpit is allowed to teach. We've lost several of the best teachers because of this ridiculous rule."

"It doesn't stop the children from learning about spiritual things in church. Let the two be separate if the government is more comfortable that way."

Katarina sat up. "I don't care if the government is comfortable or not." Johann put his finger to his lips and Katarina lowered her voice. "It won't end here," she continued. "You'll see. We have to plan to leave when we can."

"I don't know, Katya. It's an enormous decision to leave one's homeland. Canada is not heaven, you know."

"Johann, if my grandfather had emigrated in the '80s when the opportunity came, my family might be together now. My father would not have been murdered."

"You're getting dramatic, Katya. 'As ifs' and 'if only' are poor arguments."

Katarina jumped out of bed and rummaged through a dresser drawer. She found what she was looking for and thrust it in Johann's face. He knew what it would be: the letter from her Uncle George, received a year ago with the first food parcels that had given them hope. *It's a land of opportunity and promise,* he had written, *a land of peace and space and tolerance.* Well, Johann knew it was also a land of hard work and risk. Not that he was afraid of work, but he was a teacher, who would likely have to become a farmer in the new country if they went.

Katarina sat cross-legged on the bed, waiting for Johann's response. Her curls sprang out from her head, making her look like a girl instead of the woman she had become. For a moment he forgot their present impasse, but the fire in her eyes reminded him. With a sigh he relinquished his desire and tried to formulate a response that would pacify his wife. No, she would recognize that ploy. She did not respond well to placation.

"What if we go and are unable to make a living there? We can't come back, you know."

She raised her eyebrows. "I know that, dearest, but there's a better chance we will do well there. If we stay here, we will be forced to conform to the whims of people like Stalin. He frightens me."

"You shouldn't worry about things you have no control over."

"There, you've said it yourself: we have no control over this government."

"Neither did we have control over the tsarist rule."

"But we would have some say in Canada. Uncle George says it's a democracy. We could all have a part in that."

Johann yawned widely. "Katie, could we continue this conversation in the morning? I am weary and would like to go to sleep."

"Of course. You know when you are losing an argument." She got up again to return the letter to the drawer, but not before he caught the hint of a smile on her face. She tried to remain aloof, but ended up laughing along with Johann. He tried to shush her, but they were both lost in giggles.

"Katarina," he whispered fiercely, "I must insist you quiet down before you wake the entire household."

She responded by covering his face with her pillow, and the fight was on. She won eventually, and so did he. They saved the emigration argument for another day.

ഇഇഇ

"I've found a way out for Susannah," Johann told Kornelius. "If she is a widow, she doesn't have to pay taxes for herself or her children. Hannah, also a widow, is exempt as well."

"That is good news," said Kornelius, a touch of sarcasm in his voice. "Now all we have to do is convince Susannah she is a widow."

Johann looked long at Kornelius. "You have not lost your attraction to her, have you?"

Kornelius shook his head miserably. "Now I see her heart beginning to change for the better and I love her even more. She is very beautiful, Johann—perhaps I shouldn't talk that way to you. She told me you and she used to be an item—but she grows lovelier each day. I love the children as if they were my own. Either I must win her or go away from here altogether."

"It eats at you, doesn't it?"

"Yes, I'm sorry. I shouldn't have mentioned it."

"No, you misunderstand. Susannah and I were good friends when we were younger, and if I hadn't had the urge to go off and seek my fortune, as it were, we may have married and settled down. But that's not what happened and we are nothing more than good friends.

"What I am referring to is my former attraction to Katarina's younger sister."

Kornelius's eyebrows shot up in surprise.

"Yes. She was—is—a beauty. I suffered severe infatuation and she toyed with me as it suited her whim. Sometimes my heart nearly broke, and I thought I would need to go away to maintain my sanity. Then I was called to serve in the *Forstei*, and when I returned, she had not wasted a moment pining for me. Yes, Kornelius, I know the perils of caring for someone who doesn't return the feeling."

"Did Katarina know all this was happening?"

"Oh yes. She stood back, suffering my blindness in silence until I finally realized my stupidity of wanting someone I could never be happy with when my true match was right there all the time."

Kornelius mused on what Johann had revealed to him. "Thank you, my friend, for confiding in me. Sarah and I always knew we were meant for each other, but this with Susannah, this confuses me."

"Give her time," said Johann. "I'll pass on something Katarina's father once told me. He said he had learned some things about women. He said, 'Love them, yes, but understand them, never.'"

Kornelius raised one eyebrow and nodded. "That is a truth."

"Do not give up easily, Kornelius. Nothing worth having is without its cost. I will go back to the office tomorrow morning and try to find a trail on Gerhard Warkentin. Perhaps there is something I have overlooked in the past, something that would convince Susannah that she is indeed a widow."

ꕥꕥꕥ

"Good news, Susannah," said Kornelius as he entered the kitchen where she peeled a few wrinkled potatoes for the noon meal.

"We never get too much of that," she responded. "What is it?"

"Well, I have two items of good news. Which would you like to hear first?"

Feigning irritation, she replied, "Tell me in the order you heard it. Just tell me."

"Well, I talked with Johann this morning, and on certain condition, neither you nor your mother should have to pay any taxes."

Her hands stilled, water dripping from them. "What? What is the condition?"

Kornelius cleared his throat and forged ahead. "Widows are exempt from the taxes." He watched for her reaction.

She turned back to her potatoes. "Mother is certainly exempt then. We don't know my status for sure, do we? Although everyone seems bent on convincing me to forget Gerhard."

"Mrs. Warkentin, that is not our motive. Gerhard must have been a special person indeed to so capture your heart. I envy him."

She stopped again, a potato in her hands. "Mr. Penner," she said in measured tones, "I believe we have had this conversation before. You are a fine man and I appreciate your help here and the way you have taken to the children. But Gerhard or no Gerhard, I am not romantically attracted to you. Please accept that fact."

He sat down at the table and ran his hands through his hair. "My head knows it, Mrs. Warkentin, but my heart won't accept it. I cannot get the two to agree."

She turned and looked at him with an expression of pity.

"What is the other news?" she asked softly.

He raised his head, trying to remember. "Ah! The cow has freshened. She gave birth to a bull calf sometime during the night. I just found it now when I returned from Johann's."

A smile lit Susannah's face and she turned and clapped him on the back, disregarding the water dripping from her hands and the knife she still held.

"Excuse me, Madam," he said, "but I'd be grateful if you'd not come at me with a knife. Makes me a little uncomfortable and what would the children think?"

"Oooh!" She returned to the sink. A wet spot soaked through Kornelius's shirt. "I'm sorry. I forgot myself."

She dried her hands on a towel and came to join him at the table. "Do you know what that means? Milk for the children, and cream and butter for baking and to sell. And I could get 50 million rubles for a good bull calf."

"Sixty."

"Sixty then. I could pay off the tax for myself even without the exemption. Thank you for bringing me this wonderful news."

The joy in her eyes and the release of tension in her posture did nothing to still Kornelius's pounding pulse. She encouraged him not to look at her as a man looks at a woman, and then her very presence contradicted it. What was he to do?

If he hadn't turned his back on God, he would pray, but . . . perhaps he still could. They said God was merciful. Perhaps he would make an agreement with God: if he would bring Susannah to the point of accepting him, he would reconsider his opinion of God. Once the prayer was whispered in his heart, it became a commitment, and Kornelius sat back spiritually to await the outcome.

Susannah hurried back to her potatoes, but she could not stop the song that sprang to her lips at the joyous news he had revealed to her.

ജജജ

"Katarina, would you be free to walk with me?" Johann had come home from the village office with something on his mind, and Katarina wanted to share it with him, whether good or bad.

"Yes. Give me a little while to clear up the supper dishes and I will come."

"You two run along," said Oma. "Anna and I will wash and dry. We are quite capable, you know."

Katarina hesitated only a moment before she untied her apron. "Thank you both. We shouldn't be long."

"How do you know that?" teased Johann. "I may be kidnapping you."

"You couldn't take me against my will," she retorted.

He took her hand and pulled her outside. They would finish that argument later.

"Where are we going, Johann?"

"Nowhere in particular, Katya. I needed to talk with you, without an audience."

"So talk."

Instead, he reached into his pocket and took out a piece of paper. "I found this today."

She took it from him and read it while he explained. "Kornelius came to me about Susannah. As you know, he is falling for her, but she won't give him the time of day. I've been searching for something to prove that Gerhard is actually deceased. I almost didn't want to find it because he was my friend and I miss him, but I think Susannah needs to know one way or the other. It will give her the freedom to make her decision about emigration based on facts instead of wishes."

Katarina looked up from the paper. "Oh Johann. From this information, it seems as if Gerhard was one of the casualties in the Red Army. His name was listed on more than one report?"

He nodded. "Yes. No body, but that's not uncommon. If I would guess, based on usual procedure, they just kicked him to the side of the road."

She shuddered. "Don't they bury them?"

"No. They would have stopped at the next village and commanded some poor soul to go back and do that. But I have no way of knowing where he would have fallen and who would have buried him. We will never know that."

"So now we must tell Susannah."

"We have tried to tell her before and you helped me then too. She did not accept our report then. I wonder if things have changed?"

"We have to try."

Susannah sat silently across the table from Johann and Katarina. She had read the words on the paper he gave her. It lay crumpled in her hand. No one spoke.

"Mama! Mama, drink!" Little Gerhard ran into the room, unaware of the company or the atmosphere. He buried his face in his mother's lap and whispered, "Drink, Mama."

She dipped water from the pail on the counter and held it for the boy to drink. When he had finished, she patted him on his bottom. "There you go, my little man. You find Marianna and both of you go visit *Grossmama* in her room for a while. I'll call you when it's bedtime."

"Yes, Mama," he sang as he ran off toward the parlor. "Yanna! Yanna, where you be?"

"He's adorable," said Katarina wistfully.

"He's precious. At first I wondered why God would give me another child to care for on my own, but I'm so thankful for him."

"I suppose we should go," said Johann. "I'm sorry we always seem to bring bad news."

Susannah shook her head. "It's not news." She thought of

Kornelius's words and repeated them. "My head tells me you are correct, but my heart refuses to accept it."

After looking in on Hannah, Johann and Katarina set off again for home. "They'll wonder where we are by now," she said. "We've been gone a long time."

ꝏꝏꝏ

B. B. Janz met with the VBHH executive in late spring of '23 to discuss the progress of their push for emigration.

"I thought registering for visas under one name would be more efficient," said Philipp Cornies.

"And it was," replied Janz. "I appreciate your effort on that front."

Another member, Peter Dyck, nodded. "Who was to know they would change their policy and demand that everyone apply individually?"

"*Ja*," said Janz. "At least that snag did not stall us for as long as I had expected. The Foreign Commissariat in Moscow has now approved the embarkation of the first three thousand emigrants from Chortitza, and in spite of their economic problems, Germany has agreed to take any who are rejected for health reasons. Now we must make sure they are prepared to leave by June."

"I will go to Moscow in May to confirm the agreement," offered Cornies.

Janz nodded. "Perhaps we shall go together. I must speak with a number of officials as to the remaining emigrants. They are also prepared to leave. Many have sold their belongings and even their homes. They cannot exist much longer in that situation."

"Perhaps two are better than one in the meetings?" Cornies eyed Janz.

"I work better alone, for the most part," replied Janz, his

answer no surprise to Cornies or Dyck, "but it will be good to travel together."

ഌഌഌ

"Anna, Oma, where have you been?" asked Katarina. Her sister and grandmother had paused outside to wash their hands thoroughly under the pump. "I worried when you didn't appear for the noon meal, and now it's almost suppertime."

"Errands of mercy, sister," answered Anna. "There are some families who are suffering from illness who need a visit and a helping hand. We do what we can."

Katarina's eyes questioned her grandmother.

"Mostly TB patients," said Oma. "We visited Hannah, but Susannah has her well cared for, and the children brighten her day with their chatter and play."

"As long as you don't come down with it yourselves," said Katarina. The rest of her thought went unsaid: *You are too old to take such chances and Anna is not strong.*

"When we do the Lord's work, we don't worry about that," said Oma.

Johann, who had arrived home to hear most of the conversation, commented, "I heard someone else say that once. He died of typhus. He wasn't yet thirty years."

"Well Johann, then I have him beat. I have passed thirty years twice and then some."

Johann chuckled. "Never argue with Oma," he said sagely.

Anna is only halfway there, thought Katarina. What about her?

Smiling, the old woman sat at the table and Katarina noted the exhaustion she tried to disguise.

"Don't look at me so, child," Oma said. "I am tired. I am almost eighty years old—it's allowed."

"Just don't overdo it, or you will come down with something too, and then how will you expect to emigrate?"

Oma's silence caused Katarina to pause in her work. "Oma?"

The woman sighed. "Don't worry, child."

Katarina suspected that this day was not the first such mission of mercy for Oma and Anna. The two Annas worked well together; their thoughts often ran along similar lines. But with medical examinations at any time, none of them could afford to be sick. She didn't know how she would cope if one or more of them did not pass the medicals. Anna had been gaining strength, but she was a fragile child since her ordeal at the hands of the bandits.

Another worry was Oma, simply because of her age. Would the authorities allow her to embark on the long and arduous trek to a strange land? Did she want to go?

And Peter. What about Peter? The Canadian government had made it perfectly clear that they did not accept those with physical or mental handicaps. Could Peter somehow get by? On a good day without too much aggravation, he could pass as quite normal. Besides being skinny, which most people were these days, he seemed normal if you didn't look into his eyes.

Katarina was afraid for Peter. Of course they would look into his eyes. My goodness, the doctors put trachoma at the top of their lists. Eyes were inspected and treated if needed. Except for a miracle, Katarina knew, Peter would never pass his medicals. But then, Susannah said she wasn't going anywhere, so Peter could stay where he was if need be.

What if Susannah changed her mind? Hannah would not be allowed out of the country. Where would she stay if Susannah left? Would Susannah ever leave without her mother? Katarina herself had spoken to her many times on that subject. She had strongly encouraged her to go for the sake of her children, but so far she had refused.

So many questions made Katarina's head ache. Sometimes she felt as if she could almost hear her father and his father before him, telling her to go. *Take your family and leave this place. It is no longer a haven for us.*

Johann was coming round to her way of thinking. Just last week the government cracked down on religious teachers. Now all teachers were commanded to travel to Moscow for training—indoctrination. Johann was beginning to see that this antireligious bent was only the beginning.

The clincher came when Anna asked to be baptized. She wanted to obey the Scriptures and publicly proclaim her salvation, but the new law stated: *no one under eighteen years of age is allowed to be baptized.* There it was. The church and state had been separated, and now the state began to set foot in the church's business again. It didn't make sense, except that Katarina felt an iron grip closing around herself and her people. Thank goodness Johann was finally beginning to feel it too.

"I've resigned my position with the village office," Johann reported in mid-May. "It's a matter of ethics. They've called in a new mayor, and he is despicable. I cannot work with the likes of him."

"Johann, what a thing to say," she chided.

"It is the truth. He reeks of deception. I cannot be associated with such as him."

"But how will you correspond with B. B. Janz? The government post seemed the most expedient for that."

"Janz doesn't need me, Katarina. He has been generous in informing me of his progress, but he is a man who keeps his own confidence. I have learned much from him, but I will not irritate him now with my questions. He is attacked enough by others."

"What do you mean, attacked?"

"Katarina, one person cannot please everyone. I sense from some of his memos and letters that he has become a target for Mennonite complaints of all shades."

"What can people blame him for? He has given years of his life to the work, and right now has achieved the release of the Chortitza groups."

"Nevertheless, there are many who blame him for the slow progress of the emigration, for changes in visa application, for failure of medical tests. We have learned to blame from our original father and mother."

"Adam and Eve. Yes. Even without wicked people around them, they blamed the only ones there: each other. We are fickle, aren't we?"

"If only Janz continues his task until those who wish to leave are able to do so. The way the Communists change the laws, you never know when they will be in a bad humor and renege on their previous position. I think it would be a good idea to keep praying fervently on these matters, Katya."

And she had. She prayed as she worked and as she walked, in the daytime and in the quiet stretches of night when she lay awake.

Chapter 22

"This first group left Chortitza yesterday," said B. B. Janz to Peter Dyck, "and today they have arrested Philipp Cornies. All four groups were originally registered under Cornies's name. What will happen now?"

Dyck was quick to reassure. "The first group has been allowed to leave; they should pass through Sebezh into Latvia in about ten days. If the authorities let the first group go, I see no reason for them not to let the other groups through."

"You see no reason. Your reason is definitely not theirs, Peter. For now we will pray and continue as planned. What else can we do? Already the crowd is after me for not making all things right for everyone. I am only one man, Peter."

"I will go to Moscow to see what I can do for Philipp."

ꕥꕥꕥ

"I don't think I shall go to church today," said Anna in a thin voice. "I am too tired."

Katarina hurried into her sister's room to check if she had a fever. "You couldn't have gone anyway. They've canceled it."

"Canceled it? The preachers?"

"No. The government. No more public religious meetings of any kind. New rule."

"Oh, Katie, I don't like all their new rules."

"That's why we are going to leave, Anna, as soon as they

let us. You are warm but not very. What did you and Oma do yesterday? Where did you visit?"

Anna seemed hesitant to divulge the information. "We . . . we stopped for a few moments at Regehrs'."

"Regehrs'? Good heavens, Anna, I heard Mrs. Regehr had the cholera. Why ever did you stop there?"

"They were in need, Oma said, and so we stopped and gave them some soup and bread. The baby looked poorly and cried a lot. I don't know if the tiny thing will make it. Their little Nellie died of typhoid fever last winter, and now the mother is sick. We couldn't just pass them by."

"You didn't hold the baby, did you?"

"No, but Oma did. Listen, Katya, I'm sure I'm only tired. I couldn't have come down with cholera overnight."

"I am going to call on Dr. Bittner to check on you as soon as possible. Meanwhile, you are to stay in bed today, and we will see how you feel in the morning. Illness attacks a tired body much more quickly than a rested one."

"Katya?"

"Yes, child?"

"Would you check on Oma for me? She was very tired yesterday. I worried about her all night. She doesn't stop, you know, going here and there every day. I couldn't bear it if anything happened to her."

"Of course, I will check on her. If she is under the weather, I will insist that she stay in bed too."

Katarina knocked and quietly entered her grandmother's room. The woman lay beneath two quilts in the warmth of a July morning, shaking with fever.

"Oma!" Katarina's heart raced. "What is it?"

Oma muttered something, but her chattering teeth made it hard to understand her.

"I am calling Dr. Bittner immediately, Oma. You must

remain here until I return. Promise me."

The old woman did not argue, but nodded her head. Katarina gave her a drink of water, bathed her fevered brow and tucked her in again. She would forestall home remedies until the doctor had confirmed the trouble.

Katarina found Dr. Bittner on the way to Lichtfelde. He reversed his direction for her and followed her home to examine the patients. His diagnosis was not comforting.

"Anna does not exhibit traditional symptoms of any one of the diseases or ailments that have been ravaging the colony in the last years, but she is not strong. My suggestion is that you give her lots of water to drink and regular doses of this tonic for her constitution. She should remain in bed until I give instruction otherwise. Try to allow fresh air into the room, as long as she is not in the draft."

"What does she have, Doctor? Is it TB?"

"I rather doubt it. Possibly a strain of influenza, but we must watch against pneumonia. Even in warm weather, it can be deadly." He glanced at Katarina's desperate expression and added, "I think that with your nursing ability and Johann's advice and my experience, we should be able to pull her through."

Katarina sighed her relief, but with the next breath she asked, "And Oma?"

The doctor scratched his head as he returned his instruments to his bag. "Katarina," he said, "her prognosis is not so good."

Katarina clenched her hands in her lap and waited.

"Frau Peters is nearly eighty and not as able to fight off disease as those younger."

"But she has a strong constitution."

"Yes, she does, but even those with a strong constitution do not live forever. She has overextended her strength. She has exhausted herself in the care of others until the weakness has overtaken her. It doesn't look like cholera, possibly the same type of influenza Anna had earlier."

"What can we do for her?"

"I have given her a sedative. Make sure she drinks as much as possible and keep me informed."

"Poor Oma. I warned her. I told her she would not be able to come with us if she got sick. Why didn't she listen?"

The doctor pondered for a moment. "Did she agree to accompany you?"

"What do you mean?"

"My guess is that she knows she will not be allowed out of the country, or else she feels the journey and the new beginnings will be too much for her. Instead of worrying about it, she set out to use her time to help others. If she happened to come down with a dreaded disease, well, her decision would be made for her and you would not have to worry about her any longer."

"Dr. Bittner, you cannot mean that! Oma would not deliberately set out to infect herself."

"I'm not saying she did, but she was not afraid of the risk."

Katarina stood shaking her head.

"Come, Katya. It's not Oma who has made herself sick. The good Lord has allowed it, and He knows the end from the beginning."

"I can't take it in," said Katarina, thoroughly shaken. She promised the doctor she would do her best for both patients and watched him walk away, his shoulders bent from the weight of responsibility and the pain he saw every day.

"Janz writes that 639 emigrants from the Chortitza groups have been rejected on medical grounds, mostly trachoma," said Johann. "The inspections are extremely diligent."

"What do they expect from people who have been through hell?"

"Nicholai!"

"It's true and you all know it," he insisted. "Especially in Chortitza, where so many starved. Hardly a family remained complete and many have diseases. Isn't that right, Kornelius?"

"Yes, it is true. For those of us who lived through that, any place would be better. By the way," he addressed Katarina, "how are Anna and Frau Peters?"

"Anna is doing somewhat better, but Oma does not respond. It's as if she has lost her will to live."

"I'm not surprised," commented Nicholai. "What does she have to look forward to? Watching us leave?"

"We will not leave without her, Kolya."

"Oh come, Katya. We all know she won't be allowed to come."

"Could she not stay with Hannah? Then Susannah might be convinced to leave, knowing her mother was not alone."

Katarina shook her head.

ꙮꙮꙮ

"How are emigration plans progressing?" asked Philipp Cornies, now released from jail.

Benjamin Janz answered with cynicism. "Besides the medical fiasco, we are faced with the problem of Red Army conscripts. A number of families who should have left the country already have refused to leave without their sons who are in the army."

"What are you supposed to do about that?"

"Work a miracle," exclaimed Janz. "I have been speaking with the authorities in Kharkov and Moscow about this problem —Commissar Manzev in Kharkov is especially helpful, but he has confided to me that he may be sent to Moscow—and I believe they are listening, but I have no idea how long it will take to locate these young men and see them released from service, and then examined and passed. It is another major hurdle for us.

"The Canadian Board is also concerned with the number of medical rejections. I ask you, are we all sick now? People are being rejected for a thumbnail bruise caused by an errant hammer. Do the authorities possess no reason? This is a matter of life and death for us here and they quibble about bruises and broken fingernails."

"Can we expect any more help from abroad?" asked Cornies.

"*Ja, ja.* David Toews works untiringly from Canada. He has literally put himself on the line financially to assure that the money asked for by the CPR will be available. B. H. Unruh is also working from Europe. Some of our people have made it as far as England and there have been rejected for trachoma. They've been sent to a place called Atlantic Park in Southampton. Unruh is negotiating for them there."

"It sounds like there is no end to the hoops we must jump through. Do you still think it is worth the risk?"

"From time to time I am tempted to doubt, my friend, but I must not give in to it. I have been called, not only by the Union, but by God."

ꕥꕥꕥ

> *No further exodus is being allowed at this time. So many are rejected by the doctors and there is no place for them to go. I am doing all I can to find a solution to this problem.*

The note from B. B. Janz was read to the congregation of the Alexanderkrone Mennonite Brethren Church on a warm July morning, and immediately murmurs broke out in the assembled group.

That afternoon Johann, Katarina, and Anna sat in the

shade of the apricot trees. Katarina had baked zweiback, not as good as Oma's but much better than black bread. She would roast them for the journey. Now she and Anna sewed travel bags from flour sacks.

"Oma is asleep," said Katarina. "She seems better today, but her chest is still painful and she finds it hard to breathe."

Tears began to fall from Anna's eyes onto the rough fabric she stitched.

"Anna, what is it?"

"I shall miss her."

Katarina moved to her sister's side. "We will write letters. I'm sure the postal service will improve eventually.

Anna shook her head vehemently. "No, Katya. I don't think she's going to get better."

"We will pray that she gets better, Anna."

"I think God wants her to come home, Katie. I think he needs her now. We must let her go, but I am so sad about it."

"We cannot know the future, Änya," comforted Katarina, partly to deny Anna's words in her own heart. "God's way is best and we will see what that is. In the meantime, we needn't cry when Oma is here with us."

"Where is Nicholai?" asked Johann, thinking to change the subject to one more cheerful.

Anna sniffed and wiped her eyes. "He's off walking with Justina, I would assume. That's where he always is in his spare time these days."

"Hmm," said Johann. "I suppose it's better than sitting in the shade with his siblings."

"I don't know," said Anna. "I like nothing better. No matter where we end up, I shall always remember the smell of the warm breeze, the taste of the apricots, the peace of home and family. Today is a day of peace. I cherish it."

She gathered her sewing materials. "I am going to sit with Oma."

ജജജ

"He's gone again," said Paul Gregorovich. He had walked into Alexanderkrone pulling a cart of vegetables for the market.

Johann pretended to inspect the beans and potatoes. "What did he do now?"

"Can't say for sure, but the new mayor, the one you refused to work with, has had a streak of bad luck of late: memos and letters have gone missing enroute to Kharkov, village funds are pilfered, arrested men disappear from jail, things like that."

Johann's eyebrows went up. "Our friend has been busy."

"Yes, but they will not be amused if his part is proven. This may be the last straw, you know."

"He should have been more careful to hide his actions," said Johann, throwing a few choice new potatoes into a sack.

"I don't think he cares," responded Tekanin. "Besides us, he has no one, you know."

Johann silently picked out beans for soup and inquired about the price.

"For you, I have a deal," said Tekanin. The men laughed together, but their hearts continued heavy as they thought of their friend Grisha. He was on his own, partly by choice, partly because that was all that was left for him.

"Can you contact him?" Johann fished in his pocket for the ruble notes and paid Tekanin the required amount.

"That is doubtful. Pava and I have moved to a *kolcho* on the outskirts of Ackerman and I must report for work if I am to receive my allotted food allowance. I cannot wander off as I once did. All I know is that he passed through and bid me farewell, and the mayor is complaining bitterly about the troubles he is having."

Autumn drifted in on the heels of warm summer, and the year began to show its age. Schools opened again under the Communist agenda, and unfamiliar teachers stood at the front of the classes, spouting new and unwelcome ideologies.

"I have given up hope of opening the kindergarten again," said Katarina to Johann as they prepared for bed. "I received a letter from the village office that all private schools have been ordered to close."

"I'm sorry, Katya. You enjoyed that work through the last few years and helped many children to learn and take their minds off their problems."

"Yes, the kindergarten has been a help to them and to Anna and me. I had hoped to open it again until Christmas, but it is November already, and I don't know if it's worth the effort. I'm too tired to quibble with the mayor about it. Even now that we have better food and more of it, I can't revive my energy."

"Katya, are you ill?" Johann did a cursory examination, worry in his eyes. "Have you caught something? We have to be well enough to face the inspections that will undoubtedly come when we leave."

"I'm just under the weather. Too much worry and fear. I think the poor food we've eaten over the last two years may be catching up with us."

"Take time to rest when you are tired. That, as you told Anna yourself, is one of the best offenses against sickness."

"Yes, Dr. Sudermann," she teased, lying back on the pillow. It felt so good just to relax and lie down. A whole night ahead to regain her strength. She was sure she would feel better tomorrow.

ꙍꙍꙍ

"The VBHH has succeeded," exclaimed a jubilant Peter Dyck. "Benjamin, this government letter acknowledges our request to be exempt from direct participation in military affairs. One of our goals has been realized."

"Yes," said Janz. "I am aware of that and it is an answer to prayer, but I must persevere in the other mission to which I have been assigned, namely emigration. I head for Moscow again tomorrow."

"Perhaps this is the opportunity we've been waiting for, Benjamin. If we are allowed exemption from military involvement—"

"—direct military participation," corrected Janz.

"Yes, and if we are allowed to continue rebuilding our economy and creating our own markets, why are we still pushing for emigration?"

"We have good land here," added Dyck, "much better than in Canada. It only needs working and seeding."

Janz and Dyck were guests of the Isaak family that evening of December 22. Their discussion was interrupted by a knock at the door.

"A message for Benjamin Janz," said Mrs. Isaak, worry in her tone.

Janz felt his chest tighten. He rose and walked to the door. The messenger, a man wearing a black leather jacket, passed him an envelope and left.

He opened the envelope in the presence of the Isaaks and Peter Dyck.

"It is a summons," he said aloud. "I am to appear immediately at the State Political Administration, the GPU headquarters in Moscow. No reason is given."

"Ah, Benjamin, we will pray for you. We will contact as many people as we can and we will form a wall of protection around you. Go with that assurance in mind."

Janz rose from his chair wearily, then straightened his

shoulders and lifted his chin. "I have nothing to hide and I have the Lord God on my side. I will face them with confidence."

ꕤꕤꕤ

The *Gosudarstvennoe Politicheskoe Upravlenie*—the State Political Administration—headquartered in the building on Lubyanka 2. B. B. Janz stared up at the beautiful architecture, at the stone angel carved above the gable. He wondered what kind of angel would guard a place like Lubyanka. He knew personally men who had been taken to Lubyanka Prison. It was said that few who walked in ever walked out.

He comforted himself with the fact that he had not been officially arrested. He had, in fact, been trusted with the responsibility of presenting himself of his own volition. He had reasonable hope that when the secret police had questioned him, he would return to Kharkov, but there was also the chance that he would be arrested and incarcerated here. He counted on the prayers of his church family.

"Room 178." A stern clerk pointed down the hall.

Janz moved resolutely toward the room and knocked on the door.

"Enter."

His inquisitor sat in a chair behind a table. He directed Janz to the only other chair.

"State your name and address."

"Benjamin B. Janz, No. 4, Butovsky, Kharkov." He extracted the necessary documents from his briefcase to prove his identity.

"Why have you come to Moscow?"

"I have business here on behalf of the Union of Citizens of Dutch Lineage, sir, an organization approved by the government."

The man leaned forward over the table, his menacing scowl fixed on Janz. "You are here to meet with Alvin J. Miller of the American Mennonite Relief to scheme for the emigration of the Mennonites to America."

Janz strongly denied the accusation, but the man persisted in hammering home his accusation. Janz responded with his own persistence. Eventually, the man moved to the topic that Janz deemed his original concern: that of young Mennonite men requesting release from the Red Army in order to emigrate. For this Janz had facts.

"If I may show you the papers, sir, you will find them in order. The young men in question all belong to families who are indeed emigrating. Their names have been submitted to Red Army personnel during the summer, and all were approved for release. They have also been cleared by authorities here in Moscow."

"How do you know these things?" demanded the questioner.

"Because I personally transported the letter from the Revolutionary Military Council to the Foreign Commissariat."

"How can you prove this?"

"I have the envelope, which they stamped upon receipt." Janz fished around in his briefcase. "I cannot seem to find it."

"Show it to me!"

Janz calmed himself and looked once more, a prayer in his heart. "Here it is." He handed the stamped envelope to the man, who then took the entire contents of Janz's briefcase with him out of the room. Janz sat waiting, wondering what would happen next. He had done nothing wrong. He had given no false information, only given it in such a way as not to discredit the entire emigration process.

The door opened again, and the man stepped in and handed all the papers back to Janz. "All is in order," he said politely. "You are free to go."

Janz stood and faced the man. "You have put me under a severe interrogation here. Now it is my turn. What is your name?"

"Solovyov."

"Well, Comrade Solovyov, what is the opinion of your government? Do you not wish to see the poor Mennonites sent to America?"

"You have done everything on a legal basis, everything is in good order and I can only tell you to continue in this manner."

"But I would like your opinion so that I may avoid similar unpleasantness in the future."

"I cannot tell you more than what I have already said. Your business is in good order and you may continue your work. Good-bye."

Janz nodded and Solovyov stamped the entry permit so Benjamin could leave.

Janz was confused. What had brought this situation about? They said all was in order, but something or someone had tipped them off. He must not make any mistakes. He hoped he would know how to avoid them. He walked from the building without looking back and sucked in a deep breath of clean air.

As he walked to the train station, he considered his next goal. He would stay in Moscow over Christmas in order to meet with A. R. Owen of the Canadian Pacific Railway in order to try to arrive at an agreement. After all, there were a good number of Mennonites who could afford to pay their own passage to Canada. Surely the CPR would accept them.

Chapter 23

"Katarina." Johann called her name as he entered the house. "Ah, there you are."

She stood leaning on the table, gripping it with both hands.

"Katya, would you . . . Katya?" He rushed to her side, but not before she slipped to the floor in a faint.

"Katya!" He lifted her in his arms, carried her to their room and placed her gently on the bed.

She blinked at him as she came out of the faint. "What happened?"

"Shh, you fainted. Have you been feeling poorly today?"

"Not bad, just tired as usual. I think . . ."

"Katya, you must rest more. You don't show signs of TB or typhus or influenza, but your weakness frightens me."

Katarina did not meet his eyes. "Oma is so ill and Anna is not strong enough to care for her. I must keep going and I get tired."

"I will look after Oma. I must insist you rest."

"I'll try, Johann, but I'm sure I will be fine."

"How can you be sure?"

"Johann, I . . . I know the reason for my tiredness."

Johann paled, thoughts of disease and death swirling through his mind. He opened his mouth to continue his questions when the truth hit him, and he sat with his mouth open. Katarina reached out and pushed up his chin.

"You and I are going to be parents, Johann."

It took him a moment to process the announcement. He

jumped up from the bed, emitting a shout of excitement, then stopped. "Are you sure? How long have you known?"

"I am sure now. I only just realized what all the symptoms pointed to. I've been so wrapped up in everyone else's troubles that I have paid no attention to my own. But I know it now. Congratulations, Papa!"

He knelt beside the bed and stroked her face. "I can't believe it. We've waited so long, I had put it out of my mind. Imagine! We're going to have a son."

"Or a daughter."

"Katie, I don't care which it is. This is wonderful news." He kissed her tenderly and she smiled up at him with those deep green eyes that found their way into his soul. "Oh Katya, I love you."

Joy coursed through him as he thought of the future, and then fear hit him in the pit of his stomach.

"What is it?" asked Katarina.

"I was thinking of when this little one might arrive, and it dawned on me that we might be on our way to a new land. What will we do if the baby comes then?"

Katarina reached out and touched his face. "Babies come when they come, dearest. Let's not add that to our worries."

Her confidence relaxed him.

"Shall we tell Anna?"

Katarina nodded.

"Anna!" he called from the door of the bedroom. "Anna, come."

Anna appeared in the doorway, concern on her face. "What is it, Johann? Katya, why are you lying down? Are you ill too?"

Katarina patted the bed and bade Anna sit beside her. "You, my dear, are soon to be an aunt. I am expecting a baby."

Anna's mouth formed a perfect circle as she stared at her sister.

"Oh Katya! No wonder you have been so tired and out of sorts. You poor dear. And all the time it was the baby. Did you know for a long time already?"

Katarina shook her head. "I attributed some of the symptoms to the famine and our lack of proper diet. It's a relief to know the reason for my discomfort."

"May I go and tell Oma? We never know how long she will be with us, and I want her to be able to rejoice with us."

"Of course, Änya. You are ever the thoughtful one. I will rest for a bit, Johann's orders, and then I will look in on Oma too."

"I will cook supper tonight, Katya, in honor of your news."

As Katarina lay on her bed trying to relax, she began to think of the effects of her condition. She would be limited as to her energy when it came to packing, she would most likely be sick on the journey. If she did not take proper care of herself or if for some reason the baby came early, it could be born on the way, as Johann had suggested, or it could arrive when they reached Canada, a difficult beginning for a new mother.

In spite of her confident words to Johann, the possibilities frightened her. Perhaps if their names came up, they should postpone leaving until the baby was born. On the other hand, would the journey be any easier with a babe in arms? She turned her face into the pillow and tried to block out the heart-stopping anticipation and the shouting fears.

Nicholai arrived home from the mill as Johann returned from an errand in Kleefeld. They met at the door.

"Have you heard?" asked Nicholai.

Johann's forehead wrinkled. "How did you find out so quickly?"

"Well, from Mr. Baerg at the mill."

Johann shook his head. "How could he possibly know our personal secrets?"

"Personal secrets? Johann, what are you talking about?"

"About Katarina of course. About the baby."

"Baby?" Nicholai was completely confused.

"Katarina is going to have a baby, yes, but how did Mr. Baerg know?"

Nicholai's face broke into a grin, then he threw his head back and laughed until he almost lost his breath. "Johann, we are talking about two different pieces of news, life and death, actually."

Nicholai's laughter irritated Johann, along with the fact he still did not know what the other news was.

"Congratulations, Papa Johann," said Nicholai, pumping his brother-in-law's hand. "I rejoice with you both."

"What is your news, then?"

"My news? Lenin is dead."

"Lenin is dead?"

They stared at each other, then Johann opened the door and ushered Nicholai in ahead of him.

Katarina placed a bowl of soup on the table while Anna sliced bread at the counter.

Nicholai threw an arm around Katarina's shoulders and kissed her cheek. "Wonderful news, sister."

"Thank you." She couldn't keep the smile from her face. "Now what were you saying about Lenin as you came in the door?"

"He's dead," said Johann.

"Is he really dead this time, or is this more propaganda to lure us into false relief?"

"It is true, my skeptical wife. Kolya told me."

"And how did you find out, Kolya?"

"Mr. Baerg at the mill. He heard from the mayor himself."

"Yes, well," said Katarina, "we all know how he can be trusted."

Johann grimaced. "I don't think he would lie about this."

Anna had remained silent. She slipped from the kitchen and headed for Oma's room. They gave her a few minutes before they sat down for supper.

"What does this mean for us?" asked Katarina. "Will things ease or get worse? Who will take his place?"

"Stalin's already pretty high up in the Party," said Johann. "I'm sure he and his henchmen have already moved in. I don't know what the future holds, but it seems to me most of this *svoboda* was Lenin's idea. With him out of the way, I'm afraid the socialists may pull the reins tighter." He shrugged. "Who knows?"

ꕤꕤꕤ

"Do you know what Lenin's last words were?"

B. B. Janz sat with A. Ross Owen, Canadian representative for the Canadian Pacific Railway in Moscow. Owen had kindled a small fire to ward off the winter chill. He answered his own question. "He said, reportedly, 'The machine has got out of control.'"

"Rumors," said Janz. "Probably the words of one of my Mennonite brothers."

"I disagree. I think Lenin knew he had helped create a monster, like the *Sorcerer's Apprentice*, and he had lost control of it."

Janz shook his head. These North Americans tended to be melodramatic. "Back to our discussion and my proposal: allow the Mennonites into Canada who are able to pay their own way. All previous barriers to this proposal have been taken care of."

Owen pursed his lips and nodded. "I will submit your

proposal to my government for their consideration."

"Please remember, Mr. Owen, that while you are presenting and they are considering, our time of opportunity is passing. Many of my people have sold all their household goods and animals. They have passed preliminary medical inspections and their visas have expiry dates. Their lives hang in the balance, as it were, until there is an agreement with your government. Remember also that these people I speak of are potentially valuable citizens."

Janz stood, put his hat on his head and nodded farewell.

Owen stood as well. He knew there would be more meetings with this man until his purpose had been accomplished.

ꕥꕥꕥ

"I am happy for you, Katya," explained Susannah. "My only concern is that the voyage may be too hard for you in your condition."

"I cannot be the only expectant mother in these circumstances," responded Katarina. "Life carries on around and among us."

"No doubt you are correct, and I would vow to help you all the way if I were coming."

Katarina grimaced. "Susannah, do you still refuse to consider emigration? Think of your children."

"I am thinking about my children. We have a home and enough to eat, thank the Lord for the continued generosity of the American kitchen. I am exempt at this time from taxes, and have a little money if more should be required. Why would I now uproot Marianna and little Gerhard? Besides, I cannot leave my mother here, ill with TB. What do you expect of me?"

Marianna looked up from where she sat at the table, drawing pictures on a wrinkled piece of paper with the stub of a pencil. "Where are we going, Mama?"

"We are not going anywhere, Marianna. Tante Katie and I are just talking."

"Are you angry?"

"No, my dear, we are sharing our opinions."

"Do 'pinions hurt?"

Susannah raised her eyebrows and Katarina grinned.

"Where is your brother?" asked Susannah.

Marianna smiled too. "My bruvver is wif 'Nelius. He's alys wif 'Nelius." She drew a large, rather crooked stick man on her paper. "This is 'Nelius and this"—a smaller stick man—"is my bruvver."

"Very nice," admired Katarina.

"Why don't you go find your brother and play with him for a while?" suggested Susannah.

"I don't think so, Mama. I like to lissen to you and Tante Katie."

Susannah rolled her eyes. Retrieving a basket from the porch, she said, "Here Marianna. Go collect the eggs now, before the hens eat them."

The little girl slid off her chair and took the basket. She stopped in the doorway and looked back at the two women. "I hafta obey," she said, carefully pronouncing the new word, "but I think I will hear the 'pinions from outside. Grossmama says I have big ears wif little pitchers."

Katarina and Suse suppressed their laughter until Marianna left the house, and then they laughed until the tears ran down their cheeks.

"What a blessed girl," said Katarina, wiping her eyes. "I can hardly wait to be a mother."

"It's not all laughter," said Susannah, "but looking back, there is a lot of joy." She put an arm around Katarina's shoulders. "I think you will be fine, whether you have your baby here, on the journey, or in Canada. God's timing is always best."

"Thank you for your encouragement. Will you consider changing your mind about coming with us?"

Susannah shook her head. "As long as Mother is ill, I cannot leave her. If she were to be cured, I might change my mind, but that is not likely to happen. Besides, if I stay, I can keep Peter here with me and save you much worry about his future and well-being."

"I cannot reconcile myself to leaving Peter behind. I still hope he will be allowed to go."

Susannah did not answer.

"What about Kornelius?"

Susannah shrugged and looked away.

Katarina nodded and gave her a hug. "We will each maintain our own 'pinions for now, but I will be praying." She paused in the doorway as Marianna had done. "I'm not sure I want any of my loved ones staying here. I don't trust the future of Russia."

"We shall see."

"Yes. Good-bye for now."

As Katarina walked home she wondered how she would ever say good-bye forever to Susannah and her children, to Peter, to Hannah, to so many others who were determined or destined to remain in Russia.

ꕥꕥꕥ

Benjamin B. Janz traveled to the southern villages of the Molotschna in early spring of 1924.

"You need to apply for 'permission to return' for Anna and also for Peter. It is imperative if they are rejected by the doctors."

Katarina's freckles stood out against her pale face. "Where would they go? We would all have to return."

Janz inclined his head. "There are many difficult decisions to be made these days and this is one of them."

Katarina tried again. "Is there no chance Peter could be accepted?"

"Highly unlikely. I've seen the checks, the inspections. They are thorough."

Katarina leaned on the table, thoughts whirling in her head. She understood Susannah's decision to stay behind. This all seemed too difficult, too impossible.

Janz made as if to leave, and then turned back to Katarina and Johann. "Friends," he said, "work as if everything were up to you alone, and at the same time, rely on God because it is all up to him. Now, I must go. I have many people waiting for me at home, and children who hardly remember me. Little Martha knows me only as a stranger by the name of 'Papa' who visits occasionally. Let us pray that we will soon be allowed to start a new life in a new country."

Janz's home in Tiege overflowed with visitors. His wife, Maria, maintained the supply of weak coffee but could not offer food to so many visitors.

"What should I do, Brother Janz?" asked an elderly man. "My wife is not well, but I am afraid to stay here in this country."

Another asked, "If we take our names off the list, can we put them back on later when we are more sure what to do?"

"Here is a list of my family," said a young man from Ruekenau. "Their travel documents are all in order, but they expire in October. Will we be gone by then?"

Janz spoke compassionately with each one who asked for his help. He nodded humbly at those who came to scold him for his slowness in acquiring their freedom. "I must be prepared now to be the most hated man among my people," he had told his wife earlier, "for not being able to part the sea for all."

Maria Janz took note of her six children. The boys had

gone to sleep in the loft and little Martha slept in her parents' bedroom, but the girls, who slept on the pullout sofa in the parlor, could not go to bed until all the guests left. They sat leaning against the wall, yawning wearily.

Mrs. Janz closed her lips firmly and made more coffee. She would be a helpmate, not a burden. The children would survive. Once Benjamin left, they would have peace again. How she wished they could share that peace as a complete family. Perhaps someday. Perhaps in Canada.

ᛟᛟᛟ

"Katya?" Anna's cry of alarm brought Katarina, Johann and Nicholai to Oma's room.

"What is it, Ännchen?"

The old woman, who had been quietly wasting away before their eyes over the last number of weeks, pulled at her covers and tried to rise from the bed.

"Oma, shh. Oma, I'm here. Tell me what bothers you." Katarina prayed fervently while Anna cooled her grandmother's face with a wet cloth.

Oma cast troubled eyes around the room, finally settling on Katarina in recognition. "Katie! Katie!"

"Yes, Oma, we are all here. Tell us what is on your mind."

"Children, you must leave this place; you must emigrate."

"Of course, Oma. As soon as you are better, we will all go."

"No! Promise me you will go as soon as you are able. And don't look back when you leave Russia."

"We promise. We all promise."

Frau Anna Peters relaxed and blinked her filmy eyes. She looked at each face gathered anxiously around her and smiled tremulously. "I love you all. I will see you in heaven."

Her eyes flickered closed on her thin, fevered face and she

lapsed into semiconsciousness. Within an hour, the woman whose love and wisdom had carried them through many dark times, slipped beyond them. Anna cried in Katarina's arms and Johann knelt with them beside Oma's bed. Nicholai leaned against the wall, his shoulders trembling, his tears dripping onto his shirt front.

They stayed there until twilight, in the room filled with whispers of memory, floating from heart to heart and mind to mind. They talked softy of shared sorrows, and laughed at Oma's sharp wit. They felt her presence still, just beyond their reach.

"Grisha would be sad to know," said Anna. "He loved her very much."

Cleansing tears coursed down their cheeks as they bade farewell to the woman who had already gone. Johann went to fetch Cornelia Reimer to help Katarina prepare Oma's body, and Abram to build a casket.

They buried Frau Anna Peters in the new cemetery near the Juschanlee River, among the graves of others, old and young, who would never see the new world.

"I don't think she minds not seeing Canada," said Anna, kneeling in the dirt at the graveside. "Heaven will be so much better."

"The teachers are all being sent to Moscow again for training," reported Nicholai a few days after Oma's burial. "They are being told what to teach and how to teach it."

"And most definitely what not to teach," commented Katarina. "No religion whatsoever."

Anna shook her head. "Why are the Communists so afraid of Jesus? He died for them too."

"They don't believe in God." Nicholai said as he stood to leave.

"Where are you going, Kolya?" she asked. He winked at her

and she raised her eyebrows. "Walking with Justina again."

Nicholai smiled and left. Some time later he returned, with Justina. "Anna, would you like to walk with us?"

Anna's pale face lit up and she turned to Katarina.

"Of course, Änya," she said. "Take a shawl.

When they had gone, Katarina looked at Johann. "It was kind of Nicholai and Justina to invite Anna to walk with them, but the house is too quiet with just you and me. Could we go walking too?"

He smiled. "I would be honored, my dear." He took her hand, kissed it and pulled it through the crook of his arm. They walked through the garden and out beyond the orchard.

"Look, the tulips are in bloom. Oh Johann, how beautiful and brave they are."

They walked on through a field until they came to a small meadow. Katarina exclaimed in surprise. The meadow smiled with pale purple crocuses, their petals closed for the day. Katarina knelt to get a better look.

"They are long-stemmed. We will have a good growing season this year."

"The drought we once thought would never end is over."

"So the crocuses predict."

They started back, lingering in the sweet evening. The brilliant pink and orange of the sunset spread across the horizon and stretched into the sky behind them.

"I feel surrounded by God's love," whispered Katarina, not wanting to break the spell of the moment.

"I believe we are."

"What are we going to do, Johann? About Peter. And about Anna if she doesn't pass the medicals? The doctors are expected next week again."

"She's doing much better, Katya."

"I know, but what if . . ."

Johann sighed. "Look around you, Katarina Sudermann.

Do you not think the God who paints the sky each morning and evening can oversee the results of one girl's medical examination?"

Katarina stood still and watched as pink and orange blended and faded into serene blue. Finally she spoke. "I know God is in control," she said, choosing her words carefully, "but his plan may not be the one I wish and hope and pray for."

"Would you want something that was not in God's will?"

"I only want us to be together and free."

He took her arm and led her along the path through the orchard and back to the main road. "'Neither life nor death, neither angels nor demons, neither the present nor the future, nor any powers, neither height nor depth, nor anything else in all creation, will be able to separate us from the love of God that is in Christ Jesus our Lord.' Someday we will be with Christ in heaven—all of us together."

"I wish our journey could take us straight to heaven, instead of stopping in Canada first!"

"Katarina, think of it as a grand adventure."

They chuckled together, and each felt the peace that cannot be explained, the inner assurance that the One in whom they had put their trust would not fail them.

"Some reservations on the part of the previous doctor," stated the doctor making the examination of Anna. "I will need to do a complete checkup. Please step into the other room and the nurse will prepare you."

"May I stay with her?" Katarina had prayed long for Anna to overcome the trauma she had experienced on that day of horror almost four years ago. Mostly it seemed like a bad dream, but she did not want to leave her sister alone with a stranger who did not understand.

"Why would that be necessary? Is she not able to speak for herself?"

"She is quite able," returned Katarina, "but she has experienced things that have left her with a fear of strangers. I would prefer to be in the room with her. I will not interfere."

Frowning, the doctor said, "Very well, but hurry. There are long lines of people waiting."

The doctor's examination was thorough and professional, and Anna handled it well. She and Katarina rejoined Johann, Nicholai, and Peter as they awaited the doctor's decision.

"Seems well. No trachoma that I can detect. Anna Hildebrandt is fit to travel. See that she stays that way."

What an unreasonable comment, thought Katarina. Does he think we would endanger her in any way at this time?

Johann, Katarina, Nicholai, and Anna had now all been passed. Katarina had insisted they bring Peter along with them. She could not bear to part with him, even with Susannah's promise. It was now his turn with the doctor.

"How do you feel, young man?" asked the doctor, looking not at Peter but at the records. "You have not had previous medicals?"

"He had not planned to leave," explained Katarina.

The doctor turned to her. "Does this one need you to speak for him as well?"

"I'm sorry."

Turning back to Peter, he said, "Changed your mind about going?"

"Changed your mind about going?" repeated Peter.

The doctor glared at Peter. "No need to be sarcastic. Just answer the questions."

"Just answer the questions."

"Young man, I want to hear you say one of two things. Either you say 'I am not feeling well' or 'I am feeling well, thank you'."

"I am feeling well, thank you."

The doctor's eyes narrowed, but he continued his examination. “Hmm. Yes. Thin fellow. Why are you so thin? Have you been sick?”

“He’s been thin all his life,” volunteered Nicholai. “Takes after his mother, I’m told.”

The examination completed, the doctor said to Peter. “I find nothing physically wrong with you, young man, but your attitude could use some work.”

“Your attitude could use some work.”

These last words found the end of the man’s patience. “Out, all of you. Get out of here and out of the country. The sooner the better.”

Hearts pounding, the family gladly left the makeshift medical station. Their relief flooded over into lighthearted banter and jokes, but the relief would be short-lived. The Russian doctor had given them all a clean health report, but the Canadian examinations still loomed ahead.

Abram and Cornelia Reimer still waited in line. She suffered from trachoma, the painful eye disease that afflicted many of the Mennonites since the civil war, and the treatments had not so far helped her condition. Only time would tell.

ຮຮຮ

Through the long months, B. B. Janz waited for word from the Canadian Mennonite Board of Colonization and the CPR. Neither had sent any correspondence whatsoever. He worked mostly in Kharkov with frequent excursions to Moscow. He knew the way in his sleep already.

“Grant me patience and strength, O Lord,” he prayed. “May I live pleasing to thee this day.”

This day proved to be a day of soul-warming sunshine. It was the first of May, and Benjamin decided he might as well join the crowds as they celebrated May Day in one of the Kharkov parks. He smelled the heady perfume of myriad flowers in their kaleidoscope of color, and the sweet scent of new green leaves and grass. A glorious day. Yes, he would be thankful for this day, even though he wondered why his progress for emigration had melted like the winter snow.

Janz enjoyed the parade. It distracted his mind for a bit, and the music buoyed his heart. It had a certain spirit-lifting quality. Humming, he made his way back to his apartment and discovered there a surprise, a gift.

Chapter 24

The telegram addressed to Benjamin B. Janz read as follows:

> THE CANADIAN GOVERNMENT AGREES TO ACCEPT 5000—FIVE THOUSAND — IMMIGRANTS FROM RUSSIA ON CREDIT, AS WELL AS ADDITIONAL NUMBERS WHO ARE SELF-FINANCED.

"Five thousand! On credit!" Janz tucked the telegram into his jacket pocket, packed the few things he needed into his suitcase, and strode off to the train station. He must thank Mr. Owen. He had planned to travel to Moscow within a few days anyway.

ꙮꙮꙮ

"How long do we keep the cow?" Katarina skimmed cream off the milk in the pail and set it aside. "When and how do we start preparing ourselves?"

"I think it's time," said Johann. "Our neighbors are beginning to bring their possessions to the public auctions, or else they are holding private ones. Everyone is preparing to leave and there will soon be no one to buy."

"Johann, I'm afraid." She ran her hand over her growing middle in a protective gesture. "I often wake up in the morning thinking I am in my room at Succoth, that the last ten years have only been a dream."

"Don't wish that, *Liebchen*. Your last ten years include me."

"My cowardice is creeping up on me again. I have faced huge crises in the past and come through, with the Lord's help, but now I cannot seem to come to terms with this looming change."

"I have a hard time seeing the end of it too. For a time the fear of emigration kept me in denial of its necessity. I can't imagine myself in a country on the other side of the ocean, of starting a new life there."

They sat across from each other in the parlor. He reached over and took her hands. They leaned toward each other until their heads touched.

"We will survive this together," he said. "You help me and I will help you."

She sat back. "And who will help Susannah? I'm sure she would come if not for Hannah. I think she's afraid to stay, but she won't admit it."

"What would you do?"

"I don't know. I wouldn't leave my mother either. Her sister, Helena, is leaving as well."

They sat in silence, neither one of them finding a solution to Susannah's dilemma. Finally, Johann said, "I think we should sell the cow soon. Prices are dropping sharply with so many animals for sale."

"Wait until after Easter, Johann. I need milk and cream and butter so I can bake *paska*. And we need to color eggs. I also need to roast more *zweiback* for the journey."

"Make sure you hide them from your brother or you won't have any left when we leave."

"I don't know what will become of the Reimers. Cornelia's eyes aren't improving. I don't know if she will pass her medicals in time."

"Katya, if Benjamin Janz has his way, ours will not be the last train out of Russia. They may be able to leave later."

"Is Justina's family leaving too?" Anna asked Nicholai.

"Yes. They have all their papers in order."

"So do we. Johann made sure of everything, and God made me well again so I can get away from here too."

Nicholai watched her as she spoke. "Did you think we would leave without you?"

She returned his gaze. "Not really, but I didn't want to be the one to hold you back. Nicholai, I want to move far away from here and never come back. I would go to Paraguay or Mexico even, as long as I can leave."

Nicholai blinked in surprise. He had never heard Anna bare her soul to this extent. To her, Russia had become the dragon, the one who had breathed fire on her and scarred her soul, the one she expected at any time to return to finish the job. She would leave this place and its memories if she had to walk all the way.

"We are all going together, Anna—soon."

"Even Peter?"

Nicholai didn't respond.

"Peter has a clean medical report," she said, as if he didn't know.

"Anna, don't count on Peter."

"Kolya, don't tease."

"I wouldn't tease about this. The Canadian doctors will be looking for mental problems. Their government has declared that they will not accept anyone with mental deficiencies."

"But how can we go without Peter?"

"I don't know," said Nicholai. "We have to think of something, another plan in case this one falls through."

ꙮꙮꙮ

"Dietrich, we must have a plan in place in case they don't let Peter go to Canada." Maria had read the letter from Katarina many times over.

"Something tells me you have a plan already in mind." He smiled at her as she sat on the edge of the sofa. "How do you manage to mix beauty and brains as you do?"

"Dietrich, be serious. I need your help."

"I am serious, my love. Please hand me my crutch."

Maria allowed the laughter to bubble up. "If I pick up that crutch, I will bring it down on your handsome head. Now help me think. How can we help Peter?"

Dietrich sat back in his chair and laced his fingers together behind his head. "They might let him out of Russia if he is guaranteed support from the border on. Germany won't accept any more of the medical rejects. Lechfeld has a higher population than our country ever anticipated, and they will not let it get any higher."

"What do we know about Lechfeld?"

"It's not far from Schwandorf, actually. Used to be a military training camp. About four years ago it was converted into a relief center by German Baptists and a Bavarian Mennonite who gets support from America."

"Is it a temporary accommodation?"

"Depends. Some people find employment in the surrounding area while others work in Lechfeld itself."

Maria stood to pace the room. "Could we find employment for Peter there in advance? Do you think there would be something simple and repetitious he could do that would qualify him to go there?"

"I'm not sure, Mika, but it doesn't make any difference, because as I said before, Germany has declared its borders closed to any more medical misfits."

"Peter is not a misfit."

"Mika, you know what I mean. He is not mentally sound."

He saw a light come on in her eyes and waited for her to explain. "Why don't we talk to Herr Schmitt?"

"Fritz?"

"Yes, Fritz. He has contacts here in Berlin. I can't approach Mr. Unruh because he is involved with the unfortunate medical cases in Atlantic Park, in England. But you have acquaintances and friends in the army and the new government. Between you and Fritz, you should be able to pull a few strings."

"How many strings? I am sensing a whole ball of yarn, a tangled ball of yarn."

"We could guarantee Peter's care if they allow him out of Russia. Confirm our commitment to supporting him."

"And if Lechfeld says no?"

"Then we take him in ourselves. Dietrich, we have to try. Otherwise what are Johann and Katarina to do? They would have to stay in Russia, all of them."

They sat lost in thought, each on their own track.

"Dietrich?"

"Yes?"

"What would you think of moving back to Schwandorf? I miss it and I miss your family. We could visit Lechfeld also, and if Peter were accepted there . . ."

"Why do I feel like I should have gone for a drive this afternoon instead of staying home with you?"

ຣ໓ຣ໓ຣ໓

Ross Owen frowned at the telegram. "Seems too good to be true, Benjamin. I don't know what to think."

"Surely this communication is not sent without adequate consideration," replied Janz. "We have often had trouble with the Russians, but surely the Canadians are more united in their decisions."

Owen paced the floor of his office. "I do not wish to discourage you after all the ups and downs you have already experienced, but I have a feeling there is more to this than meets the eye."

Janz nodded. "I appreciate your honesty. I will be in contact."

Benjamin spent his time visiting officials in the Russian capital, finalizing the next wave of emigration. He sent word to the Molotschna that they should be prepared to leave by early June. He was not expecting the next blow to fall, but fall it did.

"Germany is not accepting any more immigrants." The official from the department of emigration reworded his statement. "There is no more leeway for medical rejections in Germany. No one can leave Russia unless they are proven absolutely healthy."

"What about Kharkov? What if we register there?"

"Kharkov and Moscow have both been approached by the German emissary. They are united in their stand."

Fine day for that unexpected achievement, thought Janz irritably. Now what? He would become the scapegoat for a failed plan, but that was not his primary concern. He believed his people must leave and that opportunity was swiftly passing by.

After leaving that office, Janz walked for several hours in the park, methodically reviewing his actions, digging for options, searching for an alternate plan. Desperate prayers for wisdom wove through his thoughts like strands in the backside of a tapestry. Nothing seemed clear to him. Loose threads hung confused, patternless.

Eventually, he walked to his place of accommodation and fell to his knees. "Oh my Father," he prayed brokenly, "has it come to this? Has it all been for naught? I did not ask for this task—thou knowest that—but I have done my best. Now I am at the end and I beg thee for guidance."

His prayers continued all night. At times he dozed, to be awakened by cramping muscles, and then he would pray again. About dawn, he lay down on the bed and fell into a light sleep. He awoke a couple of hours later with a name on his tongue.

"Manzev!"

He rose hurriedly and changed his clothing, splashed water on his face, combed his hair. He must not look desperate, even though he was. All the while he kept murmuring, "Manzev!"

Manzev, formerly Commissar of International Affairs and head of the Ukrainian secret police in Kharkov, welcomed Janz into his new Moscow office.

"Welcome, old friend! What brings you to my office today?"

Janz removed his hat and shook Manzev's hand. "Good to see you, sir. How are you enjoying your new location?"

"Have a seat, Benjamin. As you know, Moscow does not compare to Kharkov in natural beauty, but this position is a promotion in the Party."

Janz nodded.

"So what brings you here? Merely a social call?" The man raised an eyebrow.

"You know me too well for that, sir. I have long ago given up social involvements."

Manzev leaned forward on his desk. "Speak then."

Benjamin took a deep breath. "Comrade Manzev, when I last spoke with you at your Kharkov farewell, you said something to me that I have kept in my pocket."

Manzev raised the other eyebrow.

"You said, 'If you are ever in trouble, come see me.'"

"And you are in trouble?"

"Comrade Manzev, I am in great frustration with our government about this next emigration. My people are ready and waiting to leave, they have passed their medicals, their exit visas are in order, they either have their own funds or credit approved by the Canadian Pacific Railway. Now the government has again backed out of their promise. I am coming to you for help. There is no reason not to clear this emigration. We have been through all the particulars."

Manzev sat back and steepled his fingers. "Give me some time," he said.

Janz shook Manzev's hand again, firmly, and took his leave.

ꕥꕥꕥ

"Dietrich, Mika, I have a suggestion." Kristoph joined them in the parlor of his parents' home in Schwandorf, where they had recently returned to live.

"What great scheme have you cooked up now, little brother?" asked Dietrich.

Kristoph refused to react to his brother's belittling statement. He probably didn't even realize how it sounded. Perhaps Mika did, but she was too much in love to think about it for long. Which was why he, Kristoph, must go away. He could not daily witness the love between the two. It hurt him too deeply.

"I have decided to go to Berlin, to enroll at the university there. Pursue my education, as it were. I would gladly contact some of the officials and army personnel involved in gaining permission for Peter Hildebrandt to come here."

Maria's face brightened. "Really? You would do that for us? But why are you going to Berlin when we have only just returned here?"

"I need to carry on with my life. If you point me in the right direction, I will do my best in this matter."

"You shall do wonderfully," exclaimed Maria. "You were

so confident and persevering when we were searching for Dietrich. I'm sure you will be able to accomplish it, if anyone can. Dietrich, will you contact Fritz Schmitt? Oh, thank you both for your concern and help."

"Anything for you, my lady," said Dietrich.

Kristoph left the room without them noticing. His heart felt heavy in his chest. It was best that he go away for a time. He sighed and went to pack his things.

ଓଓଓ

"The cow sold for eighty-five rubles." Johann dropped the money on the table and Katarina stared at it.

"Only eighty-five rubles?"

"It's supply and demand," said Johann. "Too many people need to sell now, so the price comes down. That is capitalism."

"Well, I suppose it's better than the Communist solution: we are forced to sell and the government takes it all."

"Another group of doctors has set up in Neukirch. We have to go through the inspections again. They are extremely stringent."

"What if Peter doesn't make it?"

"Katarina, let us leave that in the hands of God. You know Susannah would keep him."

"Yes, but if she does decide to go, Peter will deter her."

"We have prayed about it, Katya. Let us trust now." He stood to leave, then patted his pocket. "Oh, I can't believe I forgot. A letter from Germany."

"From Mika?" Katarina dived at the letter and opened it with trembling hands. She began reading aloud, then forgot herself and read silently, her face flushing with the contents. Looking up at a curious Johann, she said, "God has answered our prayers."

"What? How?"

She handed him the letter and began explaining at the same time. "Mika and Dietrich wish to take Peter. They are working on getting permission from the government, on the condition that they support him for the rest of his life, and that they meet him across the border in Latvia. At Rezekne."

Johann read the letter himself. "This is truly a most unexpected answer to an impossible situation. I find it hard to believe. Mika and Dietrich. Do you think they can do it?"

"Apparently Dietrich's brother in Berlin is making all the final arrangements. He is sending documentation to us." She bit her lip to keep the tears away, but a few escaped. "It will be hard for Peter; he doesn't really know them."

"If God arranged this, surely he will help Peter to adjust. We need to discuss it with Susannah."

"Of course. As soon as possible."

The medical examinations at Neukirch did not go well for Peter. Physically he passed, but the doctors saw through his mental limitations. They declared him unfit to emigrate and denied him an exit visa.

"But we have a promise from someone who will take him in Germany. He will travel with us to Rezekne and the couple will meet him there."

"I have no official documentation from the German government to that effect," replied the doctor. "I cannot allow him to go."

Johann sputtered. "Fine. I will find the necessary documentation."

Outside the medical tent, he met Katarina, and she knew from the expression on his face the results of Peter's medical. "Did you show them the letter, Johann?"

"It is not official. They need government documents."

"Then we will get them. We still have time, possibly as much as a month."

"That is not a lot of time for government bureaucracy."

"It is all the time we have."

Susannah, who had walked along with them at Katarina's plea, returned from her examination with positive results. "Too bad we aren't going," she said. "We all three passed with ease."

"Peter didn't."

Susannah digested that. "Are either of you surprised? His passing of the previous test made me uncomfortable. It merely signified that you would have to go through the rejection sometime in the future, most likely in a place where there was no one to take him in. Now we know he stays with me."

Katarina glanced at Johann and then said, "Susannah, we need to talk about Peter. One day you may wish to emigrate as well, but Peter will not be allowed to. By keeping him, you sacrifice your freedom to leave."

"I have thought of that. I have made my decision. Remember my mother?"

"We . . . we have received a letter from Mika and Dietrich. They have offered to meet us at the border, and to take Peter to live with them, providing we can convince the authorities here to let Peter travel that far with us."

"To Germany?"

"To Germany."

Susannah was silent.

"Susannah," said Katarina tentatively, "if by some miracle your mother were healed and Peter allowed to go to Germany to live with Mika and Dietrich, if all that was somehow achieved, would you come with us?"

Susannah sighed heavily. "*If* can be a dangerous word."

"But would you?"

"I . . . I suppose I would consider it, yes, but it won't happen, so that's the end of it."

They walked through Neukirch at a moderate pace to

accommodate Katarina; her gait became more ungainly every day. Since they were in Neukirch, Susannah decided to stop at her sister's house.

"I haven't seen Helena in months, with all our sickness and her preparations. She will also be in the process of selling her possessions. It will be an ordeal for her, with four children to care for."

"The older ones are not babies anymore, Susannah. They can help her."

"Yes, but without a husband to talk to, to lean on, the task will be overwhelming."

"We will stop at Johann's uncle's, just across the street. Call us when you are ready to return home."

They parted in the street and Susannah knocked at Helena's door. Marianna and little Gerhard stood beside her, waiting.

The door opened and Helena met them with cries of relief. "Oh, you have come. Someone has come." Instead of inviting them inside, she came outside. Susannah's children cowered behind her skirts and began to whimper.

"Helena! What has happened?"

"Gretel and Abie! They have been rejected! We are not allowed to leave!"

"Why?" asked Susannah, her arms around her sister, trying to calm her. "Trachoma?"

"No. Nothing that common. They have smallpox. Neta and Jake are over at Langemann's so they don't get it too. We are supposed to be ready to leave. What am I to do?"

Susannah calmed herself first. "Lena, I am going to take my children across the street. Johann and Katarina are there. Then I will come back and we will talk."

"Oh, hurry, please. I am beside myself."

Susannah ran across the street and back in no time. She let herself into her sister's house and found her weeping at the table. "Helena. We must be strong now and discuss this."

Helena wiped her tears, but others always came in their place. "I don't know what to do."

Susannah had been thinking quickly. "I will take Neta and Jake to stay with me. We are not far away, but they cannot be near Gretel and Abie. They are old enough to understand."

"Neta's nine and Jake is only five."

"What does the doctor say about Gretel and little Abie? How serious are their cases?"

Helena pressed the hanky against her eyes again and sobbed. "Bad. I don't know if they will pull through."

There were no words to comfort. Susannah sat beside her widowed sister, waiting for the wave of sorrow to wash away for the present. When Helena had caught her breath, she said, "Susie, I know this much: I cannot go. I must stay here with my children, whether they live or die, but I want for Neta and Jake to experience freedom, to have the opportunity to live in a new country. I want you to take them to Canada."

"What do you mean? I am not emigrating. You know that. I have our mother to care for."

Helena grasped Susannah's hand so hard she winced. "Susie, think! You are staying behind to look after our mother. Now I have to stay behind to look after Gretel and Abie. That means my other two, and you and yours, are denied the opportunity to go.

"I cannot leave my children," she choked again on fresh tears, "so I must stay. I will take Mother here, or at least very near here until the children recover, and you, Susie, must take my Neta and Jake, and your two young ones, and go to freedom."

Susannah stared at her sister in disbelief. "How long have you been planning this?"

"It only now became clear to me, and then you knocked at my door in confirmation."

"I cannot be that selfish. I will stay also and we will help each other look after our children and our mother."

"No! Susannah, listen to me. Please! Take my children to Canada, far from this place. That is the most loving thing you could do for me." She blew her nose and cleared her throat. "Mama and I will get along fine. She will regain her strength given time to rest. And then, if my little ones leave me, we will have each other."

Susannah shook her head in bewilderment.

"Think, Susie. It's the most sensible way."

Susannah rested her head in her hands, elbows on the table, and allowed the disturbing, frightening thoughts to swirl and gel. Slowly, she saw the painful wisdom of her sister's plan. In a hoarse whisper she said, "I will do it, Lena. For you and for your children. I will go." She continued to shake her head as she walked across to collect her children and her sister's.

"I will take them now," she told Helena. "We are all to report to Halbstadt for more medicals on May 31. They need to be with me. Say good-bye to them now, and we will come again to see you before we leave. I promise. We will find a buggy to bring Mother, if you find a temporary place for her to stay."

"There are many places vacant."

Johann and Katarina distracted the children and promised them adventures in the future. They did not tell them their next good-bye would be their last. There was time for that yet.

Neta kept looking back at her mother as they led her away to Alexanderkrone.

ജജജ

The required documentation allowing Peter to travel arrived from Berlin via diplomatic courier. Katarina thanked the Lord it had come in time.

The households of emigrating families took on a beehive quality. Katarina baked and sewed while Johann traded and auctioned. Then Benjamin Janz sent word that the emigration would be delayed:

> *The passports of the young people have been sent back to Moscow for some reason. We must postpone our departure until these documents are returned. I will contact you as soon as the way is clear.*

"We have been overlooked again," some said.

Other's comments were more pointed. "That Janz, always trotting back and forth from Kharkov to Moscow like a self-proclaimed dignitary, while we are left here with hardly a roof over our heads."

"We cannot live like this anymore. Where is Janz hiding now while we wait again?"

Johann stood up for his friend whenever he could, but bitterness spread among the impatient and disgruntled emigrants.

ཆཆཆ

When Johann, Katarina, Susannah, and their entire entourage boarded wagons headed for Halbstadt on May 31, they wore their best clothes.

"We've never had our photograph taken," said Susannah.

"Nor had I until I went to work at Succoth," said Johann. "A photographer was invited down from time to time."

Katarina smiled at that. "I used to hate it when we had to pose for pictures. Mika loved it, of course. Said we needed to be able to show our children how we looked in our youth. I always said I hoped to improve with age."

Johann winked at her and she blushed. Seven months of pregnancy had only added a glow to her features, he thought.

He gave her a seat with a lean, but the journey would tire her anyway. He wondered why they bothered to put Peter through the strain of another inspection, but Katarina had insisted. When they received permission to take him along to Germany, he must at least be declared physically fit.

Benjamin Janz mingled with the crowd from the south villages who had come up to Halbstadt for what they hoped would be the last inspections before the actual departure. Johann spoke to him while waiting in line at the medical facility.

"What have you heard regarding our departure date?"

"We still await the return of the young people's passports," he said, "but thanks to an old friend in Moscow, the second group has been cleared to leave this week. God willing, your turn will come soon."

"I appreciate what you are doing, Benjamin, and I am sorry about the attitudes and sharp words of some of my neighbors."

Janz shrugged his shoulders. "When people are backed into a corner or find themselves grasping the end of their rope, then the blame flies like the contents of a manure spreader. I try not to take it personally."

"You are a strong man."

Benjamin eyed him. "I have a strong God. Without faith I could not continue, but I must move on; there is much to do."

"We have been cleared to go!" Johann burst through the door of his home. "Katya! Katya!"

She ambled out of the bedroom where she had been sewing bags for the roasted zweiback.

"We are to be in Lichtenau at the station on June 23. Katarina Sudermann, we are going to America!"

"Canada," she corrected.

"I will run over and tell Susannah. Kornelius will help her get ready."

After he left again, Katarina lowered herself carefully into a chair and sat there thinking. She looked around her at their house. It wasn't stately Succoth—she had already been forced to relinquish her hold on her old home in Crimea—but it had been home for almost five years. It was comfortable, it was familiar. To what were they heading? They had no idea where they would end up, although Uncle George had sent a vague promise to look after them.

Anna appeared in the doorway with Nicholai, both wide-eyed and excited.

"We are leaving," he said. "In a few days."

"Katya, are you feeling ill?" asked Anna.

Katarina shook her head and reached out her hand for help. "No, Anna, I was just overwhelmed by the magnitude of our decision." She grasped Anna's hand and pushed herself out of her chair.

"It is an enormous decision, sister," answered Anna, "but that is the direction our journey takes us on from here. We cannot stay, we cannot wait. We can only go forward. I will help you. Don't worry."

Katarina dropped the sack she had been sewing and wrapped her arms around Anna. "Thank you." She pulled a somewhat reluctant Nicholai into the embrace as well. "We are going together; we shall survive."

Nicholai pulled away. "We will do more than survive. I can hardly wait to get to Canada."

"Yes," said Anna coyly, "apparently Justina's family is going as far as Winnipeg. Her older brother went on ahead of them."

Nicholai stood tall at nineteen years of age. Katarina was proud of him. "I would find it difficult, almost impossible, to go without her," he said. "I mean to marry her one day."

His sisters grinned.

The emigrants had been instructed to arrive at the Lichtenau station by noon on June 22.

Johann and Kornelius drove the rented horse and wagon to Susannah's in Lichtfelde the afternoon before and loaded up her things. Her sister's children, Neta and Jake, stood solemnly watching the activity.

"Here you go, Jake," said Kornelius, throwing the boy a sack of bedding. "Neta, could you look after Marianna and Gerhard for Tante Susie while we pack?"

The children moved eagerly to help.

Susannah watched the children out of the corner of her eye as she worked, wondering how they could carry on with such a load on their hearts. The farewells at Neukirch the day before had been heart-rending and exhausting. They had lost their little brother, Abie, and Gretel's life still hung in the balance. At least Grandmother Hannah had been there with their mother. She would be company now that they were gone.

They're not the only ones, she reminded herself. Many families had made last-minute adjustments, sending young men ahead to avoid the draft, or sending children with relatives until the parents had been cleared of trachoma or whatever disability prevented their departure. They would meet again soon, they said. They hoped.

When packing was completed and all the rest left behind for Helena and Hannah, Susannah's expanded family climbed onto the wagon and rattled back to Alexanderkrone.

Katarina awaited them in some excitement. Now that the first shock of reality had hit, she tried her best to adapt. She would not dwell in the past; she would remember dear Oma's words. Five years ago, Katarina had said her good-byes upon leaving Succoth. She had knelt at her parents' grave in the little cemetery beside the chapel, and bade a tearful farewell to her home.

Now, here in Alexanderkrone, she had been forced to bid farewell to Mika and *Aufwiedersehn* to her dearest Oma. There had been more than enough separations for one lifetime. From now on, she would look forward. She was going to Canada. She would learn to speak English, and so would the child she carried.

All along the street, people were packing and shouting instructions and crying. Abram and Cornelia Reimer stopped by to bid farewell, promising to follow as soon as the authorities granted permission. Katarina thought Cornelia would willingly have climbed into a box if she could have gone with them, but Abram stood strong by her side, his arm around her waist. They planned to go as far as Ontario when their turn came. Katarina prayed it would come soon.

The next morning, although bleary-eyed, all of them were ready to leave. They had waited long enough.

As Johann's wagon prepared to pull away from their little house, a voice called his name.

"Johann! Wait!"

Chapter 25

Johann glanced around him and noticed a figure walking toward them.

Paul Gregorovich. His heart lurched.

He pulled back on the reins, handed them to Katarina and jumped from the wagon. The two men approached one another, high emotion in their faces.

"Well, old friend," said Paul, "You are really going then?"

"Yes, we are really going. I have had my doubts from time to time, but I believe this is best for my family."

Paul nodded and shuffled his feet in the dust of the street. "Good day to travel."

"Yes. Warm and sunny. Listen, have you heard anything from Grisha?"

Paul shook his head. "No, nothing. I have a feeling I never will." He cleared his throat. "When do you leave Lichtenau?"

"Monday; tomorrow. The train cars are there already. We are all to assemble today so we don't have to wait for stragglers."

"Well, I will let you go then. Safe travels. I hope the promised land is what you expect."

They stood for an awkward moment. Of what importance were mere words at such a time of parting? They clasped each other in a strong embrace and clapped each other on the back.

"Take care, my brother," said Johann, a tear falling unbidden from each eye. "My regards to Pava."

Paul sniffed and blinked, his voice betraying him. "I . . . I will." He strode over to the wagon. "All the best, Katarina. Good-bye, little Anna."

Anna, uncharacteristically brave, reached down and threw her arms around Paul's neck. "Good-bye."

Nicholai had jumped off the back of the wagon when he saw Paul arrive, and now stepped forward. "Thank you for your friendship, Tekanin."

Paul returned his strong handshake and smiled. "You marry that girl and make a good home for her in Canada."

Nicholai grinned.

Paul sighed and looked again at Johann. "Good-bye," he said. Then he turned away and walked briskly down the road, his boots raising puffs of dust in the morning sunshine.

Johann climbed up into the wagon again and clucked to the horse. Katarina slipped her arm around him. He tried to blink his eyes clear. Time to get to Lichtenau. No looking back.

Johann and Katarina and company arrived in Lichtenau before noon. Even now, the station yard was crowded. At nightfall, the women and children created room on the wagons to sleep, while the men bedded down underneath. Katarina assumed most people were too excited to sleep anyway.

Tension fairly crackled next morning as more and more wagons pulled into Lichtenau to bid farewell, and to reclaim conveyances and the animals that had been used to pull them.

It was blisteringly hot and dry. Johann kept his eye on Katarina, who kept hers on Anna. Kornelius hovered around Susannah until she requested sternly that he relax and allow her to do the same. Nicholai, with Peter nearby, sat with Justina in the shade of some poplar trees, talking in low tones, their excitement thinly concealed.

"We are thirteen hundred people for fifty cars." Johann figured. "That would be about twenty-eight per car."

"The windows are very small and high," commented Katarina, beginning to feel claustrophobic.

Susannah, Gerhard on her hip, whispered in her ear. "Katarina, just breathe deeply when you feel closed in. Exhale slowly and think of the wind blowing across the steppes, free and wild."

Katarina sent her a look of gratitude.

"I've volunteered as representative for our train car," said Johann, "and I will also be on the train committee."

"Am I supposed to be surprised?" she answered with a smile.

"Time to board. You and Susannah stay together with the children. Our car is number 26. Kornelius and Nicholai will look after the luggage. I need to help move people."

The boxcars stood on the track, awaiting passengers. The car representatives moved from group to group, calling out names and dividing the people among cars. Johann, with three other car representatives, VBHH representative J. J. Thiessen, and an advocate from the Canadian Pacific Railway, made up the train administration. Thiessen, from Tiegenhagen, would go as far as the Russian border.

"Look how they organize themselves," said one of the government officials watching the procedure. "I expected total chaos today." Katarina smiled to herself when she heard his statement. If the Mennonites were anything, she thought, it was organized.

"Nicholai, Kornelius." Johann approached the two as they waited to board their car. "Talk to our car members and gather some coins so the car can be washed out before everyone climbs on."

Thankful for something to do, the two men arranged for the washing of the car.

"Cleanliness is next to godliness," said Susannah to Katarina as they waited for the car to be cleaned out.

"I'm glad they are doing it; smells still bother me sometimes."

"I hope they finish soon. I just want to crawl on and sit down. It is fearfully hot out here in the sun and the children are nervous and fidgety."

Katarina worried that Anna's fragility would create problems, but such worries seemed unfounded. The girl entertained Susannah's brood, visited with Nicholai and Justina, and even found a few friends her age from Alexanderkrone and Lichtfelde.

Katarina and Susannah made their way slowly through the throng. Susannah carried Gerhard and Anna held Marianna's hand tightly. The inside of the car dried quickly in the heat with both side doors open, and the women and children soon climbed aboard, along with the others in their group. Boards had been nailed to the walls of the cars to form bunks. Katarina claimed one next to Susannah and sank down onto the hard boards with gratitude.

His responsibilities taken care of, Johann also boarded the train. Kornelius accompanied him, but Nicholai was nowhere to be seen.

"Don't worry about him," Johann assured Katarina. "Justina is in car number 32 down the line behind us. I imagine he will know his way back and forth. Where is Peter?"

"He is here."

Most of the travelers had already found their places and a strange hush fell on the crowd. A choir from one of the area churches began to sing, but the Russian soldiers stopped them. Benjamin B. Janz, dressed in a light colored suit and hat, climbed the step to the deck of car number 25 and stood in the entrance.

"Brothers and sisters," he said, his voice carrying over the crowd, "the time has come for us to bid one another farewell. This time of waiting has been a tremendous trial for many.

Behind us we leave loved ones, familiar places, memories of horror and memories of better times. Ahead, we envision some difficulties, yes, but also a whole new life in which to serve and praise our great God, to whom all glory belongs. Let us beseech the Lord for traveling mercies and courage for the days ahead, both for those leaving and for those remaining behind."

Some of the soldiers began to make their way to Benjamin Janz to put an end to this public speech, but when Janz began to pray, they stopped where they were and waited until he finished. Then he waved a hand and stood down from the train.

"God's blessings," he cried.

The train clanged and banged and then, very slowly, began to move. People stood in the open doorways, waving, weeping, hanging on as the train picked up speed. No singing had been allowed, but spontaneously, both groups of people joined together in the hymn, *Now Farewell to my Beloved Homeland*. Harmonies filled the air, mingling with the smoke of the engines and the tears of the people. Handkerchiefs waved as car after car rolled down the track toward Alexandrovsk at the edge of the Chortitza Colony.

Anna also stood near the door holding Marianna safely against her. It was a gloriously sunny Monday morning as they pulled out of Lichtenau Station. "We are going to freedom," Anna whispered.

Marianna looked up at her. "Freedom," she repeated. "Freedom."

Susannah lay on the bottom bunk with Gerhard, who had fallen fast asleep. She stroked his plump cheek and brushed a tuft of blonde hair from his eyes. She thought of her husband's soft blond hair and the blue eyes that could look straight into her heart. She remembered how he had enjoyed Marianna as he recovered from the typhus.

"Your Papa never knew you," she whispered to little Gerhard as he slept. "I will tell you all about him as you grow, and perhaps you will be like him. You certainly look like him." She pulled her son close to her chest, her tears falling on his head like a sacrifice for which she'd had no choice.

She became aware of someone next to her and turned to see Kornelius sitting on the floor beside the bunk. He looked with concern at her tear-stained face. He reached out a hand to wipe her tears but stopped and pulled it away again. They held each other's eyes.

Such a kind man, thought Susannah. Kind like Gerhard, but certainly not as handsome. No one can compare with Gerhard. But I have a whole life ahead of me. What will I do alone in a strange country with four dependents? Is kindness enough to live on? Could I learn to love him?

She smiled and he offered her his handkerchief. "Gerhard finally fell asleep," she whispered.

"Yes. Such a fine little man."

She stroked her son's cheek until she herself fell asleep, under the watchful eye of a kind friend.

Anna joined Katarina on her bunk. "How are you feeling?"

"Not too bad," said Katarina. "I'm glad they leave the doors open. The fresh air helps."

"The landscape is changing already," said Anna. "More willow thickets and poplar bluffs. More trees, and the land is not so flat anymore. Look, Katya. There's a windmill like we have at home—I mean where we used to live. It's not our home anymore."

"Russia has been our home all our lives. We will miss it."

Anna remained silent for a while. "Succoth was home. Alexanderkrone was never really home. Succoth is gone forever, so I can dream about my new home. Canada. I wonder how it will be."

Katarina sighed. "They say Ontario is quite nice, but farther west the land is very flat. Not many trees."

"Well, the steppes don't have trees, and people live there. I think it will be lovely."

"You are lovely," laughed Katarina. "I've been so worried about you and now you look as healthy as ever."

Anna smiled and leaned into the wind.

The train slowed to a stop at a small station in a lush green valley several hours north of Chortitza. Johann stood and walked to the open door. "Find your teakettles," he directed. "Hot water will be available at the station. Please do not wander away from the train. Necessary stops should be taken care of immediately. The train waits for no one."

As soon as the car slowed enough, Johann turned to wink at Katarina and then jumped off to find the other train leaders and direct the people to water and privacy—men on one side of the tracks, women on the other.

"Anna, help me down," said Katarina. "I thought we'd never stop, all this jiggling and rocking. Will you help Suse watch the children? I will be right back."

She excused herself through the press, and people moved out of the way for her, reading the urgency in her face. The women then took all the children to the trees and meanwhile, teakettles steamed with boiling water. Kornelius, Peter and young Jake joined them from the other side of the tracks and each took cups of tea.

"Mmm. Even on a hot day, this goes down smooth." Kornelius smiled at Susannah.

"Smoove," crowed Marianna, and they all laughed.

"Moove," copied Gerhard, wanting some of the attention too.

Neta reached out and tickled him. She missed little Abie.

Johann was already moving through the crowd. "Back to

the train now," he ordered. "Time to go, everyone. We will stop again later."

Katarina slept after that, finally giving in to the exhaustion of the hectic predeparture days. Anna and Neta sat on the bunk with her, but neither of them could sleep. They sat by the window again and commented as quietly as they could about the sights passing swiftly by their eyes.

In a dim corner of the car, on the floor along the wall, sat Peter. He looked no different there than he had in Susannah's home, in a world of his own.

Eventually, the rocking of the train lulled the girls into sleep as well and the car became quiet.

"Katya." Anna gently shook her sister awake. "I'm sorry to wake you, but I think you might want to get up for a bit." Her eyes shone with a secret.

Katarina blinked and pushed herself into a sitting position. "Where are we? I can't believe I didn't feel the train stop."

"You were sleeping soundly. We are in Feodorovka and will be here long enough to cook supper at the station. Come, Katya. I'll help you down."

Katarina clambered down. The side doors were open most of the time, and she was feeling more settled. She wondered why Anna was in such a hurry if they had time here.

Johann stood at the side of the car helping individuals off, and when he saw Katarina, he smiled broadly. She grew more suspicious. Were they planning some trick? She accepted Johann's help and the quick kiss he gave her as he set her on the ground. She walked toward the station, teakettle in hand, and someone called her name. A voice she had not heard for a long time.

Chapter 26

"Katarina Sudermann!"

She turned in the direction of the voice and dropped her kettle. "Agnetha! Wilhelm! How did you get here? Were you in Lichtenau? There were so many people."

They laughed and cried and hugged. "Let's make supper together and then we can talk," suggested Agnetha.

"We came up to Feodorovka on a passenger train in the afternoon," Agnetha said as they mixed the biscuits. "Wilhelm thought with the extra distance from Crimea, we may as well come this far in comfort, but now we join you. Car number 24."

"Oh Agnetha. I knew you were planning to leave this year, but with all the craziness of the last weeks and months, I never dreamed we would travel together."

"I know. Too much on our minds. Katarina, look at you! How are you?"

"I have been quite well, although right now I am tired. I haven't even spent one night on the train, and I'm exhausted."

Agnetha nodded. "Yes, but you have been preparing for a long time already. Now that you can do no more, it catches up with you."

"I hope I don't have to pay too dearly. I need my strength to help Susannah with the little ones."

"How many does she have?"

"Two of her own and two of her sister's—did you hear about her Gerhard?"

Agnetha nodded. "Very sad. So much for her to suffer."

"He was taken before little Gerhard was even born. The boy never met his father. The older two are her sister's children. Helena's husband was killed by the Machnovitz, and then her younger two came down with smallpox shortly before we were to leave. Little Abie died before we left, and we don't know about Gretel yet."

Unshed tears glistened in Agnetha's eyes.

Katarina continued. "Susannah was determined to stay back, partly because she held a slim hope that Gerhard would return, but mostly to care for her mother who has TB. In the end, Helena took their mother, since she could not leave her children."

"There are many such stories," said Agnetha as she mixed biscuits. "I know of a family who left their son behind. He was very sick and not expected to live, and the family's name came up, you know, and they didn't know what to do. If they stayed, they gave up their opportunity to get out."

"Don't tell me they left their sick child."

"They left him with a relative. My heart broke when I heard it. The wife nearly lost her mind, but her husband was determined to go. He had a hard time during the civil war and couldn't leave soon enough. I don't know how she will ever live with it."

Katarina was silent, putting herself into that horrendous situation. "I would rather die myself. Even leaving Peter with Maria and Dietrich is going to be heart wrenching."

"I know. These are times of great tragedy all around." Agnetha placed the mounds of dough over the heat. "The separation of families has to be the worst."

Katarina looked around her. "I wonder where Anna is. She always helps me."

"I told her to go visit with Sarah and Tina. They were all a little shy at first, but I think by now they will be having a wonderful time. Our David doesn't mind keeping an eye on Peter either. Anna looks well."

"She has been fragile during the last years. She—Agnetha, I hate to speak about it—"

"Then don't. I'm pretty sure I know what you are going to say. Many women and girls were molested at the hands of bandits and soldiers. Why sweet Anna? How is she now?"

"I don't understand it at all. The journey should be wearing on her, but she has remained healthy. She is excited and anxious for this journey to continue."

Agnetha thought about that. "She is leaving the terror and evil memories behind. Makes sense to me."

"Do you think?"

"Katya, she is sixteen years old. She is a young woman now, no longer a child. She is trying to prepare for a whole new life without the old one pulling her down."

Katarina considered Agnetha's words.

After supper break, they tried to prepare themselves for their first night on the train.

"I'll hold up this blanket, Anna," said Katarina. "You girls change behind it, and then you can hold it up for me."

"Maybe we can rig it up like a curtain that we can pull when we need it," suggested Susannah. "We will be many more days on the train."

Katarina scanned the ceiling of the car. "Hmm. How about . . ."

"Hook the corner of the sheet on that nail and tuck this end behind the bunk."

"Done. Now pull it around the front—there! We have privacy!"

Katarina jolted awake. The train had stopped at the station at Katrinovka and Johann had already jumped off the car to take note of who got off and on again. Wrapping her blanket around her, Katarina hurried to the trees. She stood for a few moments watching the beauty unfold as the sun spread its first shimmering rays across the Dneiper River Valley. A morning mist covered the low lying areas in a fairy tale haze. As it lifted, she saw the Dneiper winding through the valley, glistening like a silver serpent in the fresh light of morning. Taking a deep breath of the clear air, she hurried back to car number 26.

They stopped again in Alexandrovsk, long enough to cook a good breakfast, clean up the dishes, and even wash out a few clothes. The warm sun dried them quickly. Boarding again, they passed through Molzevo and on to Sofiyevka, where they stopped for a couple of hours.

Anna stretched leisurely and smiled into the sunshine. "What a beautiful day. Are we in a fairy tale, or is this reality?"

Katarina smiled. "I was thinking the same thing this morning as I watched the sun come up over the valley."

"Maybe God is beginning to bless us again. Maybe he is giving us a taste of what our future will be like."

Katarina watched Anna with concern. As Johann had said earlier, "Canada is not heaven." What kind of dream was Anna building in her mind?

"I am going to find Sarah and Tina," said Anna. "I will be back in time to go."

"Why don't you ride in their car for a while? As long as I know where you are, it's fine with me."

"Really? Then I think I will. Thank you, Katya. I will come back when we stop for supper."

They chugged through Slavgorod and then stopped for two hours in Sinelnikovo. There they found themselves surrounded by thick forest.

"Katya!" Nicholai and Justina appeared through the crowds and found her and Anna preparing supper. "Did you know there's a market behind the station? Come and see."

Katarina felt irritation. She was tired, her back hurt, supper needed to be tended to, and these two thought only of sight-seeing.

"Mrs. Sudermann, I will watch the supper if you would like to go to the market with Nicholai."

Justina's offer surprised Katarina.

"Go ahead, Katya," encouraged Anna. "Justa and I can make supper, and then she can eat with us."

Looking from one to the other, she finally agreed. Nicholai offered her his arm, and, with a wink for Justina, he guided his sister in the direction of the market.

"I should have stayed to help Susannah," said Katarina, as they checked over the produce and fresh baked goods in the stalls. "She has four children to watch."

"She also has Kornelius, who has no other duties like Johann does, and she has Neta who is more than capable of helping. And since you eat together, she does not have to make her own supper."

"Hmm. Well, you have certainly thought it all through."

"Katya, you have to take care of yourself too." He said no more about her condition. One did not usually speak of it with men, not even a brother and sometimes not even a husband. This job was hers alone, but she had to admit, the short reprieve from responsibility refreshed her.

"Where do we stop next?" she asked Johann as they ate their biscuits and tea and sausage.

"Next village is Losovo, I think. And then Kharkov."

"Will we stop there?"

"I'm sure we will, but it will be in the middle of the night."

Katarina caught sight of a brightly colored headscarf as a figure came through the trees toward them. It was a woman from the village.

"Please," she said in Russian, "do you have extra? My children and I have not eaten in three days."

Katarina's eyes widened and her heart softened as she remembered the pain of hunger, and the more intense pain of knowing her family suffered also. She gathered the remaining food into a cloth and tied it up for the woman.

"Take it and God bless you."

The woman thanked her profusely and with tears. Other people came through the trees as well, begging for a little food. They looked so thin and weary. Katarina held Johann's hand as they walked back to their car.

"We are not the only ones who suffer," she said and he nodded.

After a two-hour stop in Kharkov in the dark of night, the train carried on, stopping only briefly in Belogorod. The slim track was a ribbon of steel forging its way through dense forests that leaned bravely against it.

On Thursday they reached Orel very early and stopped there for most of the day. It was cool out, a welcome break from the beautiful but hot sun. Johann sat on the incline of the track talking with the other men. Anna, Sarah, and Tina played with Neta, Jake, Marianna, and little Gerhard. David Enns walked with Peter, speaking to him of their surroundings, even though Peter offered no response. Susannah washed little clothes and hung them on branches to dry. Katarina cooked a large pot of soup while visiting with Agnetha.

When Justina had done her washing and helped her mother and sister with cooking, she walked with Nicholai toward the town.

"How is your mother handling the journey?" he asked.

She shrugged. "Like she handles most everything: She does what needs to be done, talks as little as possible, endures whatever comes. She's never been the same since . . ."

He squeezed her hand. "I'm sorry."

She looked up at him. "It isn't your fault, Kolya."

"I know, but I hate to see the suffering those devils caused. I get so angry sometimes."

"Nicholai, you must learn to let your anger go. It cannot accomplish anything."

He raised his chin and looked off into the trees. "You don't know. You are a girl—I mean a woman. You are concerned with preparing food and washing and cleaning and family. It is the men who must deal with protecting and providing. It's very difficult to protect when one has no means to do so."

"I think you should know that I am also concerned with matters of safety and provision. We have no man in our family anymore, except my older brother, who is already in Winnipeg."

"Well, it shouldn't be that way. You shouldn't have to worry about it. That also makes me angry, that women should be put in that position."

"I think you carry far too much anger, Kolya."

He frowned and put his hands in his pockets. "Some things cannot just be forgotten."

"Not forgotten, but accepted. Put behind us. Anger only tarnishes the future."

"You do not understand."

She walked beside him in silence, knowing she could not alter his reasoning. She prayed for him, that time would do what she could not. Slipping her arm through his, she pulled him through the trees to the edge of a hill.

"Look, Kolya."

There before them nestled the town of Orel, with the Oka River flowing through it, darkly reflecting an overcast sky. Churches dotted the town, reverently displaying large gold crosses. Red and white houses scattered themselves prettily along winding streets.

Nicholai looked long and silently. They walked down through the town, arriving back at the train at suppertime.

"May I ride in your car for a while?" he asked her.

"Of course. Have supper with us and stay until night falls."

He took her hand again as they found her car. After supper they traveled to Naryschkino and stopped for a few minutes.

"This must be the most beautiful place yet," commented Justina, gazing across the wooded hills. The tranquility was a balm to her soul. It seemed to have a similar effect on Nicholai.

"Goats," he said. "You hardly see a cow here, just goats."

"They are funny creatures. They probably do better than cows on these steep slopes. Kolya, would you help me with something?"

"What?"

"Help me collect pine boughs. I want to decorate our car. Fix it up a bit."

With a shrug, he agreed. Many others joined in, using what God had planted to transform the dreary boxcars into sweet-smelling havens. When they left Naryschkino, Nicholai and Justina sat in the door of her car, their feet hanging over the edge, the wind blowing in their faces.

They stopped again in Charatschevo and the sky darkened. Justina squealed as the clouds opened and pelted rain down on them. They ran for the train and stood in the doorway watching until they began to move. Then they settled down to play a game of guessing as the train charged through Mylinka and finally stopped at Belyje Berega.

"White mountains," translated Justina. "Aren't they beautiful?"

They were indeed, acknowledged Nicholai, leaning in the doorway, watching the freshly washed landscape move by as the train picked up speed again. The last stop for the day was Bryansk. Nicholai jumped off and began to walk in the direction of his car, but stopped and ran back.

"Justa! Listen a moment." They heard music. "Come, quickly."

Chapter 27

Grabbing her hand, he pulled her down the incline of the track and ran through the trees. There, in a park on the outskirts of the village, they spotted a band playing folk music. Couples danced, smiling into each other's eyes. Nicholai put his arm around Justina.

"I'm sorry about before," he said in a low voice. "I know my anger is not good. Have patience with me."

She said nothing, only put her arm around his waist and her head against his shoulder. "Someday I'd like to dance like that," she said.

He raised his eyebrows. "Really? With whom?"

She turned to face him. "With you, Kolya. Only with you."

He leaned toward her and she could see the lantern light reflecting in his eyes. The train whistle sounded and they both jumped. Laughing, they raced back through the trees and clambered up the slope. He helped her into her car and waved to her, then raced ahead to catch his own car before it left him behind.

"Kolya! We almost left you!" Anna's face showed alarm, but seeing his grin in the dimness, she relaxed and whispered, "I'm glad you made it. Did you have a good time?"

His broad grin answered her question and she playfully pulled his ear.

Susannah winced as she looked out on the clamor of the train station in Dubrovna. She had been awake ever since their brief stop at Trosna at sunrise, but she hadn't prepared herself for the press of people and the noise.

Wearily, she helped her children and Helena's through their morning rituals and made a pot of tea. The children munched on roasted *zweiback* while she began washing clothes. She hung them out to dry and then joined Katarina and some of the other women to clean the car. Each car group was in charge of their own car.

She had just gathered the stiff, dry clothing together when the whistle sounded.

"I'll get the children," called Anna, running to where they played close by.

Nicholai helped Anna hoist them all onto the boxcar and gave Anna a boost in. Then he fell back to catch Justina's car. Anna gathered the children together on one of the bunks and told them some of the fairy stories Katarina had told her when she was younger.

Susannah sat on a wooden crate near the open door watching the world go by. Johann had asked Kornelius to help on one of the other cars, and she missed his presence.

As the train passed Lipovo she noticed irrigated fields. "What are they growing there?" she asked Johann.

"Looks like potatoes. Fresh potatoes would be nice, wouldn't they?"

"Mmhm." She saw cows grazing in pastures, and was tempted to go for a short nap when the train began to slow again. *Roslavli*, the station sign read. *Canteen*. Susannah looked around for Kornelius and again remembered he was not in this car. Well, she would go to the canteen herself. As soon as she had taken the children to the woods, or the toilet, whichever was available.

By the time Susannah had completed the necessary tasks and put hot water in the teakettle, she wondered if she would have time to go to the canteen. As usual, Anna saved the day.

"Let me stay with the children," she offered. "You go ahead. Katarina wants to go too."

So Susannah and Katarina, like two schoolgirls, walked to the canteen and surveyed the offerings there.

"Fresh potatoes," said Susannah. "I've been hungering for them ever since we passed Lipovo."

Katarina noticed the ready-made bread. "I hope it tastes good. I suppose anything will taste good if I remember the awful, hard, black bread we ate during the famine."

Susannah sobered. "Those were terrible times. I hope I shall never have to live like that again. If there is food available, I plan to eat well."

"And so you should. You need to stay strong for your family."

Susannah stood back, watching people look over the food in the stalls. "Do you think Neta and Jake will ever feel like part of my family? Do you think I will be able to look after them? Helena has entrusted me with her very heart."

Katarina put her arm around her friend. "Suse, you are already doing a wonderful job of including them with your own. Neta loves Gerhard—she misses Abie so much. And Jake, well, he will be the older brother for Gerhard, and he loves Kornelius."

Susannah looked up at her. "And what do you think about him?"

"What do I think about Kornelius? I think he is a kind, gentle, lonely man, wondering what will motivate him in the new land. He loves you. He needs you and your children to fill his life. Would it not be better than being alone?"

"I knew what you would say. I know it in my heart, but what if—Katarina, don't be angry with me for saying this again—what if someday Gerhard comes back from wherever they have taken him? What if he is alive yet and we don't know it? What if he comes and I have married Kornelius?

What would I ever do?"

"Suse, Johann showed you conclusive evidence that Gerhard died. What more proof do you need? There are many, many of us Mennonite women whose men have gone missing and who will never receive any word at all of their fate. At least you have something to give you reason to close that chapter of your life. Remember him and let him go. Embrace your future for your sake and for your children."

"And for the sake of my kind, gentle, lonely friend. *Ja*, I know you are right. Please pray for me. As the time for our new life nears, my heart quavers within me at the decisions I must make."

Katarina hugged her. "I do and I will. God will help you. Trust God. Even when you don't feel as if he is leading, or you wonder if you have missed the signs, just trust. As Johann said to me: 'He knows the end from the beginning.'"

"He knows the end from the beginning. Thank you, Katya. I will take those words with me."

They walked back to the train together, to find that Kornelius had returned. He had placed the teakettle on board and was busily loading children. When everyone was aboard, the train lurched ahead. Kornelius steadied the kettle.

"Anyone for more tea?" he asked.

"Not for me," Katarina whispered to Anna. "Then I can't make it to the next stop."

"You are getting very big," said Anna.

"Thank you," said Katarina dryly.

"I am so excited. Soon you will have a child of your own and I will be a real aunt."

"Yes, well, let's hope this baby waits until he or she can be born on Canadian soil, and hopefully we can be settled into our new home first."

They rested awhile and then the train jerked again, slowing for yet another small secluded station. Little Marianna had been playing on the floor of the car, and when the train jerked, the kettle tipped and landed near her, splashing her with hot water. She squealed and cried, and Susannah ran to her.

"Shh, child. Mama's here." Susannah quickly dipped a cloth into the small pot of drinking water and bathed the child's arm.

"It hurts, Mama," cried Marianna. By now Gerhard was wailing too. It was a noisy interlude in Alexandrovskaya. Susannah managed to quiet them all, rubbing ointment on the wound and wrapping it loosely with clean rags, while Kornelius carried Gerhard out into the sunshine.

"Officials at the station at Panskaya refuse to allow our train to pass," reported Johann after a brief conference with some of the other car leaders and the CPR representative. "I'm not sure how long we will be here. Please, do not wander far from the car."

Immediately, Nicholai jumped off and ran back to Justina's car. Along the way, he picked up various other young people.

"There are wild strawberries here," said one of the girls. "I saw them as we waited."

"Where?"

"On the hillsides, silly."

They ran helter skelter in search of the strawberries, laughing and singing. Their free spirits inspired some as they watched, and irritated others.

"Why can those young people not be content to stay quietly in their cars until it is time to move again?" Mrs. Fast from car number 32 frowned her disapproval. "Such a commotion over a few berries."

After more negotiations, permission was finally granted and the train whistle blew. Even Mrs. Fast chuckled as she watched the youth scrambling up the steep bank, delayed by fits of laughter, panic, and hands full of strawberries.

Nicholai helped both Anna and Justina, and they all three clambered aboard Justina's car instead of trying to catch their own further ahead. They fell onto the floor of the car, panting and laughing.

"*Nach dem Lachen folgt das Weinen.*" Mrs. Fast reminded them of the saying they had all heard as children, that after the laughing would come the crying. She had forgotten they were not children anymore, but young adults. Their laughing, instead of leading to tears, led to singing, and soon the entire car harmonized in folk songs and Russian ditties, as well as hymns.

When the singing died down, Justina sat with Nicholai and Anna in the door of the car. The Dneiper flowed nearby; they could see it off and on through trees and mountains.

"Look, look!" exclaimed Justina. "A castle."

"Sure enough," said Nicholai. A small castle reigned supreme on one of the mountaintops above them in the clouds. They had to move back and shut the door then, as rain fell in torrents, washing all the world clean again. They stopped for an hour in the midst of nowhere. The rain had stopped, and they watched the sun set before finding their own cars again.

That night Anna slept more soundly than she had since they had left Alexanderkrone. Possibly better than she had since that fateful day.

"Vitebsk!" announced Johann to the still sleeping inhabitants of the car. He knew many of them would need a stop. The station was pretty and well kept.

"What's the next stop, Johann?" asked Katarina. "Will we have a chance to buy a few things there?"

"They said we would be next at Polotsk. A Jewish city. I don't see why you couldn't buy goods there."

But Katarina was to be disappointed. Although Polotsk was a nice city, almost the entire town was closed; it was Sabbath. Katarina had to content herself with a loaf of *challah* from the Gentile canteen owner. She would wait until the next stop. It seemed like the rest of her life would be like this: frequent, unpredictable stops at strange places where she never knew what she would find. Everything in the air. Nothing planned or scheduled. No routine.

The train turned northwest after Polotsk and the landscape changed again.

"The crops don't look very good here," commented Johann. "Too sandy and swampy, but I think we are heading for more forest."

Sure enough, the next stop found them in the middle of a dense forest. Ferns and moss grew thickly in the woods and crept up to the station in Rossino. Susannah took care of Marianna and Neta while Kornelius led Jake and Gerhard away. When they returned, Gerhard held out a bunch of flowers for Susannah in his chubby little hand.

"Oh *Liebchen*," she cried. "Forget-me-nots. They are lovely. Thank you." She leaned over and kissed Gerhard, who ran laughing with Jake beside the train.

"I thought they were the exact color of your eyes," said Kornelius.

Susannah allowed herself to look at Kornelius then as she had not before. It didn't seem to matter anymore that he was not handsome. He was good.

She lifted the little bouquet to her face and inhaled its fragrance. "Thank you, Kornelius."

"I thought I was *Mr. Penner* to you."

Susannah blushed. "For a long time. Perhaps too long. Would you mind if I called you Kornelius?"

"I would be delighted . . . Susannah."

The wind sang through the pines as they stood together in peaceful silence. His heart soared, and hers reached again for hope.

"Susannah!" The cry jolted them both. She turned to see Justina running toward her. "Susannah, there's been an accident. Mrs. Fast fell in her hurry to get out of the train, and she has hurt herself. Could you please come and look at her?"

"Of course." Susannah ran with Justina while Kornelius jumped aboard car number 26 to get her emergency bag. She never went far without it since her nursing years. He knew she would want it.

The men carried Mrs. Fast to her bunk and Susannah examined her while asking questions. The injury was not as serious as first thought, but when others realized Susannah was a nurse, they asked her for help as well. She was tired by the time she and Kornelius returned to their car for the night.

The next day, Susannah awoke to a beautiful sunny Sunday morning in Sebezh. Johann had told them all that they would most likely be there for the day. After tending to the children's needs and making a breakfast of porridge, she found a quiet place at the side of the station and began a letter to her mother Hannah and her sister, Helena. She had wondered many times through the long, uncomfortable nights on the train, how little Gretel fared. Had she joined Abie in heaven or did she stay behind to bring some joy to her already bereaved mother? Was Hannah improving or had the move worsened her condition? All these thoughts and more poured out onto the page as Susannah sat alone.

"Excuse me, Ma'am," said Kornelius. "Would a beautiful forget-me-not agree to a walk by the lake?"

Susannah smiled up at him and reached out a hand. "She would. Let me put this letter into my bag and I will join you. Do you think Anna will be all right watching the children?"

"Yes. I already asked her."

They walked a long time, reveling in the beauty of the clear, cold lake, mirroring the forested mountains in its glassy surface.

"What a wondrous day," said Susannah, breathing deeply of the mountain air. "I feel like I am in a dream."

"So do I."

"No, I mean I feel so free and at peace. And happy, I think. I can't remember the last time I felt truly happy."

"My dream is similar."

Not sure she wanted to encourage the conversation in the direction he was going, she exclaimed over the beauty of the sun off the smooth surface of the lake.

"Susannah."

She stopped and turned her attention to him.

"Susannah, my dream, no matter how beautiful, is never complete without you."

"That is kind of you to say, Kornelius."

"I am not trying to be kind. I am attempting to describe to you how I feel when I am with you. My whole being feels full of hope and possibility. Susannah, can this dream come true for us?"

She gazed out across the lake again. Squirrels chattered in the treetops and in the distance she could hear the subdued sound of people busily spending their day.

Her voice was small when she finally answered. "Kornelius, I am afraid to hope. Sometimes dreams come true and then they shatter. I don't know if I can trust in life again, if I can ever relax in a blessing. What if something happens to you and I am alone again? How will I bear it then?"

"Do you ever wish you had never met Gerhard?"

"Kornelius! That is cruel. Of course not. I would never give up a day I had with Gerhard." She caught his implication even as she spoke and looked down at her feet.

"So if we have a few years, perhaps that would be better than nothing. And if we have a lifetime?" He waited, his eyes full of hope and love.

She raised her head and searched his eyes. "What if . . ."

"What if Gerhard comes back from the dead? Susannah, don't you think that even if by some unbelievable chance he survived, that he too would be changed? If he lived, and I have strong reason to believe he did not, he would also carry on as best he could. The life you and Gerhard shared is no more. Let us place it gently but firmly in your memory. I will never ask you to forget him, or expect you never to mention his name again. I think if I had known him, I would have respected and loved him. I too have my memories, Susannah.

"In Gerhard's absence, and perhaps even in his place, allow me to take you on from here. Accept me for your future. I love you."

She sighed. "I know you are correct in what you say, and I know you love me." She sought his eyes. "Will it be enough for now if I say I admire you, I appreciate your kind and gentle ways, I love watching you with my children, and I am comfortable around you? Would you be willing to wait until I can say the rest from my heart?"

"If you would marry me, I would be content with what you are prepared to give and hope that with time, you will come to love me as I do you."

"Kornelius, are you sure that would be enough for you?"

"Yes. It would be enough."

Tears swam in her flower-blue eyes and she leaned her head against his chest. "I will pray sincerely about it, Kornelius. Please be patient with me."

He smiled then, a warm smile with a hint of sadness in it that tore Susannah's heart.

When Susannah and Kornelius returned from their walk by

the lake, the travelers had been dealt another crisis.

"Thank goodness you are back," said Johann to Kornelius. "Would you mind going to car number 40 again? There will be baggage inspections this evening, as well as personal searches. The car has no leader since Jakob Dueck became ill and they need someone to be in charge."

"Of course. Susannah, I will see you tomorrow. I will most likely stay with car number 40 for the night to make sure they are settled."

She nodded, and wondered again at herself. When he wanted her, she pushed him away; when he left, she missed him. She turned back to her own car and her children. Baggage searches. What did they intend to find? What would they declare illegal?

The guards who descended upon the Mennonite company that evening were impersonal and businesslike, but not overly thorough. They followed certain guidelines given them by their superiors: all items belonging to the state must be given over. That included lanterns, boards and ladders used for the makeshift beds, and shovels and hoes the emigrants had hoped to use in the new country.

Following what Katarina called the theft of their beds and tools, each person was searched.

"At least the women were searched by women," whispered Katarina to Susannah later. "I hate to think what Anna would have done otherwise. I shudder at it myself."

That night they all slept on the floor side by side. Even the "curtain" that Katarina and Susannah had rigged up had been taken down. No more allowance for privacy. The searches and inspections took many hours, and the train pulled out of Sebezh at three in the morning.

Everyone slept with their eyes open that night. Even the children felt the tension. Would they be turned back at the border? Had more obstacles come about since they had left home? Who would be rejected because of some defect or other? By the time the sun began to lighten the sky, everyone had dressed and they waited in silence.

Within sight of the border, within sight of the Latvian flag waving red and white in the early morning breeze, the train shuddered to a halt. The doors of the boxcars, closed for the night, scraped open and Russian soldiers jumped aboard. They randomly searched some of the bags again and asked questions of a few people.

Screams broke out in a neighboring boxcar. "No, not my husband, please. He has papers. No!"

Katarina shuddered and turned pleading eyes to Johann in the dimness of the car. Almost imperceptibly, he shook his head. She hugged Anna to her. Who would be next? Would they find some reason to tear away one of the family?

Susannah sat against the end wall, her four charges huddled against her. She wished Kornelius were there with her, but in truth, she knew they were all in the hands of God. Only he could see them through.

Katarina sat beside Susannah with Anna. Nicholai stood beside them and Johann tried to ease the trauma for his carload.

"You!" called one of the soldiers, pointing to Peter, sitting stiffly beside Susannah. "Stand!"

"Stand up, Peter," instructed Nicholai, helping him to his feet.

Katarina panicked. "Johann?"

"Quiet! You are Peter Hildebrandt? Get off the train."

Johann pulled some papers from his inside pocket and explained to the soldiers in Russian. "This young man has been cleared as far as Rezekne. He will be staying in Germany. Everything has been cleared."

"Get off the train," the soldier repeated. Johann took Peter by the arm and kept him by his side.

"Do you go against specific orders from Commissar

Manzev in Moscow?" Johann demanded. "He has guaranteed this man's safety to Germany into the company of relatives. I cannot allow him to be taken."

One of the soldiers finally took a moment to look over the papers and changed his approach. "All seems in order. He will disembark in Rezekne."

"I will see to it," promised Johann, reaching again for the papers, which were already halfway into the soldier's pocket. He relinquished them to Johann and they stomped off the train, rolling the doors shut behind them.

The train sat silent and unmoving, a stone's throw from freedom, and the people huddled together and waited.

Chapter 28

After an interminable wait, the train slowly began to roll again, closer and closer to the border, to the flag of freedom. With a great cheer, they passed through the border gate topped by a large star—the Red Gate—and the train kept rolling.

"We are free!" Anna's cry touched the heart of every passenger.

"We are free," they repeated, tears of release pouring down their cheeks. "Praise God, we are free."

"*Nun danket alle Gott*," sang a middle-aged man from the far end of the car. "*Mit Herzen, Mund und Händen.*" Voice by voice they joined in sweet harmony, their thanks overflowing to the God who had brought them out of their bondage. "*Der grosse Dinge tut an uns und allen Enden! Der uns von Mutterleib und Kindesbeinen an, unzählig viel zu gut, bis hierher hat getan.*"

Eventually the train stopped again, but this time on free soil. Latvian hosts gave the weary travelers a breakfast of porridge and black bread.

"Like watery soup," commented Mrs. Fast, none too quietly.

Katarina frowned at her, but heard others complaining as well. Their attitude embarrassed her. How could they, so recently recovered from starvation and currently without a home, be so ungrateful and disrespectful?

Johann raised his eyebrows at her from across the

enclosure, and she knew he felt the same. He made his way toward her. "We are going to hold a church service here before we move on. Mr. Wiens from Ohrloff is prepared to preach."

Katarina enjoyed the service, their first since leaving Alexanderkrone. After Wiens had finished speaking, several of the youth brought out instruments. The guitar carried them through the melody while the mandolin sang a sweet descant. Katarina's heart lifted in worship with the music and she felt renewed. She noticed Susannah also seemed touched by the service, although her preoccupation remained.

"We are coming into Zilupe." Johann stood in the open doorway of the slowing train. "Please gather all your baggage; we change trains here."

As the groups moved from one train to the other, a Canadian Pacific Railway representative handed out small gifts. Each person received a small pin in the shape of a sheaf of wheat, with the letters C.P.R. engraved underneath it. They were also handed postcards of a ship. Even little Gerhard held one.

"Boat. Boat," he cried excitedly.

"Kornelius has been preparing the children for what lies ahead," explained Susannah. "They are very excited."

"So am I," answered Katarina, "but Johann is not. He was very sick on the Black Sea when he served in the *Forstei*. I think he is worried he will fall ill."

"And you? How will you manage?"

"Oh, I shall be fine. My queasiness is past. Now it's just my size that impedes me."

"*Ja*, I remember," laughed Susannah. "You feel like the engine car of the train."

"Or a big boat."

"Boat." Repeated Gerhard, proudly displaying his already crumpled treasure.

Johann came for Kornelius. "We could use your help again. There are fewer boxcars on this train; we must reorganize."

Children cried and mothers scolded. Men shouted and gave orders that no one followed. Johann and the other car leaders began at the first car, transferring groups as they had been divided. When all the new cars were filled, they began dividing the remaining car groups between the already occupied cars, keeping families together.

The Mennonites now had themselves organized, but the Latvians were apparently in no hurry to depart.

"Their trains are not scheduled like the Russian trains," commented Johann dryly. "We leave when we leave."

The train pulled away from Zilupe and arrived at Rezekne at three in the afternoon. Katarina's stomach churned, not from the baby within, but because this is where she would say good-bye to her brother, Peter. She had ignored it, pushed it out of her mind, but now it must be faced.

What would you think, Papa? she asked in her soul. Is this the right thing? We really had no choice, you know. It was either bring him to Mika or leave him in Russia. I hope you understand, Papa.

Somehow, in the depths of her being, she knew this was the only way. Katarina's heart pounded. What would it be like to see Mika again? Was she finally happy with her Dietrich? Would they manage to take care of Peter? Would he ever understand why he could not come with them to Canada? How would Susannah bear the separation?

She felt Anna's hand on her arm and returned her encouraging smile. They would stay on the train another night and face a new day tomorrow.

Katarina could not find a comfortable position for herself that night, even though Johann and Nicholai had given her their blankets to make a softer surface to lie on. The baby squirmed and hiccupped within her, and her mind ran through a thousand scenarios of what was to come.

"Everyone up," instructed Johann the next morning.

Groans and sighs answered him as the car came to life.

"All travelers and baggage will be disinfected here, and then we will all be moved into barracks. We cannot meet all your requests. Keep your families together and be thankful for temporary housing."

The disinfection process caused humiliation and discomfort for all concerned, but they knew it to be necessary and routine. After everything had been cleared from the boxcars, these too were disinfected, and the people moved to the barracks.

Women busied themselves with washing and cooking, girls ran after siblings, trying to keep them out of danger, and men met in groups to discuss their future and the rate of monetary exchange, which had risen sharply.

"The food is good," said Anna appreciatively. "Not like home, of course, but we are not home, are we?"

"You are correct in that," said Katarina, weary already and it was only noon.

"Katie, you need a good sleep this afternoon. I will look after clearing up the lunch. You go to the barracks and lie down. Agreed?"

Katarina tried to argue, but her weariness got the better of her. "Agreed. Where is Nicholai?"

"He went into the town. He heard there were good prices on boots."

"Oh. Well, I am content to stay here. It's chilly out and I think it is about to rain again."

"Yes. I had better clean this up quickly. Go to the barracks now, Katya."

Katarina lay on the thin mattress amid the bustling activity of the barracks. It was not the noise and commotion that kept her awake, but the never ending circles of her thoughts. She forced herself to remain lying down for the sake of the baby she carried, but she did not sleep.

Later in the afternoon, she must have dozed, because she awakened slowly to familiar voices.

"Has she been well?" whispered one.

"Yes, but tired. We hope the baby doesn't come early," said another.

A low, quiet voice asked, "Where is Peter? Did you have any trouble getting him across?"

Katarina's eyes fluttered open. She tried to get her bearings. Oh yes, the barracks. Anna insisted she come lie down. Baby was quiet now within her. Suddenly her mind became fully awake and she pushed herself to a sitting position. Eyes wide and blinking, she stared at them, gathered around her bed. Mika. Dietrich. Anna.

Mika bit her bottom lip and smiled, her dark eyes filling with tears. "Katya? Oh Katya!" She threw herself to her knees beside her sister and hugged her fiercely, then stared up at her through her tears. "You're going to be a mama. You will make such a good one."

Katarina's words stuck in her throat. She held her sister and rocked her, content to feel and not speak. Her own tears fell on her sister's dark curls. They touched foreheads, as they had done as children, and Katarina held Maria's face in her hands.

"You are as beautiful as ever." Her eyes strayed to the man who approached them. "And you have found your Dietrich."

He leaned his crutch against the wood bed frame and sat on the mattress beside her. "Excuse my forwardness," he explained, "but I have trouble kneeling." He took her hands and kissed her cheek. "You look wonderful as well, sister. Different, but wonderful."

She smiled with some embarrassment at her condition so publicly alluded to.

"Have you seen Johann?" asked Katarina.

"Not yet. We met Susannah and her brood, and Wilhelm and Agnetha and their growing children. My, how things change." Mika shook her head in wonder.

"Did you meet Kornelius?"

"Who?"

"Kornelius. He came to us two years ago from the Old Colony, hoping to avoid starvation until such a time as he could secure passage to America. He has become quite attached to Susannah."

"And she to him?"

Katarina shrugged. "She cares for him, but past that I cannot say. She still wonders if Gerhard might come back."

"And there is no hope of that?"

Katarina returned Dietrich's gaze and remembered that he too had been assigned to the company of the deceased, but he had been alive all along.

"Johann found two separate memoranda that point to his death. He had not yet recovered from typhus when they took him away to the army again, and they left him behind somewhere when he became too ill to walk. We do not know where, or if someone would have found him, but I am sure that if he had survived, he would have returned to us long ago. As it is, I truly believe he has gone on ahead to his reward."

Dietrich's mouth tightened and he nodded. "That seems conclusive."

Anna's eyed darted from one speaker to the other, waiting for them to finish. "Could we go find Peter?"

Maria put her arm around her sister. "You are afraid he will not know us. That he will suffer coming home with us."

Anna smiled through threatening tears.

"Then let us go and find him." Dietrich stood with the aid of his crutch and gallantly offered Katarina his hand.

"Thank you, kind sir," she said, a shy smile on her face.

"We should find Peter so we can all eat supper together this evening. When do you leave?"

Maria looked to Dietrich for confirmation. "Not until you have gone. We have moved back to Schwandorf."

"I thought you had found a place in Berlin?"

"We had. Now that we have found Peter, we decided to move back south where we have family. A smaller city as well."

"We are close to Lechfeld," said Dietrich. "We thought to help out somewhat if we could. There are many people from the colonies who have been detained there for trachoma and other ailments. Sometimes a familiar face eases suffering and separation."

"You always were my favorite German soldier," said Katarina boldly, to the surprise of the others. "You are blessed, Mika."

"I know it," her sister answered, slipping her hand in her husband's arm. "Every day I thank God for him."

"I must ask you to sit here," directed Johann. "We need to fill these tables first."

The couple in question glowered at him, then glanced with disdain at the already seated family. "We prefer our own kind," they said.

If I could place all of your kind in one area and partition you off, thought Johann, I would do it gladly. "These are your fellow Mennonites from south Russia," he said patiently.

"They are from the Old Colony. We are from the Molotsch."

"And so?"

The woman raised her eyebrows. "My dear sir, you must realize there are differences."

"Only in geography, Ma'am. This is where you will sit and I must carry on my duties. Excuse me."

"Well!" he heard behind him. "Such inconvenience." They seated themselves, pulling their chairs away from the others, who huddled together in an effort to be inconspicuous.

Johann shook his head. Glancing in the direction of the door of the dining hall, he saw Katarina, and with her, the entire family. His eyes fell upon Maria and Dietrich. He was glad for the opportunity to see them again. He admired Dietrich, even though they were often diametrically opposed in their opinions and beliefs. Mika had finally met her match. Johann had thanked God so often that she had not settled for him. It would most certainly have been an unhappy alliance. He smiled at Katarina, trying unsuccessfully to hide her girth under a cloak, and waved them over to the next table.

"Over here, if you please," he said.

"Johann!" Maria hugged him and Dietrich shook his hand firmly. "So you are in charge here, too?" they teased.

"Not in charge," he said. "In fact," he lowered his voice, "it was easier to work with *Forstei* recruits. At least they listened to me."

"Well," said Katarina, "we will obey. Come, everyone. Sit."

Johann joined them later. He sat next to Katarina.

"Did you sleep?" he asked her.

"A bit. I feel much better now."

He tilted his head at her as if he didn't believe it. They spoke then of their journey thus far, of Maria and Dietrich's journey from Schwandorf to Rezekne, of the government bureaucracy—both Russian and German—they had to wade through in order to gain permission to take Peter home with them.

"I'm so thankful you stuck with it," said Susannah, who sat across from them with her four charges and Kornelius. Peter sat next to Kornelius. "We could not have left him in Russia. There was no problem as long as I thought I would be staying back, but when Helena begged me to go and offered to take Mother, I had to think of Peter too."

"He miraculously passed the preliminary medicals," said Johann, "but we knew he would not be allowed into Canada. That's when we received your letter, your offer. It could not have come at a more appropriate time."

Dietrich ate heartily of the beef stew. "We worked on the matter for a long time. One of the men who accompanied my brother and Mika in their search for me," he cleared his throat self-consciously, "has many government contacts, and I have my connections through military channels. We persevered until we had clearance here, and then approached Moscow. If B. B. Janz had not spoken for us, Peter would not be here now."

"That man is a miracle worker," said Johann. "I greatly admire him."

"He did not take the first train out of the country either," added Katarina. "I believe he will stay back until he has done everything humanly possible to keep the emigration going."

"Are you ready to go to Germany, Peter?" asked Nicholai.

"Are you ready to go to Germany, Peter?" said Peter.

Susannah smiled in spite of her breaking heart and patted his arm. "You will enjoy it there, Peter Dear. I know you will."

"I know you will."

A pall settled over the gathering. Tomorrow morning the train would depart very early and only God knew if and when they would meet again. An ocean would separate them.

Johann broke the spell. "I suggest we all get a good sleep. We are to present ourselves at six tomorrow morning."

Yawning with weariness and emotional fatigue, they retired to their respective corners of the barracks. Some of the emigrants came from the Chortitza settlements, but most from Molotschna. Some had money, some had nothing but their travel debt. Young and old, rich and poor, haughty and humble, all were housed together in this temporary shelter. No special preferences were awarded, subsequently negative attitudes flourished and tempers flared.

"I can hardly wait until we are on the ship," remarked Johann in disgust as he lay beside Katarina when all the lights had finally been extinguished. "I am so tired of being papa to them all."

Katarina reached out and stroked his cheek. "You need to get used to being a papa. It won't be long now."

He held her close as the night passed and rose before anyone else had begun to stir.

"Good-bye, dear sister," said Katarina through a torrent of tears.

"Shh, Katya. Don't upset the baby." Maria also shook with sobs. "Oh, to meet after such a long time and then bid farewell again. It is too difficult to bear."

The sisters clung to each other, then Maria hugged and cried over Anna and Nicholai. She gave Johann a firm hug and charged him with the care of protection of her family. Dietrich said warm farewells all around.

Peter stood back, seemingly unaware of the situation, in a world of his own. With a deep breath and a promise to be patient with her brother, Mika linked her arm in his. Susannah wept against Kornelius's chest while Anna and Neta tried to comfort the little ones.

"So many good-byes; so many tears," remarked young Neta, dry eyed.

"Someday we will all be together," Anna assured them all, trembling in her effort to maintain composure. "Then no one will ever separate us again."

"*Aufwiedersehn*!" Maria called as the refugee train pulled away into the sunrise.

By eight in the morning, the train had passed through Pespenga. The scenery changed much as they passed through

Pura and approached Riga. Treed land became rocky outcroppings, and these in turn gave way to fields of waving wheat and eventually more forest, poplar and pine linking arms, blending shades of green.

At the last train change, there had been fewer cars again and the travelers were packed tightly together. In car number 26, people settled in with songs, stories, and recitations.

"It reminds me of the camaraderie of the Concordia Choir," said Katarina.

"Tell the story of *Ashenputtel,* Katya," begged Anna in a lull between stories.

"If anyone wishes to hear it."

"Yes, yes. The Brothers Grimm. Say on."

Nicholai listened from the doorway where he watched the Dvina River winding its silvery way across the valley. So much beauty. He wondered why men always destroyed everything. He would dearly love to make a home with Justina in one of the idyllic valleys along a bend in the river, but he knew some government or other would make life difficult or impossible. He would have to wait and see what Canada offered.

He was thrilled at the prospect of making a home in the new country. He was a young man now, and although he would accompany his family to their new home, he would soon be looking for a small beginning for himself and Justina. He wanted to dream, but the details were so fuzzy he had to give up as often as he began. The only part he knew for sure was Justina, and that knowledge went a long way to dispelling the anger in his soul. He felt the weight of it lift as the versts slipped past beneath the iron wheels.

The train rolled into Riga several hours later and another train transfer demanded everyone's attention. The impossible was accomplished in half an hour. Swift medical inspections sent some unfortunate souls to Lechfeld, the former army base near Schwandorf. Hopefully, those rejected would be able to catch up with their families later. Some whole families stayed back in hopes of proceeding together.

"Look at the streets," said Katarina as she and Anna waited in their new train car for the next leg of the journey. "They are cobbled."

"Just like at Succoth."

"The houses are so tall and skinny, as if there isn't room for ordinary houses."

"I like the white curtains in the windows," said Anna, "and flowers in boxes. They look friendly."

"I don't like the busyness. There are trams and automobiles and trains everywhere. It's a wonder anyone can find their way home."

Anna looked off toward the Bay of Riga. "I love the sea," she said. "It is so free. I could watch it all day."

"And you will, once we board the ship. You may wish you had never seen it."

"I don't think so."

"Well then, enjoy it while you can. I think that once we are in Canada, you will not see ships very often."

The sun set and the air cooled. They rattled on down the track through the night toward Libau Harbor.

"The ship. The ship." Anna patted Katarina awake. "Look at it. *The Marglen*."

Chapter 29

"There it is," said Anna. "Our ship."

Katarina took a deep breath and hoisted herself to a sitting position, then Anna gave her a hand to stand. "Thank you. I feel rather like a big boat myself, barging ahead."

Anna giggled. "You look more like a ship than a boat," she teased from a safe distance. "The S.S. Katarina." Her giggles turned to laughter which, even though it was at Katarina's expense, also sent her into a fit of laughter that made her hold her stomach.

"Enough! Now, help me gather our things."

They helped Susannah and Kornelius, and Johann returned from checking other cars to help transport their belongings to the dock.

"What huge cranes," commented Anna as she watched crates and boxes being loaded onto the ship.

"They could certainly take more care," added Nicholai. "Look, they almost broke that box open. Just dropped it instead of placing it."

"You could do better?" Anna teased again.

"Yes I could. In fact," he tweaked her nose, "when we arrive in Canada, I may take a job on the docks."

"Then you will be carrying, not working a big machine."

"You wait and see. I will surprise you."

"You always do."

"Come, you two. We have to go." Katarina ambled in the

direction of the ship and they followed her, mimicking her gait.

"What has happened to Anna?" Nicholai helped Katarina carry her bags onto the boat while Anna fell back to help Susannah with the younger children.

"What do you mean?"

"I don't know. Her feet hardly touch the ground."

Katarina smiled. "It is her turn. She deserves to look ahead to a new future."

The *Marglen* weighed anchor at four o'clock that afternoon. Johann stood with his family at the rail. Just the thought of riding on the waves caused his stomach to lurch, but he did not speak of it. They would know soon enough.

"We have been assigned to one of the lower decks," said Johann. "I think you will like the arrangements. All meals are taken care of by the shipping company. No more tea on the go."

"Show me our room," begged Katarina when they had pulled away from shore.

They walked the lower hallway to their cabin and Katarina cried with delight. Anna was right behind her.

"It's so white and clean."

"Electric lights," explained Johann, pulling the cord.

"And our own tiny lavatory," marveled Anna. "I only hope you can fit in there, Katya."

Her sister cast an irritated look at Anna, but the younger girl merely smiled.

They stowed their hand luggage in their rooms and wandered back to the dining room for lunch.

"I think I must be in heaven," murmured Nicholai to Justina seated beside him. They sat at white linen covered tables set with silver and china. Their first course consisted of beef bouillon.

"Mrs. Fast will complain about the thin soup again," whispered Justina.

The soup was followed by beefsteak, potatoes, cabbage, white bread with butter and apple jelly.

"This is a feast such as I have not seen since Succoth." Katarina seemed almost overcome with the bounty, and although Johann also voiced his appreciation, he ate little.

"I think the ship's crew needs your help again," said Kornelius to Johann. They looked up to see an obviously wealthy family push their way in front of a poor woman and her young children. More pushing and shoving followed until the crew was able to settle everyone down.

"I'm glad we arrived early," said Katarina. "If they pushed me down, I don't know if I could get up again."

"I won't let anything happen to you, Katya."

"I was joking, Johann."

"I was not. I've seen what happens when the mob takes over. You stay with me until things have settled."

As it turned out, Johann spent much of his time at the rail, and Katarina did not care to stay at his side. The Mennonite administration formed committees to handle the mealtime chaos, and people were called forward by cabin numbers.

Wilhelm and Agnetha had been assigned berths at the far end of the boat, so Katarina did not see them often. They also stayed occupied with their family, although they took advantage of shared meals.

That evening the Mennonite passengers held a service on board the *Marglen*. Mr. Wiens spoke again, his text being Psalm 46:1, "God is our refuge and strength, an ever-present help in trouble." Gerhard Enns directed a small, impromptu choir, which Katarina felt paled when compared with Concordia. A few other ministers also said a few words: Jakob P. Friesen, Jakob P. Wiens, Peter F. Goertzen, and Elder Heinrich Martens. Later, the group that remained sang Russian songs to the accompaniment of a piano.

Johann was forced to make his way back to the cabin and take up his position there, alternating between the lavatory and his berth. A storm had crept up during the evening, and rain pelted the decks.

"The lightning is snapping like fireworks tonight," commented Anna.

"I think I shall sleep well in spite of everything," said Katarina, then looked doubtfully at her husband huddled on their berth with his teeth clenched. "Poor dear."

"I love to look at the water as it swirls around the porthole," said Anna.

Johann cracked an eye open and glanced toward the little window. He shuddered and hurried again to the bathroom.

"I think he's claustrophobic too," whispered Katarina. "I'm afraid he is going to have a bad time of it. We've hardly left land. How are you feeling, Anna?"

"I feel wonderful." She twirled around in the tiny space not occupied by berths and bags and fell smiling onto her bunk. "This is an adventure."

Katarina marveled at her sister. Fragile Anna. Shy Anna. Suffering Anna. When she left Russia behind, she also left her fears, her wounds. She had taken her Oma's advice literally and never looked back. Katarina rejoiced with her. Both young women slept like the dead that first night on the water.

The next morning, finding herself with nothing to do, Katarina took out her journal, pen and ink.

> *Friday, July 4, 1924. Somewhere on the Baltic Sea between Libau and Germany. I woke to the sound of a foghorn this morning. An eerie sound, but one which excites Anna. I cannot completely understand the change in my sister. She has left all negative thoughts behind and embraces the future with a joy that continually confounds me.*

I am eating an apple I took from breakfast. The food is wonderful and plentiful. We can eat as much as we wish. I sit on the second deck now—it's quieter—and watch the waves crash against the hull of the Marglen, *the ten thousand ton ship that will take us from Libau to Antwerp. I found out this information from a crew member at breakfast. Johann used to be my source of information, but I believe we have lost him to seasickness for the duration of the voyage. So far I feel fine myself, but I don't know if it will last. Many people are taking turns standing at the rail or lying on their beds.*

According to the steward, we are passing between the islands of Bornholm on the north and Reugen on the south. Now that the wind has blown away the fog, I can see a lighthouse on the coast of what must be Denmark. This traveling is such a pleasure. If only we had a home awaiting us at the end of it. Always, that worry sticks in the corner of my mind, coloring everything I see. I pray that I could enjoy this passage with at least some of Anna's exuberance.

"We are entering the lochs of the Kiel Canal, Johann. It was built by Kaiser Wilhelm between 1908 and 1914." She consulted her brochure. "I wish you could come watch with me. It's all very interesting the way they raise the water level and then lower it again."

"I'm sorry, Katya," he murmured. "I cannot raise my head without losing the contents of my stomach, which is surely minimal by now."

"I understand. We are not allowed to leave the ship anyway."

On Monday the *Marglen* anchored off the coast of Holland near Vlissingen.

"We have to wait for high tide before we can navigate into Antwerp Harbor," said Anna. She brushed the hair from Katarina's perspiring forehead and held the pail for her again. "You and Johann are not having a very interesting time, are you?"

Katarina sighed. "I'm not too bad, but I have to keep sipping water and juice for the baby, and I have trouble keeping it down. Just pray that the baby stays where she is."

"She?"

Katarina nodded. "I've decided I'm carrying a girl."

"Boy."

"What did you say, Johann?" They had begun to ignore the limp figure lying pale and unmoving on the bed beside Katarina.

"I said boy. Baby is a boy." He clenched his teeth and groaned with the effort of speaking.

"Of course," she answered, and winked at Anna.

Anna bathed their faces with cool water and fluffed their pillows before heading out again to the deck. She didn't want to miss the ship's navigation through the narrow channel to Antwerp. She wanted to see the new ship. It was reportedly much bigger, fit for the ocean voyage. She could scarcely wait until they were on the high seas.

As she strolled the deck, her face up to the caressing breeze, several aircraft buzzed overhead. Instinctively she ran for cover, huddling in a corner behind a staircase, her hands covering her ears. The planes flew on and she heard laughter.

"What's the matter, girl? Afraid of bombs?"

"The war's over, my dear."

Anna slowly raised her head. Her cheeks blazed and she felt the old familiar fear clawing at her insides. Sobbing, she ran down the hallway, headlong into one of the stewards.

"May I help you, Miss?" he asked politely, holding her elbow.

She tried to speak, but the words couldn't get past the sobs. The two who had taunted her entered the passageway. She looked behind her in terror. Memories carefully buried filled her with such fear her stomach roiled.

"What is going on?" demanded the steward. "You have no right to bother other passengers." He still held Anna's arm.

"Listen, man, we didn't do anything. Just laughed at her. She thought those planes were going to drop bombs."

"Why were you following her then?"

They looked from one to the other. "We felt bad for making her cry. War's a bad memory. We should not have taunted her."

"Well, see that it doesn't happen again. Miss, I will see you to your cabin."

Anna nodded hesitantly.

He took her arm and offered her a clean handkerchief. She wiped her eyes as they walked along. He whistled a tuneless song. "Must have some fearsome memories to react like that."

She wrapped her arms about herself and lowered her head. He could see her disappearing inside herself.

"Hey now, miss. You don't have to tell me. We all have memories. We all have to deal with them. Where are you going?"

"C . . . Canada."

He whistled again. "Big country. Very big. Lots of room for new people."

"You . . . you've been there?"

"Me? No. Just what I've heard."

They had arrived at the cabin and he released her arm and bowed. "Is there anything else I can do?"

"No, thank you." She managed a tight smile and let herself into the room she had begun to call the sickroom. Katarina sat on Anna's berth writing a letter, looking somewhat better. Johann still lay as he had earlier. Katarina started when she looked up and saw her sister's face.

"Anna! What happened? Did you get lost? Did someone harm you?"

The tears came again and she crawled onto her berth and curled up in a ball. Katarina moved to make room and rubbed Anna's back.

"*Liebchen*, tell me what happened."

Through tears and sobs that even managed to raise Johann's head, she told her embarrassing story. Katarina listened and nodded.

"Poor Änya. Sometimes I have flashbacks too."

"Flashbacks?" Anna's voice quavered as she wiped her eyes and blew her nose.

"Yes. I remember distinctly events from the past. Like the night Papa died. Sometimes it comes in my dreams and I wake up in a cold sweat."

Anna sighed. "So you have them too. They don't last?"

"No, love, not like when it really happened. You will recover. I'm sure you will feel better soon."

A weak voice came from the next berth. "Take Nicholai with you when you go out."

The women looked over and smiled in pity. "Yes, Johann," said Anna. "I will, but then I will need to take Justa too, because where he is, she is."

Katarina kept her talking for a while to remove the intensity from her soul. Eventually the girl fell asleep and slept until they were interrupted by a steward.

"Everyone must report to the infirmary area for inspection and treatment."

"Another humiliating experience," exclaimed Katarina. "We are all tossed into the same basket. Someone develops head lice, we all must have our hair washed."

Anna sat on her berth against the wall. "Must we, Katya?

You know, they don't always use clean water for each person, and it makes me shudder to think of it."

"I know, Anna, but it is easier if we comply. Soon—very soon—we will be in Canada, and they won't bother us anymore with their interminable inspections. Besides, if we meet Sarah and Tina Enns, you may go spend some time with them when the medicals are done."

Anna nodded and slid off the berth. She straightened her dress and smoothed her hair. Katarina reached for her hand with a smile and then turned back to give Johann her other arm. He said nothing, but his green-tinged face gave him away. He grasped a small bucket in one hand like a drowning man holds a life preserver. Slowly, the three made their way to the infirmary.

The ship had been stopped off the coast of Holland near the city of Vlissingen in the morning, waiting for the tide to rise. As it did, the *Marglen* raised anchor again and began the slow, careful navigation of the narrow, twisting Shelda River into the harbor of Antwerp.

Katarina and Anna had just completed their inspection and ritual hair washing and, having delivered Johann again to their cabin, stood watching the city come into view. Boats and ships of all description filled the harbor.

"Katya, look!" Anna pointed across the harbor to a large ship sitting at anchor. "The *S.S. Minnedosa.*"

"That's our ship."

Anna studied it. "It's not much bigger than the *Marglen*. I thought it would be bigger."

"It's a good size, Anna. I'm sure it will take us safely across the ocean. Whatever the case, I believe it is time to pack up again. I think if we can get Johann up on deck and into the fresh air while we are anchored, he will be able to have at least a short reprieve from his illness."

"Poor man. He looks awful." They hurried to their room

as many others did the same. "He didn't feel very well on the train either, did he?"

"No," said Katarina. "That was one reason he stood at the open door as much as possible. It wasn't always to keep track of us all, but to give him fresh air and space."

On boarding the *Minnedosa*, the emigrants were once again subjected to medical examinations and hair washing. Then they were shown to their cabins.

"Much like the *Marglen,*" remarked Anna, rolling between her hands the orange she had received upon boarding.

"I may as well eat my orange now," suggested Johann. "while I still can." He sighed and Katarina touched his face with her hand. "The sooner we get this journey underway, the sooner you can get off the ship, dear."

"If I live to walk off again."

Anna peeled her orange and enjoyed the succulent juiciness of the fruit. "Mmm. I shall dearly miss the cherries and pears this year. Remember the yellow cherries we had at Succoth? And the apples and peaches?"

Katarina nodded, concentrating on catching the juice before it stained her clothes. "These are very good oranges."

Anna wiped her hands clean. "I would dearly love to go stand at the rail this evening. I like to watch the harbor in all its busyness."

"We will all go," said Johann.

They stood on deck later, watching the harbor lights wink on as the sun set ruby red. Anna noticed that Johann looked better than he had since they boarded the *Marglen* five days ago. She dreaded the next week for his sake, but anticipated it with joy for herself. Every leg of the journey was one step farther from Russia. She would not look back.

By the next day at noon, all passengers and their belongings had been transferred to the *Minnedosa*. A number of people, mostly older women and children, had been taken immediately to the ship's hospital.

"I think they are entirely worn out," said Katarina. "I'm surprised Susannah is not among them."

"I've helped her as much as possible," said Anna, "but her cabin on the *Minnedosa* is a little ways from ours, so it will be more difficult now."

"I wish she would have married Kornelius, and then he could stay right with her and help her."

"Is that a good reason to marry?"

"Well, not usually, but this is a most unusual circumstance in which we find ourselves. Sometimes we need to do what is necessary."

"Would you?"

Katarina made a face and smiled at Anna. "You are right, of course. I am far too romantic for that, but I am sure those two would benefit from the arrangement, both now and in the new country."

Anna smiled.

"I wish I had brought more books to read," said Katarina. "Johann will be lying huddled on the berth in the cabin for the next week and I don't know how I shall spend the time."

"We have our handwork. I love to sit on the deck and listen to the waves hiss against the bow and feel the sea spray as it showers onto the deck. I will find the Ennses, and they can join us."

Johann poked his head between them. "I'm sorry to disturb you, but we are all due for inspection again before we leave."

"But they just examined us," wailed Anna. "We haven't come down with anything in the last day."

"This is the Canadian Commission. They have the right and the responsibility to make sure we all fall within their regulations."

The women sighed and turned to follow Johann to the

hospital area. They were fortunate to pass all the tests. Sixty-four of the emigrants were not. They would be held back at Antwerp for treatment and would catch up later.

That evening after bidding farewell to the busy harbor and the chiming of the cathedral bells, and before settling in to sleep in their new rooms, the emigrants who were well and able gathered for a short service led by Nick Thiessen, a missionary to Java.

He has also traveled far, thought Anna as she listened to Mr. Thiessen's stories. He has gone to foreign and even hostile lands in obedience to the call of Christ. I am merely going to a new home where I plan to stay for the rest of my life. She admired him for his bravery and his willingness to answer the call from God. At that moment, she forgot her one and only goal of leaving Russia behind and claiming Canada as her new home, and wondered what calls the Lord might yet place on her. After all, she was only sixteen. She had a whole life ahead and she knew God had a plan for her.

Wednesday evening the *Minnedosa* approached Southampton, England, by way of the North Sea.

"Where is Anna?" Katarina asked Johann.

"With Nicholai. I wouldn't worry. He will take good care of her."

"Yes, but we are to go to bed now."

Johann winked at her. "So we are."

"Oh, Johann, be serious. I worry about her."

"I am serious, my dear." He reached for her. "Give Anna room to grow, Katya. She needs to find her own way some of the time."

Katarina's mind swirled with further argument, but she did not say what she was thinking. Perhaps Johann was right. Anna was safe and she would be back shortly.

Chapter 30

"I should go to my room, Kolya." Anna held back as Nicholai and Justina prepared to climb up to the top deck to watch the waves in the moonlight.

"Anna. Come on. It will be beautiful."

"Yes, but you don't need me to see that."

"We want you, Anna." Justina took her hand and pulled her along.

"But we are supposed to retire to our cabins and put out the lights." Anna's whisper was desperate with fear and excitement.

"Shh. Come."

Nicholai led the way, then Justina, pulling Anna by the hand. They reached the top deck and stopped to see that no one was watching, then ran over to the rail in the stern of the ship, partially hidden behind huge pillars.

Sea spray misted them with cool water as they leaned over the railing. The sea was smooth, but behind them, the *Minnedosa* left a huge wake, like a parting of the Red Sea. Small sailboats dotted the seascape beside them, heading for harbor.

"What's that?" asked Anna, forgetting herself in the beauty and excitement of the moment.

"What?"

"There. If you watch, every once in a while there are little shining objects on the surface of the water."

They watched intently. "Dolphins," said Nicholai.

Anna made a face at him. "Kolya, are you making that up? You always have to have an answer for everything, even if you don't know what it is."

"Shh, Anna," he grinned. "Don't tell Justina all my secrets."

"Then don't tell me lies."

"It's not a lie. I heard them saying the dolphins like to play in the evening, and you can see them bobbing on the surface of the water. Those really are dolphins, ladies."

"Hey, you there! What are you doing?"

The angry voice made all three of them jump. "Don't say anything," whispered Nicholai.

One of the crew strode up to where they stood watching at the rail. "I asked you what you were doing. You are all supposed to be in bed. Besides, this deck is reserved for those who have paid for the privilege."

"Just taking a bit of air before retiring," said Nicholai. "Are you telling me we are not allowed to come on deck?"

"You know that. You're only allowed to walk between decks. Now get outta here."

"Good night then," said Nicholai, with a strong touch of sarcasm.

"Filthy emigrants!" they heard as they descended the ladderlike staircase to the lower decks.

Anna was trembling and near tears. Nicholai was grinning still.

Justina scolded him. "Nicholai, you are never afraid of trouble, are you? Now Anna is all upset."

"Anna's upset? Why?"

"Kolya, he had to scold us and tell us we can't be there. Did you hear what he called us?"

"So what? We saw some pretty sights, didn't we? Don't mind his words. They can't hurt you unless you let them. Now, I must deliver you both to your cabins, ladies."

Justina shook her head. "You do beat all," she said, not without a certain admiration.

"It's been a long while since someone told me when to go to bed," remarked Johann wryly.

"They could surely treat us with more respect," said Katarina. "We are grown-ups, not children."

"Well, I for one will not argue," said Johann. "I am exhausted and I have a battle ahead of me yet once we set out to sea."

Katarina studied his face. "You've done well since Antwerp."

"I've kept my meals down for one day. That is not worthy cause for praise."

"But perhaps for thanks."

He smiled and kissed her. "Yes, my love. I am thankful for my day of reprieve. Please ignore me and my groaning for the next week, and I will recover and rise again to my role of protector and guide once we achieve the promised land."

She kissed him again and prepared for bed.

The *S.S. Minnedosa* docked at Southampton late on the ninth of July. The next day, Johann joined some fifteen of the Mennonite travelers as they went ashore to purchase supplies. Meanwhile, Nicholai and Justina watched the loading of the ship's provisions.

By one o'clock that afternoon, the *Minnedosa* pulled away from England and struck a southwest course for Cherbourg, France. Anna marveled at the experience.

"Imagine, Katya. In one week we have seen Russia, Latvia, Germany, Holland, England, and France, with sights of Sweden and Denmark. We've ridden the Baltic Sea, the North Sea, the English Channel, and soon we shall be steaming out into the Atlantic. What amazing stories we will be able to tell."

Katarina stared off into the distance where the coast of France drew nearer. "Perhaps you shall be the one to tell the stories, Anna. You could make them live so that this little one I carry will someday know of our experiences."

"You can tell her yourself, Katya. You're a good storyteller."

"I will tell her stories, I'm sure, but you are more observant. Each of us sees our surroundings in a different light."

The Channel crossing went smoothly, contrary to what they had been warned to expect. Katarina was thankful for Johann's sake. He had enjoyed his short tour into Southampton, having his feet on firm ground again, and dreaded boarding the ship again.

Katarina and Anna watched as new passengers walked up the gangplank of the *Minnedosa* for the ocean voyage. Tomorrow they would venture out of sight of all land. Tomorrow would be another adventure.

ஐஐஐ

Benjamin Janz sat across the desk from a representative of the Canadian Pacific Railway in Moscow.

"We must insist that all immigration to our country cease," announced the CPR agent without preamble.

Janz broke in immediately. "What is the reason for this sudden change of heart? There are still thousands of emigrants who have sold their belongings, acquired visas and endured endless medical inspections in anticipation of this journey. Why do you now deny them their opportunity to start afresh in a new land?"

"Things have not gone according to plan from the beginning, Mr. Janz. First of all, there are many more people wanting to go than was originally expected, second, the funds from North America are not coming in as we need them to, and third, the rate of medical rejections far exceeds any reasonable expectation and you lack facilities to handle this problem."

"When last have you spoken with the Mennonite leaders in Canada?"

"We received a communication from David Toews of Rosthern, Saskatchewan, last week. He would guarantee his own entire life savings if that would help, but we need a large amount of money before we can accept any further Mennonite programs. No matter how much we would like to accommodate you and your people, we still operate a business, and cannot do so at a loss. We depend on payment from our passengers, and many of your people cannot pay."

Janz leaned forward, his index finger raised.

The CPR agent held up a hand. "I know what you are going to say, Mr. Janz. You have been through a terrible time of war and famine. I assure you I am a compassionate man, but our ships and trains are not fueled by compassion. Those are the facts. Until these rather important details are taken care of, we must insist that all travel of your people by CPR cease."

Janz lowered his hand and sat back in his chair. "Very well, then, sir." He stood and shook the hand of the agent. "I thank you for your time. I will return when these matters have been dealt with."

"The man never gives up," muttered the agent as Janz closed the door behind himself.

Janz placed his hat on his head and marched with determination in the direction of the telegraph office. He would send a telegram to Rosthern himself. The Canadians must pull it together on the other side of the ocean. He had done all he could from here, besides hounding the officials.

He knew the Mennonite Central Committee currently fed seven thousand of his brothers and sisters in Siberia, where they had settled or been sent during the war and revolution, and that some were still being fed in the colonies, but this generosity could not continue forever, and the crops in the South did not look good this year. He had to find a way to rescue his people. His soul cried out to heaven as he walked, beseeching the Lord to hear his prayer, not for his sake, but for the sake of those who had already suffered much. Surely there must be a way.

ꕤꕤ

Anna and Nicholai sat at breakfast the next morning, enjoying hot coffee with sugar, fried ham, eggs, white bread with butter, and for Nicholai, cereal as well. They were the only two of their intimate acquaintances who had the stomach for food this morning. They had hit the high seas immediately upon leaving the shelter of Cherbourg harbor.

"I think Katya will be better soon," said Anna. "She has a pretty good stomach."

"Johann is finished until we reach land." Nicholai shook his head in pity and took another bite of the ham and eggs. "Delicious," he said with his mouth half full.

"Nicholai, remember your manners," Anna chided him. "What would Justina say?"

"What? I am enjoying my food."

Anna stared around her as she ate, noting the huge mirrors on the walls of the dining room. Luxurious draperies graced the windows and large fans decorated the walls.

"Have you seen the parlors?" asked Anna.

Nicholai nodded. "There are two for the men and two for the women. Of course, I haven't seen the women's, but Justina was telling me they are elegant."

"Apparently the women's parlors have pianos and comfortable couches and chairs. It's like a dream."

"Yes, as long as you don't count the long, slippery, smelly

passageways we have to walk now that we are banned from the upper deck. It's worse when people are constantly getting sick wherever they are."

"Kolya, please." She changed the subject. "How many do you think they can fit in here at one time?"

"In the dining hall? I think about four hundred."

Anna's eyes widened. "That's a lot of people to feed."

Behind them, a middle-aged Mennonite couple complained loudly about the food. "The coffee is bitter," he said.

"And we have no cream for it. Just milk for the cereal."

"Which is cold."

The wife looked at her husband. "You should have ordered porridge if you wanted hot cereal."

He glared at her in response while the attendant tried to please them both.

"That is embarrassing," said Anna. "So much food and yet they complain. Next they will be demanding *vereneke* or *rollkuchen* and fresh watermelon. What do they expect?"

Nicholai grimaced. "We are used to living among our own people. We have our customs, our foods, our language. It is hard to adapt."

"We could certainly adapt with more grace," she insisted. "Whatever the case, I must go check on Susannah. They are all sick and I should help where I can."

"Of course. I will deliver you there and then meet you again for lunch."

They both gave their sincere compliments to the man at the door of the dining hall.

Nicholai dropped Anna off at Susannah's cabin and continued on to see how Justina and her mother and sister were doing.

In the next cabin to Susannah's, Anna heard groans.

"I think I will die!"

"Oh Heinz, you will not die. Unless I kill you myself to put you out of your horrible misery and suffering."

More desperate groans and retching. "I want to go back to Russia. I want the hard ground beneath my feet once more."

"There is firm ground in Canada. That will have to do."

"Why, oh why did we ever leave? Why were we not content with what we had?"

"You mean nothing? It was difficult."

Anna smiled in spite of herself.

Susannah, pale but composed, sat on one of the berths with Marianna on her lap and Gerhard asleep beside her. The room smelled of sickness, but there was little she could do about it. The portholes did not open, obviously, but sometimes Susannah felt it would be good to let a gush of water in to purify the small cabin of its foul air.

Neta lay listlessly on the other cot. Anna stroked the girl's head.

"How are you, Neta?"

The girl groaned and attempted to look at Anna through slitted eyes.

"It's all right, Neta. Don't talk. I'll wash your face and maybe give you a tiny sip of cold tea. I'll do the same for all of you, Susannah."

"Thank you. Gerhard finally fell asleep and I don't want to move to wake him. It is close in here."

"Yes. I wish I could get some air moving. Perhaps if I just crack the door open a little." She did so and went about her ministrations to the children.

"Where is Jake?"

"Kornelius has taken him up on deck. He is not feeling too bad. How are Katarina and Johann?"

Anna gently brushed Marianna's damp hair back from her forehead. "Katya is getting a bit better, but her condition makes her stomach more queasy from smells, and this ship is full of strange smells. Johann is out for the count, as Nicholai says. He won't perk up until he stands on land again."

"Sounds like only you and Nicholai are well."

"Yes. He gets a bit queasy sometimes too, but he has to stay healthy to check on his Justina. She got sick when we hit the big waves. Most of us Mennonites are ill now. We are not used to the incessant rolling."

"How do you avoid the seasickness, Anna?"

Anna sat beside Neta and stroked her face lightly. " I suppose God has blessed me so I can help others."

"You are an angel to us here. Even your presence is a highlight in this self-imposed sea of sickness."

Concern rose to Anna's clear features. "This is not self-imposed sickness, Susannah. This is necessary. This unpleasantness is the sacrifice we make for our freedom, and even if I were sick as well, I would gladly suffer for a week or two in order to gain my freedom. Would you not?"

"Of course, you are right. It's hard, though, to watch the children suffer too."

"We have all seen children suffer," responded Anna. "Your children do not wander the streets of the villages without shelter, food, or family. They lie on your lap in a comfortable place. They will survive."

Anna bent to kiss her forehead as she left the room. "I need to check on Katya and Johann," she said.

"Come again when you can, angel."

Anna smiled as she quietly closed the door behind her.

It rained Saturday morning, but by afternoon the sun shone again on the dark water. After doing what she could for her sick charges, Anna sat on second deck and watched the dolphins play in the waves. They amused her for hours with their humorous antics, their chirping speech, and the great athletic leaps and dives which seemed to be executed for the entertainment of the faces lining the railing of the *S.S. Minnedosa.*

Due to the widespread sickness, the Mennonite preachers did not call a service. Instead, Nicholai and Justina took Anna with them to watch a movie in the theater. They marveled at the scenic pictures of China, Japan, and Canada. The Canadian movies concentrated on Ontario, and Anna wondered if perhaps they could stay there. She saw familiar orchards of cherries, apricots, peaches, and pears, and fields of watermelons. Her mouth watered at the recollection of the sweet, sticky juice running down her chin. Maybe there were watermelons in Saskatchewan too.

After the scenic movies, a gentleman changed the reels and played cartoons. Neither Justina nor Anna had ever seen cartoons before, and howled with laughter, to the irritation of some of the other movie watchers. The laughter raised Anna's spirits even more. She forgot to ask Nicholai where he had seen cartoons before.

As they were leaving the theater, Anna noticed a young bearded man and a very pretty woman with him. They were speaking a dialect that intrigued her. It was not German. Not exactly.

The man and woman looked at her with furrowed brows. She had done it again. Been caught staring.

"I'm sorry," she said in her best Russian. "I should mind my own business. I just heard the Russian and wondered what your accent was."

The man still frowned, but the woman's face relaxed into a smile. "Our first language is Yiddish," she explained, and she said a few words in that tongue.

Anna smiled and answered her in German.

"Would you like to sit on the deck and visit until supper?" the woman asked. "My name is Miriam and this is my husband, Silas."

Anna colored but nodded her head. “My name is Anna. We could watch the dolphins play.”

In a mix of Russian, Yiddish, and German, Miriam and Anna spent a wonderful hour. After a supper of beef bouillon, potatoes, peas and applesauce for dessert, they parted and promised to meet again the next day.

As Miriam turned to follow her husband along the corridor in the opposite direction, she inadvertently bumped into one of the Molotschna Mennonites.

“Hey, watch where you’re going,” he exclaimed, pushing his way past her.

“Pardon me,” she said in Yiddish

“What? Can’t understand your jabbering. Learn to talk like the rest of us.”

Anna could not believe what she was hearing. It made her blood boil. With uncharacteristic boldness, she approached the scene and spoke in clear German.

“Excuse me, sir, but you are very rude to my friend, Miriam. She has the same right to ride on this ship as you and I do.”

“And who do you think you are, Jew lover?”

“I am neither Jew nor Greek,” answered Anna. “We are sisters on this voyage and I take exception to your rudeness.”

He glowered at her and continued on his way.

“I am sorry, Miriam and Silas. Some of my people are very insensitive. We are used to living among our own, and so have developed a rather biased view of others.”

“No need to apologize, Anna. You were not the one who was rude. See you tomorrow as planned.”

They moved away again, careful not to get in anyone’s way, and Anna felt shame for the attitudes and actions of the man who was supposedly her spiritual brother. They had much to learn upon entering a new country. There would be many refugees from many countries, Nicholai had told her, and they would all need to get along together.

Throughout Sunday and Monday, Anna nursed her friends and family. Outside, a cold rain fell, and wisps of fog stretched phantom fingers onto the decks. Nicholai and Justina even experienced a few snowflakes on one of their forays onto the deck. Anna hugged her sweater around her.

"It is July and I am freezing," she commented as she looked after Susannah's brood. Katarina, well enough now to help, offered to entertain a few children whose parents were too sick to care for them properly. In fact, anyone who felt well enough pitched in to help.

On Monday, the loudspeakers proclaimed another medical inspection.

"Medical inspection! How do they expect to know if someone is otherwise healthy?" Katarina was appalled at the lack of compassion shown by the medical examiners. "How am I going to get Johann out onto the deck?"

"I will find Kolya," said Anna. "He won't be far away."

It was a sorry lot that limped and stumbled their way to the ship's hospital that morning. The cold Labrador stream added to their discomfort, and doctors could do little to ease anyone's condition or properly assess the status of their health. All faded inoculations were reprocessed.

Anna passed all examinations with a clean bill of health, but she felt exceedingly uncomfortable with the ship's doctor. She said nothing about it until Katarina commented on it after the supper meal.

"I cannot believe the gall of that doctor. I have been through many examinations to this point, but he was rude, insensitive, and rough. Was he unkind to you, Anna?"

"Well, I did feel quite uncomfortable with him, but perhaps we will not have to go again."

"Johann, if you feel better soon, could you look into this? It is not acceptable for him to treat us as second-class people."

Johann lifted his hand in a gesture of promise and

remained motionless on the cot. Katarina grimaced. "I am so tired of this," she whispered to Anna.

"So'm I," came the raspy voice from the berth.

By Tuesday, some of the sickness began to fade, except for Johann's.

"His is the worst case I have seen," said Katarina, looking over at her husband.

"The worst you have seen, perhaps," quipped Anna, "but not the worst I have heard. Some of the desperate ones say such funny things."

"Anna, where is your heart?" chided her sister.

"I don't know, but my stomach is tiring of beef bouillon, as good as it is, and longing for a good bowl of cabbage borscht with lots of pepper in it."

"Mmm. Or a plateful of *vereneke* with cream gravy, and sausage."

"Or deep fried *rollkuchen* and fresh cool watermelon."

"Or—"

"Pleez!" gasped Johann from the cot. "Go outside to discuss this."

Clamping their hands over their mouths, the sisters retreated to the corridor, giggling guiltily.

"Come on deck with me, Katya, and see the dolphins. Johann won't be going anywhere."

"Well, all right, for a bit. I would like to see the dolphins you were telling us about. "

They settled in a couple of creaky deck chairs and looked for dolphins, but what they saw completely surprised and overwhelmed them. Anna gasped. "Katya!" She grasped her sister's arm and stared out at the sea.

A huge black mound rose above the water and shot a blast of spray. "It's a whale!" exclaimed Katarina. They stood at the railing now, along with many others on all decks, watching in fascination as the great sea creature swam and blew. Its size astounded them.

That morning, all the emigrants were processed through a delousing station set up at the hospital. Anna felt the humiliation again, but not as keenly as some who were found to actually carry lice. Their names were kept on a list and they were checked regularly. So far, the vermin had not spread to Anna's section of the boat.

In the evening, as many as were able sat on deck for an evangelistic meeting led by Martin Kroeker. After the service, a good number of the company remained on deck to visit and enjoy the ever-changing sea air. Suddenly, a shout rose up that sent shivers up and down their spines.

Chapter 30

"Land! We've sighted land!" Cheers went up all around as the ship glided past Belle Isle into the Strait of the same name.

Anna was too excited to sleep that night. She told Johann over and over that they would soon be on land. He and Katarina finally both feigned sleep to stop her nervous chatter.

The next morning, Wednesday, July 16, Anna rose with the dawn to watch the ship's progress from the railing. Nicholai and Justina came as well, and Kornelius with Jake. Sarah and Tina ventured out with their older brother David and their young stepbrother Philipp. More and more people began to gather at the side of the boat.

"That is Newfoundland," Nicholai pointed out the land to his left, "and opposite is the coast of Labrador."

He would have gone on, but at that moment a small bird flew on deck, landing on Silas's hat. It sat for a long moment before taking wing.

"It is a sign, a good omen," said Miriam. "God will bless us in this new land."

They slid between the mainland and wooded Anticosti Island, into the mouth of the St. Lawrence Seaway. As if to celebrate, a number of whales made appearance.

The ship's doctor continued his unprofessional ways, encouraging the druggist to do the same. Complaints reached the ship's captain, and the druggist was suspended, pending arrival in port.

"I'm glad they put an end to that," said Anna. "I hate to complain, but he was not very nice to many of the women and children."

"It was a legitimate complaint, Anna," said Katarina. "That man should not be allowed to continue in that manner. Other than those two, the crew has been very proper."

"They certainly have," agreed Anna, remembering her painful experience on deck and the subsequent rescue by a steward. She had seen him several times over the course of the journey, and he had always saluted and smiled.

In anticipation of their arrival in Quebec City, all immigrants were again examined. Women and children were asked to gather in the dining hall, while the men remained on deck. Anna's heart beat in her throat as a few families were held back, to be quarantined for a period of time on one of the small islands.

At least the families were not separated, she noted. Now that they were in Canada, surely nothing evil could befall them.

In the late afternoon, the *S.S. Minnedosa* arrived at Quebec City. The passengers disembarked with their personal baggage and filed into Immigration Hall. Johann, his equilibrium returning, stood in line with Katarina, Anna, and Nicholai. He was still very pale and had lost weight through his ordeal, but he was incredibly thankful to be on land again.

Nicholai watched with narrowed eyes the young men who apparently worked for the immigration office. They did not dress as the Russian young men did, with shirts worn loose over pants, belted at the waist. No, in Canada a man tucked his shirt into his pants. He made a mental note to do the same as soon as he had opportunity to find a clean shirt.

After the voyage, exhausted passengers secured transportation to their destinations. The Mennonites, however, had no homes here. They were billeted, again by the C.P.R., in dormitory-type facilities that were clean but crowded. On the morrow they would move on again.

Katarina's weariness showed in her face, in her voice, in her manner. Johann watched her for signs of pain. He knew she would not complain unless her condition warranted attention. He hoped and prayed they would arrive in Saskatchewan before the baby made its appearance, but he knew they faced a long and arduous train ride west through rugged country. Well, they may as well get at it.

Next morning, the immigrants were awakened at five o'clock to continue their journey. After breakfast and another inspection, they were transported to the train station. As they approached the train, they noticed two Canadian women, one standing on each side of the line of passengers, handing out pamphlets. One of them spoke in English, the other in German; they passed out the papers according to the language of the traveler. Katarina scanned hers and realized it was an evangelistic tract. She showed Johann.

"Jesus is here too," she said, "even across the vast ocean."

Johann put his arm around her shoulders and pulled her close. "Of course he is. He never left us and he never will. Although," he smirked, "I had a few doubts on that awful voyage."

Katarina smiled back at him. "We are here," she said, "in Canada at last." She took a deep breath and determined to be strong for the remainder of the journey.

At the baggage room, everyone collected their belongings and was given direction as to their destination. Only about one hundred of the group planned to continue on to the West. The rest had chosen to remain in the fertile fruit belt of southern Ontario.

Throughout the journey, Susannah had been silent about

her plans. Johann now reminded her that she was welcome to accompany them to Saskatchewan. "There is plenty of room there, and we will help you get settled."

Susannah blinked rapidly and looked around for Kornelius. He was not far behind, Jake in tow and Gerhard in his arms. He saw her discomfort immediately and came to stand beside her.

Clearing his throat, Kornelius spoke. "I met a gentleman on board ship who is planning to work on a vegetable farm in the Vineland area. He asked me to join him."

All eyes rested on Susannah. She tried unsuccessfully to speak. Kornelius came to her rescue.

"I have asked Susannah to marry me and she has accepted."

Katarina squealed with joy before she could stop herself. She covered her mouth in embarrassment.

Kornelius cleared his throat, joy shining through his eyes from somewhere deep inside. "She and the children will accompany me to Vineland."

Susannah put on her bravest face. "I am grateful to the Lord for sending me Kornelius, to help me in Alexanderkrone and in Vineland and every place between. Without him I would have been lost. I shall miss you all desperately, but I will go with Kornelius now. Where he lodges, I will lodge. We will build a home together, for each other and for the children."

"Mama," interrupted Marianna, "I want my new house now."

"New house," repeated Gerhard.

"Well," said Johann, "we shall ride the train together as far as Montreal, so we have some time to bid each other farewell."

Johann and Katarina led their family to the train, and although they rode third class, the upholstered seats, little tables and wide windows seemed first class to them, a vast improvement on boxcars. With food and drink served to them, the passengers were free to wander and watch the ever changing scenery. Justina sat with Nicholai, her mother and sister in the seat behind them.

Now that Johann felt better, Wilhelm Enns and Kornelius joined him. They visited for hours, talking of the future, of what they expected, hoped for. Johann appreciated the perspective of these other men, men who also had families to consider.

Katarina cherished her time with Susannah, and visited a good deal also with Agnetha. The old camaraderie returned without effort.

"Remember, Katya, when you helped to deliver little Philipp? How thankful I was that you were there with me."

"You did well. You were very brave. I only hope I can maintain some dignity through it all."

Susannah had joined them, her brood temporarily under the competent eyes of Anna and the Enns sisters. "Forget about dignity, Katya, just get the job done."

Agnetha agreed.

Montreal amazed them with its tall, narrow, flat-roofed buildings. In the countryside, rectangular farmhouses were planted here and there, painted brightly and decorated with colorful flowers in the front yards. Long strips of farmland sat along the river, and churches sent pointed steeples gracefully into the blue sky.

At the station in Montreal, Kornelius and Susannah, Marianna, Gerhard, Neta, and Jake changed trains for the last leg of their journey down to Vineland, south of Lake Ontario, on the tip of Lake Erie. Wilhelm and Agnetha also planned to stay in Ontario. "If we don't like it," he said, "we will come west."

They bade one another fond farewells filled with promises of visits someday when they became established, and the southbound train left, many faces pressed against the windows, many waving hands on board and on the station platform.

Katarina looked a little peaked, so Johann settled her on a bench outside the station, sheltered from the sun but not the afternoon breeze. Anna stayed with her while Johann and Nicholai went in search of food. They bought bread and sausages for the train ride to Winnipeg, enough for them and for Justina's family as well. Then they boarded the westbound train.

Once in motion, the train's steady rhythm lulled Katarina to sleep. Johann stayed beside her.

Anna did not sleep, but watched the scenery out of the wide window. The land here was mostly forested, with a variety of evergreen and deciduous trees. Silver poplars shone in the brilliant sunlight, and many other trees for which she did not yet know names.

Nicholai noticed that many of the fields were fenced for livestock. He thought of the days of his childhood in Russia, and the village shepherds who collected the animals in the morning, watched them during the day, and returned them to their stalls each evening. This was a different system.

In some areas where more unforested land was available, people were busily making hay. He thought he would like to help with that. Perhaps Uncle George would show him how when they reached his farm. The other crops were still too green to harvest.

"The crops are later here than they were at home," Nicholai commented to Johann. "We will have to get used to that."

"We will have to get used to a good number of things," replied his brother-in-law. Nicholai glanced at him and realized this was no easy move for a former teacher. He had sacrificed much to leave his homeland, but then again, he had no real choice. Freedom versus familiarity. And even the familiar was swiftly changing in the land of his birth.

Nicholai did not spend much time with the Sudermann family on the last two days of the train ride. He had other things on his mind. Justina's elder brother would meet his mother and sisters when they arrived in Winnipeg while the Sudermanns would go on their own to Saskatchewan to meet Uncle George Peters. Nicholai spent every spare minute now with Justina.

The two young people talked of many things, their heads bent close to hear whispered words.

"I will work hard, Justina," said Nicholai. "I will come to see you at Christmas, and we will plan more. As soon as I can support you, I will come for you."

"What of my mother and sister? I cannot leave them."

"They will be settled by then and your brother is there."

Justina leaned her back against the seat and smiled at Nicholai. "I know we will be busy and the time will fly by, but right now it seems a long time until Christmas."

"We can write letters. The Canadian postal service is much more reliable than ours was in Russia."

She nodded.

"Justina, will you wait for me? Will you promise to wait?"

"Of course I will wait. I never wanted anyone but you."

"Justina, do you remember when you told me I carried far too much anger? That it would only harm me?"

She lowered her eyes. "I'm sorry, Kolya. It was not my place to say it."

He lifted her chin. "Yes it was, Justa. Your words worked at my heart day and night. I want you to know that you have helped me deal with the anger. I know I still need to change, but you bring me such joy." His words caught in his throat. He blinked away the emotion and clasped her hand firmly. "You will make a wonderful wife, Justina Epp."

Her joy shone through her eyes. "I think Christmas is on its way."

ꙮꙮꙮ

As the Ontario train headed south, Susannah watched the trees thicken again and then clear to reveal more farmland. Fruit trees displayed their cherries and peaches. The train followed the edge of Lake Ontario and arrived in Toronto by early evening. Her eyes stared in wonder at all the cars. Everywhere she looked, people were driving, tooting their horns, and busily going somewhere. People waved to them as they passed.

They left Toronto behind and set off in a buggy for Vineland. Once there, they would pledge their vows to each other, she and Kornelius. He would become a father to all four of the children, and they would settle into a home.

Although her heart was heavy with changes and farewells, Susannah felt a strange, almost unreasonable hope rise in her chest as the buggy rolled down the picturesque roads of rural southern Ontario. A whole new life awaited them, and she decided to embrace it with all her heart.

ꙮꙮꙮ

On the golden morning of July 19, the westbound train passed through more hilly country and into a rocky, sparsely treed terrain. Katarina was glad they did not have to stay there. The trees were stunted, as if they could not dig their toes into the soil, but were forced to cling tenaciously to the stone escarpment.

After what seemed like weeks, the train pulled into the city of Winnipeg. Katarina assumed the whole city did not look like the train yard, or she would have felt very sorry indeed for Mrs. Epp and her daughters. As it was, she felt compassion for her brother Nicholai as he bade his Justina farewell. He would see her in five months, Lord willing, but they had never been separated before. Alexanderkrone and Lichtfelde had been within easy walking distance from each other.

She turned away as Nicholai bade Justina farewell and wondered why the villages in Canada should be so far apart. She hoped they would have neighbors.

Katarina had been unusually quiet since the train pulled away from Winnipeg and continued through the vast open prairie into Saskatchewan. When she supposedly slept, Johann watched her face and noticed the tightening of pain.

Please God, he prayed, let us reach our destination first. Please hold this child back until we have a doctor and a place to stay.

Katarina blinked and gasped, her attention consumed by a tightening around her middle. Johann immediately gripped her hand.

"Katya, is it time?"

"I don't really know, Johann. I've never done this before."

"But you have seen it. You helped Agnetha give birth."

"Each one is different, Johann. I will try to relax and see what happens."

Johann left to get her some tea and to ease the tightness he felt himself. He had seen many men suffer during his years with the Forestry Service medical corp, and he himself had suffered, but to see Katarina in pain which he had caused, that was more difficult for him.

When he returned with the tea, Katarina had fallen asleep and slept for almost two hours.

"Obviously not time yet," she said when she awoke. "I think my body and the baby are both reacting to the discomfort of our journey. Do you realize we have traveled for over a month now?"

Johann heaved a sigh of relief. "Hold on to that baby a little while yet. By tomorrow morning we should arrive in

Swift Current. Uncle George will meet us there and it is but a short drive then to his farm."

"Does he know when we will arrive?"

"I sent a telegram from Montreal. He knows."

"Is he aware of my condition?"

"I mentioned it."

Katarina was silent, thinking ahead. She had had no opportunity to prepare for this baby. The only items she had brought with her were a silk baby gown sewn by Hannah, and a small blanket Oma had crocheted. These she had packed carefully with their clothes in the trunk that rested in the train's baggage car.

She would have to purchase soft fabric to sew diapers and more blankets and a few baby dresses. Would the baby be a boy or a girl? She realized it did not matter in the least which it was. She cherished memories of sweet little Marianna, with her angelic face and shining eyes, but also of Gerhard, pudgy and affectionate. She sighed in anticipation.

At her sigh, Johann leaned toward her, all concern.

She shook her head and smiled. "Don't worry, my love. I was just thinking about our baby. She will be so beautiful. I can hardly wait to hold her."

"Katarina, please do not sigh so loudly. My poor heart cannot withstand much more of this strain."

She chuckled softly and slipped her hand into his. "Get used to it. I will have much to sigh contentedly about when we are settled."

After a light meal of buns and cold meat and cheese, Johann and Katarina settled into their seats for the night. Anna slept deeply in the seat behind them. Nicholai dozed, but woke repeatedly.

The long, low whistle of the train woke Katarina as it chugged into the station.

"Swift Current," bellowed the conductor. "Ain't the end of the world, but you can see it from here."

Johann had already gathered their belongings in preparation for leaving the train. He sat on the edge of his seat looking out the window into the first light of morning.

Katarina winced at the stiffness of her joints. She needed a washroom, but would have to wait until they reached the station. She hoped Uncle George would be there to welcome them.

She woke a still sleeping Anna and they stood to leave the train, Johann supporting her.

"Are you feeling well this morning?"

"I don't know yet. Once I have found the ladies' room, I will feel better."

They waited their turn to descend the steps. The conductor offered a firm hand to make sure she didn't trip, and other passengers gave her extra room to move. She appreciated that.

"Keep your eyes open for the women's room," she whispered to Anna. "I am desperate."

Anna grinned and nodded.

"Katya," interrupted Johann, "what does your uncle look like? How will we recognize him?"

"Didn't you decide on a manner of identification when you sent the telegram?" she teased. "He looks like my mother."

"Katie, don't tease. I never met your mother."

"Well, he is a farmer—"

"—as are most of the inhabitants here. Is he tall, short, fat, thin, cheerful, sour?"

Now Katarina laughed in earnest. "Johann, he left Russia in the '80s. I was born in '98."

Johann's eyebrows raised. "You don't know what he looks like either?"

"No, but I think we will recognize him. Somehow we will know. It's not a very big place."

Anna nudged her and pointed at a sign.

"Excuse me, Johann," said Katarina, "Anna and I will be in restroom. See if you can locate Uncle George."

He watched her waddle into the ladies' room. He would never understand women. At the moment of truth, they teased. He and Nicholai gathered their luggage and two trunks, as well as the wicker basket that still carried a few blankets and clothing. The roasted *zweiback* had long since been consumed. Then he paced the station, looking for a man he did not know.

The strangeness Katarina had been feeling concentrated in her belly. A painless pressure warned her to stay where she was for the moment.

"Anna?" she called. "Please find Johann. I may need some help."

"I'll get him."

Anna ran out in search of her brother-in-law and found him outside shaking hands with a young man about his own age. He turned to her as she approached. "Anna, meet your cousin Henry. He has come to pick us up—Anna, what is it?"

"It's Katya. She says she needs help."

Henry joined Johann and Nicholai as they ran back into the building. They slid to a stop at the door of the women's room while Anna entered.

"Katya? How are you?"

"If you help me, I should be able to walk out of here. Did Johann find Uncle George?"

"Yes. No. He didn't come, but our cousin Henry is here. He has a buggy, I think."

"Good. We will have to find someplace in the village to wait until the baby comes."

Anna gave Katarina her arm, and the two made their way out of the washroom. A woman approached them at the door.

"Is there a problem? Are you having your baby now, Ma'am?"

Katarina gasped. A sudden pain hit her hard and tightened the bands around her. Johann held her other arm to support her. She breathed quick, shallow breaths and nodded to the woman.

"Do you have a buggy?"

Henry took over. "Right outside. I will take her to Dr. Friesen's office."

"Fine. I'll leave it to you then."

Between them, they managed to get Katarina up into the buggy. She felt like one of the whales she had seen in the Atlantic. And the pain . . .

Henry clucked to the horse and they moved up the street to a small building off Main Street. He jumped down and ran in to see if the doctor was in. As he ran back to them he called, "Come. Dr. Friesen is in the back."

They had to wait for the next contraction to end before Katarina could climb down. She was ushered into the presence of an older man with a pleasant expression. "Good timing," he said. "I just returned from a house call. Come lie down on this bed here. Nurse!"

Dr. Friesen settled Katarina in the room in the care of his nurse and Anna, and ushered the men back into the waiting room.

"You fellows may as well go to the Chinese diner on Main Street and have a hearty breakfast. We will find you when we are done."

Johann kept glancing over the doctor's shoulder in an attempt to see Katarina, but the door had been shut. He felt he should not desert his beloved at this time, but apparently the doctor had everything under control, and had seen this many times before.

"Go on, now. She'll be fine, and we'll call you as soon as

there is something to tell. Is this a first baby?"

"Yes."

"Then we may be awhile. I may come join you for breakfast."

No sooner had the men left in search of breakfast, than the nurse emerged from the back room. "Doctor," she said, "I think this may happen sooner than we think."

"I will be there immediately." He stooped over the little basin to wash his hands thoroughly and joined the women behind the closed door.

By ten o'clock the July sun shone hot and dry on the dusty main street of Swift Current. Johann sat staring out the window of the diner, seeing nothing. His heart pounded. He could not swallow his food. He felt as if he would become ill as he had been on the ship.

He pushed back his chair, startling his companions, and announced, "I must go see what is happening. Something must be wrong."

He met the doctor at the door.

"What has happened? How is Katarina?"

The doctor beamed. "She is fine, and you, my good man, are the father of a healthy little Mennonite girl. This one's no Bolshevik! This baby is a Canadian!"

Johann stood staring dumbly at the man.

The doctor grabbed him by the shoulder. "Come on, son. Come see your family." Nicholai and Henry followed eagerly.

"Isn't she precious?" Katarina held the baby close to her side. Johann stroked the baby's fine blond hair and then pushed the curls from Katarina's forehead.

"You've done well, my love." He couldn't stop the grin that spread over his face. Their eyes shared the love they did not speak. The moment would be etched forever in both their memories.

Nicholai cleared his throat. "Excuse me, Katya. I'd like you to meet our cousin Henry. He is the one who picked us up and brought us here."

They all laughed. Katarina said, "I'm sorry not to take time to formally introduce myself. "

He nodded to her and smiled at the sight of the new baby. "I will stay on until tomorrow, and then we can take you home. We have a little cabin ready for the four—now the five—of you."

"Thank you."

"Now," said Dr. Friesen with authority, "everyone out of here except Anna. Come back tomorrow after breakfast and I will have the ladies ready for the drive to the farm."

"It's not more than ten miles," assured Henry.

Chapter 32

August 1924
Swift Current, Saskatchewan, Canada

Johann stood on a hillock a few yards from the cabin. Katarina stood beside him, holding baby Elizabeth. A breeze stirred the wild rye and switchgrass, wafting up the dusky smell of sage. A Richardson's ground squirrel popped out of one of the mounded burrows that dotted the field and stood upright, tiny paws clasped in obeisance to the sun.

"Not a tree in sight, save those twigs the Stirlings have planted," said Johann, his voice thick with nostalgia. "Not much of anything to see at all, actually."

He remembered Succoth as he had seen it the first time, that grand mansion surrounded by orchards and parks, flowers, and regal beauty. His eyes scanned the flatland of the Saskatchewan prairie and a sudden wave of homesickness and something akin to fear shuddered through him. He was a Russian German teacher. What on earth was he doing here?

He glanced sidelong at Katarina. She too had memories. She spoke often of the good times, but carefully guarded the door to the evil days of the past.

"Did you hear the coyotes last night, Johann? They were calling to each other, telling about their day chasing gophers and mice and rabbits. And the frogs," she smiled into the sun while the wind tugged at her curls, "singing their boastful songs far into the night."

She pointed into the dome of pure azure above them at an eagle that glided on lazy air currents. "Look at him, Johann. He flies with freedom and confidence. We are free now too. There is beauty here, in the earth itself, in the life that springs from it, in the family we have begun." She kissed Elizabeth's downy head.

Johann clasped Katarina's hand to his chest. "Those who hope in the Lord will renew their strength . . .

"... they will soar on wings like eagles . . .

". . . . they will run and not grow weary . . .

". . . they will walk and not faint."

THE END

Epilogue

Praise our God, O peoples,
let the sound of his praise be heard;
he has preserved our lives
and kept our feet from slipping.
For you, O God, tested us;
you refined us like silver.
You brought us into prison
and laid burdens on our backs.
You let men ride over our heads;
we went through fire and water,
but you brought us to a place of abundance.

Psalm 66:8-12

Glossary

AMR—American Mennonite Relief Agency

Anwohner—landless Mennonite people who lived on the outskirts of the villages

Cossacks—historically nomadic horsemen from the Don Valley; their troops were loyal to the tsar

Cheka—Communist secret police

Das Vedanya—good-bye in Russian

Forstei—Forestry Service; a Mennonite instituted and maintained alternative to military service; duties included road building, reforestation, and medical service

Jugendfest—youth festival

Jugendverein—youth gathering

kolcho—communal farm

Liebchen—sweetheart

Machnovitz—followers of the bandit Nestor Machno

MCC—Mennonite Central Committee, formed in July 1920 by the AMR

Mensch, Ärger Dich Nicht—a German game similar to Aggravation or Parcheesi

muzhik—a fool

Nun danket alle Gott—a popular hymn sung by the Russian Mennonites in German, the translation is "Now thank we all our God, with heart and hands and voices; / Who wondrous things hath done, in whom His world rejoices; / Who from our mothers' arms hath blessed us on our way; / With countless gifts of love, and still is ours today."

paska—Easter bread rich with eggs, butter, and cream

Prips—a coffee substitute made by soaking grain in milk, roasting it in the oven, and grinding it

pud—weight measurement equal to 36.11 pounds or 16.38 kilograms

Reds—Bolsheviks, Communists

Selbstschuetzler—those who served in the Selbstschutz or Self Defense Corp, a Mennonite defensive organization during the civil war

Studienkommission—study commission

trachoma—a chronic inflammatory disease of the eye; the largest single cause of blindness in the world

VMSR—Verband der Mennoniten Süd-Russlands (Union of South Russian Mennonites); this name was later changed to Verband der Bürger Holländischer Herkunft (Union of Citizens of Dutch Lineage), or VBHH.

Weinachten—Christmas in German

Weinachtsmann—the Christmas man or Santa Claus in German

White Army—a.k.a. Volunteer Army; anti-Bolshevik forces loyal to the monarchy

zolotniks—weight measurement equal to .33 ounce or 4.26 grams

Historical Timeline

- 1914: Alexander Kerensky, premier of the Provisional Government at the time of the revolution, fled to Paris, then lived in the United States until his death in 1970.
- 1924: Stalin sent Trotsky into exile in Mexico where he was murdered by Soviet agents in 1940.
- 1925: 3,772 Russian Mennonites were able to emigrate to Canada.
- 1925: The Communist government forbade the VBHH to further involve itself in emigration matters.
- 1926: 5,940 Russian Mennonites were able to emigrate to Canada.
- 1926: Benjamin B. Janz left Russia with his family mere hours before the Kharkov GPU began a search for him. He and his family arrived safely in Canada.
- 1926: Truth about the extent of the regicide of the Romanov family was finally published, almost ten years after the fact. Rumors circulated until the 1970s that Anastasia still lived, but recent DNA testing has proven otherwise.
- 1927: 20,000 Mennonites were contracted for emigration, but only 847 managed to get out.
- 1928: 511 emigrants came to Canada from Russia.
- 1928: Baron Peter Wrangel (General of the White Army in the Russian civil war) died.
- 1929: The New Economic Policy (NEP) was ended, although it had effectively ended in 1925.
- 1936: Lev Kamenev and Zinoviev were executed as plotters.
- 1953: Josef Stalin, dictator of the Soviet Union, died in Moscow.

Acknowledgments

This project has been a work of love and gratitude to those who have gone before me, but most of all, to the God who continues to lead and guide. I would again like to acknowledge a number of people who have contributed to the writing of this book: my editor at Herald Press, Sarah Kehrberg; Hugo and Katherine Jantz, for encouragement, information, and promotional help; Dr. Helmut Huebert, for his excellent resources (*Mennonite Historical Atlas*, *Events and People*), and his willingness to answer questions both geographical and medical; Sarah Klassen for the use of the poem "Train: 1929," used in my prologue; Nichole Nordeman for introducing me to the song "Gratitude," which fit so well into the story; and all those who were willing to endorse and comment on these books. To my husband, Wayne, and our family, for your unflagging encouragement and love I thank you (thanks especially to Wayne and Lorraine for proofreading the manuscript). To my Lord and Savior, Jesus Christ, You truly are the best.

The Author

Janice L. Dick lives with her husband Wayne on an organic grain farm in central Saskatchewan. Both her first and second novels, *Calm Before the Storm* and its sequel, *Eye of the Storm*, won first place in the historical fiction category of The Word Guild's Canadian Writing Awards (2003-04).